HER CAPTOR'S VOW

He raised himself on one elbow, searching her face in the moonlight. "Who said I was going to rape you?" he demanded.

"Y-you did!"

Her posture clenched, Thea held her breath as his hand cupped her face then slid the length of her throat and came to rest upon the soft swell of her breast. Her heart began to pound. As if it had a will of its own, her nipple hardened against his thumb as he grazed it through the stiff linen fabric.

"You do not pay attention," he murmured. "I have no intention of raping you, fair lady. I am no Cosgrove. Ros Drumcondra does not rape his women. He does not have to. What I said was, he ought take care because you are a winsome lass and I am tight against the seam." He drove her hand down to his sex to prove the point. He was thick and hard. "I also said that, just as in days of old, I will have you before him, and that when I'm done, you will want no other."

DAWN THOMPSON

The Falcon's Bride

LOVE SPELL NEW YORK CITY

For DeborahAnne MacGillivray,
for her friendship and support,
and for all the great Ladies in Waiting.

LOVE SPELL®

September 2006

Published by

Dorchester Publishing Co., Inc.
200 Madison Avenue
New York, NY 10016

ISBN 0-505-52679-4

Visit us on the web at www.dorchesterpub.com.

The Falcon's Bride

Chapter One

Cashel Cosgrove, County Meath, Ireland, December 1811

Thea Barrington hugged herself for warmth before her bedchamber window. Outside, unprecedented snow swirled, falling and lifting, borne upon a fickle wind that hadn't ceased to blow since she and her entourage arrived in County Meath. The blizzard was a phenomenon seldom seen in the region, which never got more than a dusting, or so she'd been told. It had been a harsh and bitter season at home in England as well. This winter it had even snowed in Cornwall, something that only happened every ten or twenty years. Was it a sign, an ill-boding omen? Under the circumstances, it certainly seemed so.

Thea shuddered, pulling her shawl closer about her shoulders. Not even the blazing hearth fire could warm the turret cubicle; and to think, this cold inhospitable place was soon to be her home. How had she ever let them persuade her?

"Fie, miss," her abigail said. "Such a Friday face. Why,

1

you'd think you was headed for a funeral instead o' a weddin'."

"The snow has covered our carriage tracks already," Thea replied, avoiding a direct response. "It's as if the brougham never even passed this way—as if it didn't exist. Could it all be a dream, do you think?"

"A dream, miss?"

"I wish . . ." Thea couldn't finish the thought. How could she expect the simple maid to understand when she didn't herself?

She should be ecstatic. Nigel Cosgrove, the second son of the third earl of Ridgewood, just home from the Peninsula on half-pay, was the catch of the season. He was tall, and handsome enough—a blue-eyed Adonis with hair the color of burnished gold and a nearly sterling reputation, except for that one unfortunate incident concerning the Covent Garden lightskirt. But he couldn't have killed her. They wouldn't have acquitted him otherwise, would they? Thea pushed that to the back of her mind. Again.

"What is it ya wish, miss?" the abigail asked, jogging her memory.

"Nothing, Annie, I'm just tired. It's been a long journey, and I'd much rather take myself off to bed than face a formal dinner downstairs in that dreadful dining parlor. Why, it's so vast, I shall have to shout to make conversation, and if a fire won't warm this little cell, I shudder to wonder how I will survive the meal down there without my chinchilla fur pelerine."

"You've got the prenuptial jitters, is all," said Annie. "That's what my mum calls it. You've got ta go down. You heard Mr. Cosgrove, her ladyship is anxious ta meet ya. Ya can't be disappointin' his mama. No doubt she's wore the cook out preparin'."

Well, I'm not all that anxious to meet her, Thea thought ruefully. If her ladyship was so anxious to make her acquaintance, why wasn't she downstairs to welcome her upon arrival? By all accounts, Annabella Cosgrove, Countess Ridgewood, was a termagant of the first order— at least, so went the tale. Why else would she be exiled to such a horrid place, the most distant and desolate of all the earl's properties, while he languished in Bath with his mistress in style?

Thea almost laughed. Her own family was no better. Hadn't her mother cried off from making the journey, feigning an attack of pleurisy and staying behind on their Cornwall estate? Hadn't her viscount father excused himself over "Crown business," when everyone knew he was keeping a Drury Lane doxy in Town, and couldn't bear to miss her Christmas performance? Oh, he would arrive in time to give the bride away, of course. In the meanwhile, Thea's brother James, older by one year, an architectural student under the tutelage of John Nash on Christmas recess, had been recruited to serve in his stead for proprieties' sake. And it was the last thing James wanted, smelling of April and May himself, with a girl of his own left to fend for herself in Town over the holidays. Were all marriages so fractured? Would Thea's be the same, with no love to recommend it— at least on her part? She expected so.

"What say you come away from that window, miss, and let me tuck some ribbons in your hair before ya go down?" the maid asked, interrupting her thoughts. They needed interrupting; Thea was becoming positively forlorn. "These pretty blue ones?" the maid chirped on. "They'll look so fine against your black hair, and they match that frock just perfect."

Thea started to turn away from the diamond-shaped panes in their lead fretwork, an obvious addition to apertures that were scarcely wider than arrow slits, when movement below caught her attention. Someone was walking across the courtyard. *Walking*, in such a storm? It was a woman, her gait more a stagger as she plowed through the heavily mounting snow that had already buried the well-manicured grounds.

Where had she come from? There was nothing but rolling hills for miles in that desolate stretch, where the River Boyne wound its serpentine way through the valley. The villages of Drogheda on the east and Slane on the west were each at least five miles distant, so she'd been told. Even Oldbridge, the nearest hamlet, was a good two miles downstream.

The woman couldn't have walked from any of them. Not in such a storm. The closest structure was the curious burial mound Nigel had pointed out on the way. New-grange, called *Si An Bhru* in the old days, he'd told her, a strange Megalithic passage tomb, where supposedly only once a year, on the winter solstice, sunlight shining through the roof box lit up the chambers for seventeen minutes. A curious tourist attraction, but certainly no one *lived* there. It had piqued Thea's interest, however, and she had made up her mind to be among those who would witness the phenomenon two days hence, weather permitting. That didn't seem likely now.

"There's someone out there," she said.

"Where, miss?" The maid craned her neck for a view through the narrow window.

Thea pointed. "She's coming here. Never mind the ribbons, Annie. I shall go down as I am."

Without a second thought, Thea made her way below just as the heavy iron ring on the front door banged like thunder on the dented plate beneath. The sound echoed along the empty stone passageways. It ran her through like a javelin. James met her on the landing, and followed her down to the sound of raised voices funneling up the stairs.

A tall strait-laced butler was standing in the open doorway, his arm across the span barring a ragged-looking woman from entering. Snow making little whorls about his feet dusted his shoes and trouser legs, which were snapping in the wind. The woman's shawl and head scarf were caked white, suggesting that she had been out in the storm for some time.

"Well, you cannot come in here, madam!" the butler said, opposing the woman who was pushing on the door from the other side. "Be off with ye! We don't take in Gypsies. Be off, I say! Or I'll call the lackeys to put ye off."

"It's not charity I'm beggin'," the woman shouted over the wail of the wind. "Just ta warm me weary bones by your fire, and speak me piece. There's one inside who needs me. . . ."

"None here needs the likes o' you!" the butler assured her. He seemed to be trying not to hurt her, but he was clearly out of patience.

Thea gasped, drifting toward the commotion.

"What the deuce?" her brother muttered, sprinting along behind.

They reached the great hall below, flooded now with others drawn there by the din, her fiancé among them.

"What seems to be the difficulty, Regis?" Nigel Cosgrove asked, his tall form alongside the vexed butler blocking Thea's view. She crept closer for a better look at the woman still begging admittance.

"This person, sir," said the butler. "She refuses to leave."

"My man has told you to depart," Cosgrove said. "We do not admit your kind, and even if we did it would never be by way of the front door. Be off, unless you'd rather I summon the guards from the Watch at Drogheda."

Struggling with the wind in the doorway, he tried to close the door in the woman's face, but the wind was too strong of a sudden. The heavy gusts slamming against it seemed to have risen out of nowhere, and Thea stifled a gasp, laying a gentle hand upon her betrothed's bottle-green superfine coat sleeve.

"Nigel, please, she's nearly frozen stiff!" she said, drawing his eyes. "What harm to let her warm herself beside the fire for a bit before she moves on?"

"And have her rob us blind for our pains?" he asked, incredulous. "You do not know these tinkers, my pet. Like as not, the rest of her band lies in wait close by. You have one in and you have the lot on your hands. She knows the rules. Bold as brass, these cheeky thieving Gypsies, by God." The last was spoken through clenched teeth as he wrestled with the heavy door and the woman's remarkable strength.

"For me . . . ?" Thea persisted. "She's old, and I see no others about. How shall she best you—a poor frail shadow of a creature against a man of your stature, not to mention the servants at your command? You could handle any situation that might arise in a trice. Please, Nigel, 'tis Christmastide."

Nigel stared down at her, his face a study in exasperation. The faint laugh lines that punctuated his thin lips deepened in a frown that took in his eyes as well, darkening the clear, sapphire blue to cold slate.

"This is not England, Thea," he said, as though he were speaking to a child. That he was restraining himself was clearly evident. He had a temper. She'd seen it in action, but never directed at her. Was she testing the waters, or tempting fate? He didn't give her the chance to decide. "These creatures are like locusts," he went on. "They swarm over the land, picking it clean as they go. They know their place, but they stray from it with no compunction whatsoever, and it is up to us, their betters, to keep them in it. You have only just arrived, puss. You are not yet accustomed to our Irish ways. You would do well not to interfere."

"I do not think any of that has one thing to do with Christian charity," said Thea, defiant. "That, and that alone, is my concern. One would not turn a dog out on such a night. Besides . . . I've heard tell that it's bad luck to turn a Gypsy away without a token."

Nigel rolled his eyes. He'd given over fighting with the heavy old door and the woman in the way. Regis and several liveried footmen had come forward and laid hands upon her.

"Please? For me?" Thea asked sweetly, hugging herself and dancing in place. The biting wind was raw and bitter, tearing through the twilled silk frock that bared her arms and décolleté. Already a dusting of white had blown through the open door, spilling over the sill. She had been cold before, but now she was fairly numb.

Nigel glowered, spoiling his handsome face. "Very well," he said, with a dramatic, arm-sweeping bow from the waist. Waving the servants off, he said to the Gypsy, "Go 'round to the servants entrance in back. Regis, tell Cook to see she's warmed and given bread and broth before she continues *on her way*." The last was said while dosing the woman with a meaningful glare. She turned with a nod, but Thea's hand shot out and gripped her bony arm through the snow-caked shawl.

"Through those drifts?" she said to her betrothed. "They are knee deep!" Then, to the woman as she pulled her over the threshold, extracting a collective gasp from the gathering: "Don't be afraid, go with Regis. He will see you're cared for, won't you, Regis?"

The butler's jaw dropped. The Gypsy stared at Thea long and hard, her wrinkled lips twitching, her long gray hair straggling out from beneath the snow-covered head scarf. Thea took a chill not bred of the frosty night, staring into eyes that resembled a raven's—small, shiny, and black. They shone with approval.

"I'm not the one who needs ta be afraid," the woman said with a sly wink, her voice like gravel. " 'Tis you that needs ta hear me words, young miss. 'Tis you I've come ta warn." She slid her hooded eyes the length of Nigel Cosgrove, standing arms akimbo, the toe of his polished Hessian boot tapping the rhythm of his annoyance on the terrazzo underfoot.

"That will be quite enough!" he said, slamming the door with a crack that echoed. It had suddenly become quite manageable. Closing it, and then Thea, with a withering glance, as if the whole unfortunate business were *her* fault, he took hold of the Gypsy and steered her toward the flabbergasted butler. "Deal with this at once and have done!" he charged. "My fiancée evidently has a soft spot in her heart for strays. I am not so disposed."

The Gypsy dug in her heels. "Not before I speak me piece!" she said. "And there's no need ta cross me palm with coin o' the realm for it, neither—but it ain't for the likes o' the rest o' you lot, what I've got ta say. . . ." Wrenching free, she staggered back, cupped her wrinkled hands around her mouth, and whispered in Thea's ear.

The Gypsy's breath was hot and foul, smelling of garlic and the ghost of strong ale. Thea shuddered as it puffed against her skin, and at the words themselves. The blood drained away from her hot cheeks and she scarcely breathed. The only sound then was the thumping of her heart and the wail of the wind outside, plaintive and forlorn, like a woman sobbing her sorrows in the night.

The Gypsy had scarcely stopped speaking when Nigel seized her arm, none too gently, and remanded her to the reluctant butler's custody. "See her fed and send her off!" he gritted through clenched teeth, "before I change my mind entirely. My patience is at low ebb—I warn you, one and all."

"Remember what I've told ya," the Gypsy said as Regis led her away. "Ya heed me words, young miss . . ." She said more, but out of range, and Thea turned back to the others, perplexed. While she didn't understand the woman's message, the urgency in its delivery was crystal clear.

"So this is Theodosia," a high-pitched female voice shrilled over the discordant murmur leaking from the gathered servants. The speaker stilled them with a hand gesture.

Nigel took a firm hold of Thea's arm, his anger palpable, and she sketched a curtsy.

"Yes, my lady," she said, "but I prefer to be called 'Thea,' if you please."

"Mmm," said the countess, "how common. Well, I do *not* please. I shall address you as 'Theodosia.' It is a fine name—a respectable name. No need to cheapen it with a sobriquet." Then, to Nigel, as if she weren't there: "She needs taking in hand. She is not mistress of Cashel Cosgrove yet, m'boy. See to it. Now, then! If we are finished with theatrics for the moment, our supper grows cold."

The countess turned, jutting her elbow for Nigel to latch onto and lead her into the dining hall. He obliged, and James, silent throughout the strange occurrence, seized Thea's arm and inclined his dark head close.

"Steady, little sister," he said in a whisper as they followed behind. "Your cheeks are positively crimson. Don't let the old peahen get your goat."

"So much for good first impressions," Thea said dourly. "She's dreadful, isn't she?"

"Quite so, but you will charm her."

"I don't think I want to, James."

"Stuff! You're not marrying the countess, Thea. It's Nigel that matters, and the chap's quite smitten."

Smitten, yes, but not bowled over, Thea decided, monitoring Nigel's bearing. Granted, she'd overreached herself, but he hadn't defended her in a gentlemanly fashion. Instead, he had berated her before the servants—before *his mother.* She glanced behind. Regis and the Gypsy had disappeared in the shadows, and she drew a ragged breath feeling very alone all of a sudden. Even her brother was inclined to side with her betrothed. It did not bode well.

"What was all that back there?" James asked, calling her back to the present. "What set you off like that? Surely you realize you were out of line."

"I . . . I don't know," Thea admitted. "It seemed so heartless to evict the poor creature in such a storm. That would never be the case at home. I am not liking Ireland, James."

"Taradiddle! You'll get used to it. 'Tis the winter that's put you off; it's heavenly in these parts in spring and summer. The land hereabouts is wild and beautiful then. The hunting is top notch. Edgar Farbershire bagged two awesome stags in the wood south of Drogheda last season. And the fox hunting! I shall be your perpetual gentleman guest, sister dear."

"Nigel stands to inherit Cashel Cosgrove," Thea went on, scarcely having heard. "He means for us to *live* here meanwhile . . ."

"Have you talked to him about your misgivings?" James asked, clouding.

"I don't know as I have misgivings exactly. It's just that . . . Oh, I know, he is the catch of the season amongst the crop of second sons in the offing. He's from one of the richest families in the ton, he's handsome—everything a girl could want in a husband. But . . ."

"But you aren't in love with him. Is that it?"

"Father says that will come in time. You know how he wants this match. The Cosgroves are high in the instep. He means to tap that resource. And Mother! She has visions of *following the drum*, as it were, of coercing Father into buying a property hereabout, and setting up housekeeping as far from his doxy as she can range herself. She thinks that will end the affair. No! I shan't go into Mother."

"What's come over you?" James asked, studying her. How clear and violet his eyes were. Were hers really as bright? She hoped so. Everyone always praised them, but Divine Providence had a way of favoring the male of the species before the female when it came to looks, and she'd always thought him handsome, and herself drab by comparison.

"Nothing," she lied. His look told her she hadn't gotten away with it, and she sighed. "All right," she said. She had never been able to flummox him. "He could be more attentive, James, and I didn't care for the way he embarrassed me in company just now."

He laughed. "Is that all? I was set to take you to task myself, and would have done if he hadn't. That independent streak of yours is legendary, sister dear. It was refreshing when we were young, but we are not children now, and these are not accustomed to such . . . outspokenness in a young lady of quality. All Irish aren't bog-stomping muck savages. The Irish aristocracy strives more diligently than we English to rise above a negative image. You needs must behave, unless you fancy putting on your caps. You're one and twenty after all. You've had two seasons with no takers. Is that because you are choosy to a fault? Have you set your standards too high? You'll never convince me that you've been passed over because of your looks." Avoiding his gaze, Thea didn't answer. "Well," he went on, clearing his voice, "you aren't likely to do better than Nigel Cosgrove now and everybody benefits. You ought to thank your lucky stars that Father interceded. You were well on your way to becoming a proper spinster."

Thea supposed so, though she didn't say it. James wouldn't understand. He was a man after all. Men looked at such things differently. Besides, how could she tell him that, while she longed for a man who would revere and cherish her, she secretly fantasized giving her virtue to a man possessed of lusty passions that would awaken her own, like the heroes in the scandalous novels and poems she wasn't supposed to be reading? The gentlemen she'd met during her two failed seasons either showed promise in one of those areas or the other, never both. Nigel had come close to her heart's desire at home, when he was courting her and on his best behavior, but now . . .

They had nearly reached the dining hall, and the mere thought of sitting at table with the countess now was having its way with Thea's resolve. The way Nigel danced attendance—albeit with disdain—to his mother was nauseating. He reminded her of a trained bear she'd once seen at Astley's Amphitheatre: dancing along obedient as you please at the end of its chain with the slightest tug, but a dangerous killer once shot of it. It was clear who ruled the roost, and he obviously resented it. Was this why he was so insufferable with everyone else? She shuddered.

"You're trembling," James remarked. "You took a dreadful chill back there. Shall I go up and fetch your shawl?"

"No, no, it's just that . . . I do not relish facing the countess after . . . you know . . ."

"Mmm. Can't say as I blame you, but it must be done. Enough now! Bear up! You've got some serious fences to mend, my girl."

"You're a good brother and a capital friend, James Barrington," she murmured fondly, squeezing his arm.

"And well I know it," he replied with a wink. Then he

clouded. "Look here, what did that blasted Gypsy say to you?" he asked. "You went absolutely white—like you've just done now."

The dining hall arch loomed larger than life before her, and so there wouldn't be time to tell it even if she were willing. Instead, Thea laid a finger over her lips and put on her bravest face as her brother handed her over the threshold. The Gypsy's cryptic message would have to wait. She was still trying to sort it out herself. She'd sensed something untoward the minute she saw the woman trudging through the snow from her chamber window, and the chill that riddled her now had nothing to do with the cold in the drafty old castle.

"Never mind," her brother agreed. "'Tisn't important, it's over. You'll never see the odious old crone again."

But entering the drafty dining hall on her brother's arm, Thea didn't believe that for an instant.

Chapter Two

Thea was ill at ease all through that first dinner at Cashel Cosgrove, though no mention was made of the earlier incident with the Gypsy. Nigel seemed distant through the first two courses. It wasn't until they'd cleansed their palates with fragrant lemon and rosewater ice before the meat course that he took part in the conversation. It probably wouldn't have happened at all, thought Thea, if James hadn't inquired about the history of the castle. She almost wished he hadn't. She was set to cry off and beg to be excused from the table once he'd gotten past the Great War of 1641 in his narrative. He was giving an account of Oliver Cromwell's march on Drogheda, when a name was mentioned that froze her spine rigid in her chair. *Drumcondra*. After that, wild horses could not have dragged her from the table.

"In addition to the soldiers defending the place, there were three thousand unarmed and unsuspecting citizens in Drogheda when the conflict began," Nigel said. "Only thirty Irish remained after the slaughter. One of them, a half-breed Gypsy, Cormac Drumcondra, lived to father the most infamous libertine ever to prowl Irish soil—Clan Chieftain Ros Drumcondra, archrival of the Cosgroves, a fearsome giant of a man who once owned this castle and surrounding lands and commanded a formidable army of local supporters. But he was betrayed by the powerful nobles in England."

"What happened to . . . D-Drumcondra?" asked Thea, swallowing the dryness in her throat while Nigel paused to sip his wine.

"Patience, pet, I'm coming to it," her fiancée said, punctuating his narrative with little stabs of his fork in the air. He scowled. "Though I would have expected you to be more concerned over what happened to *our* ancestors." Wary of his tone, Thea made no reply and he cleared his voice before commencing again. "When King Charles II died and was succeeded by King James II, a Catholic, the Irish populous rejoiced, believing that King James would restore their lands, but the English nobles, unwilling to give up their power here so easily, called upon William of Orange to be their king. In 1688, William defeated James, who fled to France to regroup. He returned a year later and won a few skirmishes, in which the Drumcondras and the Cosgroves took part—on opposite sides, of course. Then, in the summer of 1690, William landed with his army and defeated James in the infamous Battle of the Boyne—"

"That site is nearby, isn't it?" James interrupted.

"Yes, how astute of you, old boy, just two or three miles downstream from here at Oldbridge. The land hereabout is rich in history, and baptized in blood."

Thea shivered, not entirely from the chill in the dining parlor despite a blazing hearth. "It's hard to imagine this peaceful, pristine place a bloody battlefield," she said.

"Must we have this dreadful discourse at table, Nigel?" the countess spoke up. "It's hardly fitting mealtime conversation."

"I am proud of our heritage, Mother," Nigel replied, "and the tale is nearly told. Now where was I? Oh yes, Drumcondra, with his army reduced to no more than a ragtag band after the carnage, was driven into the hills where he strove to win back this castle to no avail. Meanwhile, the Penal Laws imposed by the English reduced the Irish Catholics to nonentities in their own country. Cosgroves owned this castle and surrounding land, and have done since, having seized it from Drumcondra in their own private war amongst the clans."

"Evidently Drumcondra wasn't quite the fearsome warrior you painted him," James observed, "if he could lose his holdings so easily."

"To the contrary," Nigel replied. "If he had been in residence, it would have had a different outcome entirely. He was raiding in the north, and our ancestors took advantage of his absence and their alliance with the English nobles to seize the castle. There's more, of course, but what remains is quite unfit for a lady's ears. There were four Cosgrove brothers holding this keep at the time, each more bloodthirsty than the next."

"And naturally the eldest took control," James presumed. "There must have been fierce rivalry amongst them."

"No," Nigel said. "The Penal Laws abolished the policy of the eldest son of a Catholic inheriting his father's land. Instead, it was to be divided equally amongst the sons when their father died, unless one of them opted to renounce his Catholic heritage and embrace the Protestant religion. Then he would inherit the property entire. It was our ancestor, Cian Cosgrove, the second eldest—Ros

Drumcondra's arch nemesis—who did just that, which is the reason this branch of the Cosgrove family is Protestant today. The other three brothers were weak, and would not have been able to stand against Ros Drumcondra's constant efforts to take back his land. Bad judgment in battle soon cost them their lives. Cian Cosgrove was a fearsome lord, and he held it. Some say he had otherworldly help, that he did so by supernatural means. At any rate, he held on to the land, and that is why you dine tonight in Cashel Cosgrove and not Cashel Drumcondra."

"What caused the feud between Drumcondra and the Cosgroves?" James asked, earning him a strained look from Thea. Having heard enough, she really wanted to escape, but she dared not—not until she'd heard it all.

"What started it is lost in the mists of prerecorded Celtic history," Nigel said, "and dates back to medieval times. What fueled it at the last was that Drumcondra captured Cian Cosgrove's betrothed, whisked her off to another of his keeps, and made a love slave of her. The tale stops there. No further written records exist."

Silent until then, Thea found her voice. "But, what happened to Ros Drumcondra . . . and the girl?" she asked in a small voice.

All eyes bore down upon her.

"Why would you care?" Nigel blurted, taken aback. "That's twice now you've shown partiality."

"I . . . I don't," she replied, setting her fork down to keep it from clattering against her plate. "And being curious is hardly showing partiality. You've told a one-sided tale, and I always like to hear both sides of a story."

The countess rolled her raisinlike eyes, and leaked an exasperated grunt. Thea nearly laughed, recalling how often Nigel made the same rude sound and gesture.

"Sometimes you amaze me, Thea," Nigel said, his voice

cold. "I should imagine you would be more 'curious' about the Cosgroves, since you are enjoying their hospitality under their roof and are about to become one of them."

"I'd like to know, too," James spoke up.

Nigel's eyes became daggers cast across the table, his lips curved in an acid smile. "Curiosity runs in the family, does it?" he said. "Well, I'm afraid I really cannot help you. No one knows. They were never heard of again. Ros Drumcondra simply vanished from the pages of our family's recorded history. Some say he ended his days in hiding at Newgrange. He was a Gypsy, remember—at least by half—and leader of his clan. He and his band evidently found a way inside the cairn that was no more than a mound of earth then, because that is where many of their bones were found when it was excavated in 1699. But Ros Drumcondra's bones were not among them."

"How would it have been possible to tell?" James challenged. "Bones are bones, I should imagine."

"He was such a hulking giant, it would have been easy to identify his remains," said Nigel. "Some say his ghost walks this very castle, still seeking to claim it. The servants will attest to that. I do not suggest that you encourage them. Others swear they've seen Drumcondra stalking the hills, his falcon on his shoulder. Some say the bird was his familiar. That's why the peasants and nobles alike called him The Black Falcon. Still others say his spirit lives within the passageways of Newgrange, and that each year at the winter solstice, when the sun lights the tomb, he ventures forth to try again to win back the castle. He has become the stuff of legends. I say, you can take your pick—it's all balderdash. Fill your heads with such nonsense, and you may as well credit the ridiculous Gypsy tales of time tunnels hereabout that sweep men away and carry them from place to place. Or the Loch Ness monster!"

Thea hadn't touched her roast mutton. It had grown cold on the plate. She let the liveried footman take it away, and cried off when he offered the removes. Rising from the table, she set her serviette alongside her plate and cleared her voice.

"I hope you will excuse me," she said. "I'm quite exhausted after the journey, and I am really more in need of rest than food."

"I'll see you to your chamber," James said, rising also.

"No!" cried Thea, a little too loudly. If she were to let him, he might ask her about the Gypsy again. She couldn't tell him now—especially not now, maybe not ever. "Stay," she murmured. "Finish your meal. I'm quite capable of finding my chamber without an escort."

Nigel was on his feet as well. Thea knew he wouldn't offer to accompany her; it would hardly be proper. Besides, it was all too plain that he was still cross with her. When she turned to go, his voice addressing one of the footmen froze her in her tracks.

"Digby, light her way," he charged, nodding toward the candlebranch on the sideboard. "It's probably best that you do retire and reflect, Thea," he said. "We're off on the wrong foot. Perhaps tomorrow we might begin again on more amiable ground."

The footman took up the candles and escorted her toward the dining hall arch. The countess's shrill monotone echoed along the corridor. Thea didn't have to hear what she was saying to get the gist. Her very tone exuded her displeasure. But that was the least of Thea's worries now that she'd heard the tale of Ros Drumcondra. Still, the acoustics in the ancient castle were such that she did hear fragments of the conversation echoing along the drafty hallway, the countess's voice in particular dominating the others.

"You, sir, are her brother," she was saying. "Surely you can take her to task. For centuries the Cosgroves have fought to upgrade their image. We are no longer barbarians, sir. We entertain here, and proper decorum is essential. The child has no concept of it. Thea, indeed! She shall be called *Theodosia*. We shall begin with that, and *you*, Nigel . . ."

Thea would like to have heard her brother's response, but it was just as well that the footman led her out of range. It didn't matter. She was what she was. Nothing the venerable Countess Ridgewood could say or do was going to change that.

She was having serious misgivings, however. She might not be ready to confide that to others, but she never lied to herself. Why had she agreed to her father's edict? Why had she allowed it to go this far? Why hadn't she held out just a little longer in search of the man of her dreams? Granted, such marriage arrangements were politically correct and quite commonplace amongst the ton, and it was good that her father settle her well, and himself into the bargain, but what of *her*? Did her feelings mean nothing? Why had she bent to his will? The answer to that was distressing at best, but simple enough: because she no longer had a choice. The marriage was brokered. She had no say in the matter. It was simply the way things were done to save face when a girl was on the verge of passing her prime. She was hardly the only young woman in England to be trapped in a loveless marriage for the betterment of others. She would just have to make the best of it.

If she were to be honest with herself, she had to admit that in the beginning she'd been dazzled by Nigel's good looks, suave manner, and cultivated charm. But no longer. Upon closer inspection she found him to be seriously flawed, possessed of a vile temper, prone to black sulks, with a propensity for holding grudges. Nonetheless, things had gone too far to turn back. They'd come all the way to Ireland to align with the Cosgroves, and everyone was expecting a wedding in a fortnight. By then, her father would have arrived. There was no hope for it but to see things through to the bitter end, to join the ranks of her martyred mother and settle for what consolations the ton afforded such women. She would content herself with her children once they came, while her husband languished with his Cyprian—an acceptable arrangement, all supposedly very civilized.

They reached her chamber, and Thea thanked the footman and stepped inside. Annie was waiting to ready her for bed. Her nightshift and wrapper had been neatly laid atop the counterpane. The maid dressed her before the fire, then brushed out her shoulder-length curls before the vanity looking glass. She was the image of a Gypsy herself, with her hair, dark and wild, loosed from its combs, falling from a natural center part.

Thea hadn't quite been won over by the new short hairstyles, nor had she the patience for keeping long hair, since Annie was not clever with coiffures. She opted instead for something in between that could be swept up from the nape of the neck and styled in loose curls and tendrils in such a way that she didn't resemble a skinned cat.

Once her toilette was complete, she dismissed the abigail, whose cell adjoined hers, blew out the candles, and went to the window, tugging her shawl about her shoulders over the rest. The cold damp was penetrating despite the blazing fire. Outside the snow was still falling, blowing, drifting, and would be until morning, she had no doubt. The night sky had an eerie pink glow about it. There was no sign of the old Gypsy woman; the snow had long since covered her tracks. It was almost as if she had never come. But she had. The whole household could attest to that.

But for the wail of the wind and the soft hissing of snow blowing against the panes, there was no sound until a mournful screech rent the silence, riveting her to the spot. Soaring above the battlements, a great peregrine falcon dipped low, black in silhouette against the eerie snow-swept sky. Thea estimated its graceful wingspan at nearly four feet across. It screeched again, swooped low—almost touching the window—and as if borne on an updraft of the wind, wended its way skyward again. Up, up, it climbed, to sail off and disappear in the night.

A cold chill snaked its way along Thea's spine as she watched the magnificent bird's performance, for that is what it seemed. Was it a welcome, or an ill omen? She couldn't be certain. Nevertheless, she stood at the window for a good long while hoping for another glimpse of the creature. It did not return.

Standing there, Thea felt a throbbing start deep inside—a shuddering pulse that beat at her very core—and she realized in surprise and dismay that the exhibition had aroused her.

"Ye do not belong with this lot. Ye have come here for another. Two days until the solstice and ye see Ros Drumcondra, the Black Falcon, in the flesh. Beware the Cosgrove clan. Ye are the Falcon's bride. . . ."

The old Gypsy's words came to Thea again and again in her dream. What did it all mean? How could she be the bride of a warrior long dead? She tossed in the bed, disturbing the covers, displacing the feather mattress, the counterpane and cold linen sheets. When the sound came, she wasn't sure if it was the blood-chilling scream that woke her, or the cold draft that had snaked its way beneath the covers.

"Annie?" she cried, swinging her feet to the cold bare floor. The scream came again, and her heart nearly stopped at the sound.

Shuddering in involuntary spasms, Thea snatched her shawl from the floor where it had fallen, whipped it around her shoulders and burst into Annie's cubicle through the adjoining door. The girl was whimpering in the corner, babbling and trembling, her mousy brown hair straggling from beneath her nightcap, both hands clasped over her mouth as if to keep more shrieks from escaping.

"What is it?" Thea asked, shaking the maid. "Stop that infernal caterwauling for pity sake, and tell me! Is it rats? *What?*"

"I-it was just like they said," Annie stuttered. "The housekeeper, Mrs. Mabley, Regis and the others. I seen 'im! I seen 'im plain as day. Leanin' right over my bed, he was, with that eagle on his shoulder!"

"Someone was in here?" Thea cried. "Who, Annie?"

" 'Twas *Ros Drumcondra*! I seen 'im, I *did!*"

Frantic pounding at the door and shouts from the corridor outside sent Thea to answer. Nigel and James burst into the room, a troop of lackeys and footmen decked out in their night rails pouring in after them.

"What the devil's going on up here?" Nigel demanded, cinching his dressing gown about his middle with rough hands.

"Are you all right, Thea?" James urged, before she could answer.

"Uh . . . nothing . . . er, yes, James, I'm quite all right. Annie had a dream . . . a nightmare, that's all. I'm sorry if we've disturbed you."

"A *dream?*" the maid shrilled. " 'Tweren't no dream. I seen 'im plain as I'm seein' all o' you."

"Who?" James and Nigel asked simultaneously.

"Ros Drumcondra is who!" Annie wailed. "Standin' right over my bed, he was!"

"A figment of her imagination," Thea explained. "The servants have filled her head with tales of the ghost that's supposed to haunt the castle, and frightened her half out of her wits. Leave her to me . . . please. She'll be seeing specters in every shadow now. Go back to bed. I'll sit with her awhile."

Leaking an exasperated sigh, Nigel shook his head and stalked from the room, his bare feet slapping the floorboards. He grumbled a curt command that the others follow, but James hung back.

"Are you sure, Thea?" he asked, a look of genuine concern in his violet eyes. "I shall stay with you if you like. I shan't sleep again now in any case."

"No, James," Thea responded, stirring the fire to life in the grate. "I'll be fine. Run on and leave it to me." She went to him and, under the guise of a kiss on the cheek whispered, "We'd best not make too much of this. I'll settle her down. Oh, and thank you."

"For what?"

"For not calling me Theodosia."

"You heard that, did you?"

"I did, and I bring it up only to let you know that arguing the point is useless—just in case they'd convinced you."

"Fat chance, little sister."

"Good! Now, go back to bed, and let me see if I can calm her. And if you happen to see Ros Drumcondra lurking about, kindly tell him he's caused quite enough trouble for one night, since he isn't supposed to be abroad until the solstice. Now, shoo!"

James quit the chamber then, with a lopsided smile that had always put Thea at her ease, and she turned back to Annie.

"I don't care what ya say, miss," exclaimed the maid, "I seen 'im. I *did*, and he weren't no pigment o' my imagination, neither."

"You *saw* him, Annie," Thea corrected her, "and he wasn't a 'pigment,' but a *figment* of your imagination."

"Yes . . . no . . . you're mixin' me all up now!"

"Yes, well, let us leave that, and talk of pleasant things for a bit. Then, when you've calmed, we shall both go back to sleep." Inspiration struck. "I know!" she said. "There's a decanter of sherry—at least I think it's sherry— in my chamber. What say we both have a glass?"

"Oh, no, miss! I couldn't."

"Nonsense," Thea argued, padding toward the door. "I'll just be a minute. Oh, now, what a face! Don't worry, I shan't get you foxed. A little spirits will be just the thing to relax you, so you can fall back to sleep."

"I don't think I'm ever goin' ta sleep another wink in this horrid ol' house!" the maid grumbled in a low mutter.

The decanter was on a drop leaf table beside the door in Thea's chamber—left there no doubt as a remedy for chill rather than a welcoming gift, she surmised. The fire had nearly gone out, and but for the opalescent shimmer the snow cast through the window, the room was in bleak semidarkness.

Thea took up the pewter salver that held the decanter and glasses, and shivered at the touch of the cold metal in her hands. Turning back, she pulled up short, trembling from head to toe as waves of crippling chills knitted the bones rigid in her spine. She staggered back a pace. There, in the shadows, stood the misty image of a towering black Irish warrior, his raven-colored hair worn long in stark juxtaposition to his bronzed, clean-shaven face. He wore wide-top turned-down boots over dun-colored leggings that left nothing to the imagination in the region of his well-turned thighs. A mole-colored leather jerkin girded his torso. His muscular arms were bare but for the leather caps on his jerkin and the studded leather gauntlets beneath a cloak made of the pelts of a short-haired animal that was slung over his left shoulder and fastened with a silver brooch. The look in his eyes riveted her like cannon fire. Those eyes were deep set and the color of tarnished copper flecked with gold, like the eyes of a wolf bearing down upon her in the eerie light filtering through the window. They held her relentlessly.

Shocked though she was by his sudden appearance, come so soon after Nigel's chilling account of the man, it was the scandalous firestorm those seductive eyes set loose inside her that drained her senses. They stripped her naked. And to her horror, she *let* them. In stark terror she stood, her gaze locked with that of a ghost—a ghost that aroused her with a look alone.

She swayed. Someone screamed. The sound rang in her ears. Had it come from her own parched throat? Thea saw no falcon, but the flapping of its wings was suddenly all around her. She blinked, and the specter was gone, taking consciousness with it. But the palpitating sensations in her most private regions remained.

The scream came again as glaring white splinters impaired her vision, then the light failed altogether and Thea's bones seemed to melt away underneath her skin. The salver and everything on it hit the floor before she did.

Chapter Three

"So you, too, have made the acquaintance of our resident ghost," Nigel said tongue in cheek the next morning. At his request, they had climbed up to the battlements after breakfast. He'd insisted that she accompany him there under the pretext of showing her the breathtaking view, but Thea surmised that the interview was to take on the form of a lecture, and she'd steeled herself against it.

"Nothing of the sort," she said. "Annie's nonsense had my imagination playing tricks upon me is all. That and the gruesome tales you told at table last night were enough to make any girl swoon."

"Hm," he grunted. "You don't believe in ghosts, I take it?"

"I've never given them much thought."

"Well, the servants in this house do, I'm afraid. Most of them are locals, and they are a superstitious lot. In these parts some folk still leave their front and back doors ajar at night to permit the fairies to walk through unhindered. Pay them no mind, and do try to control your imagination

27

in the future. That little scene on top of Annie's hysteria won't bear repeating. As it is, the unfortunate business will have them buzzing below stairs for weeks."

"I shall do my best," said Thea, gazing out over the grounds. The falcon had returned, or another like it, sailing lazily aloft, dipping and soaring overhead as if it were watching them. Everything for miles was pristine white. Even the distant trees wore thick snow mantles. The snow had stopped, but the gray sky threatened more, bleeding from zenith to horizon like a watercolor painting. It outlined a distant mound she recognized as Newgrange, its menhirs and wet kerbstones silhouetted black against the drifts. Pulling the hood of her fur pelerine closer about her against the wind, Thea nodded toward it.

"What is that place exactly?" she asked, hoping to divert his attention from the scolding he'd intended to deliver out of range of the others' hearing. "You only touched upon it briefly when we passed it on the way here."

"Newgrange is our mysterious antiquity," he replied, "a passage tomb constructed some odd five thousand or so years ago."

"A passage tomb?"

He nodded. "An ancient burial mound, supposedly a link between the living and the dead, and a passageway to the Celtic gods they serve—*An Dagda*, father of all the gods and goddesses, his daughter *Brighid*, goddess of wisdom, *Lir*, god of the sea, and *Balor of the piercing eye*, whose own grandson is said to have put his eye out with a spear, to name but a few. There are several such in these parts. For centuries it appeared as nothing more than a hilly mound of earth. Then, when excavation began in 1699, the stone mound underneath and corbelled vault that forms the roof of the inner chamber were discovered." He pointed. "Look there," he said. "You can barely see . . . a circle of twelve menhirs surround it. Archeologists say that these curious upright boulders and the tomb itself were once the focal point of pagan ritualistic celebrations."

"Tomorrow is the winter solstice," Thea remarked. "I want to see what happens."

Nigel seemed annoyed. "In all this snow? What ever for?"

"I shan't get the chance again for a whole year," she replied. "I would like to be there at dawn when light fills the chambers."

Nigel shook his head. "You want me to wear out old Beadle the stabler hooking up a rusty old sleigh that hasn't been used in years, just to drive round to that dreary old place in such weather as this is? I think not. Look at that sky! There's more snow on the way. You know, you're becoming quite tiresome, Theodosia. That odd business with the old Gypsy woman yesterday, for one thing, not to mention the ridiculous brouhaha over ghosts. Mother says you're just courting attention. Is that it? Or is this something of a different nature? I thought I was paying you more than enough attention. We need to settle these matters now, before the wedding, so that we understand one another going into this."

"If you wish to cry off, I shan't stand in your way," Thea suggested, hoping he'd jump at the opportunity.

"Of course I do not want to break our engagement," he said, turning her toward him. "I simply want to start us out on the right foot. I realize you're young, and I've taken that into account. With nearly fifteen years difference in our ages, there are bound to be . . . difficulties. I merely want to keep them to a minimum. But I cannot do this alone. You need to grow up, Theodosia. The world does not dance to your whims, at least not here at Cashel Cosgrove. Others' feelings must be taken into account. Mine—"

"And your mother's," Thea interrupted. The wind whipped tears into her eyes, and she narrowed them. *What an insufferable wretch! Could he really be so full of himself?*

"Yes, and my mother's. What is wrong with that?"

"Well, if you are too dimwitted to see, I shan't waste my pains pointing it out. Suffice it to say that I am not the only one who needs to take stock, Nigel Cosgrove. She pulls your strings like a puppet master in Drury Lane. I thought I was marrying a *man*, not a marionette!"

"You doubt my manhood, do you?" he asked through clenched teeth. Seizing her upper arms in a viselike grip, he crushed her against him and took her in a savage kiss, drawing blood as one of his canine teeth bit into her lower lip. He tasted foul, of gin and undigested food. Thrusting one hand beneath her fur wrap, he groped her while tethering her to him with the other. "I've had no complaints in that department," he said, his voice husky with desire. "It is all I can do to keep my hands off you, Theodosia." All at once his eyes darkened. Traces of her blood glistened on his mouth, fixed in a sneer, and he licked it away with the tip of his tongue. "Why should I?" he said, wrenching her hard against him. "We're as good as wed, and you, miss, need a lesson to show you who is master here."

Terror caught Thea's breath in her throat. Blood rushed to her head. Cruel, pinching fingers tore at the décolleté of her frock until he'd bared her breast to the icy wind. He bent her arm behind her back with such a savage wrench she feared it would break, meanwhile sliding his ravenous mouth the length of her throat to the trembling flesh he'd exposed beneath, and bit down hard upon her nipple. Pinned against the crenellation, she struggled in his arms, striking what she could reach of him with her free hand balled in a fist. Her legs were useless; the bruising pressure of his sex, his rock-hard thighs and muscular torso crushed against her prevented her from raising them to her defense.

"Do not struggle," he spat in her ear. "Struggling only stimulates me." Thea cried out as he forced her free hand against his arousal. He shook her roughly. "Scream again and I'll have you here and now. You have no idea how your pain excites me . . ."

He had hold of her wrist, but not her fingers. And she summoned all the strength she could muster to seize his member like a vise, digging her nails into the soft buckskin breeches drawn taut over its bulk until he cried out and let her go.

Thea tugged the gaping frock back over her nakedness, drew back the hand she'd dug into Nigel's groin, and lowered the flat of it hard to his face. "I smell the Blue Ruin on your breath—and at this hour!" she snapped, struggling to free herself, for all she'd accomplished was to provoke him to seize her again, and more cruelly. The bear was loose of its tether. He was trying to force her to her knees. Adrenaline surged, and she fought him with all her strength. "Any beast in the field can satisfy its urges," she snapped at him. "Lust is no measure of a man. You had best ponder that, and come to terms with what *is* before we take this relationship any further."

"This is just the sort of willful defiance I'm speaking about," he snapped, buffeting her to a standstill. "You will not dictate to me. Not to *me*! You will do as I say, Theodosia. You will speak when you are spoken to, and stay in your place—or I shall be forced to put you in it however needs must."

"Just as you did last night—humiliating me in front of my brother? In front of the servants and your mother? She is horrid! A harridan! Why not teach *her* some manners

while you're about it. She would benefit greatly from a lesson or two in how to treat guests in her home."

"Ahhh, but it *is* her home, Theodosia."

"I will not respond if you continue to address me thus.
You know how I despise that name."

"Oh, you'll respond all right," he growled, yanking her
against him again, his fisted hands clamped around her upper arms. Their strength was bruising even through the
thick fur. "You will respond indeed, my little spitfire."

He lowered his mouth again over hers, forcing his
tongue between her teeth and nearly choking her with it,
despite her muffled cries and her tiny fists beating him
about the head and chest. Terror washed over her in sick-
ening waves. She'd never seen this side of him. She was no
match for his strength. All at once she realized that he
could hoist her off her feet and toss her over the curtain
wall in a trice. All that came to mind was the lightskirt's
murder. Had he killed her in a fit of passion as he'd been
accused, after all? In his arms now, at the mercy of his rage,
she was convinced that it was a distinct possibility.

Had his father's money bought his acquittal? Was that
the reason the earl had been so quick to broker a marriage
arrangement with her father—to see his wayward second
son settled in the Irish wilds under his mother's thumb before some new scandal surfaced? Was that why he wasn't
even going to attend the wedding? It was more than likely.
There had been rumors of something unwholesome having occurred in Spain as well.

Thea wrenched her head aside and panted, "Let me go,
you brute, or I shall scream this house down!"

But she didn't get the chance. Out of nowhere the falcon came, diving at incredible speed between them. Batting Thea away with its slate gray wings, it drove its sharp,
hooked beak straight for Nigel's eye. Screaming as the

great bird tore his flesh and beat him about the head and shoulders with its wings, he released Thea with a shove that sent her sprawling on the cold stone floor of the battlements underfoot.

Blood was everywhere—on Thea's hands, her face, on the soft chinchilla fur pelerine. Nigel was covered with it, struggling with the bird, its talons trying to rip that which it could not bite.

Scrambling to her feet, Thea screamed, and the falcon flew off in a fit of flapping frenzy, its harsh voice like a victory cry echoing back on the wind.

Blood was pouring through the fingers Nigel held over his eye. He'd gone down on one knee, his head bowed, his moans siphoned off on the wind. Thea scanned the sky for some sign of the bird, but it had vanished. Had the creature come to her defense? It certainly seemed so, and she took a sudden chill recalling the legend, the Gypsy's words and the bird that had visited before at her chamber window last night.

"Get up from there and let me help you below, before that hawk returns," she charged, tugging at the sleeve of Nigel's caped greatcoat. "Such birds are dangerous. The scent of blood will bring it back! And do not hold your head down like that. The blood will flow all the more. Nigel! Have you heard me?"

Only his moans replied as he swatted her hand away, and she flew toward the recessed stone stairwell that led below. "Stay down, then!" she cried. "I will fetch help."

What followed was a screaming scene of mass confusion as Thea ran through the castle halls collecting servants to assist her. The countess's shrieks soon joined the noise, and her maids took her in hand while James rode to Oldbridge for the surgeon. Three footmen carried Nigel to his chamber, and the housekeeper promptly banned Thea while all worked to stop the bleeding with pressure compresses made of bandage linen. It was just as well. So many emotions were vying for attention in her that she needed time to sort them out.

She wasn't given long. James returned in less than an hour with the surgeon, and took her to the drawing room to wait for his report. Beside herself over the damage to her son's handsome face, the countess had retired to her chamber with smelling salts and herbal tinctures brewed by Cook to blunt the edges of her upset. Meanwhile, Mrs. Mabley, the housekeeper Thea had not met until the crisis, was hard pressed running back and forth between the two patients. Still, she promised to come at once or send the doctor with news once he'd seen to Nigel upstairs.

"What happened up there, Thea?" James asked, offering her a cordial from a decanter on the sideboard.

Thea waved the glass away. "A bird," she said. "A falcon, I think. It swooped down and attacked Nigel—dove straight for his eye. Nigel had hold of me. We were quarrelling and he . . . he . . . It tried to push me out of the way with its wings, James. Stretched out full measure, those wings had to be nearly four feet across. There was so much blood. . . ."

James looked surprised. "Hawks usually do not attack humans without provocation—unless they are starving or obeying a command from their master."

Thea shook her head. "It couldn't have been hungry. The grounds are overrun with rabbits and squirrels. Their tracks are everywhere in the snow, and there wasn't another soul in sight as far as the eye could see."

"You weren't harmed?"

"Not in the slightest."

"What color was this creature?"

"His head and neck were jet-black, his wings slate gray

with a bluish tinge at the tips. He had a buff-colored throat, and his breast was streaked with black. The streaking was heavier and crosswise on its underbelly. He was a beautiful creature, with the blackest eyes I've ever seen on a bird. They almost looked human."

"If you weren't harmed, how did you get that bruise on your lip there?"

Thea's hand flew to her mouth. She hadn't even noticed the swollen lip crusted with dry blood Nigel's teeth had caused. No wonder Mrs. Mabley gave her such a shocked look earlier. And that was the least of it. Thank the stars the worst of his ravages were hidden from view.

"Well?" James asked.

"That was my fault," she said, averting her eyes. "I challenged his . . . manhood. You see how he behaves with his mother, and he . . . took exception."

"*Nigel* did that?" James said. "Don't tell me I've got to call him out now, Thea. Outstanding!"

"I hardly think it need come to that. He'd been drinking, and—"

"At this hour?" James interrupted, clearly angry. "What the deuce were you doing up there alone with him in the first place? You know better, Thea!" Just brief intervals unchaperoned until the wedding, and then only when servants are likely to be close by.

"Tell that to him! He took me up there to lecture me about my inconsiderate behavior in this house, and . . . things went beyond the pale. I think that's why the bird attacked him. You know, I really believe it was trying to come to my rescue."

"Stuff! Birds don't gallant ladies in distress, *men* do. By god, if I'd been there . . . !"

"Well, you weren't there, and despite what you say I think this bird did, James."

"Zeus, girl! You've gone and put me in the position of having to challenge a one-eyed man!"

"Oh! You don't think . . . Oh, James, no . . ."

He waved her off with a hand gesture, and raked his hair back roughly. "I shouldn't have said it. Forgive me, little sister. We must hope for the best, of course. You've addled me with all this. I never did like the chap—not really. That charm of his is too· sweet to be wholesome, as Grandmama used to say."

"Tell me you won't challenge him. Promise me!"

"You do love him after all, then?"

"No! It's you I love. I only have one brother, and I love him too dearly to risk him in a foolish duel, of all things. Now promise me!"

He scowled. "This speaks volumes to your confidence in my shooting skills," he said at last, his mouth crimping in a lopsided smile.

"Don't tease. Things are too grave for that now."

James fell silent. "Very well," he acquiesced. "I shall forgive him this once. But just this once, mind, as you say he'd been bending the elbow—though he hardly looked foxed to me. If anything of the sort occurs again, he'll feel the sting of my glove on that handsome face of his. You can bet your blunt upon that."

Thea would have said more if the doctor hadn't entered at that precise moment. She rose to her feet and reached out to James, who slipped his arm around her in support. Setting his valise down on the drum table beside the door, the portly little physician helped himself to a cordial from the decanter resting on the sideboard, downing it in one swallow.

"I couldn't save the eye," he said, pouring another. "'Twas too cleanly severed." He wagged his head. "A bird you say? A falcon, was it? In all my years, I've never seen the like. Its talons ripped the flesh halfway down his cheek—nasty sight. It's spoiled that handsome face of his. He's lost a good deal of blood, but I've stitched him up and he'll mend well enough with rest and tending. Mrs. Mabley's got her marching orders. She's an able nurse, and if I'm needed you know where to find me."

"Thank you, Dr . . . ?" Thea queried.

"McBain," the man replied, sketching an awkward heel-clicking bow due to his rotund circumference and the effects of the cordials he'd swallowed. "Dr. Timothy McBain at your service, miss."

"His mother will have to be told," said James, "and I'd really rather not. We are on such short acquaintance, and—"

"Not another word, young son," said the doctor, raising his hand. "I'll do it." He took up the decanter. "But I'll have another of these first. I'm well acquainted with the countess."

He tossed back two more glasses before he quit the room, and James turned to Thea. "Look here, you didn't even ask the man if you could see Nigel," he said. "Don't you think you should?"

"No, I don't want to see him . . . at least not now," she replied. "But there is something I do want, and I need your help, James. None here will humor me, and I don't know why, but it's important."

"What might that be?"

"Tomorrow is the solstice. I want to see the passage tomb at sunrise."

"Newgrange? What ever for?"

"I just do. I asked Nigel to take me, but he refused, and he couldn't now in any case. But you could, James. There's a sleigh in the stables. Could you have it readied before dawn and drive me round?"

James balked. "I suppose I could—but I don't know as I should, Thea. If the countess finds out . . ."

"Oh, bother the countess! What? Am I a prisoner here?
You may as well say yes, because if you don't, I shall walk."

"Ohhh no, little sister," he said, "not while that bird is
loose out there. The countess is certain to demand that it
be shot down, and if not, I shall take on that task myself."

"No! Do not dare harm one feather on that bird's body!"
she cried. "It's scary, but . . . if it hadn't come when it
did . . . Well, never mind. Just don't harm it. You know
how I have always championed helpless creatures." It was
a half-truth. Aching from Nigel's cruel embrace, she secretly feared she may have need of a champion again.

James gave a mighty guffaw in which there was no humor. "I'd hardly call that creature 'helpless,' love," he said.

Thea grimaced. "Will you take me, or not?"

"I think you've got attics to let, but I will, if that's what
you want." James sighed. "When have you ever known me
to deny you anything?"

"Good! Don't let on to anyone, not even the servants.
Not even the stabler, until we're ready to leave."

"Very well, then," said James with a wag of his head. "I
just hope we shan't live to regret it."

Chapter Four

Thea could hardly contain herself until morning. She knew it was foolish, but considering the strange events of the past twenty-four hours, she couldn't help wondering if the legend mightn't be true, that Ros Drumcondra would appear when light flooded the chamber at the burial mound and win back his castle from the insufferable Cosgroves. It *was* supposed to be a passageway between the living and the dead, after all. And she had seen him in her chamber, hadn't she?

It was madness, of course. But madness or not, the very air she breathed was palpable with a strange haunting essence of something from another time. Whatever that something was, it had captivated her waking and sleeping, like a pulse beating deep down inside that gave her no peace. That scandalous, rapturous thrumming in the blood those smoldering Gypsy eyes had set loose upon her had left her longing for more. That alone might prompt this excursion in the predawn darkness of the winter solstice.

Could she be forming a *tendre* for a ghost? Such a thing was hardly sane, and it showed the stark reality of her unhappiness in her current predicament. This was a fantasy she might indulge in, and the Gypsy's words—*ye are the Falcon's bride*—kept coming back to haunt her, heaping fuel on the fire flared to life at her very core.

Yes, something shockingly sexual had been happening to her since she'd entered the castle, and Nigel Cosgrove had nothing to do with it. Ros Drumcondra was a fantasy made to order. What harm could it do to air dream about a virile Gypsy warrior long gone to his reward or his torment? None that she could see. When she let herself, she could almost feel those strong corded arms around her, crushing her close against his hard muscled chest. She could feel the heat of his lips upon her own, and the warm puff of his breath upon her skin. She would not confide her secret fantasy to her brother—he would never believe or approve—but she would not dismiss it either.

She hadn't been to see Nigel. Deep down, she felt mildly responsible for what had happened. Not that she wished such a thing upon him; she wouldn't wish anything so horrible on anyone. But just as deep down, she was convinced that if something hadn't interfered, she might have come to serious harm at the hands of a man who evidently had little or no regard for women. That fostered fears that the accusation against him involving the lightskirt might be true after all. If that were so, she was not safe with him, nor would she ever be.

The old sleigh, rickety for lack of use since it snowed so seldom, was hitched for stealth without bells to two fine horses that were speeding downriver toward Newgrange before the first light of day.

"I hope you know what we're doing," James said as they neared the menhirs on the verge of the mound. "It doesn't look as though anyone else shares your passion for trudging out here to watch dawn light the chamber in such weather."

Thea didn't reply. James reined the horses in before the entrance, which bore a design of three large concentric circles. Beyond, the gaping mouth of the tomb loomed black against the lightening sky. James climbed out of the sleigh and lifted Thea down.

Suddenly, a soaring falcon swooped low and perched upon one of the menhirs. Thea's quick intake of breath caught her brother's attention, and he turned.

"Bloody hell!" he seethed, searching the ground for something to hurl at the bird, but the snow had covered any rocks that might have sufficed.

Thea grabbed his arm. "Don't you dare!" she cried when he unhooked the sleigh lantern and started to heft it. "I told you not to hurt it. It looks half frozen, poor creature. Put that down, James! If you harm that falcon, I shall never forgive you!"

James set the lantern back in its bracket and heaved a sigh. "There, first light," he said, pointing. "Let's have this done and return to the castle before we're missed."

"Come on, then," she agreed, holding out her hand.

"Oh no, little sister," he said. "This is your adventure, none of mine." He scowled at the perched bird. "I will wait with the sleigh."

Thea frowned. She didn't want to leave him anywhere near the falcon while he was in this humor, but there was nothing for it; light was filtering through the roof box, and so she stepped inside the tomb's inky mouth and waited.

Slowly, it began to lighten inside, revealing a passageway not quite sixty feet long that led into a chamber with three side recesses roofed by a corbelled vault. Standing stones were strategically placed as supports. The recess to the right was the largest, and most ornately decorated with neolithic art. On the floor stood two large stone basins, one nesting inside the other. They were deeply stained with something that resembled rust. Could they have once been used for sacrifice? Thea shuddered to wonder.

As the sun rose higher, the narrow beam of light filtering down through the roof box grew wider, slowly reaching the rear of the passageway until the whole chamber was illuminated with a ghostly shaft of light beaming to the very place where she stood. In awe of the phenomenon, Thea gasped, examining the carved artwork that had suddenly become clear on the roof, the walls and the standing stone supports.

She lost all track of time. The seventeen minutes of the experience seemed nearly up before they'd begun. Though it was cold inside the tomb, Thea didn't feel the chill. Her footsteps sounded back hollow in her ears, and she spoke her name aloud and listened to the echo of her voice, like ripples in a pond, spread out all around her.

All too soon the light began to fade, and she stepped into the other recesses, trying to catch it there, but it dimmed inside those also. Then there came another sound that ran her through like a knife blade; the screech of a falcon close by. Her heart leapt. Could James have gone back on his word? Had he lobbed something at the creature in spite of her pleas?

All at once the light failed, and as she ran back to the entrance the falcon screeched again. *Thank the stars he hasn't killed it!* she thought. Reaching the opening just as darkness overtook her, she stepped out into the frosty morning glare only to pull up short, her eyes flitting in all directions.

"James?" she called. "James! Where are you? This is no time for having me on. James!"

But there was no answer. Her brother was gone. Where was the sleigh? Where were the marks in the snow left by the runners, and by the horses' plodding hooves? A blanket of snow stretched out before her, pure white and unblemished. But how could that be, when no fresh snow had fallen?

She whipped around and looked toward the mound behind her, but that was all it was—a solid white mound of snow ringed by menhirs crowned with caps of white. Where was the entrance, with its elaborately carved tricircles? Was there more than one? Had she come out a different way? Where were the kerbstones—all *ninety-seven* of them—holding up the massive cairn? Gone—all gone! All but the falcon, circling above, had vanished with the light in the passage tomb.

Panicked now, Thea cupped her hands around her mouth. "James!" she shrilled at the top of her voice. "James! Stop this. What's happening? Where are you?"

But it wasn't her brother who laid hands on her from behind and threw something cold and damp over her head that smelled of horse. Someone had hold of her—more than one set of hands jostled her about and hoisted her into the air. She came down hard across a broad shoulder that she would have beat upon if her hands weren't tethered beneath the foul-smelling blanket.

The last thing she heard before something hard struck her head was the sound of a rough voice saying, "Wait till he sees what we've bagged—and right under our noses, too."

Thea's first waking sensation was of teeth-chattering cold. Her chinchilla pelerine had been removed, and so had her Moroccan leather ankle boots. Her feet were freezing. So was her body in its thin wool crepe traveling costume, which gapped open in front. Instinctively, she tried to close it, but her hands were tethered above her head, and her feet weren't touching the floor. All at once, she realized she couldn't have closed it even if her hands were free. It opened in back. The frock had been torn apart in front nearly all the way down to the hem.

A dull ache at the back of her head wrenched a moan from her dry throat. Where was she? Not at Cashel Cosgrove, surely. Why couldn't she see clearly? She wasn't alone. Several men and a woman were speaking in hushed whispers in the shadows. Paralyzed with panic, Thea strained her eyes, trying to lift their images from the waves of dizziness that came and went like a pulse beat.

All at once, rough hands spread her frock and reached inside, stroking her breasts, belly and thighs. She tried to scream but couldn't. Something stretched across her mouth was pushing her tongue back down her throat, a gag, and all that came out was a muffled whimper. Her feet were untethered, and she used them, kicking wildly at a shadowy moving target, her head swimming with vertigo. But that only spread her frock wider, and the rough hand parted her legs, cruelly exploring the soft, silken hair between her thighs.

The veins in Thea's neck bulged with the frantic scream she couldn't release. Between the cold and sheer terror of what she feared was about to happen, her whole body began to shake with involuntary spasms.

Suddenly the hand was yanked away so sharply that Thea spun where she hung, dangling from a frayed rope attached to an iron ring in the ceiling of what seemed to be a cave. Albeit blurred, her vision was returning. A chorus of muffled cries, accompanied by the hasty shuffling of feet erupted in a racket of displaced objects and raucous shouts all around her.

"We didn't mean no harm," a husky voice said. A hollow sound followed, and then more shuffling and objects clashing outside of her line of vision. "No . . . have done! I . . .

we was just havin' a bit o' fun with her while we was waitin' for you. We wouldn't have done nothin'—*No . . . !*"

Thea strained to see her captors, but the position of her arms stretched over her head and the fabric of her gaping frock blocked her vision. She only had a clear view of what was directly in front of her, and these men were off to the side.

"She's no good to us spoiled," said a booming baritone voice. It reverberated in her very bones. Their leader? It must be. Her breath was coming in heaving spasms, and relief thrilled through her. He had spared her from what surely would have been the loss of her innocence. But her euphoria came too soon. From the periphery a figure emerged and stood before her—a towering giant of a man observing her, his hard stare boring into her like tarnished green fire.

Even though her feet didn't reach the floor as she hung suspended, she had to look up to meet those gold-flecked green eyes. In the flickering torchlight, she could see her reflection in them. Recognition paralyzed her. She would know those wolflike eyes anywhere. They slid the length of her from the hair that had come down and hung loose about her shoulders, to the tips of her bare toes. It was a slow, sweeping appraisal. If a woman could be raped by a look, she was being raped now. This was no specter—he was *real*. She had come face-to-face with Ros Drumcondra.

It's happening, she thought, amazed. *The legend is true. He has come back just as they said, out of the tomb on the winter solstice to reclaim Cashel Cosgrove for the Drumcondras.* But where was she, and how could that be? This was not the dashing Gypsy renegade of her dreams, her delicious fantasy. This was a ruthless flesh-and-blood warrior, and he was dangerous.

Reaching out with one bronzed finger, he lifted away the left side of her torn frock from her body and took the measure of what lay beneath. His hooded gaze followed the swell of her breasts to the taut nipples puckered with cold, to the curve of her waist, hips and thighs. They lingered familiarly upon the thatch of raven-colored hair between them. For a heart-stopping moment, Thea thought he was going to touch her there, as the other man had, but no. Another figure sidled into view—a woman with long hair the color of chestnuts and eyes as black as coal. She was wearing Thea's chinchilla pelerine, stroking the dense fur seductively—flaunting it as she undulated against Drumcondra, her long arms wound around his neck and broad chest like snakes. So that's where the pelerine had gone!

With a flick of his finger, Drumcondra dismissed Thea's torn frock and looked long and hard at the woman who had twined herself around him. Putting her from him with painstaking control, he stripped off the pelerine in one motion, ignoring her protests, and drew a long-handled dirk from his belt.

All at once there came a flapping sound close by, like the wings of a large bird moving the still, foul air. The falcon? If it was, Thea couldn't see it, though she felt the effects of the breeze its flailing wings stirred.

Just for a moment, she caught a glimpse of something moving in the shadows across the way. A hunched old woman, her long gray hair straggling out from beneath a woolen head scarf was staring at her, a triumphant knowing look on her wrinkled face. The old Gypsy? It was. Only then did Thea see the great bird perched upon the woman's bony hand, its tethers dangling down, tether bells jingling, a plumed leather hood sheathing its head. The woman paused there for just a moment, her black eyes riveting, before melting into the labyrinth of passageways to disappear—bird and all—into the darkness, the falcon beating the musty air with its magnificent wings.

She got only that fleeting glimpse before the torchlight flashed off the dirk in Ros Drumcondra's white-knuckled fist and commanded her attention. Thea gasped and screwed her eyes shut tight, certain her next breath would be her last as he hefted the pelerine over his shoulder and came at her with the blade. But it wasn't the attack she feared imminent. Instead, he began hacking at the ropes tethering her wrists with the weapon.

The rope being weak, the blade razor sharp, and his strength greater than anything Thea had ever known or imagined, her bonds gave way in a trice, and she fell into his strong arms outstretched to receive her. It wasn't the most graceful return to earth by any means, as her half-naked body was forced against his stiff leather jerkin decorated with hobnails. The tactile experience of her soft flesh against cold studded leather was a shock to her system, as was the crush of her thighs, and the soft mound of her feminitity against the arousal challenging the seam of his skintight leggings. He eased her over it in painfully slow increments, his enormous hand planted firmly on her buttocks while setting her on her feet.

Thea wobbled at first, come so suddenly to firm ground again. Drumcondra made no move to steady her, but instead stripped the rest of her torn garments away in one sweep of his hand, and tugged the chinchilla pelerine around her. Thea squealed in fright through her gag at the first motion, then groaned in relief when the fur warmed her shivering body. Drumcondra wasn't moved by either exclamation, as he watched her struggle into the sumptuous fur wrap. He re-bound her wrists, gave pause over the gag in her mouth for a moment before evidently dismissing the notion of removing it, and shoved her down on a pelt rug in the corner. Then, without a backward glance, he stalked away.

Thea's eyes flashed about her surroundings. It was definitely some sort of cave—a well appointed cave, at that. There was something vaguely familiar. Could it be the stone basins? There were several set about, like the ones she'd seen at Newgrange. Drumcondra had seated her near a makeshift brazier heaped with peat over live coals. Fragrant smoke drifted lazily upward to escape through a hole in the roof. There were chests and sleeping pallets along the walls. Niches hacked out of the rock held torches made of rushes soaked in some anonymous rendered fat. There was a rancid odor about it, trailing acrid smoke that fogged the oppressive air. The stench flared her nostrils and made her grimace until she became accustomed. This seemed to be some kind of common room, but passageways fanning out in more than one direction suggested a much larger compound with several more rooms farther in.

It was into one of these that Drumcondra steered the irate Gypsy wench, none-too-gently, their voices raised in a Celtic dialect unfamiliar to Thea. The others had scattered, all but a wizened old woman stirring something in a kettle on a tripod over the brazier. It smelled rich and earthy—some sort of venison stew, Thea supposed. She hadn't taken breakfast before they set out, and only then did she realize how terribly hungry she was. Nothing was being offered, however, so she drew her knees up under the warm pelerine and turned on her side, content to be ignored for the moment.

Exhausted, she had just begun to doze when a strong hand fisted in the fur at the neck of her pelerine jerked her upright, and she looked once again into the eyes of the Gypsy Ros Drumcondra, his hooded stare intense. Those eyes held her relentlessly for longer than she cared to suffer them, then he unfastened the gag and stripped it away. But he didn't discard it. Holding it at the ready, he straightened up and dosed her with a warning glare, one finger placed across his sensuous mouth in an attitude that brooked no argument. Not only could the man rape with his eyes, he could speak with them as well—far more eloquently than his lips had done.

It was useless to scream, and Thea took another tack. "L-let me go. . . ." were the first words she uttered through her bruised lips. They hurt, reminding her of Nigel's assault on the battlements. She'd completely forgotten until now.

Drumcondra crooked his thumb toward her mouth. "My men did that?" he queried, his eyes narrowed.

"N-no," said Thea. "That occurred before I met your . . . 'men.'" Savages came to mind as a better description of the gudgeons that had captured her, but she thought better of saying so. "The lump on the back of my head is their handiwork, though."

He gave a dry grunt, squatted down, and laced his fingers through her hair feeling for the swelling. She winced when he found it, and he jerked his hand back as though he'd touched a live coal.

"You are the Cosgrove's betrothed?" he said. How long the lashes were, wreathing his deep-set eyes. Those eyes were hooded now, not with passion, but cold, calculating scrutiny. There was hatred in that fierce stare. No, this was definitely not the phantom of her fantasy. But if not, why did her heart beat so rapidly under his gaze, and why was his breathing so audible of a sudden?

She nodded. "Y-yes," she said, low-voiced. What sort of cruel game was this? He couldn't be real. How could a specter be real? But he *was* real; there was no question. Her scalp still stung from his fingers groping her head for the knot his cronies had left, and the ghost of his arousal still throbbed through her. She could still feel its pulsating pressure. He'd made no attempt to act upon his attraction, but neither had he made an attempt to hide it.

"Did he leave this mark on your mouth?" he asked, running his thumb along the bruise on her lip.

"That is none of your business!" Thea snapped, jerking her head to the side. His touch, though featherlight, was like a lightning strike, and she began to tremble from something other than cold.

Drumcondra's eyebrow lifted. "What were you doing at Si An Bhru?" he said.

"I beg your pardon?"

"Si An Bhru—the burial mound. What were you doing there all alone at sunrise? Do you not know that wars are waging hereabout?"

"You mean . . . Newgrange," she said. He cocked his head, clearly nonplussed. "I . . . I was lost." It was all she could think to say that he might credit as truth. She vaguely recalled Nigel saying that the passage tomb was once called Si An Bhru, and cold chills gripped her. Drumcondra would call it that, wouldn't he? He was from the past after all. How hard it was to brook that he had traveled forward through time. It was incomprehensible.

His suspicious glance proved him skeptical. "New . . . grange?" he said.

"I-I am from England, sir," Thea said, grateful for yet another inspiration. "That is what we call the place there."

He gave a satisfied grunt charged with contempt for the English, and nodded to the old woman, who filled a trencher with the delicious smelling stew simmering over the brazier and thrust it toward her. A tankard of ale followed, which was nut sweet, rich and brown. Thea devoured both while Drumcondra crouched on his haunches, watching. As soon as she'd finished, he surged to his full height and moved toward her with the gag again.

"Please," she said, running her finger over her bruised lip. "Must you? It . . . hurts my mouth."

He gave thought.

"I won't cry out, if that's what you fear."

His green eyes blazed. "Ros Drumcondra fears *nothing*!" he said, "least of all a skinny bit of English fluff. No one will hear you if you do cry out but *me* and mine." He waved the soiled rag in his hand. "I use this because I am not fond of women's puling. It grates on my patience, and I do not think it wise that you risk angering me."

"Then why don't you just let me go? What use could I possibly be to you? What do you mean to do with me?"

"I intend to hold you for ransom," he said. "My castle in exchange for you . . . intact."

Thea felt a chill. "And . . . if he will not pay such a ransom?"

"He'll pay."

"You overestimate my worth, sir."

"I can be very persuasive."

"And if your persuasions fail? What then?"

"Then I will punish him in such a way that the castle will hold naught for him but sorrow, and in the end, I'll have it anyway."

Thea stared at him. "How?"

"You ask too many questions."

"I need to know," she persisted. She was goading him, which was a dangerous game, but she'd come too far to turn back now.

"Some things are better not to know," he said. "But since you insist, if he will not meet my demands, I will resurrect the ancient rite of *prima nocte*—first night. The right of the lord of a land to take any man's bride to his bed on her wedding night. To be the first to take her maidenhead—her virtue, little lady—and give her back to him used baggage—spoiled."

"That is barbaric!"

"Yes, and it was abolished long ago, but that matters not to me. Not after what he took of mine—my wife and children slaughtered by his sword. Why such a look? I am no savage. I am a lord, well-qualified. Who is to oppose me? I am clan chieftain in these parts. Cian Cosgrove may have taken my castle and my land, but he cannot take that from me. Tara has decreed it. It is only a matter of time before I have back what is rightfully mine. So! Either way I win. I'm half hoping that he does refuse my offer. Revenge is always sweeter taken of the flesh than by merely stripping a man of his possessions. The pain of human loss lasts longer."

Thea swallowed, and her breath caught in her throat. "*Cian* Cosgrove?" she asked, having heard little past that.

"None other. What? Are you so simple that you do not know the name of your betrothed?"

"W-what year is this . . . ?" she murmured, scarcely able to hear over the the blood pounding in her ears.

He gave a start. "What year?" he asked, incredulous. "You *are* simpleminded, then, as well as insolent and foolish. It is the Year of Our Lord, 1695."

Chapter Five

The miracle had clearly worked, but in reverse. The winter solstice sunrise had not brought the Gypsy warlord Ros Drumcondra forward in time through the passage tomb; somehow it had catapulted Thea back to his time, the end of the seventeenth century. How could that be? But it was, and she was in grave danger. He would never believe her if she told him the truth, that it was *Nigel* Cosgrove, Cian's descendant nearly a century and a quarter into the future that she was to marry. Thea scarcely believed it herself.

Strangely, the one thing that threatened to make her a watering pot was worry over how frantic James must be over her disappearance, and there was absolutely nothing she could do to put her brother's mind at ease. If only he had gone into the passage tomb with her, she would have his company for comfort now. But he had not, and she had to keep her wits about her and somehow find a way to go back the way she'd come to her own time. James and the

Cosgroves would doubtless think that she had been carried off by Gypsies.

She almost laughed. Wasn't that exactly what had happened?

Making matters worse, time was passing—too much time. Thea tried to keep track of the days, but one seemed to melt into the next with nothing of consequence to mark their passing. Drumcondra came from time to time, scrutinizing her from a safe but visible distance. He said little. It was impossible to read the thoughts lurking behind those eyes boring into her, and she wasn't even sure she wanted to, taking the physical attraction she had to this man into account, and the impossibility of any such situation. Things had been a lot simpler when she only had his ghost to fantasize about. His virile physical presence was entirely too much.

All in all, she was treated well, albeit roughly. Though her wrists were still bound, they were loosely tethered in front of her. She was fed, given warm water to wash, and privacy by way of a screenlike affair behind which she could execute a satisfactory toilette. At night, she had fur rugs to sleep in, and the old woman who'd first served her the stew watched over her so that there'd be no unseemly event such as what had occurred upon her arrival.

Though she continually begged Drumcondra to release her, her pleas fell upon deaf ears. Again and again she begged, but he was unmoved, the thoughts behind those copper-lit eyes remaining his own. She could not read them; she was almost afraid to, they seemed so dark and daunting. Still, he haunted her with his silent visits, and she thrilled each time he came into view. And so it went until what seemed at least a fortnight had passed and she'd all but given up hope of ever seeing the light of day again.

Drumcondra hadn't come today at all, and she'd begun

to fear that something had happened to him. Though his presence was always alarming, he brought an odd facet of comfort as well. All day she'd worried over his absence. What if he never came? What if she were to be left at the mercy of those that, without him to prevent it, would surely slit her throat as easily as look at her? Or worse? Finally, she began to doze. It was hardly wise, half naked in a den of thieves without the warlord watching over her, but there was nothing for it. She was exhausted. She did her best to convince herself that Drumcondra's minions would not molest her again after the display she'd witnessed upon her arrival. Neither would *he*, wanting her intact for his bargain with Cian Cosgrove. That was her most calming argument. Still, there was that odd business about *prima noctea*. But surely he couldn't have been serious—all that had been abolished centuries ago. Still, she had no doubt that he would resurrect it in her case to further his own ends without batting an eye. Who would oppose him? None she'd seen so far in his domain.

The sight of the old Gypsy woman from time to time was oddly reassuring, though Thea had no idea how she could be there, unless she had been lurking in the passage tomb also. Of course! That had to be it. She had to have come from somewhere nearby Cashel Cosgrove when she'd trudged through the snow to give her cryptic warning. Could she be living inside Newgrange? Hadn't Nigel said the bones of the Drumcondra clan had been found inside when the tomb was excavated? If it were possible then, why wouldn't it be possible now? These thoughts drowned in the stuff of dreams, however. She was just too tired to care.

It seemed as if she had just closed her eyes when rough hands roused her, jerking her to her feet. It was Drumcondra. She groaned. Every muscle in her body ached from the rough handling, and from being so long housed on the hard floor of the cave with nothing to cushion it but the skimpy fur pelt.

Her hands were still bound, and without a word he seized her arm and hauled her along the passageway to the entrance of the cave, but she dug in her heels when the snow drifts loomed up before her.

"Where are you taking me?" she demanded, resisting. He tightened his grip without answering. "No! Please!" she cried. "I cannot walk out in that like this. My boots! Give me back my boots!" That she was naked under the fur pelerine was bad enough; the mere thought of stepping barefoot into those snowdrifts riddled her with crippling waves of gooseflesh.

"No boots," he grunted.

"But why?" she cried, still struggling.

He jerked her to a standstill. "You cannot run without boots in the snow," he said.

"Please, I beg you," she sobbed. "I shan't run. I'm so cold. Isn't it enough that you've ruined my frock—torn it to shreds? You cannot mean to make me walk through those drifts with nothing on my feet."

Loosing a string of muttered blasphemies, Drumcondra scooped her up in his arms and plowed through the snow. Only then did she notice the magnificent Gypsy horse tethered in a stand of young saplings alongside the mouth of the cave: a stallion as white as the snow, its feathered feet and forelegs pawing the frozen ground. It looked magical standing in the sugary frosted twilight, white clouds of visible breath puffing from its flared nostrils, like a mysterious creature of myth. One horn protruding from that proud brow would not have seemed amiss.

Without ceremony, Drumcondra hefted her onto the animal's back and swung himself up behind. Tethering her against him between the reins, he walked the horse out of the grove. Thea's hood had fallen away. She shuddered, and he tugged it back in place. The man wasn't entirely without feeling. But she wouldn't thank him for it, the great lout!

"Where are you taking me?" she insisted.

"What? You do not fancy a moonlight ride on such a fine night—upon so fine a horse as Cabochon here?" he said.

Thea didn't answer. She dosed him with a withering glance and stiffened in his arms.

His deep baritone laughter responded, reverberating through her body in a most alarming way. There was something so sensual in this experience, riding bound and naked but for the soft chinchilla fur on the back of the majestic stallion in the arms of this gargantuan Gypsy warlord. Was that his manhood leaning heavily against her thigh? He was aroused! That she could feel his sex through the thick fur of her pelerine made her heart leap. His height was evidently not the only thing gargantuan about him. Thea gasped in spite of herself, and tried to inch away, but it was no use. Her other thigh was forced against the studded pommel. She was trapped between it and his throbbing hardness. Drumcondra threw his head back and loosed a mighty guffaw.

"I say again, sir," Thea snapped, trying to ignore what could not be ignored. "Where are you taking me?"

"To Cashel Drumcondra," he said. "He may call it Cashel Cosgrove, but it will never be. It is mine, and I mean to have it back. We go to show him how that is to be, hmm?"

"You mean to take me back there?" For a moment she was hopeful, thinking of James, until she realized that James wouldn't be there. He existed somewhere over a hundred years in the future. It was madness. But it was true.

"To flaunt my conquest," he agreed, with a nod.

"How can the castle belong to you?" she asked, wondering out loud. "If you are a Gypsy, how can you be a lord?"

"My mother is full-blooded Romany," he explained. "Cashel Drumcondra has been in my family since time out of mind. The ancestors of Cormac Drumcondra, my father, were clan chieftains of this land in their turn since the Romans came. The Cosgrove may have laid siege to my castle, but I am still the border lord. It is only a matter of time before I have back what rightfully belongs to me."

"You favor your mother, then?" It was beyond impossible. How could she be sitting so calmly in this enigmatic warlord's arms, half naked, on her way to the stars alone knew where, calmly discussing his lineage? One day her curiosity would get the better of her . . . but not tonight. She knew how this all ended. Ros Drumcodra had vanished from existence almost a hundred and twenty years ago, and she meant to know how and why. This was, after all, just a dream—wasn't it? It couldn't really be happening. None of this could be real. Still, the bulk of his sex forced against her thigh was a startling contradiction to such imagined fiction.

"Not entirely," Drumcondra drawled. "My father's blood was mixed. He was descended, it is suspected, from the men of the shipwrecked Spanish Armada that landed upon our shores, and from the tribe your kind now calls *Tinkers*. There was much mixing of blood in the early days, between the Romans and Danes, the Spaniards and Gaels. The dark-haired olive coloring of our clan opposed to the ruddy-looking Irish purebreds could be the result of the mixing of any number of races who came to conquer here."

The man was an enigma at best, what with his tanned skin and hair the color of a raven's feathers, his towering height a contradiction of both bloodlines. More jarring was his voice, for it was as cultured as any London aristocrat's, not slurred and peppered with the common provincial cant, though his speech did have a pleasant Irish lilt about it.

"How do you mean to bargain, when you haven't even taken the trouble to learn my name?" she snapped.

He shrugged. "That is of no consequence. What do I need with a name, when I have the physical proof in my arms?" The last was said seductively in her ear, his hot breath puckering her skin with gooseflesh. "Believe me, before this night is done, he will know the terms of my bargain."

Drumcondra said no more as they rode on through the deepening twilight. The moon shone down on the breast of the snow-clad hills gleaming in the distance like spangles on a length of white cloth stretched out as far as the eye could see. His scent wafted past her on the breeze. He smelled clean and very male, darkly mysterious, of the earth and the forest, of musk and tanned leather and the ghost of some anonymous brew. She breathed him in deeply.

A furtive glance in his direction revealed that he had been studying her. His shuttered eyes had sunk underneath the broad ledge of his brow, and a muscle in his angular jaw had begun to tick. She quickly looked away. The look in those eyes chilled her to the marrow.

"Do not think to escape me," he murmured in her ear, meanwhile tightening his hold upon her—pulling her hard against the bulk of his turgid sex. It was a sinister warning, the words dripping menace. And yet there was a tremor—the faintest glimmer of vulnerability humming under the surface of those words. They triggered new waves of gooseflesh along her stiffened spine.

"Now, why would I want to do that?" she snapped haughtily.

He tightened his hold. "Aye, why, indeed?" he asked, the words dripping sarcasm. "You are a strange one, fair lady. Much about you is . . . different. You beg for your freedom, but I have not heard you beg to be reunited with your lover since you've come among us. Why is that, I wonder?"

How could she answer? What would he believe?

"He is not my lover, you insufferable clod," she flung at him. "We have not even met." That was certainly the truth. Did he believe her? Another sideways glance showed her that, at the very least, she'd given him pause for thought. She went on quickly, "We were on our way to the castle when your minions laid hands upon me."

"We, you say?" he said. I know of no others. Where are they, then?"

"How should I know?" she snapped. "Ask your men. I was unconscious."

"How many in your party?"

"Just myself and my brother," she said. "Judging from the treatment I have received at your hands, sir, I can only hope that he has escaped your hospitality." It was half truth, but he couldn't know that, and it sounded credible enough. Let him wear himself out over that on the animals who had laid hands upon her, and good riddance! It was no less than they deserved.

"I saw no one but you," he said, frowning, his eyes lost beneath the jutting ledge of his brow.

"Praise God!"

He tightened his grip upon her again. "My men have been well chastised for their rough handling of you, my lady," he said.

"Rough handling?" she blurted. "They nearly raped me! If you hadn't come in when you did . . ."

"Ahhh, but I did return," he pointed out. "And you came to no real harm, nor will you in my keeping so long as you do exactly as I say."

"Ha! Chastised!" she said, still dwelling upon that. "And who is to chastise *you*, sir? You are savages—barbarians—the lot of you! You are no better than they, dragging me out in the bitter cold half dressed, with no boots on my feet. Who but a savage would treat a lady so?" It was a dangerous outburst, and his posture clenched against her. He tightened his hold with a vicious wrench. How strong he was. She had no doubt that he could snap her spine like a twig. Perhaps she'd gone too far.

"I have my reasons for that," he said.

"What reasons could you possibly have for such treatment?"

"Patience, my lady," he said, in that maddening baritone rumble that seemed to penetrate the very marrow of her bones. "You will see soon enough." He pointed. "Cashel Drumcondra!" And it was—oh, it *was*—on a distant hill rising black into the night, silhouetted against the stars in the moonlight.

But there was no comfort for her in the sight. How could there be when she felt nothing but dread of the place since she'd first set foot inside those cold stone walls? What did Drumcondra mean to do? Certainly not ride right up the steep approach and storm the bastions single-handed. When he started up the grade, she gasped again. It seemed as if that was exactly what he was about to do.

She laughed aloud. "You needn't have worried about the possibility of my escaping," she said. "One man alone on horseback against *that*? You dream, *Lord Drumcondra*. They will slaughter you."

"You think so, do you?" he asked. "Watch!"

Without warning, a falcon swooped down and perched upon Drumcondra's outstretched arm. Thea hadn't even realized it had been circling aloft, and she cried aloud as it landed, its great wings stirring the air, grazing her fur hood, its feathers rustling in her ear.

"Shhh! Be still!" Drumcondra commanded. "Not a sound, or it will be the worse for you, fair lady."

Thea shrank from the bird. "Then keep that creature away from me!" she snapped.

Reaching beneath his shaggy fur mantle, Drumcondra produced a sizable stone wrapped in parchment tied with string, and placed it in the bird's beak. Then, pointing toward the castle battlements, he gave the bird flight.

"Go, Isor!" he commanded. "Go and deliver!"

Thea's breath caught watching the great bird soar toward the castle, watching it glide on the updraft of a fugitive zephyr in the cold still night, and circle the battlements. Only then did a shadowy figure pacing there become clear. A sentry was posted aloft. He looked up. Something dropped. He stooped to retrieve it, and the falcon soared back and landed again upon Drumcondra's outstretched arm.

Thea strained her eyes toward the castle. The moon had risen bright and full. In its light, she watched the sentry disappear as Drumcondra walked the Gypsy horse closer.

"What now?" she asked.

"We wait."

"For what?"

"For Cosgrove. We would have made this little twilight ride long since, had he not been off marauding in the north. He has returned."

"You actually believe he will just walk out here and speak with us?" Thea breathed, incredulous. "He will bring the army that defeated you, and God alone knows what will become of me—not that you care. Why don't you just let me go? I told you, Cian Cosgrove and I have never met. The betrothal was arranged. He will not be moved to pay ransom for a stranger—an English stranger at that. You will be killed for naught!"

Drumcondra's cold smile did not reach his eyes. "I am touched by your concern for my welfare, fair lady," he said seductively. "But disappointed in your lack of faith in my abilities." The last was said with mock sorrow. The man was insufferable. He pointed. "See? He comes!" And so Cosgrove did, backlit by torches set in brackets inside throwing golden ribbons of light upon the snow through the open doors. They were different—two, instead of just one in her own time—than the ones Thea remembered, heavily studded with spikes and reinforced with iron hinges and bars. "Where is his army, fair lady? Who dreams now, eh?"

"W-what was in that missive?" she murmured.

"It is not so important what was in it, but how it was delivered," he said. "Cian fears the falcon, and well he ought."

Thea wanted to ask him why, but her lips wouldn't work, watching Cian Cosgrove standing belligerantly in the snow-swept courtyard, his jutting chin uptilted. She gasped, and gasped again. She could have come face-to-face with Nigel Cosgrove for the uncanny resemblance. Cian's hair was slightly darker, and he was not as tall, but the rest was so similar it took her breath away.

"What do you here, Drumcondra?" Cosgrove thundered, his gravelly voice amplified by the snow. It shot Thea through with gooseflesh. "Send that bird here again and my men will shoot it out of the sky, your precious *familiar*."

"You will not shoot Isor, Cosgrove. You fear other-worldly reprisals too much for that because you have not been able to conjure any creature to match him. Besides, everyone knows you cannot kill a familiar. It will only rise up again in another, greater form—a tiger next time maybe, or a wolf. No, you won't harm a feather on Isor's body."

"Say your piece and be gone!"

"I am come to introduce you to your bride," Drumcondra said, triumphant.

"Eh?"

"Your English baggage here," Drumcondra continued. Before Thea could blink, he pulled her pelerine apart in front, seized her exposed breast, and began fondling it.

Screaming, Thea twisted in Drumcondra's arms, and the falcon jumped up on his shoulder, adding its cries to hers. Her hands were still tied in front, but that did not prevent her from delivering a scathing blow to his ribs with a well-aimed elbow. It was like buffeting steel, and her efforts produced nothing more than a barely audible grunt.

"You Black Irish Gypsy bastard!" Cosgrove seethed, taking a step closer.

"Stand where you are, Cosgrove!" Drumcondra thundered, causing his horse to rear back on its hind legs, pawing the air with its feathered forefeet. "You get her when I get my castle back!" he snarled. "She will be delivered to you intact once every stinking Cosgrove thief has left my land. I have no quarrel with her, but take care, she is a winsome lass and I am tight against the seam. You have two days. That is more than generous, considering. It's more than you gave my wife, my children, helpless in my absence."

"Let her go, Drumcondra!"

"Did you let my wife and children go? No, you raped and slaughtered them—defenseless against your horde without me to protect them, filthy coward. Now you see my justice—Gypsy justice. Two days, commencing at midnight! Then, if you have not left this place, you get her back a virgin no more. *Prima nocte*—first night! Just as in days of old, I will have her before you, and when I've done, believe me, she will want no other!"

Thea was terrified. It was getting harder and harder for her captor to control the agitated horse beneath them. The falcon had begun beating the air with its wings again, its talons sunk deeply into Drumcondra's shoulder through his shaggy fur mantle. He seemed not to notice. He still had hold of her breast. In spite of herself, the touch aroused Thea. Icy-hot waves of sensation sped to her loins as his skilled fingers tugged at her aching nipple until it grew tall and hard against his roughened skin.

Others had begun to gather in the doorway. Cosgrove held them back with a hand gesture. Drumcondra's horse began to whirl in circles, forefeet flying. He let her breast go and took the reins in both hands. It was taking all his strength to control the animal. Thea closed her pelerine in front as best she could with her wrists tied. She felt herself slipping and cried out, grabbing the tall studded pommel with both her hands. She clung to it relentlessly as the horse continued to buck and whirl, his frightened cries ringing in her ears. All at once she saw the gleam of steel in the moonlight. Cosgrove had drawn a dirk from his belt and, taking advantage of the horse's frenzy, he lunged.

Thea screamed: "Look out, my lord, he has a blade!" but too late. Drumcondra brought the animal's feet to ground just as Cosgrove sprang, plunging the dirk into his thigh. His head thrust back in pain, Drumcondra straightened his arm and gave the bird flight. Thea's eyes were wide with amazement. She had never seen anyone handle a falcon without a falconer's glove before.

"Isor—*strike!*" he commanded, and the great bird flew straight for Cosgrove's face, sinking its sharp beak deeply in, plucking out the eye like a grape from the vine, its talons ripping flesh. Cosgrove fell to his knees, wrestling with the creature in the bloodstained snow.

Thea groaned. Things were happening just as they had on the battlements with Nigel. Her head began to swim. Blinding white pinpoints of light starred her vision. The last thing she heard before losing consciousness was Drumcondra's thunderous voice shouting:

"Isor—*home!*"

Chapter Six

Thea groaned awake in a darkened chamber. No torches lit this cubicle. Elaborate sconces on the walls held beeswax candles. None were lit. A roaring fire in the hearth provided the only light. This was no cave. For a moment, she thought she was back at Cashel Cosgrove, but on closer inspection, she thought not; the trappings—even the composition of the walls—were too dissimilar. But if not Cashel Cosgrove, where was she?

She struggled upright. Her hands were no longer bound. She was lying in the center of a raised bed fitted with heavy brocade curtains that once might have been ivory in color, now a dingy brown. It was made with mounds of soft fur pelts. She was lost in them. What was she wearing? A shift of sorts, crudely made, though of serviceable stuff in a muted shade of wine, embroidered in threads of gold. It fit well, loose and flowing, the neckline square, revealing more of her charms than she would have liked. No matter that, it was far less revealing than the open-front fur pelerine, whose closures the warlord had rent and which now lay draped across a Glastonbury chair in the corner. Another chair like it was positioned opposite. From it a figure rose and stepped out of the shadow-steeped umbra of the room. It was Drumcondra.

He strolled to the bedside gazing down, his arms folded across his chest. Divested of his fur mantle, he was just as massive as he had been cloaked. How broad his shoulders were. How narrow his waist. His dun-colored leggings were torn. They outlined every sinew and cord in his muscular thighs. The left one was bound with a linen strip stained with blood. Her eyes were riveted to it.

"It is nothing," he said, answering her look. "Just a scratch." He exhibited the dirk Cosgrove had left imbedded in his thigh. "Piddling excuse for a weapon," he observed. "Not nearly powerful enough to kill a Drumcondra. But then, that was not his intent. He wants to prolong the agony." Drawing another blade from his boot, he raised it. "Now this is a laudable weapon," he said, turning it to and fro in the firelight. It was a fearsome-looking dagger, more like a sword, honed to a needle point, with a hilt of braided metal set with what appeared to be sapphires. He thrust it back in his boot.

Thea was still trying to make sense of her surroundings. That she could not was no surprise, since nothing thus far in her circumstance this side of Newgrange made any sense either.

"Is this place . . . ?" She trailed off, not quite knowing how to finish her question.

"What?" he erupted. "You think I *live* in that cave?" He burst into hearty laughter. How he could stand there laughing with blood oozing down his leg was beyond her. How he could even be on his feet was a mystery. The man must be made of iron, she decided. "You are at Falcon's

Lair, my keep on the outskirts of Drogheda. Cashel Drum-condra was not my only residence, just my finest. The stronghold my wife Maeve preferred. It was also my most vulnerable. Unfortunately, she lived to discover that and regret her preference."

"I'm . . . sorry." Thea faltered.

Drumcondra's eyebrow inched up a notch. "Maeve was no great loss," he said, stirring the coals to new life in the grate. "I was cuckolded by the bastard who did this." He slapped his bleeding thigh. "She was slaughtered, the fool-ish chit, when his horde laid siege to Cashel Drumcondra, because she was expendable. Once he had possession of the cashel, she was no longer of use to him. The bastard has mistresses aplenty. He used one of his liaisons with Maeve as a means to gain entrance, and then he killed her—or his men did. I was not there to see the deed done, only the aftermath. It doesn't matter which. He is respon-sible. No, Maeve was no loss, but my children are quite an-other matter. Your betrothed and his horde raped and hacked them to death, my son and daughter, and their mother. I have seen cleaner chambers in the slaughtering house than the rooms where they were found."

Thea was stricken speechless. She couldn't meet his eyes. He had clearly been embittered by betrayal. Her first reaction was to reach out to him, then it became all too chillingly plain: No matter what, he planned to wreak vengeance upon Cosgrove by doing the same to her. The thought chased the blood from her scalp so rapidly that vertigo threatened.

"I see," she murmured. "Y-you plan to . . . to retaliate in kind, then," she said, trying to be strong.

He straightened from his chore at the hearth, and swag-gered close. "Why did you warn me?" he asked.

"My lord?"

"You cried out a warning when the bastard came at me with this," he replied, exhibiting the dirk. "Why did you do that? If he had succeeded, you would be in his arms now . . . not in my bed."

That struck new terror in her heart. *His bed?* Of course it was. It was large enough to accommodate a giant. She should have known by the way he prowled the chamber, the way he tended the fire and emerged from the shadows as part of the architecture itself. She threw back the pelts and sprang away as though it were aflame.

"I feared for my life!" she shrilled, steadying herself against the bedpost. "Don't flatter yourself that it was a benevolent act. It was a matter of which savage was to have sway over that life. If you want the truth, I thought it was to my best advantage to stay on that horse—I had designs upon it as an eventual means of escape, you see. I want no truck with either of you!" The words were edged to wound, though there wasn't much truth in them except the bit about wanting nothing to do with either of them; and even that was suspect. How intrigued she was by this man!

And she viewed Cian Cosgrove with the same eye as she viewed Nigel, his descendant. Though Ros Drumcondra seemed by far the greater danger, somehow she felt safe in his keeping. This, despite the fact that he had manhandled her cruelly, subjected her to the humiliation of being exposed and molested before a stranger, and awakened her to secrets of the flesh without her consent. She knew he had not really hurt her, and he had prevented his men from meting out the stars alone knew what fate in the bowels of that dreadful cave.

Again, Drumcondra's lips smiled but his eyes did not. What was that look? She couldn't read it, only the accompanying clenched posture. It was as if she'd struck him with her words. She didn't regret that. She would not stroke the great lout's vanity by admitting to her attraction.

The neck of her shift slipped off her shoulder, calling attention to the garment. She jerked it back into place, depriving his eyes of the view. She snatched her skirt and shook it.

"D-did you . . . ?" she murmured, almost afraid of the answer.

He threw back his head in a burst of lecherous laughter. It ran her through like a sword thrust. This time his smile did reach his eyes. They were spangled with coppery lights in the fire's glow. He was grinning like a satyr.

"You little hypocrite," he said. "You do not mind that I've decked you in fine homespun linen—"

"Is *that* what this itchy stuff is?"

"—just that my hand might have dressed you in it, eh?" he went on above her bluster. "And this despite that I have already . . . experienced your charms. You may allay your fears, fair lady. All proprieties were strictly met."

"I am a prisoner here, then?"

"I prefer to call you my guest."

"You never answered my earlier question."

"What question might that be?"

"You know very well what question. I shan't repeat it, sir."

"That was no question. You'd made up your mind to it. Take care you do not make up *my* mind. I meant what I said to Cosgrove. It wouldn't be wise to meddle with my . . . urges—in any form."

Just then the sound of flapping wings and tinkling bells drew Thea's attention to the hearthside and the candle stand that stood there, where the falcon perched in the deep dark shadows of the chimney corner, its head hooded in plumed leather. She hadn't noticed it until that mo-

ment. She gasped and skittered around the bed, putting it
between them.

It was one thing when the bird had championed her on
the battlements. It showed her no such instincts now. Her
heart sank. It was as if the creature had betrayed her. This
was clearly Drumcondra's bird, under his command. She'd
seen what it could do at his bidding, and she was afraid.

"Keep that creature away from me!" she shrilled.

"Isor will not harm you, fair lady. He is hooded and
tethered . . . for now."

"W-what do you mean?"

"When I leave this room, he will remain, but I will loose
his tethers and remove his hood. He is my eyes when I am
not near, you see."

"You can't mean to leave me in this room with that
creature?"

Drumcondra nodded. "You will be quite safe—unless
you try to leave."

"My lord, I just saw that falcon tear a man's eye from its
socket. Is this your justice, then? Is this your retribution—
to . . . to have it maul and peck me to death? It would be
kinder to take that dirk there and drive it through my
heart!"

"I am not disposed toward kindness."

"But . . . did you not say you have no quarrel with me?"

"Just so, I have none, but that shan't stop the inevitable
from happening. Do not count upon it. You are exactly
what I have been waiting for, the means of my ultimate revenge." He slid his eyes the length of her. "And by the
look of things, well worth the wait."

His leg was bleeding badly, but he didn't even seem to
notice. Precious little of the white linen bandage remained that wasn't blood-soaked, and Thea nodded toward it.

"Don't you think you ought see to that?" she asked.

"In due course," he replied. Striding to the candle stand, he loosed the bird's jingling tethers and removed its hood. Its beady black eyes sought Thea out at once, and she hid behind the bed curtains, peeking out in furtive glances.

"You can't mean to convince me that that bird really is your familiar," she said haughtily. A familiar? A warlock's creature?

"No, fair lady, not I," he said. "I shall leave that up to Isor, himself." Drumcondra strode to the door. All that blood and he wasn't even limping! He turned.

"By the way, what *is* your name?" he asked.

"Thea . . . Theodosia Barrington," she stammered.

He gave a dry grunt. "Deuced ghastly name. Theodosia. It doesn't suit you at all. Thea will do."

"My lord!" she cried, as he seized the door handle. "How long am I to be cooped up in here with that bird?"

"Until I come to bed," he said from the threshold.

"Not this bed?"

"Yes, *this* bed, fair lady," he replied through the door. "Where else?"

And the rasp of a key in the door's lock sent shivers down Thea's spine.

Alone, she eyed the bird suspiciously. Familiar, indeed! No such thing. It was a well-trained bird, like the ones her father kept at their country estate in Cornwall, nothing more. She had enough strange phenomena to deal with without crediting Gypsy magic. She had never been a superstitious sort. Still, the creature stared at her with the most humanlike eyes she had ever seen. There was no question that Cosgrove feared it. Was that bird the sole reason his army didn't converge upon them? Were they so terrified of it? Evidently. They feared killing it as well. And she'd thought Cornishmen were superstitious.

What time could it be? She'd lost all track. How long
had she been unconscious? It was just twilight when
they'd confronted Cosgrove at the castle. What had Nigel
said of the distance—five miles . . . five *hours* to reach
Drogheda? Wrack her brain though she did, she couldn't
remember which. It wasn't important then, but it was now.
How long before he returned? Surely, he didn't mean to
sleep in that bed with her. But if not, why had he put her
in this chamber? There must be plenty of others rooms he
could have chosen.

She went to the window, wary of the bird following her
every movement with its shiny onyx eyes. Her heart leapt
when it made a clucking sound as she passed by. She gave
it a wide berth. Outside, the moon shone down, casting
dappled shadows over the courtyard. It all looked so unreal. Much smaller than Cashel Cosgrove, Falcon's Lair
stood in the middle of a wooded glen. A moat surrounded
it, its banks hemmed with mounds of snow. The portcullis
was lowered. She could see it clearly in the moonlight
from her vantage in what must be one of several L-shaped
wings. Even if she could escape her chamber, it would be
next to impossible to escape the keep. The moat was far
too deep, and the thin crust of ice crystals on the surface,
while appearing solid, was surely too deceiving to chance
crossing afoot unless the portcullis were raised to access
the drawbridge. It would surely be guarded. That didn't
bode well.

Thea turned away from the window. The massive bed
loomed before her. No! She would not sleep in it with Ros
Drumcondra. Snatching several of the fur throws off the
counterpane, she dragged them to the far corner of the
chamber, putting as much distance between herself and
the wily bird as possible, and made herself a pallet. It was a
little farther from the hearth than was to her liking, but

there was nothing for it. She would not camp anywhere near the murdering bird. Her efforts were wasted, however. No sooner had she burrowed down beneath the furs, than the falcon took flight, soared across the room, and perched upon the back of a bench that matched the Glastonbury chairs an arm's length from her. Thea groaned, and pulled one of the fur rugs over her head. Maybe the deuced bird *was* a familiar after all.

It wasn't long before she fell sound asleep, cocooned amid the soft fur blankets.

Chapter Seven

Ros Drumcondra braced himself with one hand gripping each side of the settle in the stabler's quarters. It wasn't the first time Mossie McBain, the stabler, had stitched him back together after a melee, and it wouldn't be the last— not while his enemy drew breath. Not while he roiled with bloodlust for Cian Cosgrove. Isor's attack earlier had only whetted his appetite.

"Hold now, m'lord," said the stabler, a formidable-looking needle in one hand trailing waxed thread, a jug of whiskey in the other. "There's nothin' for it, 'tis goin' ta sting like the devil, but that'll take the edge off the sewin' ta come."

Drumcondra grunted, digging his fingers into the carved whorls and feathers decorating the bench, and gritted his teeth as the stabler poured whiskey into the gaping wound in his thigh. Divested of his leggings for the operation, since the wound was rather high, he wore only his tunic and jerkin. A fresh pair lay carelessly tossed on a chair in the corner, with the boots he'd removed and set aside. Another splash of whiskey hit the wound, and he cried out in spite of his resolve not to do so.

"Bloody hell!" he roared, snatching the jug. "Better you put it in me than on me, Mossie." Upending the crock, he drained it nearly dry, then thrust it back at the stabler none too gently. "Well? Have at it, then," he snapped. The stabler stood slack-jawed, needle suspended.

Mossie jumped to attention, and Drumcondra gritted his teeth against the pain as the needle pierced his flesh. But pain had its advantages. This was the first time he'd been in a flaccid state since he'd met Theodosia Barrington.

Theodosia—a dreadful name that didn't suit her at all. Now, Thea? Yes, that suited well enough. It brought the image of a regal Greek goddess to mind. The beautiful little spitfire had struck a chord in him that hadn't been played in some time.

What was he thinking? He had no time for affairs of the heart—least of all with the means of his retribution. That little dalliance was to be something of a different nature entirely. Besides, he had Drina for satisfying those urges. Why hadn't he earlier, then?

Mossie took a deeper stitch, and Ros sucked in a hasty breath. "Dammit, man! The bastard's dirk did not go half so deep. Watch what you do! And mind my cods with that pigsticker. I may have need of them again before I die."

"It ain't my fault ya got yourself stabbed so close to your privates, m'lord. What was ya thinkin'? You're usually a mite sharper than that."

"Yes, well, never you mind. Just stitch me back together and have done. I've work ahead of me yet tonight."

The stabler scoffed. "The most work you'll do once I've put ya ta rights again'll be between the sheets, m'lord."

"And that's exactly the sort of work I had in mind. *Owwwww!* Watch what you do, damn you, man!"

"Oh, aye?" laughed Mossie, ignoring the outburst. "Well, you'll not be fit for *that* sort o' work t'night. 'Tis sleep ya need. Ya ain't invincible, ya know—for all ya make yourself out ta be."

Mossie McBain was the only soul in Falcon's Lair who could talk to him thus. The stabler had served his father before him, and he was the closest thing to a surgeon for man or beast to be had for miles. Precious few of Drumcondra's satellites could claim to have found a soft spot to inhabit in his cold heart. Mossie McBain was one of them.

"There!" the stabler said, biting the thread. "You're done till the next time." He slathered some salve on the stitched wound from a pot on the shelf and set about binding the warlord's rigid thigh with a clean bandage.

Drumcondra shrank from the odor of the ointment. "What is that stuff? It smells of horse!"

"Aye, and so do you—and well it ought. 'Twas a horse that last got the benefit o'it, this 'stuff.' He ain't complainin' like some two-legged folk I know."

Ros staggered to his feet, gingerly tugged on his clean leggings and boots, and took a few steps, testing his mettle. That done, he snatched the crock of whiskey and drained it to the dregs.

"Thank you, old friend," he said at last, wiping the liquor from his lips with the back of his hand. "I needn't tell you to look sharp. You've got the best view of the main approach from these stables. We're going to have visitors aplenty soon. Isor pecked Cosgrove's eye out tonight, and he knows I've got his lady. The joust goes on between us— this damned civil hatred that lets us meet and taunt and slay each other slowly. The grand game. There are bound to be reprisals. Just keep your eyes peeled."

"Beggin' your pardon, but ya should have left her at Si An Bhru. He never would have found her there. He never would have *gone* there. He's too afeared o' it—scared o' ghosties."

"I . . . I couldn't do that," Ros admitted.

"Why?"

"Because I couldn't. Branko and Flannan nearly raped her. I cannot trust them. And then there's Drina. You know what a jealous wench she is. I couldn't chance it. I shan't get another opportunity as sweet as this to wreak my vengeance upon the Cosgroves. She doesn't know where she was. She fancied herself in a cave somewhere. She had no idea that she was inside Si An Bhru all the while. It would have been too easy for her to escape the place if she knew. She's smarter than that lot."

"Well then, you're courtin' trouble," said the stabler, thrusting the pot of salve and a wad of linen toward him, "but ya done that since ya could stand without your knees bucklin', so that ain't nothin' new. She's got to ya, this little Englisher, hasn't she? Ya can't fool old Mossie; all the more reason why she shouldn't be here. Ya need your wits about ya now."

Drumcondra sighed. "My past is neither here nor there. She's come, and she'll never escape from Falcon's Lair. I won't lose this stronghold if you keep an eye out. So look sharp!"

It seemed as though Thea had just fallen asleep when strong arms hauled her off the fur pallet and shook her awake. Her eyes had barely focused upon Drumcondra, when he dumped her in the middle of the elevated bed and stared down, arms akimbo.

"Are you simpleminded after all?" he barked. "You cannot lie on the floor. We have rats! Why do you think this fine bed here is raised?"

"M-my lord . . . ?"

He crooked his thumb toward the pile of pelts she'd just vacated. A plump gray rodent was crawling over the fur where moments earlier her body had been. Drumcondra's bluster alerted his bird, and it swooped down upon the creature in the blink of an eye, its deadly beak and talons making short work of it in a fit of frenzied squeaking and flapping. The bloody onslaught lasted only a moment before Isor squawked in victory. Batting his wings in a triumphant display that sent loose feathers flying, the great bird returned to its perch to devour the rat caught in its clutches.

Thea turned her head away from the sight, burying her face in the eiderdown bolster. The awful crunching and tearing of bones and flesh across the way, and the bird's guttural squawks of satisfaction as it fed, threatened to make her retch, and she covered her ears to shut out the sound.

The low, throaty rumble of Drumcondra's laughter joined the noise, and she moaned, burying her head beneath the furs. Her escape was short-lived. The warlord ripped the pelts away. Caught off guard by the sudden motion, Thea cried out in earnest at the sting of the fur, at the rush of cold air, and at the formidable sight of him staring down at her. What was that look in his eyes? She was almost glad she couldn't read it. It was too intense. All traces of laughter had fled his face, and his glazed eyes were inscrutable. They seemed to glow with an inner light in the soft semidarkness. Skittering over the bedclothes, she put as much distance between herself and the Gypsy as was possible.

The fire had all but died in the hearth, and no candles were lit in the sconces. A fractured shaft of luminescent glow laden with dust motes that the moon threw across the bed was the only light source. That picked out the angles and planes in his face, accentuating the cleft in his broad chin, and cast his deep-set eyes in shadow. When he strode stiffly around to the opposite side of the bed, she uttered a strangled gasp and skittered away.

He laughed. "You think that childish display will prevent me?" he asked. "Little fool, I am getting in that bed, so you may as well give it over."

Clutching the bedpost, Thea watched him strip off his tunic. The moonlight gleamed on his broad shoulders and defined his narrow waist. She followed the shadow of dark chest hair that diminished to an arrow-straight ribbon disappearing beneath his leggings, and monitored the pulsating muscles flexing in his corded biceps. She was so mesmerized by the sight, for she'd never seen a man in such a state of undress before, he had hold of her arm before she knew it happened. Without ceremony, he lifted her off the bed with no more effort than he would have employed plucking up a broom straw, and set her on her feet.

Thea gasped as the bird across the way loosed a chorus of harsh clucks. Did the odious creature *laugh*? It certainly sounded that way. Its onyx eyes were flashing, and its head was cocked in her direction. It began clucking again, its head bobbing up and down in rhythm with the sounds. She dosed it with an ireful stare, but it was brief. Dragging her toward the Glastonbury chair alongside the hearth, Drumcondra sank into it and extended his injured leg.

"I must make use of you," he said, still tethering her arm in a white-knuckled fist.

"I beg your pardon?"

"My boots."

"Yes?"

"I do not intend to sleep in them."

"What has that to do with me?" she snapped haughtily.

Without ceremony, he spun her around and thrust his left boot between her legs, hiking her shift up to her knees in the process. "Pull!" he charged, planting his other foot squarely on her behind. "*Gently*, mind," he warned. "Disturb those stitches, and you'll sew me up again."

Thea wiggled the boot, while he pushed with the foot he'd planted against her bottom, and she tumbled forward upon the floor when it gave.

"Now the other," he directed. "You shall have to be creative here. I cannot push off with my left, lest I stress the wound."

Thea dosed him with a withering stare. *Creative, is it?* she thought. *I'll give the great Gypsy lout "creative."* Bracing her bare feet against the forward crossed leg of the Glastonbury chair he occupied, she tugged with all her might on the heavy wide-top boot until it gave; then she scrambled to her feet and crowned him with it. It was a vicious unexpected blow over the head, delivered with all the strength she could muster. Caught off guard, the attack stunned him long enough for her to make a dash for the door. Tugging the gilded handle with all her might, she cast a backward glance toward Drumcondra, who was trying to rise. It was no use. The door was locked.

"*Isor, hold her!*" he thundered at the tail end of a string of expletives as he struggled to his feet.

Thea screamed as the bird landed on her shoulder, its talons piercing the linen shift. Its wings were beating her about the head, its beak fastened in her hair. In terror, she fell to her knees and covered her eyes, her bent head to the floor in a vain attempt to escape the creature.

"Get it off me!" she shrilled.

Drumcondra reached her in two ragged strides. "Isor, enough!" he bellowed. He extended his arm, and the bird hopped onto the leather gauntlet on his wrist. Hauling

Thea to her feet with his free hand, the warlord jerked her to a standstill. "What? Did you think that piddling blow would be enough to s-subdue *me*? Dream on, f-fair lady." Giving the bird flight, he steered her to the bed and shoved her down upon it.

He was slurring his words, and Thea pounced upon that. "You are foxed, sir!" she snapped at him. "Thoroughly castaway!"

"'Foxed' . . . 'castaway' . . . ? What strange words are these? I do not know them."

"In your altitudes, bosky, half-sprung, in your cups—*drunk*, sir! You reek of strong drink."

Recognition struck. "Ah! Quite possible," he said. "I tipped the jar before this here," he explained, slapping his injured thigh and wincing. He fell into the bed beside her. "How else but drunk should a man go under the surgeon's knife?"

Thea scrambled away from him, but his quick hand clamped around her wrist dragged her back again. "I'm not *that* drunk, my lady," he said in that seductive baritone voice of his. "It will take more than one piddling crock of whiskey to 'fox' me." His fist relaxed, and he began to slide his hammish hand the length of her arm. "Mmm," he hummed. "Soft as silk."

She swatted his hand, attracting the notice of the bird. It clucked, took flight from its shadowy retreat beside the dead hearth, and landed on the elaborately carved headboard of the bed. A quick peck on the top of her head sent her under the fur pelts with a shriek.

"Keep that thing away from me, I said!" she cried. "It bit me!"

A fiendish drunken laugh rumbled up from his throat, and he reached beneath the furs and pulled her hard against him.

"It is not wise to menace me within the bird's sight," he agreed, "else you lose some vital portion of your anatomy. He is my creature after all . . . my familiar. You would do well to remember that."

"*Familiar* is it? Balderdash! It is a vicious predator, and me you have made so! You think that I will just lie here and let you rape me because that bird is perched between us? I'll see it in the stew pot first! I'll wring its scrawny neck before I will succumb to rape. Why don't you just kill me outright? That is what you mean to do in the end, isn't it? What will that serve? Will it bring your wife and children back? Let me go, Lord Drumcondra! In God's name, will you please just let me go?"

He raised himself on one elbow, searching her face in the moonlight. "Who said I was going to rape you?" he demanded.

"Y-you did!"

Her posture clenched, she held her breath as his hand cupped her face then slid the length of her throat and came to rest upon the soft swell of her breast. Her heart began to pound. As if it had a will of its own, her nipple hardened against his thumb as he grazed it through the stiff linen fabric. He began strumming the tall protruding bud. Her breath caught as icy-hot waves of pulsating sensation moistened her sex, just as they had done when he had fondled her naked breast while confronting Cian Cosgrove.

"You do not pay attention," he murmured. "I have no intention of raping you, fair lady. I am no Cosgrove. Ros Drumcondra does not rape his women. He does not have to. What I said was, he ought take care because you are a winsome lass and I am tight against the seam." He drove her hand down to his sex to prove the point. He was thick and hard, responding to her touch, albeit forced. "I also said that, just as in days of old, I will have you before him, and that when I've done, you will want no other. I call that not rape, my pretty, because before I've done you will beg me to put that which you hold in your hand inside you. But . . . not tonight."

And with that, he fell back down in the bed beside her, his wavy black shoulder-length hair fanned out on the bolster, and threw one well-muscled arm across his closed eyes, while the other tethered her wrist again.

"The wound, the whiskey, and that boot you clouted me with have had their way with me . . . for the moment," he said. "But take no comfort in it. That door is locked. Make one move to leave this bed and *Isor* will have his way with you, fair lady."

Chapter Eight

"What do you mean she just disappeared?" Nigel bellowed. His savaged eye was thickly padded with cotton wool, his head wreathed in bandages. They had kept Thea's absence from him as long as they could. He had lost much blood, and had been confined to his bed with a fever that had set in after the falcon attacked him. Now he was on the mend, but hardly fit to be up and about. That had made him surly—downright mean, thought James, looking on. The more he saw of Nigel Cosgrove, the less he liked the man, and the more he wondered if Thea hadn't staged the trip to Newgrange for the sole purpose of haring off to escape the impending marriage. If it were true, after what he'd seen of her betrothed thus far, he could hardly blame her.

"I know it sounds preposterous, but that is exactly what occurred," James said. "The bird . . . I believe it was the very same that attacked you, seemed to follow us to Newgrange. When we reached it, Thea went inside alone while I waited with the sleigh—to keep an eye on that falcon. I was of a mind to kill it if it menaced us. She was gone for some time—past the seventeen minutes when the tomb would be flooded with light. I called to her, but she didn't answer, so I took the carriage lantern and went inside. There was no sign of her, Cosgrove, and there is no other exit from the passage tomb that anyone has ever heard of. I searched the land surrounding, but there were no footprints in the snow—"

"That is absurd," Nigel said. "You must have muddled them in your search."

"I did nothing of the kind. There was one clear set of her footprints going in, but none coming out. I thought at first that she was playing a prank on me, but no. It has been too long. And where could she go? There is nothing for miles out there—nothing but mounds of snow. If there were tracks they would still be there. No new snow has fallen since."

"What then?" Nigel asked hotly, throwing his arms in the air. "You shan't convince me that anything supernatural is afoot, Barrington. And do not presume to spout that Gypsy horse shite about time tunnels to me! Save that for jingle-brained birdwits like your sister, who doubtless believes in faeries and ogres and . . . what is it you Cornish call the trolls that live in your mines? *Knockers?*"

"Now, see here. There's no call to snipe at Thea. I'm hardly suggesting—"

"You'd best not."

"I shall leave no stone unturned until I find her," James said. The insufferable gudgeon was in danger of coming up with a blackened good eye. It was beyond the beyond. How dared Thea go traipsing off and leave him with this impossible coil to unwind.

"That wretched old Gypsy crone is not exempted from this, you can bet your blunt upon it. Whatever possessed

Theodosia to champion her so? I never should have allowed the woman to set foot in the house. There's been nothing but misfortune come upon us since I let her in. They do that, you know—bring misfortune. Deuced Gypsies—Tinkers—Travelers—the whole bloody lot can go to the devil and good riddance, the heathens!"

Now who's spouting gammon over the supernatural, James wanted to say. He bit back the temptation, with hard-set lips and ticking jaw muscles.

"What did that odious woman say to her?" Nigel asked. "Did she confide in you?"

"No, she did not," said James. "I asked, but she skirted the issue and I did not pursue it."

"They've probably carried her off!" Nigel went on. "Well? What are you sitting here for? Go back out and run them to ground. Go round to Drogheda and bring the guards from the Watch. Do *something*, man!"

"I've only just come in, and I'm exhausted, Cosgrove," James said, his voice strained. Another minute and he'd tell the jackanapes exactly what he thought of him, by God! "No one wants to find Thea more than I do, I assure you." Should he speak his mind? The devil take it—yes! "Look here," he went on, "I know my sister well by half— far better than you, sir, and I'm beginning to believe that Thea does not want to be found. I wasn't going to do this, but I see now that I must. When you get up out of that bed, there are issues that needs must be addressed. I saw the mark you left upon Thea's lips, and I know what transpired between you up on those battlements—none of which befits the conduct of a gentleman, sir."

Nigel gave a dry guffaw. "Are you calling me out, Barrington?"

"I am putting you on notice, sir . . . for the present."

"What occurs between Theodosia and myself is none of your concern."

"I beg to differ," said James. "My sister's welfare and well-being are very much my concern, Cosgrove. I haven't liked your attitude toward Thea from the start. I would be remiss as her brother and her protector if I were not to speak my mind in the matter."

"Now is not exactly the hour to give me the benefit of your 'mind,'" Nigel said.

"I thoroughly agree," James returned. "Which is why I shall take my leave and be about the business of fetching the guards from Drogheda. There will be plenty of time for settling grievances once Thea is had back safely, please God." And he turned with a heel-clicking bow to quit the room without a backward glance.

Streaking past two housemaids in the corridor who had obviously been eavesdropping, he collected his multi-caped greatcoat, beaver hat, gloves, and a flask of whiskey to ward off the chill. Then, without a word to anyone, he jogged down the stairs and stalked off toward the stables.

It was scarcely midday, but the sky had darkened considerably since he had returned. He would have to hurry if he wanted to reach Drogheda and bring the guards before the threatening snowstorm. Haste was of the essence. A new snowfall would cover any tracks he might have overlooked, though he couldn't imagine where they might be. He'd combed the entire area. Not so the guards. They were trained in such things, and might detect something he had not. Beadle the stabler saddled him a magnificent Andalusian stallion, and he rode off at a gallop heading east, straight for Drogheda.

Since Newgrange was on the way, he made one last pass. The gaping black entrance of the tomb was nearly obscured now by drifting snow. Only a narrow swath re-mained, showing Thea's footprints all but filled in now. Cupping his hands around his mouth, James called to her at the top of his voice for what had to be the hundredth time. Her name sounded back in a mournful echo that lived afterward for some time, before dying off on a strong wind that had risen since he'd left the site earlier. There was no reply. If she were near, she would have heard him.

He had no means to light his way into the chamber again, but he'd gone in several times, hoping to find some secret room, some hidden chamber that he might have overlooked where she might be trapped. It was no use. He would have to leave it to the guards, and he would have to make haste fetching them. A close eye on the dark scud-ding clouds looming overhead, he turned his horse back toward the lane and continued on his journey.

The five miles to Drogheda seemed twice that distance when he finally neared the outskirts of the city. The horse was laboring. He'd driven the animal relentlessly, trying to outrun the storm—to no avail. Such weather was unprece-dented in County Meath; they'd all said so. Blinding, wind-driven snow was falling. He could barely see two feet in front of him. Ice crystals were forming on his hair and eyebrows and crackling in his nostrils. His black superfine greatcoat was caked with snow, and his beaver hat was frosted white. He should have opted for the sleigh, or one of the traps in Nigel's stables instead of the stallion. He'd thought to save time on horseback and outrun the storm, but it had overtaken him anyway. At least in a carriage, he would have been somewhat protected. There was no use lamenting it now. There was a more urgent press. It was still a good distance to Drogheda proper, and there was nothing for it. He had to find shelter somewhere before pressing on.

All at once a structure loomed up before him. It appeared to be the remains of another ruined castle. Pursuant of an architectural career, such sites held an irresistible fascination for him. Many such structures littered the countryside. He'd passed several along the way; dreary, melancholy places whose walls were crumbling from neglect, stark evidence of times gone by. This one, however, was more substantial than some of the others. One whole wing seemed intact, including the portcullis on what must have been the main entrance where the dilapidated wing opposite was attached. From that vantage, he couldn't vouch for the snow-laden roof and battlements. Still, it would at least provide shelter from the storm, and he turned his weary mount toward it, his head bent into the cruel north wind.

A deep trench all around suggested that a moat had once wreathed the castle. While the sides had fallen in over time, and were not the vertical drop they once must have been, the access was still steep on both sides and the Andalusian balked at the prospect of negotiating it. Half prancing, half slip-sliding through the drifts, James managed to coax the animal halfway down before a deep hollow hidden beneath the surface buried the horse to the withers. He climbed down, a firm hand on the ribbons, and hauled the shrieking, foundering horse out of the drift, thanking God that the fresh powder was still soft enough to manage it.

Coaxing the frenzied animal up the other side of the trench was another matter. White breath puffing from flared nostrils, its eyes crazed with fright, the complaining horse resisted. It took all the strength and skill with horses James possessed, which was not a little, to get the Andalusian out of the trench onto what once had been the castle courtyard. At that, it wasn't accomplished without thrice tumbling down the grade—horse and all—in the attempt.

Overhead a falcon soared through the snow-swept sky, circling what remained of the battlements. The sight of it sent cold chills not related to the elements racing along his spine. The wind wailed like a woman screaming, stopping him in his tracks. It sounded like Thea's voice trailing off on the wind. It came again, louder now. It seemed to surround him, just as the wind surrounded him, tugging at the capes on his greatcoat like so many curious fingers.

"Thea . . . ?" he murmured. It couldn't be. It was his imagination playing tricks upon him, that and the howling wind. It had numbed his brain. So anxious to have news of his sister, he was ready to conjure her from the very air around him, and to spirit her away from the man she was so loath to wed—despite the much-needed wealth their marriage would bestow upon the Barringtons.

Wearily, a firm albeit numb hand wound in the ribbons, he led the horse toward the ruined castle. There was no difficulty gaining entrance. The gaping hole, no more than a slag heap—all that remained of the L-shaped wing still standing—was large enough for the horse to enter as well. James assessed the soundness of the structure and decided that long ago, by the look of things, that section had evidently been destroyed by fire, at least what parts of it would burn. What remained had all but crumbled to dust and rubble over time, posing no threat now. Cautious still, he walked the Andalusian inside, out of the wind, unsaddled it, and went in search of a suitable chamber in the sound wing where he might pass the time until the storm subsided.

Thea awoke still tethered to Ros Drumcondra. His burly fist was clamped around her wrist, just as it had been when he fell into a deep sleep the night before. But that wasn't what woke her. She was cold—cold and wet!

The moon had moved on, but the sun had not yet risen. Reflected glare from the snow, tinted blue by first light creeping over the horizon showed her Drumcondra's inert form beside her. Above, the falcon still perched on the headboard. It looked docile enough, but Thea didn't believe that for an instant. Her scalp was still tender where it had pecked her. If she was cautious maybe, just maybe . . . A soft cluck when she attempted to move put an end to that fantasy. Did the creature never sleep?

Reaching with her free hand, a close eye upon the bird, she slipped it beneath the pelts, and began feeling for the source of the dampness. The hand Drumcondra had tethered was soaked, as was her leg and her shift forced against his thigh. She threw back the furs and her breath caught. *Blood!* Her hand came away red with it. He had stressed the stitches and opened the wound.

Thea tried to pry her wrist free of his grip, but it wouldn't budge, and the bird began to travel the rolled, carved top of the headboard, its sharp claws clicking against the wood, the bells on its tethers clanking noisily. Nonetheless, Thea shook Drumcondra's shoulder.

"My lord, please wake. You are bleeding, sir—badly!"

Drumcondra groaned, but did not open his eyes.

"My lord!" Thea persisted, shaking him harder. She cried out when the bird hopped down to Drumcondra's shoulder and pecked her hand. The creature was absolutely *evil* . . . or overprotective to a fault. Stupid bird! How could a mere wisp of a girl as she harm such a hulking giant? Oh, for a shoe to lob at the murderous thing. Lud! She'd hit the wrong target wielding Drumcondra's boot. Her benevolence toward all God's creatures—at least this creature was rapidly flagging. "My lord!" she shrilled in a voice loud enough to rouse the dead. "Awake at once! You are bleeding!"

Drumcondra lurched, and tightened his grip on her wrist. "Uh . . . ?" he grunted, then groaned again, and fell back against the bolster he'd sprung from. "My head," he moaned, throwing his free arm across his eyes.

She had no sympathy for the lout. Worried though she was that he was bleeding dreadfully, she'd rather swallow her tongue than let him know it.

"Get up!" she snapped. "Get up this instant and minister to yourself! You have opened your wound, sir. The bed is bathed in blood!"

He groaned awake. His hooded eyes, glazed and bloodshot, settled upon her face, and he vaulted erect in earnest, a motion he obviously regretted. Taking his head in his hands, he raked his fingers through his hair and sought her eyes again.

"What did you hit me with?" he asked.

"Oh!" she cried, slapping the furs with her free hand. "*Look!*" she said, pointing. "You are bleeding, my lord!"

"Bloody hell!" he trumpeted, attempting to rise. A grimace contorted his handsome face, and he fell back down again.

Thea's hand flew to her lips, and she watched him struggle with the pain and the blear and the obvious headache, by-product, no doubt, of the blow she'd awarded him and the quantity of whiskey he'd consumed before his surgery. His breathing was rapid and shallow. If she were brave enough to stroke his skin, she was certain it would be hot and dry to the touch. He was burning up with fever.

Now what was she to do—locked inside a chamber with a man who could well be dying? Would anyone even hear if she were to cry out for help? And if they did, would they treat her as the others in the cave had done? She would rather die cooped up in this chamber than chance finding out. At least he hadn't tried to rape her.

"C-can you kindle the fire?" he asked, low-voiced.

"If you will control that bird," she said.

"Isor . . . will not . . . harm you."

"Hmmm. Well, if he does, he will roast over that fire! The creature has clawed me once and bitten me twice. I will bear no more!"

"The tinderbox is on the mantel. J-just *do* it."

A close eye upon the bird, Thea did as he bade. There were fresh logs piled in the corner. Working the flint and combustible bits from the tinderbox until a flame sparked, she touched it to the logs and fanned the fire to life with the bellows. It took some time, and when the chore was done, she turned back to find that Drumcondra had stripped off his leggings and was plucking the stitches from his wound.

His tunic barely covered his private parts, and her hands flew to her mouth looking on. But mesmerized, she couldn't tear her eyes away. His face twisted in pain, he made no sound as he worked to remove the last strand of knotted thread. Whatever else he was, the man was a seasoned warrior. How many times had he done such as this after a battle? She shuddered to wonder. The sight thrilled and horrified her all at once. The effect of those polar emotions was so soul wrenching it drained the blood from her scalp, and she sank like a stone in the Glastonbury chair, drawing his eyes.

"You aren't going to swoon on me again, are you?" he said. Blood was running down his leg, and he jammed the soaked bandage he'd stripped away into the gash and pressed down hard.

"N-no . . ." she stammered. It wasn't the blood. It was the realization that she actually cared what happened to him that buckled her knees. "What are you doing?" she breathed.

"What should have been done before," he said. "There is no surgeon hereabouts. My stabler tends our wounded, just as he tends the animals. He is getting old. The wound is too deep for stitching. I feared as much. . . ." He started to rise, and fell back down. Swinging his good leg back up on the bed with a groan, he left the other dangling over the side, still putting pressure on the wound. "Heat a poker in the flames," he gritted.

"You would cauterize it?" she murmured, horrified.

He shook his head, his green eyes riveting. "Not I, my lady. You must. I will tell you how."

"Ohh no, my lord!" Thea cried, shaking her head wildly. "I . . . I cannot. I will not. I am amazed that you would trust me with a hot poker after . . . after . . ."

He forced a chuckle. "I have no choice, other than to bleed to death," he said. "And, my strange little creature, you are humane if nothing else."

"Which is why I cannot do this," she protested. "I could not do such a thing to an animal."

"You can, and you will—you must," he said. "Call your anger back if needs must. Just do it."

"I am no surgeon. Can you not summon your stabler and have him fix this fine mess he's made? I give you my word, I will not oppose you. Please, my lord, I beg of you. I cannot do this."

"Heat . . . the . . . poker."

The command was unequivocal. By the look of the amount of blood he was losing, it was plain there wasn't a minute to spare, and she thrust one of the iron pokers into the fire. It raised a flurry of sparks, and she backed away from the hearth.

He beckoned her closer. "The flames will slowly turn the poker red," he told her. "At first it will be the color of wine. Leave it until it turns as red as this blood here, then bring it quickly, and lay it so." He illustrated. "Hold it for a slow count of five, no matter what I do under the brand. It must be so."

"My lord, you are not thinking clearly," she said, her voice steady for all that she was a shambles. "If I come near you with that poker, the bird will tear me to shreds."

"Fetch me his hood from the candle stand," he replied.

Thea did as he bade, and handed it over.

"Isor, *come!*" Drumcondra commanded, extending his arm. The bird hopped down from the headboard and stood while he fastened the hood in place. "He will not attack what he cannot see," he said to Thea. "Fetch the poker."

Thea went to the hearth and waited until the poker glowed before she hefted it out of the flames and carried it to the bedside. Staring down at him writhing below, she hesitated.

"Do it!" he said. "Now, before it cools."

"I . . . I cannot, my lord," Thea sobbed.

Drumcondra's hand shot out and grabbed her wrist, driving the poker into the wound. She cried out as the hissing, smoking iron seared his flesh, but he held it there twisting and grimacing in pain, head thrust back and teeth bared, for a slow count of five before he let her go. Sobbing, she flung the poker across the room, and covered her face with her hands.

Drumcondra grabbed her arm and shook her. "On the chest . . . you will find a jar . . . and linens," he panted. "Fetch them here. You must bind the wound."

Thea brought them and knelt down.

"Only a thin layer of the salve," he said. "Just enough to keep the bandage from sticking so we do not have to do this again. Then bind it."

Thea uncorked the jar with trembling hands and shrank from the stench of the strange blackish stuff inside. "What

is this?" she asked through a grimace. Mingled with the
stink of blood and burnt flesh, it threatened to make her
retch.

"A Gypsy remedy," he said. "Secret herbs and oils old as
eons. It has great healing power. Mossie, my stabler has
cured many a horse with it."

Thea dipped her fingers in the thick, odious ointment,
holding it at arm's length. Anything with such a reputation that smelled so foul had to have something to recommend it. That it cured horses was encouraging. Ros
Drumcondra had more stamina than any horse she had
ever seen.

His eyes were glazed with pain he would not cry out to
release. The look brought tears to Thea's eyes—though
she couldn't think why, since he'd brought it upon
himself—as she spread the salve on the blackened smoldering crust that had mercifully stopped the blood flow.

Drumcondra groaned and shut his eyes. "You have a
light touch, my lady," he murmured, and groaned again.

Thea did not reply. This was not the groan of a man in
pain, it was quite something else, and it set her blood racing. Her hands were trembling when she unfurled the
bandage linen. Twice—three times, she reached toward
his leg and drew her hand back. Her touch had aroused
him. It was impossible, but there it was. What was the
man made of?

She had to lift his leg to wrap the linen properly, and
her hand came closer to his sex with each precarious revo-
lution. When her hand brushed the hard shaft of hot,
veined flesh beneath his tunic, she cried out in spite of her
resolve not to do so, and jerked her hand away. He smiled
that maddening smile of his that did not reach his eyes. It
was a cold expression, and yet it sizzled with inner fire.
What was he thinking? It was impossible to say, though

hot blood surged to her temples while meeting that gaze, and she quickly tied off the linen and lifted his leg onto the bed.

"A very . . . light touch," he murmured, and then he said no more.

Chapter Nine

Looking in dismay at the sleeping Gypsy warlord, Thea breathed a ragged sigh. The man had to be a sorcerer—she was convinced of it. She tossed the fur rug over him and backed away from the bed. A swarm of contradictory emotions overwhelmed her. This enigmatic virile warrior had awakened in her sensations that were frightening and new. Despite his rough bluster, he hadn't really hurt her, but what he had set loose in her was more frightening than pain.

She'd glimpsed his manhood, felt its turgid strength, felt it respond to the reluctant fingers he'd crimped around it. Something tugged at her sex, recalling the way his flesh leapt to life at her touch. That tug—over which she had no control; she was completely under his spell—was what she feared most. What had he said? *Before I've done, you will beg me to put that which you hold in your hand inside you.* No! She could not—*would* not—leave herself vulnerable in such a way. She would not give him her virtue. But he had awakened her to a thirst for pleasure that she knew only he could slake, and she hated him for it.

There was no alternative but to put as much distance between herself and this man as possible. The door was locked, but the key had to be somewhere in the room. She would never get a better opportunity to search. Now, while he was sleeping and the bird was subdued.

He couldn't have concealed it on his person. He was half naked. Her eyes darted around in search of a likely place. The room was large but sparely furnished. Except for the massive bed, the two Glastonbury chairs, a large linens chest bolted to the floor, a chamber pot and the wrought iron candle stand that doubled as the bird's perch, the room was bare of furniture. She had been sound asleep when he entered earlier. He would have had plenty of time to hide the key. But where? Ros Drumcondra was no fool. Surely he knew she would try to escape at the first opportunity.

On tiptoe, she moved about the room. Keeping a close eye on the Gypsy sleeping behind, she ran her trembling hand across the roughly hewn mantel over the hearth, then moved on to search the Glastonbury chairs, lifting her pelerine from the one beside the door, but there was no sign of the key. Crouching low, she inched along the base of the raised platform the bed stood upon. All at once, movement near the corner of one of the fur throws that had fallen on the floor caught her eye as she probed. A squeaking sound nearly stopped her heart. She stiffened as her hand brushed the long skinny tail of the huge brown rat she'd disturbed there. Thea squealed in spite of herself, fell back on her behind and skittered across the floor, drawing her bare feet up beneath the blood-soaked hem of her shift. Where were the creatures coming from?

The cold light of dawn filtering in through the window

revealed the answer. There were holes in the wall on both sides where it met the floor. The scent of blood had evidently drawn them. She was covered with it, and the brazen rat was stalking toward her.

Terror all but paralyzed her brain. She held her breath in a desperate attempt to keep the raw scream building in her throat from escaping. If only she had something to attack with—if only the falcon wasn't hooded! Drumcondra's boot, lying where she'd flung it alongside the candle stand caught her eye. A likely weapon! Leaping to her feet, she pattered to it, but when she reached out to snatch it, another rat slithered from the wide, turned-back cuff.

The scream she fought so valiantly to hold back escaped in the form of a strangled exclamation. Though Drumcondra didn't respond to the sound, the falcon did. Something clanked against the stone floor when it landed, wings flapping, on the platform. Thea stared. It wasn't little bells that she'd heard clattering against the headboard earlier; it was *the key*, braided cleverly into the bird's tethers.

Restless, Drumcondra stirred, a soft moan escaping his throat. Thea held her breath. The crafty warrior had hidden the key in plain sight—in the one place he'd evidently assumed she would never go to retrieve it. How little he knew her. Hooded, the bird was less fearsome. Drumcondra was the greater danger or rather *she* was, to herself, under his spell.

The rats forgotten, Thea crept up on the bird. As if it knew, it hopped away, clucking and bobbing its hooded head. She was scarcely making a sound. Could it be that sensitive to her motion? Evidently it was, though she couldn't fathom how . . . unless it *was* a supernatural creature. She made a fresh approach and, hooded as it was, it pecked at her, missing her hand by inches. Like lightning, she drew back then made another approach.

Gingerly her fingers inched toward the bird's tethers. But it was not to be so easy. By the third failed try, she'd begun to contemplate killing it—crushing its skull with Drumcondra's boot. But she could not bring herself to do it. She could not conscience killing a defenseless creature. And it was defenseless, hooded, blind and unsuspecting.

It took several tries and more than one wounded finger before she won the prize, and at that not before she'd snatched Drumcondra's cast-off leggings and thrown them over the creature while she worked. Tiptoeing to the door, she turned the key in the lock, breathing a sigh of relief when it opened. Then, snatching her pelerine, she cast one last look at Drumcondra behind, stepped into the darkened hallway, and locked the door behind her. *There then! Let him just try to get out without the key!* she triumphed.

Taking it with her, she crept along the corridor with no plan in mind except escaping, and melted into the indigo shadows not yet chased by the dawn.

Ros Drumcondra groaned awake to the squawking, flapping frenzy of his irate bird beating him about the head and chest with its massive wings. Half asleep still, he swatted at the creature, but that made the falcon screech all the louder. It would not be borne. His head was splitting, the aftermath of the whiskey he'd drunk and Thea's crowning him.

He struggled upright, bracing himself upon his elbows, blinking the sleep from his eyes. It was a moment before they focused. The bird was still flapping about, and he stripped off its hood and glanced around the room in search of Thea.

Free of the hood's encumbrance, the bird took flight and soared about the exposed beams above. Screeching, it dipped and soared and flapped about in a genuine rage,

Drumcondra thought. It wasn't long before he realized why. *Thea was gone!*

"Bloody hell!" he cried, swinging his feet over the edge of the bed, an action he instantly regretted. For a moment, he'd forgotten the injury. Cursing the air blue, his head thrust back in pain that manifested itself in spurts of red glare behind his screwed shut eyes, he pounded the furs beneath him with white-knuckled fists and tried again to rise more gingerly.

Snatching up his leggings from the floor, he tugged them on—no mean task with the injured thigh. The blood had ceased to flow, and his brow was running with sweat. Both were good signs. Mossie's mysterious Gypsy unction had worked some magic.

By the time he'd tugged his boots on, the bird had ceased its circling. Not a minute too soon. He was still half castaway from the whiskey, and the creature's irate revolutions were making him dizzy.

"*Stay*, damn you!" he commanded. "How did she get that key, eh?"

The bird's eyes flashed. If ever a falcon wore a look of indignation, this one did now.

Drumcondra strode to the door and seized the handle. When it didn't release, he rattled it relentlessly. Loosing a bestial howl that sent the screeching falcon, wings flapping, straight into the chimney corner, he raised the heavy Glastonbury chair and slammed it into the door, rendering the chair to splinters. The door sustained no damage. Neither dent nor scratch marred the thick old wood. Drumcondra raved again, his thunder ringing from the rafters, both clenched fists raised to the heavens.

"Bloody hell, she's locked me in!" he seethed, bearing down upon the bird hiding in the shadows beside the hearth. All that showed its presence there were two beady eyes blinking at him from the dusky recess behind the bellows.

"Oh, aye—hide, you bloody coward!" he thundered. Stalking stiff-legged toward the hearth, he seized the iron candle stand, stalked back, and hefted that against the door. It groaned, but showed no sign of giving way. He lunged at it again and again to no avail until—blind with battle madness, impervious to the throbbing pain in his thigh—he shattered the glass in the window overlooking the courtyard and heaved the candle stand through like a javelin. Before he could blink, his bird took flight and soared after it, screeching its complaints as it grazed him with its flapping wings sailing past.

The narrow window was barely wide enough to accommodate either of them, since the glass was a later addition to what amounted to no more than glorified arrow slits in the upper chambers. Below, three nonplussed lackeys patrolling the grounds stared up at the missile speeding toward them, their jaws sagging, and Drumcondra roared like a lion.

"What are you gaping at, you lazy gudgeons?" he bellowed. "Haul your worthless arses up here and turn me loose!"

Thea had escaped the chamber, but escaping the castle would not be accomplished as easily. If it had been summer, it mightn't have been impossible, but how was she to manage with no shoes and snow?

Keeping to the shadows, she crept along the cold dank passageways looking for a staircase that would take her below. What to do there she had no inkling, unless it be attempting to hide in one of the carts she'd seen from the windows coming and going. Then, if she could only find her way back to Newgrange, she might be able to access the portal she had stumbled upon that had brought her here, and find her way back to her own time. If such a thing were even possible was a mystery. Her entrance to Drumcondra's world through the passage tomb had occurred at the solstice, and that was long past by now.

Presently, she found herself in what appeared to be a gallery above the lower floor. There had to be a staircase leading below, and she hugged the musty walls bleeding with dampness and slimed with green mold in search of it. She had scarcely begun when a racket below echoed along the corridors as three lackeys came running. Flattening herself behind a column marking a recessed alcove, she held her breath until they passed, traveling toward the wing she'd just fled. From their mutterings, it was clear that they had been summoned. Could Drumcondra have wakened? The possibility of that gave her feet wings, and she raced along the hallway until she found the staircase the lackeys had mounted to reach the gallery and made her way below.

Others were milling about now—houseboys and lackeys and scullions running every which way through what she assumed to be the great hall. If her shift weren't covered in blood, she might have mingled among them undetected, but as she was, barefoot in the sumptuous chinchilla fur pelerine, there was no hope of that. The servants being preoccupied with some urgency was to her advantage, however. No one had taken notice of her yet in the confusion. If she could only reach the servants' quarters undetected, she might just be able to find a cart leaving the compound and affect her escape. It was a pleasant fantasy to be sure, but all she had to cling to as she followed the servants hoping to implement her hastily formed plan.

She had nearly reached a narrow hallway that emptied into what her nose told her must be the kitchens, when a rumpus behind turned her to face two of Drumcondra's band who had laid hands upon an intruder. The captive was holding his own in a bold attempt to break free, and two other men came running. Thea's heart fairly leapt from her breast. Stifling a scream, she gave up her shadowy anonymity along the periphery and ran back the way she'd come. Bursting into the great hall, the scream long building in her throat would no longer be contained, and she ran straight into the melee screaming:

"*James!*"

She had not taken two steps when Drumcondra's strong hands lifted her off the floor and slung her over his shoulder. Where had he come from? Her eyes having seen naught but James, she had not even seen him approach.

"So here you are, fair lady," he said. "You needn't have invaded the kitchens. I would have been happy to satisfy your appetite."

Ignoring the obvious innuendo, Thea beat upon his broad back with both her hands balled into fists. "Put me down!" she shrilled as he hitched her higher. "Ow! Put me down, I say! And turn my brother loose! If you harm one hair upon his head, I—"

"Your brother found at last, eh?" he interrupted, wheeling to face the two men struggling to restrain James. "I thought that bit a work of fiction. I couldn't imagine there to be two lackwits fool enough to be wandering the battlefields of County Meath unprotected. I stand corrected. What manner of clothes is the man wearing?"

"The l-latest London fashions, my lord," said Thea, thinking on her feet though they were off the floor. "If you were not barbarians here, you would know that, you clod! Now put me down!"

"You heard my sister, let her go!" James demanded, earning himself a blow to the mouth from one of his captors.

Thea screamed. "James, do be still!" she warned. "I think I can explain all this . . . if Lord Drumcondra will only let me."

"Lord Drumcondra?" James breathed, aghast.

"She will have to explain it to *me* first," said Drumcondra, stalking off with her. As he strode off, over his shoulder to the others he said, "Take him below and clap him in irons while I get to the bottom of this. I shall deal with him later."

Chapter Ten

Drumcondra literally dumped Thea on the bed. The bloodied bedclothes had been stripped away and replaced with fresh linens and feather beds beneath the furs. Across the way, while the floor was still littered with broken glass, a plank had been fitted in the gaping window. While it preserved some of the warmth, it diminished what little light the chamber boasted to begin with, since it was the only window.

"What have you done with the key?" he asked, looming over her.

No blood seemed to be seeping from his wounded thigh through his leggings, though he favored it, moving stiff-legged. His tight-lipped stare through eyes glazed with pain, however, told too well that carrying her back to that room had aggrieved it.

"I threw it away," she snapped, tossing her dark curls.

His eyebrow inched up. "I do not believe you," he said flatly.

"I do not care what you believe, my lord. Let me go to my brother!"

"Not . . . just . . . yet," he pronounced, studying her. After a moment, he strode to the chest in the corner and fished out a shift of cream-colored silk, richly embroidered with threads of gold in a pattern of the same concentric circular motifs she'd seen at the entrance of Newgrange. He tossed it to her. "Put it on," he said.

"I beg your pardon?"

"You are covered in blood. Put it on." .

"I will not disrobe in front of you, Lord Drumcondra!" she said unequivocally.

"Tell me, what have you got that I have not already seen, eh?"

"That is neither here nor there, sir. What you have already seen, *I* did not show you."

"A minor point." He jerked her to her feet and stripped off the pelerine. "Now the shift," he said. "Or would you rather I do it for you?"

Thea backed away. "At least turn your back, my lord," she said.

"I think not," he responded, folding his sinewy arms across his chest. "How can I see where you've hidden the key if I do that, fair lady?"

"Lud!" Thea exclaimed. Jamming her hand into the pocket of the shift, she tugged out the key and threw it at him. "There!" she cried, as he snatched it up from the floor where it landed with a clang after bouncing off his chest. "Are you satisfied? Now will you avert your eyes, sir?"

"I would have done," he said, his droll words riding a theatrical sigh, "had you been honest with me. Since you have not, I think I shall just give you a taste of what you may expect should you ever oppose me again."

His eyes, half-closed with desire, smoldered toward her

as he closed the gap between them in one ragged stride. Thea's breath caught in her throat as he took her in his arms. She thought he was going to strip her of her shift, as he had the pelerine, but to her surprise, he did just the opposite, moving ever so slowly, savoring every facet of the chore before him.

How tall he was, bending over her; the look in his eyes devouring her at close range was more than she was ready to bear. She could no longer deny her attraction to the man. But nothing could exist between them. They were from two different worlds—literally. It was inevitable that time would part them. There would be nothing but heartbreak. Besides, he only wanted her for one thing: to use her as a means of retribution against Cian Cosgrove; to take her virtue, and give her back tarnished and deflowered. That was not what those shuttered eyes were saying now, however. Should she listen to her head . . . or her heart? All at once, the old Gypsy woman's words came again without bidding: *Ye do not belong with this lot. Ye have come here for another. Two days until the solstice and ye see Ros Drumcondra, the Black Falcon, in the flesh. Beware the Cosgrove clan. Ye are the Falcon's bride* . . . What did it all mean?

There was no time to ponder. His lips were warm when they took hers, his tongue like silk. The gentleness of that first long, lingering kiss was so totally contradictory to every other encounter she'd had with the man, it stalled her brain. It was her secret fantasy, come to life in such a volatile way there was no mistaking it; only now it was no air dream, *it was real*. Stark terror and raw passion vied for supremacy. Passion won.

Before she realized what was happening, her arms were around him. As foxed by his closeness as a drunkard in his cups, she breathed in his scent. It was darkly mysterious, just as she remembered it, heavy with musk, with the heady, earthy scents of the forest laced with a hint of tanned leather and whiskey residue.

His moan aroused her. His hands, exploring her body through her linen shift, set her blood racing. Shocking waves of liquid fire pumped through her belly and thighs as the flat of his open palm splayed out on her chest, inching lower, dangerously close to the soft swell of her breasts and her nipples that had grown hard and tall beneath the fabric in anticipation of his skilled fingers. Ever so slowly, that hand came close; but they did not touch those aching buds or the puckered flesh around them. Excruciating ecstasy, so deliciously acute it took her breath away.

The arm around her waist crushed her closer to his swollen hardness, its bruising pressure throbbing against her. Again, her breath caught. What sort of man was this to be aroused, come so soon from such a serious surgery? He was in pain, and yet . . . ! And how could he be gentle and explosive at the same time? The stars only knew, but he was. A sleeping tiger lay just beneath the surface of his ardor, ready to pounce. She could almost feel its claws, its fangs—the primeval pull of its passion drawing her like a magnet. It was palpable, living in its own space—a space he had invaded, claimed, *possessed*. That space was her flesh, her sex, her very soul.

What was she doing? What was she thinking? This man was a fierce fire-breathing warrior—the Black Falcon. He had her in his talons now, and though she should resist, she was powerless against his prowess, powerless against the smoldering fire beneath the surface of this man that threatened to consume her whole. In that one wonderful, terrible instant, she would have let it. She had never dreamed this. How could she have, when she had no idea such ecstasy existed?

Her scandalous penny novels had not prepared her for

anything remotely like what was happening to her now in Ros Drumcondra's arms—what was evidently happening to him as well—those secretly read tomes, taken as gospel in her ignorance, paled miserably in comparison.

Just when she thought she could bear no more, his hand left her chest and began inching up the skirt of her shift. The fabric was wrinkled and stiff, crimson with his dried blood. He drew it away as gently as if he were peeling a delicate, succulent grape, which is just how she felt then, vulnerable—raw and moist, and his for the taking. But he did not take her. Casting the shift aside, he took the fresh one from her hand—she hadn't even been aware that she still clung to it—and slid it over her trembling nakedness.

"Not yet, my lady, but soon . . ." he murmured huskily against her hair, his warm breath sending shivers along her spine.

Blood sped through Thea's veins and scalded her cheeks. How could he humiliate her like this—lead her to the brink of heaven only to plunge her straight into hell? It would not be borne, and she drew back her hand and struck his handsome face with all the strength she could muster.

"Lord Drumcondra, you are no gentleman!" she seethed.

He threw back his head in a mighty guffaw. "I have never pretended to be," he said, soothing his cheek where a red welt was forming. "And the day will dawn that you will be exceedingly glad that I am not, because upon that day, fair lady, I will pleasure you beyond your wildest imaginings."

"I sincerely doubt that, sir," she said. Did her voice really crack? Lud!

Again he laughed that maddening laugh that did not reach his shuttered eyes. Thea raised her hand to strike again, but he caught it midswing in an iron fist, and strode to the Glastonbury chair with her in tow. Putting weight on the injured leg with a grunt and a grimace, he planted his other foot on the chair seat and threw her over his strong, sound knee.

"Here! Let me go! Let me *go*, I say!" Thea demanded, struggling. He paid her no mind, though she pounded him with flying fists, and kicked the air with her bare feet. For that was all she could reach in her precarious position as he hiked up the shift exposing her bare bottom.

"Mmmm," he murmured, running his massive hand over the curve of her naked buttocks.

Thea held her breath. The roughness of that hand against her tender flesh set fire to her blood. What was happening in the region of her most intimate self was scandalous as he stroked her. Shocking orgasmic contractions that left her weak and trembling riddled her breathless. The phenomenon was, however, short-lived. All at once, he awarded her bottom three sharp slaps, and set her on her feet again.

Tears glistening in her eyes, she faced him, rubbing her behind through the soft ecru silk. They were not tears of pain, but of anger. He hadn't hurt her, unless it be to wound her pride. He had embarrassed her, and she hated him for it—especially now in that he knew the effect he'd had upon her. How had it ever come to this?

"Disobedient children need a sound trouncing now and again," he panted, his voice gravelly. Whether that was due to the turgid arousal challenging the seam in his leggings or that he'd taxed the wound, Thea couldn't tell. Either way, his eyes, usually soulful and wolflike, were dilated and glazed, reminding her of the falcon's eyes, like two sparkling chips of onyx. "Do not think to presume to test my patience or my restraint again," he said. "You have nearly gotten more than you bargained for."

"I am no child, my lord," she fired back at him. "I did not ask to be brought here. I do not want to be here. I want to go home." She bit her lip as tears she could no longer hold back streamed down her hot cheeks. Where was her home, Cosgrove's castle . . . her father's Cornish country manor . . . the London townhouse? She couldn't go back to any of them now—not after Falcon's Lair. Not after Ros Drumcondra. Facing that was more than she could bear. Raw passion heretofore unknown to her, humiliation and anger roiled in her in fierce competition. Anger spoke. "If you mean to wreak your vengeance upon the Cosgroves at my expense, I beg you do so quickly," she said. "Take that dagger from your boot and plunge it into my heart, because that is the only way you'll have it. I would sooner be dead than let you rob me of my virtue, Lord Drumcondra!"

He stiffened as though she'd struck him. "Is the prospect of my embrace so distasteful, then?" he asked, all trace of his wry smile having dissolved.

"Distasteful?" she said. "It is frightening! Can you not tell? Can you not feel it when you touch me?"

"That is not what I feel when I touch you, my lady," he said with a guttural chuckle.

"You are mistaken."

"We shall see."

"We shall not!" she sallied. "You may maul and humiliate me, embarrass and abuse me at your pleasure, my lord, just as the cat toys with its mouse, but you will *never* have my willing love."

"So it is to be a test of wills between us, eh?" he mused. "That is a game you cannot win."

"Is your heart so hardened against your enemy that you would stoop to ruin an innocent to appease it? Does your Gypsy heritage not frown upon human sacrifice? Because that is what I am at your hands, is it not?"

He was silent apace. "Where had you really come from when my men . . . found you?" he finally said.

Should she say? Should she throw caution to the winds and tell him the truth? Would he even believe her? How could he, when she scarcely believed the truth herself.

"It is as I've said," she murmured, sinking down on the edge of the bed. The devil take it; her knees would no longer support her. "I was lost, and I became separated from my brother in the storm." James! What was happening to James? she suddenly wondered, as reason began to trickle back, jogging recent memory.

"Hmmm," he grunted.

"I want to see my brother!" she cried. "Please, I need to see him—to talk to him! I beg you, my lord!"

"Not until he has first talked to me," he replied. And spinning on his heels, he quit the chamber.

Thea threw herself across the bed and sobbed her heart dry. A woman's tears were frowned upon by society. No woman wanted to be branded a watering pot. But if there was ever an occasion for crying, this was it. And who was to know? Who was to see? For that matter, who was to care?

What would James ever say? Would he tell Drumcondra the truth, or concoct something else the warlord might believe? She didn't dare to speculate or she would go mad. If only he had let her speak with James first; but he had not, and she was on the verge of madness over that when the rasp of a key turning in the lock bolted her upright on the edge of the bed. Drumcondra had just left her. He couldn't be returning so quickly.

She held her breath as the door handle moved, and

gasped as the door came open—not in Drumcondra's hand, but in the wrinkled hand of the old Gypsy woman whose cryptic words had started her on this mad journey. At sight of the bird perched upon the woman's arm, Thea groaned and fell back down again, dissolving in fresh tears.

"Shhhh," the Gypsy said. The minute she released the bird, it flew to the candle stand and perched there, clucking, its head bobbing up and down in what Thea was convinced was a display of arrogance. She glared at it, and it responded with a significant cluck and flutter, extracting a toothless grin from the Gypsy. "Ye have naught to fear from Isor, miss," she said. "He is duty bound to protect ye."

"He has a fine way of showing it!" Thea sobbed. "That creature pecked at me—at my head, my hands." She pointed out her scratches. "It is a menace!"

"How else was he to get your attention?" asked the woman. "Ye are a willful child." She clicked her tongue. "Aye, willful, but a perfect mate for the master."

"Never!" Thea cried, her whole body delivering the word. "You came to me at the castle. How are you here? You cannot exist in two places—in two times. I saw you in the cave when I was shackled, helpless. You and that bird, the very same bird that attacked Nigel Cosgrove and followed my brother and I to the passage tomb, I have no doubt."

The Gypsy nodded. "The very same," she said. "He too travels the time corridor. He must. He is the Black Falcon's familiar."

"But . . . you were there when those men . . . when they nearly . . . nearly . . ."

Again the Gypsy nodded. "I was," she said, "and I knew Drumcondra would prevent his men from doing ye harm. I needed ye to see that . . . to know that he would protect ye. No matter what ye think ye see in him, he is an honorable man. He has what ye *Gadje* call a 'tendre' for ye, even if he may not know it yet." She winked. "I would never have let ye come to harm. Did I not bring ye here?"

"*Gadje?*" Thea repeated, puzzled.

" 'Tis Romany for all ye without the Gypsy blood."

"But why? I do not understand. Where did you come from that day on foot in that storm? The only place close by would have been Newgr—Si An Bhru. Do you live there, then?"

She nodded. "But that is not important now."

"It is to me," said Thea, "if I am to understand this. That cave those savages took me to . . ."

"It was no cave, miss. Ye never left Si An Bhru, they simply took ye back inside. Ye did not recognize the chamber—our hiding place—as it is now, in his time. It looks different in your time, after the renovation."

Thea gasped. "But why? Why did you lure me here? I do not understand."

"Ye do not have to understand, just accept your destiny," said the Gypsy, her raisinlike eyes flashing. Ye are Drumcondra's mate. I could not let ye wed the Cosgrove. He has not fallen far from the tree that grew his ancestor, Cian. His seed must not continue. It must die with him to break the feud and lift the curse. In a bloody onslaught, the Cosgrove slaughtered Drumcondra's heirs and took his land. There is a justice that goes beyond the physical world—Gypsy justice. Ye cannot oppose it, nor can ye ignore it standing here with me in his time. Ye are part of that justice. Do not tax your brain for understanding. Accept the offering. The alternative is too terrible to imagine."

"W-what . . . alternative?"

"What ye would face as wife of the Cosgrove. He has done murder. He killed a whore in London in cold blood, in a fit of jealous passion, and tried to blame it on another.

His father paid him free, as often is the case among your *ton*, and he will do murder again if ye return to what he calls Cashel Cosgrove in your time. He has already laid hands upon ye. The Cosgrove is an evil man, with much to answer for, but I would not worry over that. His hour will come. I have saved ye from a dreadful fate."

"For what?" Thea asked, on her feet now. "So that Ros Drumcondra can murder me instead? Forgive me if I am not grateful for the offering. He has put you up to this, I take it?"

The Gypsy shook her head. "He does not even know," she replied. "And ye must not tell him of my . . . interference. What is said here in this room between ye and me, must never be spoken."

Gooseflesh puckered Thea's scalp and drained the blood from her face. She did not need a mirror to tell her she had lost her color. Her skin had suddenly gone clammy and cold despite the warm glow radiating from the hearth and the heat of passion slow to subside. None of this was possible, and yet here she was, living proof of the Gypsy's words.

"I saw his ghost—I did!" Thea asked. "How can I have, when now I see him in the flesh?"

The woman's reply was as Thea had already surmised: "You see him in the flesh in *his* time. How else but as a ghost could you see him in your time? Do not trouble over that. These are things beyond human understanding."

"Why are you doing this to me?" Thea sobbed.

"I have seen Drumcondra's death," the Gypsy went on. "It is too terrible to contemplate—even for me—and I have seen many deaths, miss, in what your kind calls premonitions, and am . . . how do ye say . . . conditioned to the things I see. It is a Gypsy gift that sometimes, like now, seems more a curse than a blessing, because it hurts the heart. It is my mission to prevent what I have seen if I can—but I need your help to do it."

Thea sank back down on the edge of the bed, afraid to hear more though she knew she must.

"But why me?" she murmured.

"Because ye are the Cosgrove's betrothed," said the Gypsy. "Mine is a kinder justice all around than what Drumcondra is planning. It will lead him to his doom— and such a doom must not be. It is too monstrous."

"H-how do I know you tell the truth?" Thea snapped. "I have only your word."

"I will show ye—if ye dare."

"H-how . . . ?"

The Gypsy laid a finger alongside her nose and went to the door. She only stepped out briefly before returning with a bucket of water, which she placed upon the hearth-stone before the fire.

"You planned all this!" Thea cried. Why else had she come equipped with that bucket?

The woman flashed a toothless grin that, like Drumcon-dra's, did not reach her eyes. "Draw near and look," she replied, pointing toward the bucket.

Thea gestured. "What? In there?" she asked, padding to the hearth.

The Gypsy nodded. "Since time out of mind, Romany have seen the future in such a bucket—no need for crystal balls and other scrying fripperies, 'tis Nature tells the tale. Water, fire, wood, and stone. Look in it now, and ye see what brings ye here—what I have seen, and what will be unless ye have the courage to change it."

Thea hesitated. This was passing strange. The shadowy black water undulating in the bucket was tinted shades of red and gold in the fire glow. It seemed to beckon to her, and while she was drawn to the edge—even though she wasn't sure she credited the Gypsy's words—she feared to look.

"Looking cannot harm ye," the Gypsy assured her, "but not looking can harm him. Oh, aye. Come, then."

Thea drew nearer and stooped over the bucket. At first all she saw was the satiny breast of the water, and then . . . But no! It couldn't be, but it was. A scene took shape that held her relentlessly—a scene too terrible to be believed. She wanted to turn away, but she could not. It would not let her. Not until the fire and the blood—so much blood—subsided and became water again could she tear her eyes away.

Thea reeled back from the bucket. "No more," she sobbed. "Show me no more."

The Gypsy nodded. "Ye saw, then?"

"I saw. But I *couldn't* have seen, could I? I mean . . . tell me it shan't happen thus. Tell me it shan't!" She was sobbing openly, pacing in her bare feet, giving the bucket a wide berth and wary glances. Coming too close to the candle stand, the falcon clucked and raised one wing stirring the air. Thea cried out and backed away.

"It shan't if ye prevent it," promised the Gypsy.

"How can I possibly prevent it?" Thea asked.

"I cannot tell ye," the Gypsy said. "Ye must think. Ye already know, miss. 'Tis already written. All that's left is for ye to see it through, and ye will know how when the time comes. Aye, ye will, but time is short. When the falcon took the Cosgroves' eyes, it was begun—in this time and yours."

"How do you know this? What is it to you? Who *are* you?" Thea sobbed, her eyes brimming with tears.

The Gypsy smiled the smile that did not reach her eyes, and said, "I am Jeta, Drumcondra's mother."

Chapter Eleven

James stared at the iron-barred door, waiting for the shadows to give birth to the Gypsy who had laid hands upon his sister. It was outside of enough. What was Thea doing here in this wreck of a castle with this odd lot? How had she got here? How had *he* got here? One moment he was leading the weary Andalusian stallion through a gaping hole in the building, a close watch upon a falcon circling aloft; the next he was in a well-appointed great hall swarming with servants in a part of the structure that showed no sign of deterioration, and two lackeys had seized upon him. He wasn't foxed. Though he'd brought a flask of whiskey along to warm him on the journey, he hadn't touched a drop.

He was chained in the bowels of the castle by means of shackles that were fashionable over a hundred years ago. But for a healthy jostling, he hadn't been harmed, though one of the lackeys had taken possession of his beaver, and another had confiscated his multicaped greatcoat. Small loss. The garments were soaked through from the snow and wouldn't have protected him from the cold that prevailed in the dank castle's lower regions in any case. Mold and must frosted everything. The walls were bleeding with rising damp. He was leg-shackled to one of them by means of an iron ring set in the floor, waiting. It didn't take long. He heard Drumcondra's heavy boot heels echoing along the stone passageway long before he set eyes upon him. This was no ghost.

James got to his feet stiffly. Negotiating the moat in the snow had taken its toll on seldom used muscles. He would definitely need to take a few turns around the mattresses at Gentleman Jim's when he got back to London—*if* he got back to London. Where the devil was he?

"I mean to know how you got in here," Drumcondra said, facing him, hands on hips. "How did you gain entrance with the portcullis lowered? The water isn't frozen solid, only crusted over. You couldn't have walked across. It would never have supported your weight. Did you swim in this weather?"

"Of course not!" James said. "Where is my sister? What have you done with her?"

"She has come to no harm. Answer my question."

"The moat is dry, you fool!" James served. He was out of patience now. "I walked across—well, slid down the far bank and struggled up the near. It's not my fault that your gudgeons were asleep on their watch. I could have used an assist coming on in that storm."

"You trespass upon my land, sir," Drumcondra said. "What is your business here?"

"I've come looking for my sister, whom you have imprisoned so it seems. I demand you release her at once!"

"You demand, eh? I think not." He thumped his broad chest. "*I* demand. Now you tell me why you and your sister—two Englishers, mind—roam about County Meath in times when border wars are waging, and your countrymen invade our shores to plunder, eh?"

England invade Ireland? It was the first he'd heard of it. A hundred years ago or more, perhaps. Was the man addled? "I know of no invasion," he said. "My sister is betrothed to a . . . gentleman hereabouts, and we have come to his estate to celebrate Christmastide and make the wedding preparations."

"Mmm," Drumcondra grunted.

"What? You doubted her word, sir?" said James. He was incredulous. How dare this ignorant Irish muck-savage question the motives of his betters? Perhaps Nigel Cosgrove was right—at least in one regard: the Gypsies evidently were a blight upon the land.

"What were you doing at Si An Bhru?"

"I beg your pardon?"

"New . . . New . . . grange you call it in England."

"Y-yes," said James. The man really was a primitive if he still called Newgrange by the old name. "Thea wanted to see the passage tomb on the solstice."

Again Drumcondra grunted. "Did Cosgrove send you?" he asked.

"Well, yes, of course," James said. "Look here, what is all this about, sir?"

"She is his betrothed?"

"She is, but—"

Drumcondra raised his hand in a gesture meant to silence him. "Why did he not come himself?" he asked. "Is he . . . unwell, then, that he would send his betrothed's brother *here* unarmed on such an errand?"

"As a matter of fact, yes, he is," said James warily. The Gypsy seemed about to rejoice. "He is abed, sir, recovering. A falcon gouged his eye out."

Drumcondra froze in place for a long moment before he spun on his heel and stalked out of the chamber, locking the iron-barred door behind him.

"Wait!" James called. "Where do you think you're going? Let me out of here! Turn me loose, I say! Are you in league with that old Gypsy woman? Did the lot of you abduct my sister, and bring her here to this slag heap?"

But there was no answer, nothing but the sound of Drumcondra's heavy footfalls carrying him away.

"Please, my lord, I beg you let me see my brother," Thea sobbed. Drumcondra had returned to the chamber in a seething rage. Standing with his broad back toward her, he searched the flames in the hearth, the muscles ticking a steady rhythm along his angular jaw. "Why will you not let me go to him? What have you done with him?"

"He is safe enough . . . for now."

"What do you mean, 'for now'?" she asked. "Answer me, my lord!"

"Demands, demands—always demands," he growled. He pounded his breast with his fist. "*I* demand," he said. "I told him the same. One more day and then we shall see."

"What do you mean?"

"You heard me deliver the terms," he said, spinning to face her. "One day is gone. Cosgrove only has one more to vacate my land, bag and baggage, or—"

"Yes?" she snapped, "or what, my lord—you will give me to him ravaged?"

He glared at her. "The Cosgrove sent him!" he thundered. "I had it from his own mouth, your precious brother. The bastard is still mending from Isor's handiwork, so he sent your brother. Is he simpleminded, then, that he would march single-handed upon my keep to collect you?"

"Y-you had what from him? What did he tell you, my lord?"

"A-ha!" he blurted, his eyes flashing. "So there is something between you and the Cosgrove! You are saving yourself for him!"

"I . . . I told you we have never even met," she sobbed. "I never set eyes upon C-Cian Cosgrove until you took me to that keep!"

"You lie!" he thundered. "You were staying at the castle. Your brother took you to Si An Bhru to see the sun rise on the solstice."

Thea swallowed hard. Of course Drumcondra thought James was speaking of Cian Cosgrove. Why wouldn't he? He didn't even know Nigel Cosgrove existed. She had to get to James and try to explain before he made another blunder. Meanwhile, what could she say that this hulking Gypsy warrior would believe, and that would calm him?

"You must have misunderstood," she snapped, aiming for indignation when all the while she was trembling inside. "I said that we were on our way to Cosgrove's castle—"

"My castle," he flashed, thumping his breast again.

"Y-your castle, yes," she recovered. "We were on our way there when I begged him to pass by the tomb. We became separated, and your minions laid hold of me. He . . . he must have gone on to the castle when he couldn't find me. Look here, what does it matter? He is my brother. He has come looking for me. He has no quarrel with you."

"Indeed not, fair lady," said Drumcondra. "I have one with him. He stays below until the sun sets tomorrow. What happens then depends upon the Cosgrove."

"Now it is I who do not believe you," she said haughtily, tossing her dark curls. "He is dead or maimed or otherwise harmed. That is why you will not let me see him!"

"I told you, he has not been harmed."

"Prove it," she sallied. "Take me to him. Let me have one moment alone with him, and then you may do . . . as you will with me." She uttered the last with downcast eyes, remembering the bucket and what she had seen in the bloodied water. She couldn't think about that now. Not now. "Please, my lord."

With no more said, he seized her arm, led her into the corridor, and down the roughly hewn staircases to the lower regions.

Drumcondra was limping by the time they reached a row of recessed chambers. It was plain that his wound was grieving him far more than he was willing to admit. They stopped before one of the cells, and he had just picked out a large key dangling from a chatelaine he wore around his waist when Jeta stepped from the shadows with a smile and sly wink toward Thea, and laid hold of Drumcondra's arm. Annoyed, he bent while she whispered something to him in a foreign tongue. Nodding, he shoved Thea inside the cell and locked the door behind her.

"Here! What are you doing?" Thea called as Drumcondra strode off with the Gypsy. "You are just going to leave me here?"

"You wanted to see your brother," the warrior's voice echoed back along the corridor, "so, see him. I will return."

Inside the cell James staggered to his feet, and Thea rushed to embrace him. "You are hurt!" she cried. "I knew it!"

"No, no—just stiff as a coat rack," her brother assured her. "I had the devil's own time negotiating the trench that evidently used to be a moat around this deuced place. I entered through the ruined wing, and went in search of a suitable chamber in the sound part of this keep to wait out the storm, when the lackeys seized me. Never mind that, what are you doing here? How did you get here? You called the hulking brute that locked me in here Lord Drumcondra. This dilapidated relic is evidently his keep. Is he one of Ros Drumcondra's descendants? What the deuce is going on, Thea?"

She burst into tears. "Oh, my dear God," she sobbed, "I don't know how I shall ever tell you."

"I think you had best try," her brother said testily, rattling his shackles.

"Be careful what you say to Drumcondra," she began. "You've said too much already."

"Too much? Stuff! The blighter scarcely gave me a chance to say anything at all. He *is* one of Ros Drumcondra's descendants, then? Come, come, Thea—it is I, James, your brother. You have never, ever found it difficult to speak to me in any regard. What is all this?"

Thea drew a ragged breath and wiped her tears away. "Very well," she said. "You shan't believe one word of it, I'm sure, but I think that I can prove it if you will just be patient with me."

"Yes . . . ?"

"He is not descended from Ros Drumcondra, James. He *is* Ros Drumcondra."

"*What?* Have you attics to let? That is impossible, Thea. The man lived nearly a hundred and twenty years ago. I'll believe that you saw his *ghost* that night back at the castle before I'll believe this."

"There isn't much time," Thea said. "I need to say this before he returns, James. Please, hear me out, and if you still do not believe me after it's told, I beg you say nothing to Drumcondra."

"I am waiting," snapped James, clearly out of patience.

"I do not know how you got here, but I think I know how I did," she began. "If only you had gone into the tomb with me, I wouldn't have to explain anything. When the light failed, I stepped back out and you were gone—everything was changed. There was no entrance behind me, only a mound of snow. There weren't even any footprints, mine or yours, and no tracks from the sleigh runners in the snow. At first I thought that I had exited through another opening, but I had not. Then two men grabbed me. I was struck on the head, and awoke sometime later chained much as you are here now in what I thought to be a cave. Drumcondra saved me from . . . I daren't speculate upon what those Gypsy bandits might have done to me."

"You were compromised?" James breathed.

"Compromised?" she blurted. "Good God, James, that does not even signify here!"

"Go on," he gritted through clenched teeth.

"Newgrange is a passage tomb, is it not—a corridor between the living and the dead? At least that is what it is supposed to be—what the ancients believed it to be. When I first set eyes upon Ros Drumcondra, I thought that the legend was true, that he had come on the solstice to reclaim his castle and his land. Instead—and this is the truly impossible bit—I had somehow traveled back to his time through the corridor. He is no ghost, James. It is Drumcondra in the flesh, and you have now joined us—in the Year of Our Lord 1695."

"That is preposterous!"

"I agree, but it is true, James. If you had a view of the grounds, I could prove it to you. You say there was a trench where the moat once was. There is no trench there now. The moat is filled with water, and there is no ruined wing. The castle is intact."

"But that is impossible! I nearly broke my back navigating the drifts in that trench. At one point, Nigel's Andalusian was buried to the withers. I led that horse right through what once was a solid wall of stone and timbers."

"Do not mention Nigel," Thea said. "These know nothing of Nigel Cosgrove. It is Cian Cosgrove who lives now, and who, through some bizarre happenstance has just had his own eye gouged out by a falcon as well—the same falcon, James. Jeta, the old Gypsy who came to Cashel Cosgrove said it is so, and God help me, I believe her. That bird is almost human. There *are* time channels here, despite what Nigel said. This place and the passage tomb must somehow be connected. I cannot think how you have come here else such is true."

"At university, we touched upon such phenomenon as what the professors called *lay lines*, and John Nash has mentioned such in his architectural essays and lectures. He said that much land here and at home is rejected as building sites because of the locals' superstitious fear of them. But I have never credited occult or supernatural phenomenon, or such speculative doctrines that cannot be proven. But you do, don't you? You actually believe you've traveled back in time to 1695. They must have really beaned you right and proper. I believe the blow to the head has quite scrambled your brains."

"There's more," said Thea, "but no time to tell it. That is Drumcondra's voice I hear. He will be upon us any second! Say no more, and do not divulge what I have just told you. He has no idea that I am from another time. If it must be told, I must be the one to tell it. Do not fear, James, I will get you out of here. It matters not whether you believe me or you don't, so long as you keep my confidence. My life—both our lives—may well depend upon it."

"Thea—"

"No! There isn't time. One last thing. The ruined wing you say you entered through . . . how was it ruined?"

"It's hard to say. I have studied such sites in my travels, as you know, with much interest. It is my passion, and it appears to me that at some point what bits would burn were destroyed by fire. The rest has deteriorated over time. But that is only my opinion. Why?"

Thea swallowed the lump that had constricted her throat, and blinked back tears. "He's here!" she said in a low whisper. Drumcondra's return had saved her from answering that question. "Remember what I've said," she murmured. "Say nothing."

Chapter Twelve

Drumcondra wore a face as long as the day returning her to his chamber. Jeta was nowhere in sight. Thea wasn't certain if that was a good sign or bad. She wasn't certain of Drumcondra's mood, either, only that it wouldn't bear testing. He had a face like a thunderhead. His eyes were cold and shuttered, his sensuous mouth drawn in a tight lipless line, his jaw muscles ticking and his nostrils flared so wide that he resembled a fire-breathing dragon. Making matters worse, his leg was paining him. She could see it in his ragged gait, though he careened through the halls with all the finesse of a juggernaut.

When he threw open his chamber door, he pulled her up short of the threshold. The Gypsy girl, who had stolen Thea's chinchilla fur pelerine when she first came among them, had donned it again, with nothing underneath, and now lay writhing in Drumcondra's bed, flaunting her voluptuous nakedness beneath the fur.

Drumcondra reeled Thea into the room, slammed the

door, and reached the girl in three staggering strides. "So, this is where you've got to. I should have known, and searched here first," he seethed. "Get up out of there, Drina!" Without ceremony, he hauled her to her feet, delivering a string of reproofs in either Gaelic or Romany—Thea couldn't be sure which, since she spoke neither dialect.

He stripped the pelerine from the girl in one motion, just as he had the first time, and tossed it on the bed. Then, snatching her clothing from the floor where she'd discarded it, he steered her to the door. As she passed, the girl spit full in Thea's face, wrenching a shocked outcry from her. She wiped the spittle away. Drumcondra thundered something unequivocal in that same foreign tongue, crimped the girl's hands around her clothing, and shoved her through the door naked, locking it after her.

Spinning back toward Thea, Drumcondra glowered. "What?" he said.

"That is exactly what I was about to ask you, my lord," she returned loftily.

"Oh, I see," he said, standing with his hands on his hips. "Well, I am neither priest, nor monk, nor eunuch, fair lady—a thing I mean to prove to you before this night is done."

"I think you ought take yourself off and prove it to the creature you have just evicted. With such as that to warm your bed, you can have no need of me."

He reached her in one stride and seized her in strong arms, pulling her against his hard muscled chest. "I have a need that only you can quench," he said, bearing down upon her with his powerful gaze. "You have bewitched me, I think, with those eyes the color of Londonderry bluebells, and hair like raven's feathers. There's Gypsy somewhere in your blood; I'll not be persuaded otherwise." He inhaled deeply, and let his breath out on a soft moan. "You smell of gillyflower and of rose. You have not gotten such a perfume here. Can it be your very essence, I wonder? Neither flower blooms in the snow. . . ."

"P-please, my lord, I beg you, let me go," Thea pleaded. His closeness was like a drug to which she had become addicted, his hands like firebrands searing her through the flimsy ecru silk. Across the way his bird was perched, sleeping, though its beady eye was open, watching them. Did it always sleep thus, with one eye open? She wondered.

Food brought up in her absence stood undisturbed on the linens chest. Food always seemed to be in good supply. She couldn't help but wonder if the same was so in the lower regions, where poor dear James was chained, shivering with cold and confusion.

Drumcondra tilted her chin up to meet his gaze and lowered his lips, but she turned her head aside. "Please, my lord," she said.

He took hold of her chin again. "You say no, but I feel yes in that perfect body. It betrays you," he murmured. His deep baritone thrummed through her—through the veins that carried hot blood to her cheeks and temples. Her heart was beating against his—shuddering, thumping. Could he feel it? How could he not? Anger at her weakness flared.

"I find it quite impossible—nay, repulsive—suffering the advances of a man who intends to use me as a means to slake his lust for vengeance, sir," she snapped.

He stiffened as if she had struck him, but did not let her go. Scooping her up in his arms, he laid her on the bed and climbed in gingerly beside her.

Thea twisted away. "Neither do I favor bed sport where another has been cavorting. So this is why you left me alone with James, then—so you could have your little assignation with that Gypsy roundheels. You are caught out, my Lord Drumcondra. Now, let me go!"

He seized her arm and turned her back. "You heard me say otherwise."

"I heard a foreign tongue. Did no one ever tell you speaking so when others are unfamiliar with your speech is ignorant and impolite, sir?"

Though there was a hint of jealousy, too, Thea was stalling for time. There was only one way to prevent the horror she had seen in Jeta's bucket, but she did not know how to accomplish it. As long as Drumcondra remained in his time, his fate was sealed and imminent. And being there with him, she was not exempt from the devastation. Neither was James. Not one, but three lives now hung in the balance.

The only way to prevent it was to lure him into her time. Jeta had said it was already written. Thea did not understand the augur then, but she did now. Hadn't Nigel himself told her that Drumcondra's bones were not found in the passage tomb with the others? Had he not said that all trace of him had vanished from the pages of local history and lore nearly a hundred and thirty years ago—that he had simply disappeared? But how could she accomplish that? Jeta obviously trusted that she could, but Thea couldn't see how. If she told him the truth, he would never believe her, just as James hadn't believed her. She would have to trick him into following her back somehow. But if she knew how to get back, she would have done so on her own long since. And then there was James. It all seemed so hopeless and, though she knew the answer, there seemed no solution else she use her womanly wiles to have it done.

Out of that facetious thought, inspiration struck. Since time out of mind, women had used their sexuality to charm the unsuspecting male. She was a woman after all, despite her sheltered life and inexperience that left her so vulnerable to his prowess. If he were to break down her defenses here in his time, comfortable and complacent, he would never leave it; but if she could somehow lure him into her time . . .

Drumcondra's hands were roaming over her body through the silk shift, his skilled fingers doing scandalous things to her breasts. He bared them to his lips, and she moaned in spite of herself. She fought desperately to keep control, but her pulse was pounding in her ears and her heart was fairly leaping against her ribs. While innocence by no means meant ignorance of such matters, she was unprepared for feelings so intense they took her breath away, for the firestorms at her very core that riddled her belly and thighs mercilessly. It was a volatile awakening, made more so by the dire circumstances facing her and so little time to do what seemed impossible. It would be so easy to let him have his way with her, to welcome inside her the turgid member leaning heavily against her thigh, as he'd promised she would. The shocking thing was, this was so totally against her nature. She could only surmise that it was because of the unreal, dreamlike quality of her situation, and her girlish air dreams—but that did not make it any easier to bear. Existing in another time, it was as if these things were happening to someone else, which was making it harder and harder to resist him. That she wanted him was without question. He had seduced her to the brink of yielding to a single kiss, something she never would have credited as being possible in her own time.

Her aching nipples, at the mercy of his lips, hardened under demands of his silken tongue, betrayed her. Her moist sex swollen—aching for release—would not be ignored where the heel of his open palm massaged it through the gauzy silk. As if possessed of a will of its own, her body arched against the pressure of that hand as lightning strikes of liquid fire coursed through her, catching her breath, dulling her senses, lifting her out of herself into the swirling white pinpoints of blinding light that starred her vision.

Technically, he had already taken her virtue. All that remained was for her to give it to him in the physical sense. She was his captive. He could take her anytime he pleased. That he had not, spoke to the success of her desperate prayers that he would not unless she gave him leave. That was part of the seduction: The conquest must be total. She had to open herself to him of her own free will . . . to beg him to fill her with his life, to possess the sweet flesh of her innocence in total abandon. She was on the brink of that under his artful enchantment, despite the fact that she knew all too well she must not give in to the demands of his sex or of her innermost desires. To surrender now would break the spell that daren't be broken until they, all three—he and she and James—had passed through the corridor together.

When he reached beneath her shift and his hot, rough-textured hand began to palpate her naked sex, she pulled back, resisting. "I beg you, *don't*," she murmured, shoving the hand away.

He loosed a guttural chuckle, rubbing his fingers together. "I do not see the difficulty," he said. "By the look of this, you are deflowered already. All that remains is that you let me know you in the Biblical sense." He whispered the last directly in her ear, which he nipped in the process, beginning the damming sensations again. It would not do, and she vaulted upright in the bed and covered her breasts.

"You would like that, I am sure," she said, "but it shan't

happen here in this bed after what just got out of it. You've turned your bedchamber into a brothel, and I am no whore. If you are hell-bent upon seducing me, you shall have to find a more romantic setting in which to do it. As it is here now, I would rather take my chances with the rats."

It sounded credible enough, though she dared not offer a sideways glance in the direction of those eyes to be sure; she was that unsure of her footing and her resolve. Throwing her feet over the edge of the bed, she went on quickly, while she still possessed the courage. "Besides, you shan't claim my favors while my brother lies chained and hungry in your dungeon. That would be foolish of me, don't you think? I am no birdwit, sir."

He seized her arm. "It is inevitable, you know."

"That may well be," she returned, prying his fingers from her arm, examining the white fingerprints his grip had left behind, "but if it is, it will be in *my* time—not yours, my Lord Drumcondra," she said. Gooseflesh washed her from head to toe at the prophetic nature of her words. They all but stopped her heart. It hadn't been deliberate, but couldn't have been more aptly put. What was that look in his eyes? Did he see the hidden meaning in those words as well, or was it her stricken expression at giving the bizarre situation substance with words that seemed to have stricken him also? "Besides," she said, on her feet now, "that leg is paining you. Any fool could see it. You are in no fit condition to seduce anyone."

Drumcondra vaulted out of the bed in a vain attempt to hide the truth of her accusation. His unsteady exit brought the ghost of a smile to her lips.

"You think so, do you?" he seethed. "How wrong you are, little hypocrite. It would have been wiser of you to give way to your desires. But no matter, you need not have rats for bedfellows. I shall spend the night in more . . . welcoming apartments. Sleep well, fair lady."

Drumcondra lumbered down the hall in such a fit of foul temper he nearly ran headlong into Jeta ascending the stairs from the level below.

"Clumsy lout! What ails ye now?" she said, steadying herself against the wall.

"Where is Drina staying?" he asked, ignoring the question.

Jeta shrugged, and crooked her thumb toward the opposite wing. "Where she always stays when you two have been at it," she said. "What do ye want her for? She says ye put her out."

"I have an itch that needs scratching," Ros growled, turning down the corridor, dosing his mother with an ireful glance. Though he loved Jeta dearly, he made no display of it either in company or when they were alone. It wasn't the Gypsy way, such weakness. What existed between him and his mother was an understanding in the heart that need not be spoken with the lips.

Jeta presented him with a toothless smile in return. "Ye might just have to scratch it yourself, after what I heard comin' out of her mouth just now."

Drumcondra paid her no mind. Limping along the hall, he cursed Thea for being right about his leg. He had stressed it, and the bandage needed changing. Mossie would do it, but that would have to wait. Right now, there was a more urgent press, and smoothing ruffled feathers was not his strong suit.

He burst into Drina's chamber only to duck low as a crockery jar whizzed past his head, missing it by inches. It smashed against the wall, splattering his jerkin with some anonymous women's unction that reeked of strong perfume. Another followed that he wasn't quick enough to avoid. It hit him squarely in the chest and turned him white with talc.

"Do ye want more?" Drina said, hefting a larger missile, a coffer of hammered silver. "Ye need to find another nest to roost in tonight Lord Drumcondra. What? She wouldn't have ye—your high and mighty, milk-and-water miss? Your fine lady? I could have told ye that." She lobbed the coffer at him with a satisfied nod.

If he'd had thoughts of slaking his lust in Drina, they were no more. Her assault had eliminated the need. Dusted white and splattered with malodorous cream aside, the last missile had grazed his wound. That alone would be enough to kill his ardor, which quickly turned to rage.

"Who gave you leave to make yourself at home in my bedchamber?" he asked.

"When have I ever needed leave, m'lord?"

"Why have you come here?"

"Why?" she cried. "To see if ye had met your doom at the hands of Cian Cosgrove. Ye disappeared without a word to any of us. If it wasn't for Jeta's reports that ye'd come here with your lady wounded, we would have thought for sure the Cosgrove had killed ye!"

"So it was my mother who called you here. She will regret that."

"Ye bloody ingrate! I hope the leg rots and drops offa ye."

"Oh, aye, you showed me that just now. If you've opened the wound, you'll wish you'd stayed at Si An Bhru!"

Drina burst into laughter, watching him slap the talc off his jerkin. There was nothing to be done about the cream. Damned vixen! It would leave stains on the newly tanned leather, notwithstanding that he would be smelled before he turned the corners in the castle now. The jerkin was ruined, and it was his best.

"There is a way to put it all to rights," Drina said, sauntering toward him. He'd seen that sultry walk before. There was a time when that undulating saunter would have ended with their naked bodies entwined beneath the sheets. It wouldn't serve now. "I want that fur wrap," she told him. "Give it me, and I might just be persuaded to forgive ye."

"She was right, by God!" he said. "I did turn my chamber into a brothel."

But he said no more. Drina's shriek and another flying object—a heavy silver candlebranch—hit the door squarely where his body had been, as he backed away just in time.

"Ye will pay for that, Lord Drumcondra!" Drina's muffled voice said from behind the closed door, as yet another missile hit it. "Ye and your fine lady. Enjoy her while ye can. Ye haven't heard the last of Drina!"

Thea vaulted upright in bed when the key turned in the lock, and leapt from it when the door began to open, anticipating Drumcondra's towering form to cross the threshold. When Jeta entered instead, she sank back down, in a state of near collapse.

"Time is short," the woman said. "Have ye decided?"

"Have I a choice?" Thea asked.

"We all have choices, my lady. Ye have denied him?"

Thea nodded. "I've sent him straight into that woman's arms."

Jeta laughed. "Ye needn't worry over that," she said. "He'll get no comfort there tonight." Relieved, though she would rather bite her tongue than betray herself, Thea turned away to hide what she knew had to be in her face. "I did not bring her here for that," Jeta went on.

Thea spun back to face her. "*You?*" she breathed. "You brought her here? But why?"

"To help ye—aye, and him," the Gypsy replied. "It must play out, the destiny, the way it is designed." She gave a sly wink. "If she had not come, where would ye be right now, eh? In that bed, is where, and him content in ye—too content with his conquest done to be away before 'tis too late, because she would have come in any case and found ye thus. 'Tis all onesided between those two; he doesn't love her, and she knows it. He was honest with her from the start, but she just won't give it over. The coin will flip now. Aye, ye will see that too, is as needs must."

Thea ignored the old Gypsy's augre. "Where is he, then? Suppose he should come back and find us here together plotting . . . whatever we're plotting?"

"No danger of that. Old Mossie's tendin' what damage was done to his leg. He won't come back here after. His pride won't let him. He'll walk off his passion up on the battlements, the cold north wind his only mistress tonight. We're safe enough."

Thea gasped. "Drina opened his wound?" she cried, having heard little past that.

The Gypsy shrugged. "Whatever she's done, he won't die from it. We've both seen how that will be if ye fail. Midnight tomorrow ends Drumcondra's pact with the Cosgrove. It must be then, before the retaliation begins."

"I do not think that he will harm me, Jeta," Thea said. "Not . . . anymore."

"'Tis not that I fear, miss," she returned, "but no matter. If ye do it right, ye never need know."

Something cryptic in the last raised Thea's hackles, but

she wasn't ready to probe. There was nothing for it but to trust the woman, as bizarre as that prospect was.

"That's just the trouble," she said. "I do not even know how I came to be here, much less how to return to my own time and take two others with me. I wouldn't know where to begin."

"That is why I have arranged this little visit. To tell ye how."

"*You* arranged?" Thea raised her hands in protest. She didn't want to hear more. "We are not at Si An Bhru," she went on. That is where I was when I came among you. How can I return from here?"

"Easily," Jeta said succinctly. "Did your brother not come among us here at Falcon's Lair? Did he not see the falcon just beforehand?"

Thea stared, slack-jawed.

The Gypsy gave a smug nod. "The corridors are linked, miss, and the falcon knows the way. Did he not gouge the eye out of another Cosgrove's socket in your time? Hmmm? Now ye see, eh?"

"And Drumcondra does not know the way?"

"No one knows but me and, of course, the bird."

"You are forgetting that *I* do not know the way," said Thea. "And Drumcondra will never go willingly—not while his blood roils for vengeance here."

"I know it. Ye will have to trick him."

"He will kill me for that!"

"Shhh! He may not be abroad tonight, but others are. Be still! There is no other way. Tomorrow night at the stroke of midnight, I will occupy my son in sight of the stables. A horse will be waiting. Turn the falcon loose—"

"Oh, no! I won't go near that bird!" Thea interrupted.

"Ye *will*! Isor knows his place. He has always been your

champion, if you would only see it. Ye will set the bird free get on that horse, and follow him. Drumcondra will come after you, and the bird will lead you through the corridor."

"And my brother?" asked Thea. "What of him?"

"I will see to your brother, miss. You leave that chore to me."

"What if Drumcondra comes back here to this chamber? What if he . . . if he . . . ?"

"Do not borrow trouble; it has lent you enough already. There is only one thing you need to fix in your mind. No matter what occurs, you must follow that bird!"

Chapter Thirteen

The following day dawned cold and gray with the promise of more snow. Drumcondra kept his distance through the morning. Trusting that Jeta would free her from the chamber in time to do what had to be done, Thea passed the time trying to decide what she would ever tell him if they did manage to cross over.

Despite her efforts to keep it at bay, the hellish vision she'd seen in Jeta's bucket came to the fore and would not leave. She couldn't be certain, but the bloodcurdling scene seemed to play out in that very chamber—a fire, a holocaust where Drumcondra had been burned alive. He wasn't alone. There was a woman with him . . . a woman who looked suspiciously like herself. Not even the bird had escaped the carnage. Thea had seen it, feathers aflame, soaring aloft through the window to its ultimate death. She shuddered, reliving the experience that she had thus far managed to block from her memory, all but bits and pieces. The agony of the warrior, trapped, aware as the flames consumed him, his companion, too, was more than she could bear. Then the scene shifted, and there was blood . . . so much blood. The slaughter would drive the Gypsy band back to Si An Bhru and their walled-up fate inside the passage tomb where their bones would ultimately be found. And though she did not see it, she knew that Cian Cosgrove was behind it.

Was this the retaliation Jeta had spoken of? Or could it have been Drina's jealous vengeance that fueled this fire wiping out Drumcondra and his clan? There was no way to tell. There was nothing she could do about the latter part of the vision—neither she nor Drumcondra were involved in it—but the rest . . .

It wasn't until midafternoon that Drumcondra's hand unlatched the door and he strode inside bearing a tray heaped with food. Seated in the Glastonbury chair as far from the bed as Thea could range herself, she watched him set his burden down upon the linens chest. The Friday-faced demeanor hadn't left him. He looked just as surly as he had last night. He made no move to attempt seduction. Instead, he went to the candle stand and to her horror collected the falcon.

"What do you do?" she asked him, hoping her tone was not as desperate as it sounded echoing back in her ears.

"There is another storm on the way," he said. "Isor needs to hunt and feed before it comes. He cannot exist on a steady diet of eyeball and rat."

"There's food aplenty on that tray," she said. "Why not leave him? He hardly looks deprived."

"It is not what he is accustomed to," Drumcondra returned. "He needs to hunt for his food. Making a house pet of him will only make him weak, and of no use to me." He stopped abreast of her. "Is this a newfound affinity you have for Isor? I though you hated the bird."

Thea gave a casual shrug. Meanwhile, her heart was hammering in her breast. "I have grown accustomed to his company," she said. "Captivity can be a lonely state, my lord."

"And whose fault is that, my lady?"

"Yours!" she couldn't help herself from snapping.

He offered a crisp nod and sketched a bow, and the clucking bird bobbed its head for all the world as if it understood and mimicked the gesture. Thea snorted. Maybe the creature could be trusted, at that.

"Y-you will bring him back after?" she called out as he reached the threshold.

Drumcondra didn't answer. He dosed her with a long hard stare, then shut the door and locked it behind him.

When he did not return in a timely fashion, Thea was beside herself. She couldn't see through the window for the plank in the way, but it had to be late—at least dusk. What if he didn't come? What if no one came? What if the midnight hour passed—would it be too late? She was nearly out of her mind with worry. Her food lay untouched on the linens chest. She could not bring herself to swallow it, though her belly growled for want of something solid inside. She hadn't eaten but sporadically since she left Newgrange.

Why didn't he return? Was this some sort of punishment for her rejection? Thea was half mad by the time a key turned in the lock and the door creaked open. But it wasn't Drumcondra's hand on the latch; it was his mother's.

Thea's hand flew to her lips at sight of the woman's borne-down expression; everything about her screamed catastrophe. Rooted to the spot, it was a moment before Thea could speak. When she was finally able, the words were halting and strained.

"Something is . . . wrong," she murmured through her fingers.

"It is nearly time," the Gypsy said, handing over the ankle boots Thea had never expected to see again.

"Where is Drumcondra?" Thea murmured, tugging on the footwear.

"Gone," said the Gypsy.

"Gone where?"

"To the Cosgrove's castle." She gave a dry grunt. "How he would rail at me if he heard me call it that," she said. "I could not prevent him going. He has gone to see if the Cosgrove has met his demands."

"And the bird?"

"The bird is with him, miss. They are as one entity—inseparable. He would not venture forth into battle without Isor now."

"*Battle?*" Thea cried. "He has not gone alone? He is injured, he—"

The Gypsy raised her hand. "He has taken several of his trusted warriors. There is nothing to be done. Ye must go, miss. Your brother awaits ye in the stables. Ye cannot remain here any longer else ye share in the carnage to come."

"Go?" The prospect of leaving without Drumcondra was unthinkable—unbearable. The thought of it set off earthquakes in her heart that reverberated in her very soul. It was then that she knew for certain that somehow their souls were linked, as though an invisible cord were stretched between them that spanned the corridors of time. She could not—would not—sever that tether. "How can I go without him?" she sobbed.

"You must," the Gypsy said. "And before it is begun, while I still possess the power to help ye."

"But how can I go without the bird?"

"You forget that I, too, travel the corridor, my lady. How

else did I come to you in the beginning? Come, your brother awaits. In an hour's time, these snow-covered hills will run red with blood, and bodies of the dead will litter that cold white ground. Yours must not number among them. There is nothing more that you can do for him, my lady. I have failed. It is finished."

Thea took one last look about the chamber that had been her prison, at the bed where she had so desired to give Drumcondra her virtue, and at the vacant candle stand where the bird had perched content to bask in the warmth of the chimney corner, its hooded eyes ever alert for rats. Without a word, she took up her fur pelerine draped over the Glastonbury chair, looped it over her arm, and followed the woman into the corridor.

They hadn't taken three steps when Drina sprang from the shadows and seized the pelerine. Unprepared, Thea nearly lost her grip upon it, and a tug of war resulted for possession of the wrap. Despite Jeta's flying fists attacking the Gypsy wench about the head and shoulders, the crafty girl swooped down, bit Thea on the wrist, and won the fur. Then, waving it like a banner, she danced off and disappeared into the shadowy recesses of the opposite wing, her laughter living after her.

"Never mind," said Jeta, seizing Thea's arm in her bony fingers. "There is no more time, I will fetch ye a mantle. It will not be so fine as your fur, but it will suffice. Come."

Wrapped in a hooded cloak of indigo homespun, Thea met her brother at the stables. The midnight sky, heavy with snow that had just begun to sift down, was a ghostly shade of gray-blue with an eerie tint of pink bleeding through from the full blood moon hidden behind the clouds.

James was mounted on his Andalusian, waiting, just as

Jeta said he would be. The Gypsy seemed to walk with a slower gait, each step a weary effort. Thea watched in dismay that mother's grief for a son she knew would die in the battle to come. That she was powerless to prevent the onslaught was all too visible in the old woman's eyes.

But Thea wasn't ready to admit defeat. One look at the skeptical expression on her brother's face set her in motion, and she mounted the side-saddled Gypsy horse he was holding for her.

"What is this all about, Thea?" he barked. "Where are we going? There's a fresh storm brewing."

"'We' aren't going anywhere, James," she replied, taking the ribbons from him. "You are going home." Then, to the Gypsy as she dug her heel into the horse's side: "Which way to Si An Bhru?"

Hope glistening through the tears in the old Gypsy's eyes, she pointed westward. "Bless ye, miss," she cried. "Follow the river just so, but do not enter the forest. When the time comes, trust the bird to lead ye!"

"Will one of you please tell me what is going on here?" James barked, as the woman seized his horse's bridle.

"Send my brother home, Jeta!" Thea cried. "Send him *now!*" And ignoring James's shouts, she leaned low over the neck of her mount and drove him at a gallop over the lowered drawbridge, straight for Newgrange and Cosgrove's castle beyond, her cape spread wide on the wind.

Scarcely thinking beyond that she could not leave Drumcondra behind, Thea drove the dappled horse over the invisible snow-covered lanes, its feathered feet and forelegs flying, gouging clumps of snow from the crusted ground. Occasional snowflakes drifting down were evidence that heavier snow would soon be falling. It was bitter cold. Her chinchilla fur pelerine would have spared her much of the wind's bite, but Thea scarcely thought about that. Trusting that Jeta would see James safely back to their own time, she concentrated upon only one thing—finding Drumcondra before what he was planning brought him back to Falcon's Lair and the gruesome fate she'd seen in the old woman's bucket.

Thea's fingers were numb gripping the reins. Her cheeks were like ice. The wind whipped tears into her eyes, which she narrowed as the water froze on her cheeks and lashes. It seemed an eternity before she saw movement again. She had nearly come upon Newgrange, and she saw the falcon soaring through the gently falling snow before she saw the riders. At least a dozen mounted horsemen were coming on at breakneck speed. But they weren't headed for Cosgrove's castle; they were riding straight for Falcon's Lair, raising clouds of diaphanous snow as they came.

Thea reined the horse in on the crest of a hillock. She had a panoramic view of the land all around. The reason for their haste soon became clear: A veritable army was in pursuit of the ragtag band of gypsy renegades. Drumcondra was in the lead astride the great white stallion, his falcon circling overhead. The sight of the hulking giant of a man astride that feather-footed horse took her breath away. She had ridden on the animal with him, but she had never seen him from this vantage. Was he aware of the horde that followed? He must be. He couldn't win, not against that army—so few against so many gaining on him. He was evidently trying to reach Falcon's Lair to mobilize the rest of his own men, who were lazing unaware. Her heart sank. He would never break ranks and follow her instead, not in such a situation. Nonetheless, she slapped her horse about the neck and withers with the reins, and plunged down the hill into the valley below.

A close eye upon the bird, Thea drove her mount straight for Drumcondra. It was a foolhardy tactic with such an army in pursuit, but that army meant their death if she were to believe the old gypsy—and her own eyes. She'd scarcely reached the valley when a hitch in the warlord's stride showed recognition. He had seen her; so had the bird. It soared off farther north, though still toward Falcon's Lair. It was almost as if it traveled in a direct line from Newgrange to the castle.

Thea gasped and started to follow. Would Drumcondra come after her? She held back to be sure. If she were to pursue the bird's path without him and they became separated, how would she ever find her way back to him, or he to her? Timing meant everything. Somehow, the bird seemed aware. The tinkling of his tether bells was reassuring as he circled aloft, seeming to wait for her to catch up.

Thea glanced behind her again. Yes! Drumcondra was following. She picked up her pace, as the bird did also.

It was reckless, riding sidesaddle at breakneck speed over such uneven ground; there were pitfalls hidden beneath the snow and it wasn't long before a rut disguised by a snowdrift tripped up her horse. The beast shrieked as its forelegs floundered, and it went down, pitching her over the pommel into the drifted snow. Overhead, the bird's screams pierced her with terror. There was exasperation in the sound. Her horse could not get up, its floundering evidence of a broken leg.

Thea staggered to her feet as Drumcondra's strong hand lifted her, hauling her up on the horse in front of him. "What do you think you are about, eh?" he seethed. "Running from me, were you? Little fool! That is sure and sudden death in pursuit back there. Hold fast!" And with no more said, he turned his mount toward his ranks to the south.

The falcon continued in its northerly course, and Thea

struggled in his arms. "I wasn't running from you, my lord," she pleaded. "I was coming to help you!"

"Eh?"

"Please, *the bird!*"

"What about him?"

"It goes a different way."

"So? He knows what he's about. Be still. There is no time here now for foolish prattle. I will deal with you later. Another of my keeps is under siege! I will not see any more of my holdings taken unaware—not ever again!"

"The falcon knows a better, shorter way," she persisted. "Jeta, your mother, told me. My lord, I know something you do not. I beg of you, trust me! There isn't time to tell it here now. If you would live to see another dawn . . . *follow that bird.*"

The falcon beckoned, dipping and soaring, circling overhead before it sailed off in its chosen northeasterly course toward Falcon's Lair.

Drumcondra glanced behind him and loosed a string of oaths in another tongue. His men had scattered. Cosgrove's army was bearing down upon them, closing the gap, the thunder of their galloping mounts amplified by the heavily falling snow.

"My lord, I beg you. *Please,*" cried Thea, "Before the bird is out of sight."

Tightening his grip upon her, Drumcondra loosed a beastial roar, kneed his frenzied mount into a rear that nearly unseated them both, then set him on the falcon's course and galloped after.

Chapter Fourteen

Drumcondra drove the horse beneath him through the windswept darkness like a man possessed. Clinging to him, Thea shut her eyes. The bird was still leading them, a dark silhouette against the eerie pinkish sky, when last she'd looked, but she could bear to look no longer. Neither could she brave a glance behind to see if Cian Cosgrove's men were still in pursuit. Drumcondra did not speak, and Thea was grateful for that. Soon enough he would demand an explanation, and she had no idea what she would tell him, or if she would ever get the chance to tell him anything. If they didn't find the corridor, neither of them would live to see the sunrise.

She wracked her brain, trying to recall how it was when she'd come through the passage tomb. Try as she would, she could remember nothing significant occurring in the transition—no vertigo, no pain. One moment she'd been exploring the chambers in 1811, the next she'd been standing in the unblemished snow in the winter of 1695.

Would it be the reverse now? How would she tell? When would she know? And what of Jeta? Would she be there to greet them, or had her angst when they parted, insisting that Thea go while she could still give aid, have been because there was no way for her to avoid the coming devastation? And what of James? Would she ever see her brother again? Thea's mind was reeling.

All at once the snow stopped falling, and a structure loomed before them, black against the starry sky. Thea's breath caught in her throat. The great bird swooped down and alit atop the battlements of what had once been Falcon's Lair, exactly as James had described it, though now the portcullis was raised, and the drawbridge was extended.

Drumcondra reined in his mount so severely that it spun in circles and reared back on its hind legs, pawing the still air with its feathered forefeet. Thea cried out, clinging to Ros's mantle with both hands fisted in the fur back and front.

"What's *this?*" he thundered. "My keep in ruins? They could not have gotten here before me. They could not have!"

"N-no my lord," Thea murmured. "If you will let me, I . . . I think I can explain."

"Explain?" he said. "What have you to do with this treachery? Speak!"

"I have done no treachery. I have saved you . . . saved us both this devastation. . . ."

"Where is the moat?" he gritted out, staring wide-eyed toward the snow-clad hollow looming before them. "It was filled with freezing water not two hours ago. It could not have been drained dry in that space of time." He gazed up at the stars. A sickle moon winked down now among them in a clear sky, no blood moon hidden behind dense snow clouds. "What sorcery is this?"

"I cannot answer that, my lord," said Thea. "Your mother is the one to tell it, and I do not even know if she is here to do so. . . ." She trailed off, drawing his eyes to her dismay. He shook her gently. "Explain this," he insisted.

"Might we go inside, my lord?" she said. "I am freezing."

"What are you doing in that flimsy thing? Where is your fur wrap?"

Should she say? There was no use to lie. "Your Drina stole it from me," she said.

He loosed a string of oaths, and climbed down from the horse. "Stay here," he said, producing a gate key. "I will go first and unlock the portal."

With no more said, he strode off over the lowered drawbridge. For a split second, Thea fought against the instinct to go with him, for fear of one of them accessing the corridor again. The falcon seemed at home upon the battlements here, perched like a gargoyle on the top of the curtain wall. Taking comfort in that, she waited somewhat less than patiently for his key to turn in the lock. The rasping sound the heavy rusted hinges made from disuse— audible even at this distance—made her blood run cold. The minute he hefted the great doors open, she urged the reluctant horse on and crossed over.

Thea climbed down from the stallion while Drumcondra tethered the animal and untied his saddlebag, slinging it over his shoulder. Giving him a wide berth, she followed him as he stomped incredulous through what remained of Falcon's Lair. The stables were gone; they had burned in the fire. Thea was right: It was the wing that had housed Drumcondra's bedchamber that had been destroyed. Cold chills unrelated to the cold December night riddled her mercilessly. Her teeth had begun to chatter, more from shock than cold. For a time she didn't speak, following him through the corridors. It was almost as if he'd forgotten her presence. Then, when he threw open one of the chamber doors on the north side of the second-floor corridor, he seized her wrist and reeled her inside. Tossing the saddlebag he'd been toting down, he faced her, his arms rigid at his sides, his hands balled into white-knuckled fists.

"I will ask you again," he said. "What has happened here?"

"M-might we have a fire, my lord?" she said.

Two chairs leaned against the wall. He broke them into pieces, clearly venting his rage, and heaved them into the hearth. He seemed to be familiar with the room because he knew where to find the tinderbox. Opening a drawer in the bottom of a tall oak wardrobe, he snaked it out and lit the fire.

Clouds of soot belched from the clogged chimney, which was on the verge of collapse for lack of use. Thea fanned the sooty fog away with her hand, and buried her nose in her homespun cloak while it subsided. Then, her ankle boots crunching upon what remained of broken crockery beside the door, she drew near the fire, reaching for its feeble warmth.

"I am waiting," Drumcondra said, his sinewy arms folded across his chest.

Thea spun to face him. The time she dreaded was upon her. She could stall no longer. She drew a ragged breath and pulled herself up to her full height before him.

"My lord, do you remember how often you have told me that I seemed . . . different to you somehow. My clothes, my manner, my speech?"

"Aye. So . . . ?"

"I passed it off as the result of my English heritage. I could not tell you the truth then. You would never have believed me. I doubt you will believe me now. I was hoping

Jeta would be here to persuade you, but she is not, and . . . I am afraid . . ."

"Of me?" he asked.

"Of you, yes—and of myself . . ."

"Go on."

"I am betrothed, my lord, though not to Cian Cosgrove, but rather to his descendant, Nigel Cosgrove." One look into those riveting green eyes, and she threw her arms into the air. "Oh, it is too bizarre!" she cried, "I can see that you do not believe me already, and I've scarcely begun."

"I know of no Nigel Cosgrove," Drumcondra said.

"No, you would not," she replied. "He is not of your time. Neither am I. That is why I seemed . . . different to you. I am from the Year of Our Lord 1811, my Lord Drumcondra. I visited Newgrange, the passage tomb that you know as Si An Bhru, at sunrise on the winter solstice to see light flood the chambers. My brother James was with me. He remained outside while I explored the chambers. When the light failed and I stepped back outside, your men assaulted me. All the land around was changed, just as this land is changed here now, and you told me yourself that it was the year 1695! There is more—so much more that I do not even understand, but I swear to you that I speak the truth. You are standing inside Falcon's Lair, but not in your time, in *mine*, after the devastation—after the fire that would have consumed you, consumed us both if I hadn't found you in time. If I hadn't tricked you into following that bird through the corridor that links our times in some way we may never understand. Jeta, your mother, knew, my lord. It was she who gave me the means to save you."

Drumcondra turned away and went to the window. It overlooked the destroyed wing silhouetted against the clear night sky.

"You are standing in the proof of what I say, Lord

Drumcondra," Thea said, soft of voice, almost afraid to disturb him.

He spun to face her. "I must go back!" he said. "If what you say is true, I can prevent this!"

Thea shook her head. "If you go back, you will die in that chamber where you held me captive. I saw your death. Your mother showed it to me."

"How?"

"In a bucket of water."

Drumcondra's scalp drew back. "If she showed it to you thus, it is true. The bucket is a Gypsy mystery—one of many. We Gypsies have knowledge beyond the comprehension of ordinary men. You should have told me this before."

"She advised against it."

"And now she is likely dead."

"I pray not, my lord," Thea said around a tremor. "It was she who lured me here in the first place. It would pain me never to see her again."

"How do you mean?"

"The very night I arrived at Cashel Cos—your castle . . . You see, that *was* a lie. I did reside there briefly, but I couldn't tell you then. You thought it was Cian I was to wed. At any rate, she came to the castle and told me things that led me to that passage tomb on the solstice. I think she did so, because she meant for me to save you from a horrible, horrible death, my lord."

"And so she sacrificed herself and died instead," he murmured. "I must go back. You must show me the way."

"Me?" she cried. "I cannot, my lord. I do not know it, and even if I did I would not. I saw your death! You burned alive in that chamber, a woman at your side. I believe it was *I* in that holocaust with you! You must stay here, in my time with me."

"And do what, go where? I cannot stay here. Where shall I go? What shall I do? What shall I wear? I cannot go abroad as I am. The coin in my pouch is doubtless obsolete. Where do I obtain your coin of the realm, eh? It is impossible. I must go back—now, before it's too late."

"It is already too late, my lord," Thea moaned. "The midnight hour has come and gone. You cannot turn back time. If it were only possible . . ." She couldn't finish the thought. Besides, she didn't mean it. She would gladly brave that holocaust if the alternative meant never seeing him again.

Drumcondra kicked at the broken pottery beside the door, at a tarnished coffer amongst the debris, and spun to face her. Thea had never seen so tragic a look of devastation in anyone's face. She longed to go to him, to throw her arms around him, but she could not. She stood her ground.

"The bird brought us here?" he asked.

She nodded. "It travels the time corridor freely, my lord," she said. "Even *it* knows you must stay here now. These are truly strange happenings, to be sure, but to a purpose. I must believe that. *You* must believe that."

"A purpose, eh? What purpose to save me from a slaughter that destroys all of my people—wipes them from the face of the earth?"

"I do not know, my lord," she said. "Only that there is one. Your mother knew it." She gestured toward the battlements. "That bird knows it, and while I do not pretend to understand it, I know it, too. Your destiny lies . . . elsewhere."

"You say that Isor travels the corridor freely," he said. "How do you know this?"

"At first I did not know it. It was your mother who explained. That bird, I do believe, harbors the same hatred for the Cosgroves as you do. When he gouged out Cian Cosgrove's eye, it was not the only time he blinded one of them." Drumcondra's nonplussed expression stopped her momentarily. He had scooped up some of the pottery shards he'd been kicking at from the dust-covered floor, and was fingering them as she spoke. "That bird took my betrothed's eye in just the same manner before I came to you."

"Why?"

"He was protecting me, I think," she said, reflecting upon the incident. "Nigel had taken me up on the battlements to chastise me for insisting your mother be admitted in view of the storm. We were arguing, and he took hold of me. We were struggling, and the bird swooped down, batted me out of the way with those enormous wings, and gouged Nigel's eye out. If Nigel hadn't taken to his bed, I would never have come to you. He had forbidden me to visit the passage tomb. I coerced my brother into taking me."

"This Nigel. He did not . . . harm you?"

"No, my lord, but if that bird hadn't intervened . . . Your mother could persuade you if she were here. I have no experience with the supernatural. I do not pretend to understand any of this, but I do not think we dare tamper with it."

"I have heard of such as this," he said absently. "Since I could stand without my knees buckling, I was told the tales of Si An Bhru—that it was a passageway between the living and the dead, a sacred mystery. That is why we made it our home . . . our hiding place. The superstitious folk hereabouts gave it a wide berth. We were safe there. Everyone thought we were camped in the hills. I thought the stories were like so many other Gypsy tales, the legends of our heritage. I did not credit them as truth."

"Would it comfort you to know that your people's remains were found there . . . that many of them reached the tomb after the devastation, and evidently lived and died there? Their bones were found inside when the tomb was opened up in 1699 and renovated. *Your* bones were not among them, my lord. Our history tells us that you simply . . . disappeared and were never heard of again."

Drumcondra froze, stock-still, his green gaze riveted to her.

"Dare you tamper with that, my lord?" she asked, blinking back tears.

"You are a brave woman," he said. "You must have been . . . terrified."

"I am not brave," she sobbed, dissolving into tears. "I am still terrified. For us both."

He reached her in two ragged strides and took her in his arms. His taut muscles rippled against her. His chest, as hard as steel, flexed beneath her face, and his hands soothed her through the homespun cloak. He still held a fragment of the broken jar he had been fingering. He tossed it down and it shattered to dust.

"What was that?" she asked.

"That was what has convinced me," he said, burying his massive hand in her hair. "Not three hours ago, Drina threw that jar at me in this very chamber. It was filled with some strong-smelling women's balm that splashed all over me. I stink of it. I can still smell it on my jerkin."

Thea inhaled and gasped. "Patchouli!" she said. "An Asian scent. Very costly, very much in demand, my lord."

He raised her face until their gazes met. "I much prefer the smell of gillyflower and rose," he murmured.

All at once, he clouded. "Do you love him, this Nigel Cosgrove?" he said.

"No, my lord," she replied. "It is an arranged betrothal."

"They still do that in the year 1811, eh?"

"They do."

"You will not marry him," he said flatly.

"My lord?"

"You will not marry him," he repeated. "Our lives are linked—yours and mine. That has not changed, fair lady. I have brought you to life, and now that life is mine."

"My lord—"

His warm mouth swallowed the rest. His hand buried in her hair cupped her head. His fingers laced through her dark curls, caressed its silkiness, feeling its texture. He deepened the kiss and she sagged in his arms, lost in the power of a palpable passion.

His need was evident. His bruising hardness forced against her, riddling her with icy-hot waves of paralyzing fire coursing through her very core. As anxious as that forceful manhood was, she did not fear it anymore. There was a new gentleness in him then that totally disarmed her. He seemed transfixed in a way that contradicted his otherwise flamboyant image. And, oh, what his kiss was doing to her equilibrium!

Warm, skilled fingers roamed her body through the thin silk shift beneath her cloak. As if they had a will of their own, they knew just where to touch, just what to tantalize. Her breath erupted in a moan as his hand came to rest upon her belly. Her sex leapt as the hand prowled lower, hovering over the mound between her thighs through the clinging silk.

Her arms tightened around him, drawing him closer, charging the corded muscles in that dynamic body to flex and shudder against her. Where had her resolve gone? What was she thinking? His earthy scent had hypnotized her. The sultry baritone rumble bubbling up from deep inside him thrilled her from head to toe, those shuddering groans resonating in her throat until she feared she'd faint from sheer ecstasy. He was right. She was his. How could she ever love another after living in the arms of Ros Drumcondra?

As though he'd read her thoughts, he drew his lips away and glanced toward the bed behind them. It was stripped bare to the mattress ticking. Thea's eyes followed. There was no denying the meaning in those tarnished green eyes, in the rapid breath puffing from his flared nostrils, in the visible pounding of his heart through the leather tunic stretched taut over his hard muscled chest. Reluctantly, he slid his hands down her trembling arms and put her from him.

"The place has been looted—picked clean," he said, striding toward the door. "What little remains is not worth stealing. Stay. Warm yourself by the fire. I shan't be long."

"W-where are you going?"

"To find us some decent bedding if I can," he said, stepping into the hallway.

He wasn't gone long. His arms loaded with fur rugs and a richly woven tapestry Thea assumed had once hung on the wall, he strode to the bed and began spreading his finds.

"I found a cupboard they overlooked," he said. "Either that or others have left these over time. They do not look familiar. There isn't a spoon or a trencher left in the place."

"After nearly a hundred and twenty years, my lord, you are fortunate to find the walls still standing."

He strode to her side, and cupped her head in his hand. "You are mine," he said simply. "You shall know no other."

"What are you saying, my lord?" She had to know his intentions. She might be the love slave of a Black Irish Gypsy warlord, but there were still proprieties to be met. They had come into her time now.

"Your kind puts great store in the ritualistic religious

sanctification of marriage," he said. "We Gypsies do not. We have our own marriage rituals that are not so strict, but just as binding. The ceremonies are centuries old. This . . . situation calls for sanctification, don't you think? I would have you for my wife, Thea, before I take you in that bed, because I know your sensibilities demand it—and because I wish to prove to you that I am no barbarian. Will you marry me the Romany way, my lady?"

Thea's heart was bursting. This was not at all what she'd expected. The man was full of surprises. There was only one answer she could give and still be true to herself, because her need of him was greater than her sense of propriety. She nodded her assent. She would not give him her virtue otherwise. Though the thought of marriage to such an enigmatic warrior was daunting, the prospect of living without him now would not be brooked.

He pulled her into a smothering embrace that left her weak and trembling, in need of his strong arms for support. So, it had come to this. Truth be told, she'd known it would from the very first. She had always been of the opinion that some things were ordained in heaven. This was one of them. Thea had found her soul mate. To deny him would be to fly in the face of the Divine Providence that had brought them together through time and space and soul-wrenching calamity.

"There are several rituals," he murmured against her hair. "In some Gypsy cultures, it is enough for a man and woman to simply declare their wish to be joined in marriage to each other for the oath to be binding. But I suspect that you would require something . . . more. There is another ritual that should suffice. Come, sit." He led her to the bed and snatched up his saddlebag from the floor. Rummaging inside, he produced a chunk of bread and a flagon of mead. Kneeling down beside her, he tore two small pieces from the loaf, drew his dagger from his boot, and pricked his finger with it. Thea gasped as he squeezed a drop of blood onto one of the morsels. Cleaning the blade on his leggings, he handed it to her. "Do as I have done," he said.

Thea pricked her finger with the blade and let a drop of her blood drip onto her piece of the bread.

Drumcondra took back his dirk, and handed her his bread, taking hers in exchange. "Eat," he said, "and we are one for all time."

Thea took the bloodstained bread into her mouth, and watched wide-eyed as he did the same with hers. "For all time," she murmured, meeting his shuttered gaze.

"There should be music and dancing," he remarked, "platters heaped with food and goblets overflowing with ale and wine, but all that will have to wait." He raised her to her feet. "What we have just done is as binding as any bishop's blessing. I am part of you, and you are part of me now. It will be thus forever. Nothing can change it—not even death."

"I . . . do not want to change it," Thea murmured.

Drumcondra stripped her of her cloak and, in one motion, raised her shift up over her head. Thea stood naked, her charms exposed to his gaze. Those gold-flecked green eyes devoured her in a slow familiar appraisal, from her windblown crown of ebony curls to the delicate shape of her dainty feet. They lingered on the curve of her rounded hips and narrow waist, on the soft swell of her breasts, grown turgid with desire, the tawny nipples hard in anticipation of his touch. His look alone was a seduction.

He scooped her up in his arms and laid her on the bed among the furs he'd piled there. Across the way, the fire in the hearth had finally mellowed into a smokeless issue of radiant warmth. The glow gleamed on Drumcondra's bronzed skin as he stripped off his tunic and leggings. Naked but for the ragged bandage clinging to his thigh, he stood over her, aroused. Thea's trembling breath hovered in her throat. She had never seen a fully naked man before. Her gaze slid over his body in awestruck amazement. It lingered upon the broad span of his lightly furred chest, upon the narrow line of dark hair striping his flat middle, pointing like an arrow to the rigid curve of his sex. It followed the corded contours of his well-turned thighs, and roamed back over the whole. Her breath caught again, and his sex responded to the sound.

Favoring his injured leg, he sank down beside her and took her in his arms. Gathering her against him, he moaned. How perfectly her body molded to his despite the difference in their height, how easily their limbs entwined, as if their bodies had been designed as two pieces of a whole that had just come together.

He moaned again. "I have wanted to hold you thus since I first set eyes upon you," he said, his voice husky with desire. "I have dreamed of it . . . longed for it . . . to hold your naked *willing* flesh in these arms. To have you open yourself to me like the petals of the flower you are, so fragrant and fine."

"My lord, you take my breath away."

"You might call me Ros now, I think," he said, with a chuckle. His laughter dissolved. "But you are trembling," he murmured. "You do not still fear me."

"N-no, my lord—Ros. It is just that . . . I do not know what to do."

He laughed again. Raising her hand to his lips, he kissed her moist palm then lowered it to his arousal. "Look what you have done already," he said. "It is on fire for you. Whatever else you need to know, I will teach you. Hold me, Thea. Quench my thirst for you."

Thea slipped her arms around him. Every pore in her skin responded to the fever in her blood. Every warm puff of breath against the curve of her ear, her arched throat, sent rivers of liquid fire flowing through her belly and thighs, moistening her swollen sex. His chest hair felt like silk against her breasts. When his fingers found her nipple, she was undone. She shuddered with pleasure against him, and he spread her thighs and eased himself between.

"Your leg, my lord!" she whispered.

"Shhh, Thea," he said. "If you speak, the sound of that sweet voice alone will relieve me and end this enchantment too soon." He found her sex, and stroked her there—lightly at first, then faster, deeper until she feared she would ignite the way kindling ignited when he worked them with his tinderbox. "One brief moment of pain," he murmured. "Just this once. It cannot be helped. You are so . . . delicate, so . . . narrow . . ." He hesitated.

That wouldn't do. Thea seized his wrist. Her whole body throbbing like a pulse beat, she drove his probing fingers deeply in and groaned. There was pain, bittersweet ecstasy that lifted her out of herself, and she scarcely felt the pressure lessen as he withdrew his hand and filled her with his anxious erection.

"Thea . . ." He gasped as he entered her. Groaning, he took her deeper—took her mouth, rocking her in his arms, gifting her with the unexpected power of gentle strength that threatened her consciousness. "You have bewitched me," he groaned.

Clinging to him, she met his thrusts again and again, her body arched against his hard muscled torso. All that remained of the pain was a dull prickling of sensation soon dissolved in the heat of another sensation, one that enveloped, overwhelmed her. It seemed to lift her out of her body, all but stopping her heart like it had done before, only this time—oh, *this* time—as he moved inside her, it was as if her bones were melting. Her very soul seemed in danger of igniting as the fiery flow raced through her body. At last, she breathed, her heart thudding in her breast, echoing in her ears, and she murmured his name as the warm rush of his seed filled her.

It was a breathless moment for them both before he lifted his weight from her and eased himself to the side, his breath coming short, his skin running with sweat.

"Your leg," she moaned.

He folded her in his arms and wrapped one of the fur rugs around her. "Shhh," he murmured. "You are mine. Nothing else matters."

Thea clung to him beneath the furs. How well he had loved her. How gently he had taken her—and with such a size! Even at the end, when they had clung to each other in mindless oblivion, he had been conscious of her comfort. What would be if he ever let that pent up passion loose? Could she bear it? One day, she would know the full power of that passion. For now, it was enough that she had brought this mighty warrior to his knees. Who was the love slave now?

Exhausted, she slept, but her dreams were fitful and oppressing, threaded through with nagging doubts that his leg was not as sound as he pretended, that the fire in his skin that had become suspiciously dry again was not only due to passion, but to fever.

She had nearly pushed the thoughts aside when the sound of motion bled into her vision. Rats? No, it was a human sound. It came again, and this time there was shouting. Her eyes flew open to the sight of James looming over her Gypsy husband, the dagger that had sealed their marriage vows indenting Ros's throat.

"Get up out of there, Drumcondra!" James demanded, "or I'll run you through right where you lay! What have you done to my sister?"

Chapter Fifteen

"James, no!" Thea screamed, seizing his arm. "He has done naught that I did not want him to do. We are wed."

James hesitated. The sharp point of the dirk had pierced Drumcondra's skin, and a trickle of blood ran down his neck, though he made no sound. Thea's eyes oscillated between her brother's indignation and the muscles ticking along her husband's broad jaw. Her fingers tightened on James's wrist, and tears swam before her eyes. He had never been able to resist her tears. She prayed it was still so now.

"Please, James," she sobbed. "I love him." It was the first time she'd admitted it, much less spoken it. The words drew Drumcondra's eyes despite the blade still indenting his skin, but she dared not look then for fear she'd see in them that what he felt for her was something more akin to lust. Of that much she was certain. They had never spoken of love.

"How can he be your husband?" James snapped at her. "Who has wed you—what vicar, what priest? There are none here in this heathen nest of Gypsies to be had, and not a soul abroad for miles around." He snatched her shift off the floor and tossed it at her. "Dress yourself," he charged. "I mean to know what is going on here. You have a good deal of explaining to do. Get up, I say!"

"Do as he says," Drumcondra said. Then, to James, he added, "We are wed by Romany law. If you will put that blade down, I will explain."

"He is telling the truth, James," Thea pleaded, on her feet now, wrapped in the fur rug. "Put that blade down!"

"Stay out of this, Thea, and put on that garment. I will not stand here conversing with you like . . . like *that*."

"Avert your eyes if you would have me dress," she snapped.

James turned back to Drumcondra while Thea struggled into her shift in great haste. She had never seen such a look of rage in her brother's eyes in all her life. His mouth was white, his violet eyes glazed over like a drunkard's, and his cheeks were blotched crimson. He was livid.

"The old Gypsy woman told me a preposterous tale," James said. "I suppose you are going to tell me something equally ridiculous?"

"James, *please*," Thea pleaded. "Put that down!"

He cast her a sidelong glance. In that split second Drumcondra seized his wrist, flipped him over onto the floor, leapt from the bed and fell upon him. Snatching the blade, he held it at Thea's startled brother's throat.

"Now you will listen, I think," the warrior said.

"Oh, my God, Ros, no! I beg you, don't hurt him!" Thea shrilled.

"I am the one who is bleeding," he said. "It is not my intent to harm him, but neither will I sit still and let him run me through in my conjugal bed with my own blade. Now, sir, will you let me fetch my leggings and converse with you in a civilized manner, or are we to wage a war you cannot win?"

"James, *please*."

"If this hulking lout will get off me and make himself presentable, I will listen to what the two of you have to say. But be warned, it had best be good. As it stands now, 'my lord,' you are called out, and I expect satisfaction."

"Your servant, sir," Drumcondra growled, staggering to his feet. He snatched his leggings and tugged them on. Thea turned away, her hand shading her eyes as James got up from the floor and tugged his frock coat and waistcoat into place. Then, ordering the cloak Jeta had provided to replace his stolen greatcoat, which had twisted around sideways, and slapping the dust from his buckskins, he faced them.

"Very well, then," he said, addressing them both. "What is the meaning of this?"

"Whatever my mother told you was doubtless true," Drumcondra said.

"That was your *mother* who led us here?" James blurted.

Drumcondra nodded. "When did she speak with you? Is she here?" He was in the process of tugging his boots on, and he froze in place, his gaze hopeful.

"She is not," said James. "She led me a merry chase, then brought me right back here and disappeared—but that damned bird was waiting to attack me. It won't come after me again, by God!"

Thea gasped. It wasn't until that moment that she noticed the deep gash just above her brother's eye, crusted over with dried blood.

"You haven't harmed it?" she cried. "Oh, God, James, tell me you haven't harmed that bird!"

James stared at her, incredulous. "It nearly gouged my eye out—just as it did Nigel's," he said, thumping his brow and giving her a scathing look. "What? Was I supposed to stand still and let it have it?"

"Oh, James!" she said.

"What? I haven't killed it, I just drove it off with stones from the rubble out there, and it flew off as surly as ever."

Thea collapsed, sinking down upon the edge of the bed, her head in her hands.

"Will one of you please tell me what is going on here?" her brother bleated.

"James, I tried to tell you when I came to your cell, I did, but you weren't ready to listen. Are you ready now?"

"You mean to tell me that what you told me about traveling back to 1695 is true?"

"Did Jeta not tell you the same?" Thea asked. James stared, and she went on quickly. "When she took you out of the dungeons into the courtyard, did you not see the moat filled with water?"

"I did, but—"

"Is it filled now?"

"Well, no, but—"

"How do you account for that, James? There is so much more that you didn't see, but that alone should prove what I told you."

"Assuming that what you say is true, where are we now? You've lost me, Thea. Once, I let you convince me that you had seen Drumcondra's ghost. Now you're telling me the man is *real*? I thought you addled when you put that to me in the dungeon, but this? This is impossible."

"Was it a ghost that just bested you, whatever your name is?" Drumcondra put in.

Thea gave a lurch. "Forgive me," she said. "My brother, my lord—James Wadsworth Barrington."

Drumcondra grunted, his scowl as black as soot. "Drumcondra's ghost at your service," he said drolly. "I like this no better than you do, Barrington, except that it has given me the woman I mean to spend the rest of my life with. Do not harm the falcon. It knows where the time corridors are; I do not. Destroy it, and if my mother is alive, she may not be able to join us."

James sank down on the edge of the bed. "What year is this here now, then?" he asked, clearly in a state of hopeless confusion. He looked so lost. Poor stodgy, well-adjusted, level-headed, logical James. Of all people to become embroiled in such an illogical state of affairs. Thea would have laughed if the situation weren't so grave.

"I believe it is 1811, James," she said. "You are inside Falcon's Lair, Lord Drumcondra's stronghold at Drogheda, five miles east of Newgrange, as it exists *today*—in ruins. You were held captive in this same keep only hours ago, as that was in 1695—moat and all."

"But . . . how could you marry *him?*" he asked, waving a wild arm in Drumcondra's direction. "You hardly know him, and if all that you say is true, he isn't even human. He doesn't even exist in our world, Thea!"

"He does now," she sallied. "And I know him well enough to be absolutely certain that I do not want to live without him in *any* circumstances. James, like yourself I do not pretend to understand any of this, only that a woman knows when she has met her soul mate. Whether that happens in the blink of an eye or over time doesn't matter. Whether you believe that or you do not doesn't really matter either. It is no less bizarre than our society's so-called 'civilized' marriage arrangements and the infidelities that result from them. You hardly need look beyond our family for example."

"So, now what do we do?" asked James. "You've married a seventeenth-century Black Irish Gypsy warlord, while your real intended—scarcely five miles off, mind—is making arrangements for your wedding to *him* from his sickbed!"

Thea turned away. How was it that her brother could always manage to make something perfectly simple seem so totally illogical?

"He cannot go about here now like *that*," James said. He waved a wild hand in Drumcondra's direction, earning him a withering glance from the warrior, whose posture had expanded listening to the exchange. It was clear Ros didn't appreciate being the subject of discussion as if he weren't even there. "Look at him, Thea," James went on hotly. "That hair—those togs. Are you mad?"

"Hair can be cut," Thea argued, earning herself a scathing dose of Drumcondra's green-eyed indignation. "Or at least ordered," she amended, and he relaxed his posture guardedly. "And togs are the least of our worries. You can lend him some of yours until suitable clothes can be bought."

"Mine?" James blurted, vaulting off the bed. "Look at us! How are mine to fit—*that*?" He raked his hair back roughly, wincing as his hand grazed the falcon's handiwork on his brow. "His speech will suffice, I suppose, but you have attics to let if you think you can pass him off as one of us. Where can he stay? Certainly not here. The whole place has gone to wrack and ruin. One good windstorm and the rest will come down—sure as check. I'm surprised that flue hasn't caved in and set another fire, what with the chimney so long in disuse. Besides, who knows who owns this land now? You haven't thought this through, Thea."

"There was nothing to 'think through,' James," she said haughtily. "He—*both of us*—would be dead now if we hadn't come through that corridor. That is simply the way of it."

James was about to speak again, when a hollow pounding racket and loud shouts echoing through the musty old halls from below pulled them all up short.

"Come down out of there, whoever ya are!" a gruff voice bellowed. "You're trespassin'! I've a loaded musket at the ready. You've got till I count ta five! *One* . . . !"

"Oh, James!" Thea cried.

Drumcondra lunged toward the door, but James arrested him with a quick hand. "You cannot go!" he said. "Stay out of sight. I will handle this. Thea, put on that cloak and come with me. Say nothing. Let me do the talking. Now you'll see the folly of this bumblebroth you've boiled us in, by God!"

"*Two* . . . ," thundered the voice from below.

Steering Thea along the corridor, James called out, "There is no need for arms, good sir. It is only two wayfarers who have taken shelter from the weather. I, and my sister. Speak up, that I may follow your voice to oblige you. . . ."

"*Three* . . . ," came the reply.

"Oh, James!" Thea said.

He squeezed her arm in an unequivocal gesture that demanded her silence. "We are coming, man!" he hollered. "Please, you are frightening my sister!"

"*Four* . . . ," the voice thundered.

"We can't let him find Ros!" Thea hissed.

"Be still!" James replied in a low mutter. "It is one man alone, from what I can gather. If needs must I can take him down and subdue him. Sink me! My bristles are set up high enough by all this to do it, by God! As near as I can tell, he's in the great hall. Hurry!"

"*Five!* You were warned," the man said.

They had reached the lower landing, Thea clinging to her brother for dear life, her heart hammering in her ears as they pulled up short before a short stocky elder gentleman in buckskins and tweed, leveling an antiquated blunderbuss at them.

"And here we are, sir," said James, winded. "James Wadsworth Barrington, and my sister, Theodosia Barrington, at your service, sir."

"Englishers!" the man spat out in disgust. "I might have known."

"That, we cannot help, sir," said James. "For the trespass, we are greatly sorry. Exhaustion necessitated it, I fear. We've come . . . a long way, and we've harmed naught but a broken chair to use for kindling."

"Ya could have burnt the place down, ya bloody fools! Can't ya see all that's holdin' it up is the drifted snow? *Englishers!*" He lowered the gun, but his cold hard stare did not bode well. "I'm goin' ta bring it down meself come spring, or put it up for auction and let the next fool of an owner have the pleasure—damned nuisance—landmark or no! But wait now, only the two o' ya, ya say? There's two horses, but three sets o' tracks out there. Somebody come in here over that bridge afoot—big fella, too, by the look o' them boot tracks." The blunderbuss shot up and took aim again. Thea gave a whimper in spite of herself looking down the ominous barrel.

"I cannot speak for who else may have trespassed here recently," said James, clearly begging answers from the air. "There's no one here now but us. We've just come from the coast on our way to Cashel Cosgrove some miles west, for the Christmastide feast and my sister's betrothal celebration. She is to marry Nigel Cosgrove there in a fortnight. There is nothing untoward afoot here. We're quite alone . . . you can see for yourself, sir."

"Hmmm," the old man said, considering.

"You know who we are. Might I inquire as to who you are, sir?" James braved, "That I might pay my compliments properly?"

"Squire Michael Fitzmorris, though I don't know how that'll serve ya. I own this slag heap, more's the pity.

You've got ta go. 'Tisn't safe, and that's a fact. Don't want no 'tastrophes on me conscience."

"Oh, and we shall," said James, "Just as soon as the storm subsides."

"What storm might that be?" the squire said, with a start. "There ain't a cloud in the sky."

It was clear that James was still not sure which side of the corridor he was on, and Thea squeezed his arm. "Uh . . . we weathered a nasty one coming up from the coast," he recovered. "It quite wore us to a raveling. We were that glad for a place to rest for a bit before we continue on our way. We still have a long ride ahead of us. If you will allow, my poor sister is in delicate health. By your leave, we will rest awhile, and be on our way in the morning."

"Aye, well, see that ya are," said the squire, taking Thea's measure. "And no more fires!"

"No—none," said James. "You have my word. Do you live close by, Squire Fitzmorris? We saw neither soul nor dwelling coming on, or we might have knocked upon your door."

"Far enough ta weary an old man takin' him out on such a bitter night," he returned, "but close enough ta see the smoke belchin' outta that chimney. Ya wouldn't have passed my door comin' on from the quay, though—too far south."

"Ah!" James erupted. "That explains it, then."

"Well, I'll be takin' me leave," the squire said, "but I'll be back in the mornin', and you'd best be gone when I get here. Remember, I can see smoke risin'—no fires." He stomped off then, and Thea distinctly heard the word "Englishers," escape him as he went.

Once James was certain he had left in earnest, he steered Thea back up to the second floor chamber, but Drumcondra was nowhere in sight.

"Oh, James!" she cried. "Where could he have got to?"

"Hah!" James said. "He's able to fend on his own, I

imagine, a man like that. Perhaps he's gone back where he came from. Good riddance, I'll be bound."

"I am sorry to disappoint you," the warrior said, striding back into the chamber, his falcon perched on his studded leather gauntlet. He held the bird up in salute. "I thought I'd even the odds," he explained.

"Keep that damned vulture away from me, sir!" James charged, shoving Thea behind him.

"Isor will not harm you, Barrington . . . unless I decree it. Who was that I just saw leaving from the battlements? One of the guards?"

"No," said James. "It was the present owner of this wreck of a folly, though not for long to hear him tell. He means to sell come spring."

"*I* am the owner of Falcon's Lair," Drumcondra said, thumping his chest.

"Yes, well—no more, my lord."

"And I do not take kindly to being ordered about in my own keep!" the warrior went on with raised voice. "Least of all by a . . . a . . ."

"An architect," James concluded for him. "Well, you'd best get used to it, because you have no authority here now, and unless you swallow that pride and allow me to assist, you shan't survive a sennight as you are. Collect your things, both of you. We go now—before that fellow changes his mind and sets the guards on us."

"Go where?" Thea cried. "Now who hasn't thought this thing through?"

"The only place we can go till I unwind this coil," James returned. "Where this nightmare all began. Newgrange."

Chapter Sixteen

"That needs tending," James said, pointing a rigid finger toward Drumcondra's wound. They were seated inside the passage tomb on pallets made of the fur rugs they had carried from Falcon's Lair. Among their other loot were candles, the tinderbox, and what combustible materials they could tie onto their saddles such as mightn't be missed, should Squire Michael Fitzmorris suddenly take inventory. These consisted of chair legs and shelf boards, and discarded ledgers and tomes strewn about the place. They were even able to find bits of coal, evidently left behind by other wayfarers in the past.

The smaller stone basin in the central chamber would serve as a brazier, since it stood under the roof box where the smoke could escape. It would be used sparingly, and only at night. Though the surrounding land was barren for miles, rising smoke could be seen from a great distance in daylight. The only issue upon which they all agreed was that this had to be a temporary arrangement. In 1811, the tomb was no longer a sealed hilly mound rising from the land; it had an opening now, and though it wasn't likely to attract the curious in such weather, one couldn't be too careful.

"He is right, my lord, you have fever," Thea said. "There is a surgeon—he visited Nigel when the falcon gouged out his eye."

"Well, we certainly cannot have him here," said James. He had begun to pace. "There's nothing for it," he said. "We shall all have to go back to Cashel Cosgrove."

Drumcondra stiffened as though he'd been struck at the mention of the castle, and James stopped midpace, and faced him. Thea held her breath. These two men she loved so were destined to clash, and James had clearly reached the end of his tether.

"What?" her brother said, addressing the warrior. "It may have been your stronghold once, but it is a Cosgrove holding now, and there is nothing to be done about it."

"I think, my lord," Thea interrupted, "trying to make sense of all this, that somehow we were destined to be together, that you had to lose your castle to Cian Cosgrove, and that he had to destroy Falcon's Lair as well. Elsewise, how would we ever have met? I would never have come here where your mother could find me if it weren't to wed Nigel Cosgrove and give credence to the love slave legend. I would never have been able to prevent you being part of . . . what occurred at Falcon's Lair."

"Yes, well, we do not need you waxing philosophical on us here now, Thea," James said. "That hardly signifies."

"Oh, but I think it does, James," Thea said. "And what's more, I believe there's a reason for it—something we are destined to do, my husband and I, that we must do together. We have only to discover what that reason is to prove it to that logical mind of yours."

"You will have to come back to the castle with me, of course," James went on as though he hadn't heard. "Then I shall—"

"She stays with me," Drumcondra said.

"I am not about to leave her here to take pneumonia with you in this . . . this tomb. You would have to be mad to imagine it, sir."

"You will see 'mad' if you attempt to take her back to the Cosgrove, Barrington."

"Be reasonable, man!" James cried. "Our father will have arrived from England to attend the wedding by now. It will, of course, have to be postponed. Believe me, if we do not return, he will raise an army to comb every wood and thicket hereabout, and this will be the first place he looks."

"There will be no 'wedding,'" Drumcondra said. "She is already married to me. How will you explain that, Barrington?"

"You cannot mean to continue this . . . this charade?" James said, incredulous. "A Gypsy wedding? Such heathen rituals are not recognized by civilized gentility. Surely you know that?"

"They are for life," Drumcondra enunciated, his whole body delivering the words, "And they have been since time out of mind. Gypsy vows are more binding than any of your pompous rituals." He had struggled to his feet and reached for Thea. She went into his arms. "They are enough for us. You would rather see your sister shackled to a brute she does not love, who has abused her, than wed to her soul mate—one who has defied time and place to have her—one who would lay down his life for her? You are a fool, Barrington."

James's posture collapsed. "What do you expect me to do?" he asked, defeat in the sound.

"Get me into my castle!" Ros replied.

Thea's eyes flashed toward him. "To do what?"

"Just do it," Drumcondra said, his shuttered eyes riveted to her brother.

James threw wild arms into the air. "Oh, I see!" he said, with not a little drama. "I am to just march you into the castle as you are—Thea in whatever that scandalous frock is, and *you* in your natural state, sir, decked out for seventeenth-century battle. You look like refugees fresh from treading the boards in Drury Lane, the pair of you. How will you excuse him, Thea? What explanation will you give to Nigel for even returning if you mean to stay with your Gypsy lover? You leave the countess's hospitality—her son's bride-to-be, mind—and return nearly a month later wed to Attila the Hun here, expecting her *and* your betrothed to simply accept the pair of you with open arms because the rest of your family is camped there? Madness!"

"He needs the surgeon, James," Thea reminded him. "You said so yourself. Can we not contrive some fabrication to address that, and meanwhile give me time to talk to Father?"

"You think Father is going to sanction your marriage to *him*, when he is salivating over expected gains from an alliance with the Cosgroves? You dream."

"Just get me inside the castle," Drumcondra insisted. "Give me a chance to establish myself in your time. I have a plan for us, but it cannot be set into motion until I have done so."

"You mean . . . pretend that Thea and Nigel are still to be wed?" James said.

Drumcondra nodded. "Only until I can execute my plan."

"The wedding is certain to be rescheduled to take place

as soon as possible—certainly no more than a fortnight from now, more likely as soon as a sennight. Nigel was champing at the bit."

"It will be time enough."

"And who will you pretend to be, then, in the meanwhile?"

"Whomever you wish, so long as Thea and I are not separated. A wedding guest, a minstrel come to perform at the wedding banquet, her rescuer—however you will. Just get me inside those walls."

"You mean to lay siege to that castle!" James cried, his voice raised with discovery.

"Not . . . exactly."

From the shadowy recesses of the corner, the falcon clucked, drawing James's eyes. "What of the bird?" he asked. "Take that creature anywhere near Cashel Cosgrove and it won't live to see another sunrise. The gamekeeper has been ordered to shoot it on sight. No hawk is safe in this valley now."

"Isor is well able to fend for himself," said Drumcondra.

James shook his head. "You say you have a plan? You need to tell it. I shan't go one more step until I know what folly you are hatching that will put my sister in jeopardy, sir."

"You forget," said Drumcondra, "that keep was once mine. There is a fortune in gold hidden there—Gypsy gold that I will be able to convert to your currency. Ill-gotten, I admit, but who here now is to question its origin?"

James stared. "Surely someone has discovered it by now," he said. "After all these years, it's hardly to be expected that it still remains."

"If no one knows it exists, the odds are in my favor, Barrington. Cian Cosgrove was unaware of it. No one knew—

not even my wife, and unless the current residents are ghouls and grave robbers, it is safe to assume that it has stayed where it was laid."

"And now belongs to the current owner," James said, his tone flat.

"It belongs to *me*," Drumcondra seethed, thumping his chest, "The legacy of my father. With it, I will be able to keep your sister in grander style than your Cosgroves ever could."

James shook his head. "I want no part of this," he said. "I shan't become accomplice to robbery."

Drumcondra smiled the smile that did not reach his eyes. "Ahhh, but you will be part of the result," he said.

"And how is that, pray?"

"I mean to have Falcon's Lair back," said Drumcondra. "You said yourself that the owner is anxious to get shot of it. It goes against my grain to have to purchase my own land—to pay for what is rightfully mine—but purchase it I will if that is the only way to have it back."

"That slag heap?" James blurted. "You mean to house my sister in that crumbling pile of rubble? You, sir, have attics to let."

"That is where you enter into it," Drumcondra responded. "You are an architect. I will pay you well to see it is made livable."

James's jaw fell slack. "Now I know you're mad," he said. "The entire structure would have to be leveled clear to the foundations. Construction crews would have to be engaged—stone masons, roofers, landscapers and the like. Why, it would take a fortune. . . ."

"Which I will supply, once I retrieve it," the warrior concluded. "I cannot do that from here."

James began to pace dramatically. "So, let me see now if I have this correct," he said. "You mean to gain entrance to Cashel Cosgrove under false pretenses in order to relieve them of gold that is legally theirs, being the owners of the place. Furthermore, you intend to use this now twice ill-gotten fortune to purchase a worthless wreck of a manor, which you somehow seem to expect me to resurrect for you. Have I got it with any degree of accuracy, my lord?"

"James, how is it that you always must dissect everything put before you?" Thea asked. "You are practical to a fare-thee-well, and logical to a fault. I pity *your* intended. You haven't an ounce of romance in your soul, and even less vision."

"Hah!" her brother erupted. "Someone must exhibit logic here. Left to you, we—all three—are destined for incarceration in a lunatic's house!"

Drumcondra shrugged. "What say you, Barrington, are you game?"

"Even if I were, you cannot show yourself like . . . like *that*."

"Are there no longer shops in the area? There used to be a clothier in Oldbridge."

"I suppose . . ."

"The coin in my pouch will likely not suffice, but I will make it right by you when I have my gold."

"Yes, well, I expect there's naught to be done but go along with this madness. I leave for Oldbridge at first light." James took the warrior's measure, sliding his gaze the length of him. "We shall be fortunate indeed to find anything that remotely comes close to your stature, my lord. You never would manage it at home, by God! Count yourself fortunate that the Irish are more strongly made."

"I am in your debt, sir."

"Oh, yes!" James warbled. "And I will collect, make no mistake."

Thea embraced her brother. "Thank you, James," she murmured.

"Do not thank me yet," he replied. "Thus far, I'm only committed to making him presentable, nothing more."

Thea turned; and was suddenly afraid. Something unequivocal in Drumcondra's eyes sent soul-shattering chills racing along her spine. Whatever his thoughts were, they were his own. He would not share them. Whatever plan he was hatching had taken possession of him, and she was almost glad she couldn't read those thoughts. He was a Gypsy warrior after all, and she was seeing that facet of him for the first time. It was terrifying. But why now, when what they had just lived through had been a far greater threat? She couldn't explain it unless to call it premonition, but the specter of something that tasted of death was there in that chamber with them, as palpable a presence as any.

"W-why does it have to be Falcon's Lair?" she asked, drawing Drumcondra's eyes. They were hooded and glazed with a different kind of passion. It made her blood run cold. "If, as you say, you have a fortune in gold, why can you not build a keep elsewhere . . . start anew, where there are no sad memories to remind you of the devastation that occurred there?"

Drumcondra gave a start. The look in his eyes was incredulous. "Because of the corridor," he said—as though she should have known.

"You are trembling," Drumcondra whispered in Thea's ear as they lay together wrapped in the fur rugs. They were alone. James had disappeared into one of the side chambers to spend the night. Despite the warmth radiating from the brazier, Thea couldn't control her shuddering. It had nothing to do with the temperature.

"James is right," she said. "It is a mad plan."

"You must trust me," he replied, soothing her in his strong arms.

Thea said no more. What really haunted her then was the reference he'd made to the corridor. No longer worried that he wouldn't believe her, she now feared he hadn't severed ties with his own time. If he were ever to leave her and return to the past now, after . . . No, she wouldn't think of that, not with his dynamic body so close, so aroused in her arms. She wouldn't think about it at all if she could help it. Resurrecting Falcon's Lair was not the answer. Why, even without the obvious, to live with him so close to Cashel Cosgrove and Nigel? Madness! Somehow she would convince him of that—but not now. That coil would have to wait to be unwound. This was not the moment.

With only the glow issuing from the brazier and one feeble candle plastered to the floor with tallow for light, Thea couldn't see him clearly, though she felt the strength in him—in the rock-hard biceps, in the likewise corded thigh leaning against her. His skin was hot and dry, evidence of fever. Another would have succumbed by now, she thought. What was this man made of, this enigmatic Gypsy warlord?

His rough-textured fingers aroused her, stroking her face, her throat and shoulder. She moved against him, a soft moan escaping. The throbbing had begun inside—that wonderful, terrible pulse-beat that set fire to her sex. It was scandalous to feel such sensations, to indulge in such forbidden pleasures. But there was no impropriety here. They were joined in marriage after all. Could it be the bizarre circumstances of their vows that made the intimacies they shared seem shocking? Or was it that she'd found herself taking unabashed pleasure in things others of her sex only endured as a duty that must be borne?

They were perfectly matched; but then, she had believed that from the first moment she set eyes upon him in his ghostly form, lurking in the shadows of her bedchamber at Cashel Cosgrove. What had begun as a fantasy, an air dream, had become a reality so unreal in nature it utterly defied all reason. And yet, it was the most natural phenomenon she had ever imagined.

Her response to his advances proved the point. The heat of his hand through the thin silk shift set her heart racing. The silken feel of his skilled tongue as it entered her mouth, sliding between her teeth, conjoining with her own, wrenched a husky moan from her dry throat. That triggered a response, and her arms gathered him closer still as if they had minds of their own.

As he moved to spread her legs, the fur rug fell away exposing his broad shoulder span to the brazier's golden glow, burnishing his bronzed skin, casting their tall auburn shadows that seemed separate entities on the chamber walls.

"There is no more pain?" his husky voice murmured in her ear.

"No, none, my lord," she said.

The breath leaked from him on a long resonant moan as he entered her, his thick sex filling her so full she feared she'd burst. Every sighing whisper of air seemed to have left his lungs. His heartbeat was the only sound, pounding, thudding in her ears, the shuddering vibrations hammering against her breasts buried in the soft ebony thatch spread over his chest.

If he had driven himself hard inside her then, hammered himself against her, she would have exploded, but he did not. His sex swelled deeper. No other part of him moved, only that stretching, throbbing thickness reaching depths she did not know existed. Her breath caught. Her body arched. His had frozen in place.

The tantalizing ecstasy seemed to go on forever. Just when she thought she could bear no more, he raised her hips and took himself deeper, moving now—strong, shuddering thrusts that ignited her like firebrands; undulating plunges gaining momentum until the heaving propulsions exploded inside her, pumping himself dry, filling her with the warm rushing flood of his seed.

Afterward, he did not withdraw but gathered her close, his hot brow upon her shoulder, his breath puffing out a rhythm against her moist skin. She had not yet come back into herself from wherever his dynamic body always seemed to take her. It was as if she were above herself looking down, watching that bronzed body roped with muscle as it coupled with hers. In the magic of that moment, she almost didn't see the candle flicker, or feel the cold breath of wind that extinguished it. It wasn't until the acrid odor of the burnt wick trailing smoke reached her nostrils that she knew it had gone out. Cold chills riddled her spine despite the warm arms pressing her close. Was it an omen? She wouldn't credit it. Instead, she crowded those thoughts out with remnants of the ecstasy of his embrace still palpitating through her.

Drumcondra didn't seem to notice the sudden darkness that enveloped them, since the fire in the brazier was dwindling also. His soft moan filled the chamber, and at the end of it, almost without breathing, he said, "You are mine. Nothing in heaven or hell can part us." He found her lips with his own, hot and dry, gathered her to him, and took her again and again.

Chapter Seventeen

They left Newgrange as twilight tinted the snow mounds blue, the falcon soaring overhead, his regal wingspread silhouetted against the full moon. Thea and Drumcondra, mounted upon Cabochon, followed James's lead on the Andalusian as they rode north-northwest through the drifts toward Cashel Cosgrove.

The buckskins, waistcoat, frock coat, and caped mantle James brought back from Oldbridge, while not being bang up to the mark when it came to London fashions, were almost a proper fit. Purchasing suitable ready-made boots for a man of the Gypsy's stature, however, was quite another matter. Nothing could be found that would fit. His old ones would have to do. A straight razor dealt with his dark growth of stubble, but he dug in his heels when it approached his hair. No amount of persuasion would convince him to part with his glossy black shoulder-length locks, and in the end Thea tamed them in an acceptable, albeit outdated queue.

It was decided that they would pass him off as wayfaring gentry from the north in hopes it would explain his olive coloring. It was also decided that they not stray too far from the truth, and a story emerged from their collaborative efforts in which James had come upon them returning on his way to fetch the guards. It would be said that Drumcondra rescued Thea from a pair of thieves with intent to hold her for ransom, who had been lurking about Newgrange. They had taken her with them on their current raid. Then, when the storm came they were forced to take shelter, and were waiting it out in a ruined keep west of Drogheda, where Drumcondra, who would be called Mr. Drummond, fortuitously took refuge from the storm himself. A skirmish ensued, and the thieves scattered. This would explain his leg wound, and hopefully earn him an invitation to recuperate at the keep and a visit from Dr. McBain. Even Thea agreed it was a brilliant plan. Now all that remained was to implement it.

They reached Cashel Cosgrove at full dark. The bird immediately soared off to alight atop the battlements in a clucking, flapping exhibition of blatant disrespect and defiance. The brazen display brought the closest thing resembling a smile to Drumcondra's lips that had crossed them since the odyssey began.

He ground out a guttural chuckle. "If I know Isor, he has left his calling card aloft," he said as they approached the courtyard. "In the old days, if a sentry were patrolling there, he would be duly decorated by now."

Thea took a sudden chill, recalling the last time she rode upon Cabochon in Drumcondra's arms approaching that castle. She relived that cold barefoot ride, when, naked beneath the sumptuous chinchilla fur pelerine, her hands bound, she clung to him as they rode through the sugary-frosted twilight. A pulse stirred in her sex recalling the bulk of his arousal forced against her thigh, recalling the touch of his hand upon her breast, the cold breath of the Meath night air ghosting across her naked skin, and the arousal those skilled fingers hardening her nipple had caused. The memory was so jarring she shuddered, and he pulled her close, soothing her gently. Did he remember, too? He must have. The smile had dissolved on his lips, and his eyes were inscrutable.

"Bear up now, little sister," James said, obviously having misread her expression. Hot blood rushed to her cheeks. Her brother knew nothing of that episode, but she didn't need a mirror to tell her she was blushing just the same. A smile that did twinkle in his eyes creased Drumcondra's lips, observing what she was certain had to be her cheeks aflame, but he made no remark as they reined in before the portal and climbed down onto the circular drive.

Regis the butler staggered back from the doorway when they crossed the threshold. James had custody of Thea now. They were taken to the drawing room, and Nigel, the countess, and Viscount Nathaniel Barrington were summoned there. They did not speak while they waited. That too was arranged beforehand. Once they entered the castle, the game had begun.

The countess entered first. "Well, miss," she said to Thea. "You've run us a merry chase. What have you to say for yourself?" She took Drumcondra's measure, her steely eyes raking him suspiciously. "And who is this, if you please?"

"Mr. Drummond, may I present Countess Ridgewood," James spoke up. Nigel and the viscount had come into the room. Drumcondra's eyes were riveted to Nigel. The Gypsy warrior's scalp had drawn back, his eyes, come open wider than Thea had ever seen them, were riveted to the man and his unsightly eye patch, which didn't cover the jagged scar that spread above and below it.

"Your ladyship, Father... this is Mr. Drummond," James went on quickly. "It is he we have to thank for Thea's return, and he has been wounded in the process. Might the surgeon be summoned to attend him?"

"Father," Thea said, going into the viscount's out-stretched arms. He seemed thinner than he had when she saw him last, and his face showed evidence of strain. Still handsome, he possessed the same violet eyes as she and her brother, though his dark hair was tinged with gray. Aside from that and a healthy paunch, he could have passed for a man ten years younger.

Drumcondra's eyes were still fixed on Nigel. Thea knew the uncanny family resemblance to Cian Cosgrove was what had stunned him—that and the patch. Now, there was no question. If he had harbored even the slightest shadow of a doubt, it existed no more. When Nigel spoke, Ros stiffened as though he'd been shot.

"It seems that I am in your debt, sir," he said, "for re-turning my betrothed. What is the nature of your injury? You look sound enough to me."

"He was stabbed in the thigh," James put in before Drumcondra could speak. "He has fever."

"Mmm," Nigel grunted. "You might let the man speak for himself, Barrington." He crossed the room and yanked the bell rope. Everyone began speaking at once. Thea's eyes were riveted to Drumcondra. She tried not to make it appear obvious, but that look in his eyes was one she had never seen. It terrified her. Her father was speaking to her. She had no idea what he was saying. James had noticed Drumcondra's expression as well, and he went at once to his side. In Thea's opinion, when Regis appeared on the threshold, it wasn't a minute too soon.

"Have someone go round to the stables and see that Beadle sends one of the lads after Dr. McBain," Nigel said.

"Our gentleman guest has been injured. Oh, and Regis, see that the south wing turret room is made ready for him, and send Boon up to valet him when he's not tending me."

"Very good, sir," said the butler, disappearing.

"My, how forceful you've become, Nigel," the countess said. "How free you make with my house. One might think you had already swept me into my grave."

"We can hardly deny the man hospitality, Mother," Nigel said, his jaw muscles ticking. "He's brought our Theodosia home."

"The last occasion upon which we offered our hospitality to a stranger began this nightmare as I recall," the countess said.

That she was right didn't signify. Thea wanted to throttle her. Nigel had slipped into his condescending mode where his mother was concerned. While it used to infuriate her when he became the marionette in her presence, she was grateful now. Perhaps if he was occupied at that, he wouldn't look too closely at their little charade.

"Your ladyship," the viscount spoke up. "Credit it that Mr. Drummond is my guest. I am in his debt for returning my daughter to me safely, and of course, as my guest, he must remain to share in the festivities when Thea and Nigel are wed. You are far too generous a lady to deny me the indulgence, hmm?"

"Of course," the countess spat, as if the words were a dose of foul-tasting oil of castor.

By now the chattering had revealed the basics of their story, and thus far it was well received, except for the countess, whose sharp-eyed scrutiny had homed in upon Drumcondra with all the subtlety of a sledgehammer. Thea could not believe the harridan's rudeness, but then she had always displayed such an attitude. Drumcondra seemed not to notice her at all. He had eyes for no one but Nigel Cosgrove.

When at last the butler returned to escort him to the turret room, Thea nearly breathed an audible sigh of relief. James followed, which earned him a scathing glance from the warrior. It was clear to Thea that Drumcondra didn't want her left unsupervised in Nigel's company for a minute. It was also clear that James wanted a word alone with her enigmatic Gypsy husband. In the interest of preserving their well-drafted plan, after a tense moment, James won out, and elected their father to see Thea to her chamber in his place. There was to be a lecture; she could feel it in her bones.

As soon as the door closed behind them, the viscount gripped her hands at arm's length and took her measure. There was no escaping those penetrating eyes of his. He saw more with them than the average father, perhaps because he was such a worldly man.

"Are you really all right, my dear?" he asked. "You wouldn't try to flummox your father now, would you?"

"I am quite well, Father," she said. Why was he looking at her like that?

"Hmmm," he said. "Something untoward is afoot. You may have hoodwinked that lot downstairs—deuced boors—but you cannot hoodwink me. I've lived too long and seen too much to have become jaded in my dotage—"

"You're hardly in your dotage, Father."

"Kindly do not interrupt me, Thea, and do not presume to slather on the sauce. It won't do. Are you going to tell me what is really going on, or must I drag it out of your brother? Do not doubt that he'll tell me. The lad's no-nonsense—always has been once I've gotten him out from under your spell. Do not doubt that I shall, daughter. I mean to have some answers."

"I do not have the faintest idea what you mean," Thea said, hoping for indifference, but certain her rapid heartbeat was showing through the new dove gray muslin frock James had brought back from Oldbridge for her.

"Come, come, girl. Kindly do not insult my intelligence. I'm hardly blind. Captured by thieves? Surely you could do better than that? You hardly paid any notice to your betrothed during your reunion down there just now, but you scarcely took your eyes off that Drummond chap. What? Do you think your old father is blind? You are positively glowing. Don't tell me that colossal boor Cosgrove lit up that face, those eyes. I'll never believe it."

Thea took her hands back, and sank down on the rolled-arm lounge. This was the last thing she needed. She'd forgotten how she had never been able to keep anything from her father. She couldn't very well tell him the truth, but what on earth would satisfy him? She hardly knew. She abhorred lying—especially to him—but . . .

"Father, you know I do not love Nigel," she said. "If you want the absolute truth, if I hadn't been abducted, I would have run from this impossible marriage. The man is insufferable." It was half-truth, but close enough to evoke the emotion that made it believable. Tears welled in her eyes; she couldn't prevent them.

Nathaniel Barrington let his breath out on a long nasal sigh. "This distresses me," he said. "I had hoped . . ."

"Is this match all that important to you financially, Father?" she asked. "I mean—"

"I know what you mean," he interrupted. "I shan't trouble you with the particulars since they do not concern you, but I was hoping to stabilize our financial situation, yes. We're hardly in Dun territory, you understand, not nearly rolled up. Just swimming a bit at low tide at the moment, and I would stand to gain much should our families align."

"And . . . if they do not?"

"So that's how it is, is it? You've already made up your mind, then?"

"I have only gone along with this because I knew you were in financial difficulty," Thea said. "If it were in any respect a palatable prospect, I would hold my peace, but there is nothing to recommend it. The countess is a scheming termagant determined to restore her son's reputation by eliminating the stigma of the recent accusations against him through this marriage. I see it now. I've come to believe that perhaps the accusations against him were true . . . that he did murder the Covent Garden doxy. They found her dumped in a gutter, Father, with her throat cut. She'd been raped and brutally savaged, beaten nearly beyond recognition. Surely you remember? There was little talk of anything else in Town. The Cosgrove fortune got him out of it, saw him acquitted—enough blunt will buy anything these days, you know that. We were made to order. Don't you see? They mean to whitewash it all with this betrothal; I'd stake my life upon it."

Her father clouded, his violet eyes drawn deep under the ledge of his brow as he studied her. Thea couldn't meet those eyes. They had always been able to see right through her. That would be dangerous now.

"Has Cosgrove . . . misused you?" he asked.

"Let us just say that I can see how his vile temper could have led to something . . . unpleasant."

"Let us leave that for a bit," the viscount said. "What is between you and Drummond?"

"Mr. Drummond is a fine man, Father."

"Mr. Drummond is a Gypsy if ever I set eyes upon one. He no more fits the togs he's gotten up in than they fit him."

"I hardly thought it necessary to question him in regard to his lineage while he was rescuing me, Father," she said.

"You have no idea what I've been through." That was the truth, and she delivered it with soul-wrenching passion.

"There, there, daughter, do not put yourself in a taking." He slipped his arm around her shoulder, gave it a rough squeeze, then let it go, commencing to pace before the hearth. "Well, regardless, there's no getting around the fact that you've been compromised," he said.

"*Compromised?*" Thea blurted. "Father, where I have just come from 'compromised' doesn't signify."

He spun around to face her, setting his indigo superfine coattails atremble. "What is it that you want to do, daughter?" he asked, facing her down.

"Father, I would never have come back here if it weren't for you having come. If it weren't to put your mind at ease."

"How badly is that Drummond chap injured?"

" 'Tis serious," she replied.

"How serious?"

"H-he was stabbed in the thigh with a dirk during the confrontation. There was no surgeon at the keep where it occurred, and a stable master stitched it together, but the stitches didn't hold and . . . and the wound had to be cauterized. Now he has fever."

Her father grumbled. "I shall have a word with your Mr. Drummond, I think, once the surgeon has come and gone. Perhaps he will be able to shed some light upon this odd business, since you are unwilling to do so—can't think why. Have I ever caused you grief, daughter? Have I turned a hard hand toward you in all your life, or even rendered you a severe reproof?"

"No, Father," she demurred, her eyes lowered. Her tears had left black spots on her soft gray muslin bodice. "I have always prided myself upon the point that you have never had to. It is just . . . there is really nothing to tell."

"Mmm, of all you haven't said, m'dear, that is the most

revealing. There is much to tell, I think. It is just a matter of whom to tell it. Yes, I shall have a little chat with Mr. Drummond before we go further with this, Theodosia. Then we shall see."

He left her then, and Thea threw herself across the bed, no longer able to hold back her unhappiness. She knew she was lost the minute he called her Theodosia. He never addressed her thus, except when he was extremely displeased. That such a thing had occurred so rarely she couldn't even remember the last occasion, was little consolation. Oh, why had she come back? She never should have. All she could do now was pray Drumcondra would be about the business of collecting his gold before her father pried the truth out of him—or James—and had them all shut up in the madhouse.

Only one thing was certain then, and it hit her like cannon fire. Her virile Black Irish Gypsy husband was as ill equipped to exist in the year 1811 as she was to exist in 1695.

Chapter Eighteen

Ros Drumcondra finally succumbed to the laudanum doses Dr. McBain administered in the process of repairing the crude doctoring done to his wound. Barking all the while that he'd just witnessed treatment more exemplary of medieval practices than nineteenth-century surgery, McBain cleaned and rebandaged the wound, and had the Cosgroves' cook prepare herbal draughts of black currant, balm, and bilberry to address the fever.

The turret chamber that had been assigned to him evoked strange dreams. Once it had been the nursery where his children slept, and where they had died. He stared at the drab gray walls through his opiate haze, but saw them instead running with blood, saw pools of it on the bare floor all around him. Though no trace of the carnage remained, the memory was torture, and he welcomed sleep to chase the visions though they bled into his dreams and remained when his eyes struggled to open between doses.

It was all too bizarre. Nothing made any sense. Was it the drug or the situation itself? He couldn't be certain. Only one thing was: He had to retrieve the gold and escape the keep with Thea before something happened to her. He didn't know what that something was, only that a physical threat existed. Premonitions were part of his Gypsy heritage. He could feel it—he could smell and taste it in the very air that hung heavy with must and decay and the stench of death throughout the old keep. That, too, was tangible, made more so when Viscount Nathaniel Barrington crossed his threshold several days later.

Ros was seated on the edge of the bed. His fever was gone and his wound was mending. Boon, Cosgrove's valet, had just dressed him, complaining the while about the ill-fitting garments. Now he was alone. When the knock came and the door creaked open, he attempted to rise, but the viscount waved him off with a hand gesture as he stepped inside and closed the door behind him.

"It seems that I am in your debt, sir," the viscount said, extending his hand.

Drumcondra rose, despite having been exempted, and shook. "Your servant, sir," he said, executing a heel-clicking bow, despite the stiff leg. It didn't go over all that well in the wide-top boots. Would he ever become accustomed to nineteenth-century protocols? Did he even want to?

The viscount took a seat on the lounge across the way, and Drumcondra sank back down on the edge of the bed. It would have hurt less to remain standing, but he was too recently out of bed to tax his strength. He needed that in reserve for what he was planning once the house was asleep and in darkness.

"So, sir," said the viscount, slapping his knees. "Might I extract a straight answer from you, then? No one else seems willing. What the devil's going on, Drummond?"

"I'm afraid I do not know what you mean, sir," Ros hedged.

"To the contrary, I think you do. I shall come directly to the point. What is between you and my daughter? I know there is something. A blind man could see it. That Cosgrove has not speaks to the self-centered measure of the gudgeon. If I may digress . . . you do not like the man overmuch, do you?"

Drumcondra hesitated. The viscount seemed amiable enough, but it wouldn't do to relax his guard. His warrior instincts were flagging danger now. That had happened the minute he set foot inside the castle. Now, it was as if all his nerve endings were in tune to extrasensory vibrations he dared not ignore. He had not forgotten that Boon was also Nigel Cosgrove's valet. That had not been accidental. He got to his feet, signaling the viscount toward caution with a finger across his lips, and moved with the stealth of a tiger to the door. As he threw it open, the spindly-legged valet spilled in over the threshold, and the viscount vaulted off the lounge as the man came hurtling into the room.

"Is there something you wanted, Boon?" Drumcondra said.

"Eh . . . no, sir. I do not think so, sir."

"Good. I shan't need you then."

The valet scrambled off, bobbing like a jackrabbit, and Drumcondra motioned the viscount to follow. The two men passed through a small doorway leading to a narrow passage. It connected to an antechamber that had once served as the sleeping quarters of his children's nurse, who had also been slaughtered there.

"We won't be overheard here," he said, leading the way to a recessed settle in the corner beside a vacant hearth.

"Well, well," said the viscount. Whipping out his handkerchief, he dusted off the bench before sitting. "You certainly seem to know your way around the place, don't you, sir. Have you been exploring?"

Drumcondra hesitated. What else could he say but, "Yes, my lord. Old castles are . . . a particular interest of mine."

"Then you should get on royally with my son," said the viscount. "James is an architect, you know—at least he means to be when John Nash is through with him. Brilliant man, Nash. Have you ever met him?"

"No, I cannot say that I have."

"Mmm. Yes, well, we've gotten off the track."

"It was my pleasure to escort your daughter home from her ordeal, my lord," Drumcondra said seamlessly. "I am only glad to have been of service to her in her time of need."

"Yes. Yes, well it ain't her home yet. What happened to the thieves?"

"They ran off. When they saw me coming on with the dagger still in my leg to the hilt, I expect they thought it prudent to do so."

"Forgive me for being blunt, but I never mince words. You have Romany blood by the looks of you."

"Yes, my lord."

"Mmm, what were you doing prowling about Drogheda in such a storm? Do you make your home there, then?"

"I wouldn't call it 'prowling' exactly. I'd come from the north to purchase horses, when the snow delayed me. As luck would have it, I took refuge in the very place that your daughter was being held captive." It was more than half-truth, and he was on the verge of being quite pleased with himself . . . until the viscount spoke again.

"And then you compromised her," the man said.

"I beg your pardon?"

"You were then housed alone together for some time, I believe—were you not? Unchaperoned, that is?"

Drumcondra threw his head back in a mighty guffaw. "I was in no condition to sully your daughter's honor, my lord," he said on the wane of it. "With a four-inch dirk in my thigh."

The viscount grunted. "Well, Thea has been compromised nonetheless."

"Quite properly—before I arrived upon the scene, my lord, and she was for all of that . . . unharmed."

"All right," the viscount said, slapping his knees again. "We've danced about quite long enough, I think. You knew that valet was listening at the door. I believe you expected that he or someone would. Why? And what is your connection here? You and my daughter both must think me a bufflehead to be so easily twigged. I watched you both downstairs when you arrived. What? Do you imagine that I do not know my daughter, sir? I may not know you, but I am well acquainted with her, I can assure you. You may as well have it said. I shan't leave these chambers until you do."

Drumcondra hesitated. The man wasn't going to give up without some sort of explanation, but how much of the truth should he share? Certainly not the truth entire. The man's intractable eyes were boring into him. When he spoke, it was with as much authority as he could muster.

"Will you keep my confidence, sir?" he asked, meeting those eyes so like Thea's. "Lives could well depend upon it—your daughter's among them."

"Intrigue, is it?" the viscount whispered, those violet eyes asparkle now with new light. "Well, out with it man. I shan't breathe a word."

"Are you familiar with the history behind this castle, sir . . . that it was stolen from its rightful owner, Ros

Drumcondra, by the Cosgroves nearly a hundred and twenty years ago?"

"I've heard little else, while awaiting news of my daughter, from that braggart of a son-in-law-to-be of mine."

"Then you know that Ros Drumcondra was a Gypsy warrior, a border clan chieftain who presided over these lands in his own time." The viscount nodded, and Drumcondra went on smoothly. "I, sir, am his descendant."

"Ah-ha!" the viscount cried with a start, and gave another attack upon his knees, this time with his fists. "I knew there was something. So, all this is not exactly a coincidence, eh?"

"Not exactly. At least, not entirely. Beyond that, however, I must ask that you respect my privacy. These do not know it, and it is vital that they do not. There is something here that belongs to me—well, to my clan—that I must retrieve. These are not aware of it. Neither was their ancestor, Cian Cosgrove, but the legend has come down to me through my clan." The viscount clouded, and Ros went on quickly. "Ros Drumcondra's father, Cormac Drumcondra, left his son a legacy. I believe that legacy is still here, and if it is, I mean to have it."

"What sort of legacy, sir?"

"Gold," said Drumcondra. "Now do you see why I have begged your confidence?"

"Gold, you say? How much gold are we talking, sir, and what has my daughter to do with all this?"

"Gypsy gold, my lord," Drumcondra explained. "The fruits of a lifetime. A virtual king's ransom."

"And you imagine such as that would still be here after all this time?" He shook his head and gave a skeptical grunt.

"I do. It is in a place that none will seek it—at least not this superstitious lot."

"And where might that be, Drummond?"

"Before I involve you any further, there is something else that you must know."

"And that is . . . ?"

"In regard to your daughter."

"Continue. . . ."

"I love her, sir."

There was a long silence. "I assumed something of the kind," the viscount said at last. "And what are her feelings toward you?"

"They are the same."

"Though she hasn't said, I had that impression from her also. Why on earth did you bring her back here, then?"

"Because of you for one thing," Ros admitted. "She was loath to cause you distress. The gold, for another. It will secure our future. And . . . for justice."

"You mean to elope, is that it?"

"Something to that effect, yes."

The viscount's eyebrow lifted, and he cleared his voice. "I expect you want my blessing, eh?"

"Not without tribute, sir," Drumcondra said steadily. Involving anyone was the last thing he wanted. Much depended upon his acting as quickly and efficiently as possible. It was not that he didn't trust the man. He didn't need any others in the way of what he was planning. There were too many involved as it was.

"Am I to be bribed then?" the viscount asked.

"Not bribed, sir. I prefer to look upon it as a settlement. I will double anything you hoped to gain from an alliance with the Cosgroves. Will you help us?"

"Not for your tribute," the viscount said, rising. "I see how wrongly I have taken advantage of my daughter. I told myself it was an auspicious match—that it was for her betterment . . . for our *mutual* betterment. On the surface it was. You know, it's odd. I hardly know you, sir, and yet I see truth in you, while I see something more akin to deceit in Nigel Cosgrove."

"I do not carry tales, but when your daughter and I first met, her lips were cruelly bruised. Cosgrove tried to force his attentions upon her, attracting the hawk that took his eye. That hawk belongs to me. Let no harm come to it. It protects her also. I cannot be abroad here now to do that myself. My strategy prevents it. I beg you keep a watchful eye upon her until I am at liberty to do so again."

"Hmmm. Where is this gold that I'm about to help you steal, sir?"

"Exactly where I—that is to say, where Ros Drumcondra hid it. In his father's crypt, sir. In the very coffer that contains his bones."

Ros did not join the others in the dining parlor for dinner. He cried off, opting for a tray in his chamber. If they thought him well enough to leave his rooms, they might just deem him fit enough to make his departure, and that could not occur until he'd recovered the gold. His absence at table, however, did prompt a visit from James after the meal. Once the dinner tray had been removed and the servants dismissed, they repaired to the nurse's chamber behind locked doors, well out of earshot.

"Thea is beside herself with worry," James said, low-voiced, the minute the door latch clicked behind them. "When you didn't come down to dinner, she began imagining all sorts of horrors."

"I am counting upon you to put her mind at ease," Drumcondra said. "I do not want to appear too sound just yet . . . in case our little plan goes awry and we need more time. Besides, the less discourse I have with these the better. I have already nearly slipped up once. That won't bear repeating now."

"I shall do my best, but you do not know Thea. She has it in her head that you have taken a turn for the worse. Once she takes a notion—"

"We haven't much time," Ros interrupted, dismissing the issue. "Your father paid a call upon me earlier. Have you seen him since?"

"Yes," said James. "I only spoke with him briefly, but long enough to be certain he is not convinced our tale rings true."

"Can he be trusted?"

James ground out a guttural chuckle. "It's too late to worry about that now," he said. "You've already taken him into your confidence."

"Only to a point, and only because I had to; I had no choice. The man is keenly perceptive."

"Let us just say you two lovebirds ought not pursue a future in Drury Lane. It's a wonder Cosgrove hasn't seen it—or that harpy of a mother of his."

"If all goes well, I will be away with Thea before dawn."

"Where will we go?"

"Not *we*, Barrington. You will not be going with us. There is bound to be pursuit. I need you here, where you can forestall it if you can until we are away."

"I do not know what I can do in that regard. You will leave a trail in the snow out there."

"If fortune smiles upon us, fresh snow will cover our tracks. There is a halo around the moon. That is a sign."

"What is your plan?"

"I will need my horse brought round behind the castle. There is a service door in the northeast corner by the park. You will know it by a stand of young saplings nearby. Tether him there. Once all have retired, meet me in my rooms. Bring Thea. Have her dress warmly. It will be a long journey, and much distance must be covered before dawn."

"Where will you go?"

"Into the north for a time," said Drumcondra. "Since time out of mind, my people have had allies there. I am hoping it is still so."

"And if it isn't?"

"I will deal with that if it occurs."

"Should I tell Father?"

Drumcondra nodded. "I need his blessing, Barrington."

"I believe you already have it. He's guilt-ridden over nearly shackling Thea to these here. If she hadn't met you, she'd have gone along with it just to please him. It's how things are done in our society. Deuced barbaric, if you ask me."

"Some things are ordained in heaven," Drumcondra said, thinking of the past and all that he had suffered so that he could meet his soul mate. All the blood he kept seeing— awake or asleep—since he entered the castle, a great red sea of it everywhere, was at the root of those thoughts. He could smell it. He could taste it. The castle was sullied with the stench and the stain, albeit invisible to all save himself. No. Repossessing Cashel Drumcondra no longer obsessed him. He never thought he'd live to see this day dawn. But it had, and now his only obsession was leaving it behind forever.

"What then?" James asked, snapping him back to the present.

"We go below," he replied. "There is an underground crypt, one of many rooms that were used as torture chambers in medieval times. The one we seek is hidden behind a false wall—a secret passageway leads to it. I doubt this lot even knows of its existence. My father is buried there. The gold is with him."

"How can you be certain?"

"Because I put it there at his instruction when he died," Drumcondra said. "Another passageway close by leads to the rear service door I spoke of . . . and freedom."

"You make it sound so easy."

"It will be . . . if things go well. And if not, just be certain all in residence are asleep before you come to me. The rope does not exist that can stretch Ros Drumcondra's neck, but I would rather not at this time relish the chance to prove it."

Chapter Nineteen

It was well past midnight when they began to assemble in the nurse's chamber. The minute Thea crossed the threshold she went into Drumcondra's arms.

"Please," she said, "the horse is waiting. Forget the gold. Let us just go away before something prevents it. I have a dreadful feeling about this, my lord. They hang thieves."

"We will need the gold, Thea. I am not stealing anything from this lot. It is mine. They do not even know it exists. Now come, and make no sound."

All was still as they made their way below. The viscount was designated to stand guard, but Thea would not be persuaded to stay with him while James and Ros went into the crypt chamber. She was terrified. Not for herself, but for the outcome of the entire escapade. Nigel had been insufferable since her return. His cold hard stares and veiled innuendoes directed toward Drumcondra were more than she could bear. She was not skilled at deception. She had never needed to employ such a tactic before. It did not sit well with her, and she feared Nigel would see right through her thinly veiled protests that his suspicions were unfounded.

The countess's opinions on the other hand were far from veiled. She made her displeasure known with every toxic breath she drew, until the house literally rang with her displeasure; and yet she still pressed for the union. How that could be when the woman so obviously despised Thea was becoming clearer with every passing hour. She was desperate to settle her son well before he plunged the Cosgroves deeper into scandal.

Two candlebranches lit their way. The viscount carried one; James carried the other. When they reached the end of a narrow stairwell in the very bowels of the castle, Drumcondra motioned the viscount to stay behind, for it was the ideal spot to monitor anyone descending to the lower regions in time to give fair warning. Still, Thea refused to leave Ros's side, and she stood her ground watching him feel the cold stone walls slimed with mildew at the far end of the corridor. When what appeared to be a solid wall began to move, she gasped in spite of herself.

So long in disuse, the mechanism made a bone-chilling rasping sound that echoed, rumbling through the lower regions as the wall moved inward. Drumcondra muttered a string of oaths under his breath as he stepped inside the crypt room.

"We must do this quickly," he said. "That will have been heard above if any of the servants are about. It is the one thing I did not anticipate."

James held the candlebranch high overhead. "It's empty," he said. "Someone must have found your treasure after all, my lord."

Ros made no reply. He went to the far wall, which was constructed of large stone blocks. Where the wall met the ceiling, a border of stone carvings in the shape of lion heads and leaves decorated all four walls of the empty room. Rusted iron rings hung at intervals in the lions' mouths. Drumcondra pulled one, and another groaning, rasping racket echoed through the silence as one of the stone blocks in the wall creaked open revealing a coffin, also hewn of stone.

Thea covered her mouth with both her hands to keep herself from crying out, as Drumcondra pulled the ring again and the casket, resting upon a slab of stone, slowly emerged from the wall.

James set the candlebranch down and helped Ros slide the lid of the coffin to the side. Thea turned away as the skeleton of Cormac Drumcondra came into view, surrounded by bulging sacks tied shut with sinew.

Ros murmured something Thea took to be prayer over the body in a foreign tongue, made a strange sign over the skeleton, and reached for the saddlebags James was carrying. Together, the two men began to fill them, while Thea stared wide-eyed. She didn't want to look at the remains of Cormac Drumcondra, but she couldn't help herself. Judging from the bones, he, too, had been a giant of a man. His grave clothes had been reduced to no more than spiderwebs, and when the skeleton was grazed in removing the sacks, some of the bones fell away. The hollow clacking sound they made, and the awful stench of mildew and dust permeating the air in the confines of the small, close cubicle, threatened to make Thea retch.

They had nearly finished when the sinew gave on one of the sacks James was gathering and the sack hit the floor. Some of the coins spilled out at his feet. Others rolled off into the shadows. James gathered what he could find and had just gotten to his feet when a sound that nearly stopped Thea's heart ripped through the quiet. Her father's voice was echoing along the corridor outside, and it brought them all up short, just as another tug on the ring in Drumcondra's hand engaged the chain that returned the coffin to the wall.

"I heard a noise and came to investigate," the viscount was saying, the words funneling down the hall riding a nervous laugh. "I'm certainly glad to see you, Cosgrove. It seems I've overreached myself and lost my way."

"That was foolhardy," Nigel's agitated voice boomed. "This castle is very old, and strange noises are quite common. I heard it, too. You should not be abroad alone here at this hour. Wait where you are. There is a door beyond. I must be certain it is barred."

James thrust the saddlebag at Ros and sprang toward the door, but Drumcondra seized his arm. "I promised your father a tribute," he whispered. "I will leave it inside Si An Bhru; go as quickly as you can to retrieve it else others find it first. I am in your debt, Barrington."

James didn't answer. He darted out of the crypt, taking the candlebranch with him, and Thea went into her husband's arms holding her breath as they waited in the darkness. The last thing she saw before the light was snuffed out was the gleam of cold steel as Drumcondra drew a dirk from his boot.

"It's nothing, Father," James's voice echoed along the corridor. "There's a door back there but it's bolted shut top and bottom. It must have been the wind we heard. It's blowing a gale out there . . . Oh! I say, Cosgrove! I didn't see you there. We heard a noise, but it must have been the wind."

"The service door is locked, you say?"

"Top and bottom, yes."

"Hmmm. Well, come on, then. You do not belong in this part of the castle. It is falling to ruin from disuse down here. You could do yourselves a mischief."

Thea slumped in Drumcondra's arms and he soothed her gently. She scarcely breathed as their receding footfalls grew more distant, for fear of making a noise that would turn the men back again. They waited what seemed an eternity before Ros let her go and hefted the saddlebags.

"Come," he murmured. "Stay close beside me. The distance to the door is very short. We are soon away."

Thea had no intention of becoming separated from Ros in that pitch black chamber. Clinging to his cloak with pinching fingers, she crowded against him as he inched his way along the wall, feeling for the entrance to the narrow corridor that led to freedom. They soon reached it, and he wrapped the bolts in the edge of his cloak before throwing them open. Muffled thus, they made no sound, and he quickly ushered her out into the windswept darkness only to pull up short.

"What is it?" Thea whispered.

"Where are the young saplings that used to stand here?" he said. "I couldn't have been mistaken. James was supposed to tether the horse among them."

"They are before you," Thea murmured, resisting the urge to laugh. "Oh, my lord," she said through a giggle that leaked out in spite of her resolve. "In a hundred and twenty years, your saplings have become *trees*. See there . . . ? The horse is waiting among them. All is well."

Drumcondra cleared his voice and grunted. He did not wear embarrassment well, and that prompted another chorus of giggles, which Thea wisely suppressed. That she could even laugh in such a situation was a blessing, and she tried to hold the merriment of the moment at least in her heart as he secured the saddlebags on the stallion's back along with the small parcel of Thea's belongings James had secured there earlier. Mounting, he pulled her up alongside him.

It worked to their advantage that the saplings had grown into a forest. It allowed them to travel without leaving telltale hoofprints in the snow. All at once the sound of tether bells tinkling rose above the wail of the wind; then came a triumphant warning screech before the falcon swooped down and alighted upon Drumcondra's broad shoulder. Thea ducked her hooded head against his hard muscled chest as it landed, but she didn't fear it any longer. Its presence had become a comfort.

Drumcondra produced a morsel evidently saved from his evening meal from beneath the folds of his caped cloak and offered it. Thea's breath caught in her throat watching the great bird tilt its head at the one-word command—"*Easy*"—and take the token without touching Drumcondra's fingers. He had neglected nothing in the scheme of their escape, not even the bird. Would she ever understand this enigmatic Gypsy warlord she had married by secret rite?

The copse merged with another, even older pine forest farther east that passed just north of Newgrange. Until then, their tracks had remained concealed inside the edge of the wood; when Drumcondra rode out of the eerie green darkness that had sheltered them and into the open, Thea stiffened in his arms.

"Is it wise to leave the forest?" she asked. "Our tracks will be harder to follow there."

"It cannot be helped," Drumcondra said. "We have your father's blessing, Thea, and I promised him a tribute to replace what he was expecting from the Cosgroves. I told your brother I would leave it inside Si An Bhru, and I must do so."

"Father would not hold you to that in these circumstances," Thea said. "The settlement he means to make on me, whatever you choose to offer against it . . . these things can all be settled later. I beg you, do not stop. I have a feeling . . . I have had since we returned. Please, my lord. Keep the pace. Do not go back to Newgrange!"

As though in contradiction, the bird took flight and, screeching, soared off on a sudden updraft straight for the passage tomb looming before them, tinted blue beneath the stars. It almost looked to Thea as if the bird entered in through the gaping mouth of the cairn, past the three concentric circles that marked the entrance. It was wide enough to ride the horse right inside, though Drumcondra ducked his head low as they did. With no light to see by, he urged the horse straight ahead, where the narrow corridor emptied into the main chamber, depending upon the horse's instincts to find the way.

The bird was nowhere in sight when they entered. The horse complained when he passed too near the large stone basin on the right, and Drumcondra eased Thea down. "I left the tinderbox inside the basin," he said. "The candle is as we left it, on the floor beside it. Light it, while I untie the saddlebag."

Thea groped the basin for the tinderbox, a sigh of relief escaping when her fingers tightened around it. Kneeling, she swept her hands over the cold floor, blind in the pitch blackness for the candle, but her hands closed upon fur instead. They had taken all the fur rugs with them. Had some creature sought shelter in the tomb and fallen asleep there? Cold chills paralyzed her. Her heart leapt in her breast and she screamed at the top of her voice, praying her cries would chase it, but it didn't move. Drumcondra was beside her in seconds. Snatching the tinderbox from her, he worked the flammable bits into a spark that showed him the candle and lit it. Raising Thea to her feet, he took her in his arms, staring down toward what her hands had unearthed. It wasn't an animal after all. He stooped and snatched up something far more threatening. It was her chinchilla fur pelerine.

* * *

James didn't wait for morning to make the trip to Newgrange. There would be too much chaos then, when Thea
and Drumcondra were discovered missing. He set out at
once. Plying old Beadle the stabler with a vulgar bribe to
buy his silence, he had the man saddle him the Andalusian stallion, took up a lantern, and rode out.

It wasn't the lure of gold that put him on his course. He
was half hoping he would find *them* there. He wasn't given
over to the idea of letting them go off on their own. It was
all passing strange, and he meant to get to the bottom of it
before consigning his sister to the warrior's keeping. Besides, how could he help restore Falcon's Lair if he had no
idea where Drumcondra was, or if he'd even made the
purchase?

He rode in the same direction, following their tracks
through the woods. The wind had died to a murmur sighing through the pines. There was no sign of life. Not even
the woodland creatures spoke. It was as if the world stood
still and he was a trespasser in it, reminding him of another time, another place, when Falcon's Lair loomed before him in ruins. The night wasn't particularly cold, now
that the wind had died, but he shuddered remembering. It
all seemed so unreal, and yet he was living proof that it
had actually happened. Somehow, he had traveled
through time.

He hadn't shared that aspect of the situation with his
father. That the viscount was so easily swayed in Drumcondra's favor was no surprise. The old man was a romantic, by God. Nathaniel Barrington was a product of the
times. He knew his duty, and he honored it. His lady wife,
their mother, wanted for nothing while he strayed with his
mistress. James couldn't fault him. It was all very civilized.
It had been an arranged marriage. His long-suffering

mother was mad for Nathaniel, but his father's tastes were of a more elegant nature. Nathaniel and Nigel Cosgrove were about as dissimilar as night was from day: There was no honor, no duty in the man; it was inevitable that they clash. Ros Drumcondra, on the other hand, exuded a magnetism that was larger than life. He followed a Gypsy code that was unbending—like nothing either Barrington had ever seen. It transcended time. Oddly, the warrior did not seem to belong to past or present.

James shook those opinions free as he neared the entrance to Newgrange. So lost in thought, he'd nearly passed it by. The Gypsy horse's hoofprints were clearly visible going in, but there were none exiting the passage tomb. His spirits lifted. They were still here. He hadn't missed them as he'd feared. Climbing down before the entrance, he tethered the horse to a clump of bracken, took the lantern and entered the tomb. It only took a moment. Drumcondra had left the saddlebag in the large stone basin. He called out, but his voice reverberated through the empty tomb, sounding back in his ears, and then silence.

Could he have been mistaken? He turned to go, intending to have another look at the tracks in the snow, but soft sobs echoing from one of the side chambers arrested him. Holding the lantern high, he followed the sound. Thea lay crumpled on the chamber floor, dissolved in tears. At sight of him she groaned, scrambled to her feet, and went into his arms.

"Thea?" he cried. "What's happened? Where is Drumcondra?"

"Gone," she sobbed. "He's gone back, James. I've lost him."

Chapter Twenty

"What do you mean, he's gone?" James was saying. Thea scarcely heard. It was as though his voice, the voice that had always been a comfort, was coming from an echo chamber. Her brother was kneeling on the cold floor beside her, and yet there seemed a barrier between them, as though she weren't really there, as though she were caught halfway between time . . . not really anywhere. She was terrified.

The lantern he held up while he examined her gave off no more light than a firefly in the bowels of a bottomless cavern. The golden nimbus issuing from it seemed fractured, as though she viewed it through a spider web. She couldn't feel the heat it generated so close on her face, or even the cold all around her. Was it shock or . . . something else?

"I don't know," she sobbed. "We entered to leave the gold. It was so dark. No light filtered in past the bend in the corridor. I remember crawling about on the floor, feeling for the candle. I didn't find it. I found my chinchilla pelerine instead."

"Your pelerine, you say? I don't understand."

"There is so much you do not know, James," she said. "So much I haven't told you of my time among Drumcondra's clan."

"I think it's best we remedy that, but not here. Come."

Thea resisted. "No, wait!" she cried. "I feel so strange. Something is wrong, James. I fear to stay, but I fear to leave here also."

"Very well," he soothed, "but have it said quickly. I am not liking this. I have never seen you in such a taking. Just look at you. You're trembling. You shall surely take pneumonia. Where is the pelerine?" He glanced about, holding the lantern high.

"That's just it," she wailed. "It isn't here now. It's gone."

"He took it with him—what, Thea? You aren't making any sense."

"Sense? There is no sense. Don't you understand? I have lost him, James. He is gone . . . and I do not know how to have him back!"

"All right," her brother soothed, wrapping a strong arm around her. "The pelerine. Let us begin with that since it seems to have so overset you."

"When I first passed through the corridor and found myself in Drumcondra's time, there was a girl, a Gypsy girl who had been his mistress. Her name was Drina. She stole my pelerine. Drumcondra took it back from her and returned it to me. But she was obsessed with it, and just before we all fled Falcon's Lair, she stole it from me again. I didn't bring it back with me, James. It existed in 1695 once I returned—until I found it on this chamber floor not an hour ago . . . at least, I think it was an hour ago. I don't know. Time seems so irrelevant somehow."

"Go on," James forced. Poor James, how all this must be taxing his logical mind. His expression alone was a picture of confusion.

"Ros picked up the pelerine, slung it over his shoulder, and mounted his horse. Then he reached for me, intending to wrap me in it once I'd climbed up also. But James, when I reached out for him to take me in his arms, mine closed around empty air. He was suddenly gone—horse, pelerine and all—he was just . . . gone."

"Back to his own time, you mean?"

"It must be," she said. "I do not pretend to understand, but I think that pelerine was a trap. He never should have touched it. She has taken him back, James. I shall never see him again."

"Perhaps it is for the best," he said, his words riding a sigh. "I know it isn't what you want to hear, love, but in time I think you'll come to realize it the only practical solution. Maybe deep down he knew it himself."

"How can you say that?" she cried. "We are *wed*, James."

"That ridiculous pagan ritual?" He scoffed. "No civilized culture would recognize such a union, and you know it, Thea. He didn't belong here, and you certainly didn't belong in his world."

"But we do belong together, James. You will never convince me otherwise."

James surged to his feet and reached to pull her up alongside. "We cannot stay here, Thea," he said. "It will be light soon. We have to go back to Cashel Cosgrove before we are missed. We can sort all this out there. It will be all right, you'll see." He began leading her then. "Father won't hold you to the engagement. He knows your mind in the matter, and he is quite put off by Nigel all the way round after suffering him and that mother of his under the same roof for a sennight."

They had nearly reached the opening. Thea's head was swimming. She hadn't shaken the odd detached feeling that had overwhelmed her since Drumcondra disappeared. The last place she wanted to go was back to Cashel Cosgrove. He hadn't meant to leave her; why couldn't James see that? Drumcondra loved her; she knew he did. She had felt his love when he held her, when he kissed her, when his sex came to life inside her, respecting her innocence but at the same time fulfilling them both, awakening her to pleasures beyond her wildest imaginings. He was reaching for her when he disappeared, and she had been nearly driven mad since by trying to find the corridor; but the portal was closed to her. Her heart was breaking.

A cold blast of air funneling through the entrance almost snatched her breath away. James had a firm hold upon her arm, and he was leading her toward the waiting mount. Relaxing his grip, he stooped to reach for the saddlebag, and she dug in her heels.

"No!" she cried. "I won't go back. I cannot. It does not matter that Father won't press for the union with Nigel. He will take me home to England, to Cornwall. I will never find Drumcondra there. He will never be able to find me. *No!*"

With a mighty shove, and designs upon a head start, she caught her brother off balance as he hefted the heavy saddlebag, and he careened into the stone basin. Lifting her skirt, for it dragged on the floor, she ran through the opening, leapt astride the waiting horse, and galloped off into the star-studded night.

James's shouts rode the wind behind. They stabbed her like knives. His fury was unmistakable, but it couldn't be helped. She was sorry for shoving him; she'd heard him curse when he struck the stone basin, but there was nothing for it. He would never have let her go otherwise. She was so light-headed from the strange happenings in the passage tomb that she would never have escaped him without an advantage. That shove had given it to her, and now she rode like the wind toward Drogheda in search of the corridor there.

Drina must have found the one at Newgrange for the pelerine to have been there. A sinking feeling in the pit of her stomach told her she should have stayed, but how could she have? It would be the first place they would look for her now. Drogheda was not that far distant, and the corridors between the passage tomb and Falcon's Lair were linked, after all. She would just have to make the best of it. She *would* find him. She had to; he had taken her heart with him.

She would be going back to his time after the carnage, if she could go back at all. There was no way of knowing what she would find there. Drina had evidently escaped the Cosgrove's attack. If only Jeta had escaped it as well, she would help. Hadn't she come to her at the very beginning? History told nothing of the aftermath of the onslaught, only that it was then that Ros Drumcondra disappeared. While she rode, Thea prayed that this was not the disappearance behind those recorded words.

According to the legend, she had disappeared as well, if she were to equate herself to Cian Cosgrove's betrothed in the past. What else could it mean? There was no other betrothed. Cold chills riddled her spine until the bones snapped, as another thought surfaced. If any did escape the carnage at Falcon's Lair, they fled to Newgrange, where their bones were eventually found. Was that how the pelerine got there? Dear God, was she going the wrong way—straight into the stars alone knew what sort of danger awaiting her at Falcon's Lair?

First light broke quick with fugitive mists that reminded

her of her home in Cornwall. Drifting over the land, they seemed to pick and choose the hollows where they wished to settle. One valley appeared draped with ghostly veils, while the next lay untouched. The first gray streamers of that cheerless dawn crept westward from the quay outlining the wounded shape of Falcon's Lair silhouetted black in the distance. Thea's hopes raised and sank again in the space of a heartbeat. It would be in ruins after the devastation. Was she still in her own time? There was no way to tell at this distance. Until that moment, she had been alone. She hadn't seen a soul since she left Newgrange, not even a woodland creature prowling the snow for food, or a bird in the sky. All at once two riders appeared coming on at great speed from opposite directions. Her heart leapt. A gasp squeaked past her dry throat trying to make them out. One was approaching from behind, out of the west, his caped greatcoat spread on the wind of his motion, for there wasn't a breath of a breeze stirring. The other was charging toward her from the east, with Falcon's Lair at his back, his fur mantle scarcely moving as he galloped out of the mist. His horse's heavy hooves gouged clumps from the snow-covered ground—flinging them into the air sullied with bits of the earth beneath. Her heart fairly leapt from her breast. Could it be Drumcondra? Had she found him after all?

Thea's eyes flew between the two horsemen. The thunder of their approach shook the ground. All at once, as the morning mist lifted, the screech of a falcon soaring overhead drew her eyes. It was too high aloft for her to hear the tinkling of its tether bells, but she knew it was Isor circling above, and she gasped again looking back to the riders. Both were gaining on her, and she tugged on the reins, pulling the horse up short. It wheeled and danced, carving circles in the snow as her eyes snapped back and forth between them and the bird now as well. Would it lead her?

"Which way?" she cried aloud as both men rode out of the milling mist and presented a clear image. She screamed again, scarcely able to believe her eyes. The horseman coming on at a deadly gallop from the west she recognized as Nigel, astride his favorite gelding. She could see him clearly now. But the rider bearing down upon her from the east wasn't Drumcondra at all. *Both* men were wearing ugly black eye patches. The second was Cian Cosgrove.

It was a choice Thea couldn't make—wouldn't make. Screaming at the top of her voice, she dug her heels into the horse's sides, leaned low over its sleek neck and drove the animal hard at a gallop northward, away from both. Overhead, the great bird's screeches died off on the wind. She couldn't see it now, but then she wasn't looking for it, nor was she looking behind. The sleek Andalusian underneath her was swifter than Nigel's gelding or Cian Cosgrove's heavy, feather-footed warhorse. Blind to everything except what lay directly ahead, and deaf to the sound of any hoofbeats but those of her own fleet-footed mount, she failed to hear the whirring sound stirring the air close by until the net encased her. It struck her hard and stung, knocking the wind out of her lungs, as strong hands pulled her off the Andalusian's back into stronger arms. The horse galloped on at a greater speed, with her weight suddenly lifted, its frenzied cries trailing off on the wind.

Thea screamed at the top of her voice as the horseman tightened the net around her squirming body. Looking through the wide rope mesh that contained her, she glimpsed the hills behind, but there was no sign of Nigel now. There wouldn't be. She had passed through the corridor. She was in the arms of Cian Cosgrove, and they were heading straight for Falcon's Lair. The only constant on either side of that mysterious passageway that bridged time was the great falcon. Still, it soared above her. Why did its presence hold no comfort for her now?

"Why do you struggle?" Cosgrove asked, close in her ear. His voice was harsh—just as she remembered it from the night she'd first heard it astride another, grander, feather-footed stallion in Ros Drumcondra's arms. Tears welled in her eyes. The wind did not whip them there. She hadn't made this choice; fate had made it for her, and she was terrified. She was running from them both, and now she was where she'd set out to be, but in the arms of the wrong man. "You cost me dear enough, madam," he spat, giving the net a rough jerk. "Half my army lies dead in the snow on your account, and I do not even know your name. For your sake, I hope you're worth the price."

Thea didn't respond except to grunt and struggle with the impossible net he'd thrown over her. It was scratchy and hard, and smelled of tar. The mesh was large enough for her tiny fists to fit through, and she used them, beating him about the chest and shoulders until she'd scraped them raw on the rough hemp.

"Put me down!" she gritted out. "Let me go!"

"I think not, madam," he said. "I've waited too long for you." He shook her. "Stop that! It won't buy you free. You're mine now, what's left of you. Did he keep his promise? Has he had you, with his bloody *prima nocte*, the black-hearted Gypsy bastard?"

"Drumcondra and I are wed!" she hurled at him. "Now, let me go!"

"Wed, is it? Ha! That won't save you, madam. It only makes my job easier. I won't have to break you in then, will I? Not after he's rutted you. I had his first wife, too. You may as well stop struggling. I paid good Irish gold to have you carted here from England as a token of good will. I mean to get my coin's worth."

Real fear gripped Thea now—fear that could be tasted, cold and metallic, like blood building at the back of her throat. They had nearly reached Falcon's Lair. In close proximity now, she saw the devastation as it was in Drumcondra's time—smelled the slag and char and stench of burnt flesh. It rose in her throat with the deathlike taste of her fear, and the unwashed odor of her captor. Bending over, she could not help but retch.

Cosgrove laughed. It was a bone-chilling sound. "Not exactly perfume from the London shops, eh?" he said. "You'll get used to it. We'll be here awhile before we head back to my keep with what spoils my men can carry—long enough for us to get to know each other . . . in the Biblical sense, that is." Thea shuddered, and he threw back his head in a mighty guffaw. "Oh, aye, we will," he said.

"You are naught but an animal to have done such as this," said Thea. The passage of time had softened the devastation. It was a horrible sight now, having just occurred.

"Ahhh, but I did *not*," he said. "You've Drumcondra's Gypsy whore to thank for it. I only came on after to avenge *this*." He tugged at his eye patch. "And you. He put up a good fight, did Drumcondra, but as you can see, I have taken this keep from him as well. A pity he was so . . . distracted. Was that because of you or that whore of his, eh?"

"I don't know what you're talking about!"

"Drina, his Gypsy whore set the fire. I only cleaned up after it," he said. "The jealous bitch thought to burn the both of you in your bed, but you weren't in that bed, were you? She paid with her life in that blaze."

"Drina is *dead*?" Thea breathed. How could that be? How, when it was the pelerine that had taken Drumcondra from the present? "Where is Ros?" she demanded. "What have you done with him?"

"He tried to save his ragtag band, and failed," said Cosgrove. "My army was too great for him. It has always been thus."

"Where is he? What have you done with him?"

"Done with him?" Cosgrove asked. "Why, I have killed him, madam. Ros Drumcondra is dead."

Chapter Twenty-one

When would her death come? When would she disappear as Drumcondra had done—as history had set it down? These were the morbid thoughts overwhelming Thea then, as she sat grieving for Ros, locked in yet another chamber in the remains of Falcon's Lair. *Drumcondra is dead.* She could scarcely believe it. Had all her efforts to save him from death in the fire been for naught? Had he only returned to meet his inevitable fate in spite of those efforts? Perhaps she hadn't changed history after all. Perhaps it couldn't be changed. Perhaps it was his time to die. But what of her if that were so? Why was she still living? Her head ached for those thoughts banging around in her brain. She was exhausted, and they gave her no peace. She dared not sleep in any case. Cian Cosgrove had locked her in one of the chambers off the gallery over the kitchens that the fire hadn't reached, and left her there. It was only a matter of time before he returned, and she was terrified.

The chamber cell was one she had never seen. It was

smaller than Drumcondra's chamber, and was likewise sparely furnished, boasting an elevated bed, a boot chair, and a small drum table. The floor was bare, the hearth unlit. Thea was freezing, but she would not light it. She would in no way cater to Cosgrove's comfort in her husband's house—even if it meant sacrificing her own. Instead, she dragged a fur throw off the bed and wrapped herself in it over her woolen cloak. He would not find her waiting in that bed when he returned. She curled instead in the stiff-backed boot chair. At least its rigid antiquity would keep her from falling asleep. Only one goal drove her then—escape. She would not become Cian Cosgrove's love slave. She'd sooner be dead.

How she wished she had wings like the great bird and could take flight. She shut her eyes and imagined herself sailing on the wind high above the wounded battlements. She saw herself dipping and gliding, borne upon an updraft . . . free. She hadn't seen the bird since she drove the Andalusian north to flee both pursuers. She almost laughed. She actually missed the creature. What she wouldn't give to see it now.

Dragging herself to her feet, she tugged the fur rug close about her and went to the window. Every sinew in her body ached from the rough handling of her capture. Squinting through the dingy glass, she searched what scant scrap of land and sky she could see for some sign of the bird. There was none. The sky was gray with the threat of snow, and empty of life, which in itself seemed odd, since birds always gathered inland before a storm— especially sea birds, and Falcon's Lair was close to the sea.

Had the falcon extracted its revenge? Had it deliberately led her to this end, captive of a barbaric border lord who seemed more medieval in his thinking and methods than a seventeenth-century Irish chieftain? She was loath to believe it. But even if it were true, she longed to see it again, his familiar, because it was her only link to him.

When the door opened at her back, the glass rattled in its casings. Only then did she feel the puff of cold air coming through. The glass was cracked in two places, hanging by a thread. One sliver had already fallen to the floor. A stiff wind would likely dislodge the rest. Could it have burst from the heat of the fire? A pity the chamber wasn't on the main floor of the keep instead of two towering stories high. The window frame was wide enough that she might have crawled through it if that had been the case.

Thea spun to face Cian Cosgrove as he entered bearing a crock, and a basin heaped with fruit and cheese. He slapped the burden down on the drum table, and faced her, arms akimbo. He was not the giant Drumcondra was, though he was taller than she remembered of her first glimpse of him in the courtyard at Cashel Cosgrove. Then she had viewed him at a higher vantage, however, from the back of Drumcondra's Gypsy stallion. He was fair, his hair the color of summer wheat and did not quite reach his shoulders. His eyes were smoky blue, tucked well beneath the ledge of his sun-bleached brows. But for the scar the falcon's beak and talons had left behind that ran the length of his face from eye patch to chin, he might have been considered attractive. His resemblance to Nigel was even more uncanny at close range. She gasped in spite of herself, taking his measure.

"So," he said. "Our wedding night has come at last."

"There has been no wedding," she snapped. "I see no priest."

"I am no papist."

"Vicar, then," she served.

"And where did Drumcondra find a priest?" he asked. "Or did he marry you by Gypsy rite as I supposed, the heathen?"

Thea didn't answer. He had begun to circle her, raking her familiarly with his cold-eyed stare. Despite all her layers of clothing, she felt naked under his gaze.

"How did you kill him?" she asked, backing away as he began to close the circle. Though she dreaded to know, she had to hear.

"Easily," he pronounced.

"I want to know how he died." She persisted. "You owe me that."

"*Owe*, is it? A curious word. I owe you nothing, but I will tell. The tale will be told by the fires and in the camps of men long after you and I have turned to dust, madam."

No, it shan't, Thea wanted to say. *I have heard the history of Ros Drumcondra, and no such tale glorifying Cian Cosgrove was ever recorded*. This, however, was not the time to share that news, and when she spoke it was to take a different tack.

"So, what harm to tell it, then?" she said, as calmly as she could manage, considering that he had come so close she could smell the unwashed odor of him drifting from his dingy, soot-stained clothes and skin.

He shrugged. "None," he agreed, folding his arms across his broad chest. "He brought it upon himself. He had come to my keep with some of his Gypsy minions to see if I had given in to his ridiculous demands. I knew he would, and I was ready for him."

How well Thea remembered the night she left James behind and fled Falcon's Lair in search of Drumcondra, to lure him into the corridor and save him from the fire. Cold chills gripped her hearing that event recounted from Cosgrove's lips.

"My soldiers by far outnumbered the scraggly few he'd brought along, and he retreated. It would have ended then, because he could not win against us, but then you appeared. At first I thought you were escaping Falcon's Lair—returning to me—but I see now that it was quite something . . . else. We will come back to that. Drumcondra broke ranks and followed you. The others scattered, and in the confusion you and Drumcondra escaped us heading north. So you see I knew he was not at Falcon's Lair when we reached it. That is why we came on instead of turning back when his band dispersed, to take the keep in his absence like we did before. The place was already ablaze when we reached it; the whore who set the fire plunged from the battlements in flames before our very eyes. We heard the tale from those who lived long enough to tell it afterward."

"None of you tried to find him?" said Thea. "Strange. I would have thought it the first thing you would do, considering your bloodlust for the man."

Cosgrove shrugged again. "Not really," he said. "Life was much more interesting while he lived to spar with me. I wasn't out for his blood. Drumcondra and I are old adversaries, madam. Our feud is rooted in the mists of time—"

"What started it?" Thea interrupted. She had always been curious about that.

Again he shrugged. "A woman, what else, eh?"

"If, as you say, you did not want to kill him, why did you?"

"He gave me no choice."

"G-go on . . ."

"Taking Falcon's Lair was not difficult. The few remaining lackeys and sentries and pitiful excuses for fighting men that did not meet us in battle fled without their leader to marshal them. He should have never returned, but he did. He rounded up and regrouped his men, and marched on us here. You were not with him, madam. Where did he have you?"

"At Si An Bhru," she flung at him, her whole body loosing the words, "Where you would not come because you fear its magic."

He growled. "Take no comfort in my supposed fear of *anything*," he said. "I know it not. Cian Cosgrove fears neither man on earth nor devil in hell."

"You have not told me how you killed him."

"You will not like hearing it."

"I need to know."

He studied her quizzically for a moment. "Why?" he asked at last, his tone suspicious.

"To . . . to put it all behind me." She faltered. "I have no body to bury, sir—not even that. The least you, his murderer, can do, is tell me why and how you killed him. I should think such would appeal to your bloodthirsty nature."

"You will have—a body to bury, that is—once the snow melts," he said. "He died by my sword. I ran him through in defense of my life. The snow ran red with his blood. A new storm covered his remains, just as it did many others. You will find them littering the land where they fell, come spring."

Thea gulped down tears. She would not give him the satisfaction. There was a sense of smug pride in his delivery; he would have no reason to lie. Inside, it was as if her heart were bleeding. She was devastated to think that Ros lay below within her reach, but too late. How could she bear it?

Cian seized the fur rug wrapped around her, and she tightened her grip upon it.

"Come, come," he said. "Your modesty does not suit. I have already seen what lies beneath all those layers. You have your 'husband' to thank for that. He made it a point to show it me, if you recall."

"That does not signify," she said haughtily, yanking the fur rug out of his hand. "I did not give myself to him until we were wed. What makes you think I would give myself to the likes of you without benefit of clergy?"

"I could easily take you, madam."

"You could," she replied. "But if you did it would be the last, because if I could not kill you, I would kill myself. My life means nothing without Ros Drumcondra. You will not demean me. I may not bear a title, sir, but I am still a lady, and I will not heel to rape."

"You will 'heel' to whatever happens to be my pleasure, madam," he said, gravel-voiced. The muscles along his angular jaw line had begun to tick, and his nostrils flared. "You needn't fear that I will trouble you overmuch. I have whores aplenty to service me. But our union will make legitimate heirs, and you will suffer it. That is why our marriage was arranged."

"Take me now, and your 'legitimate heir' may be Drumcondra's issue," she sallied. It came to her in a flash, and not a minute too soon, judging from his leering expression.

"Eh?" he grunted, bearing down upon her with shuttered eyes.

"I have had no courses since I last shared Drumcondra's bed," she said, backing away from the look in his smoky blue eyes. "If you would be sure of an heir, you had best curb your urges until I am past my next monthly flow."

"You speak strange words," he said. "Do all Englishers speak thus?"

"What would you prefer, 'until I have come again in season'? You understand my meaning, sir. You must wait . . . or you might never know whose son I bear. Unless, of course, it does not matter to you? It does not matter to me, you understand. I would welcome raising Drumcondra's son no matter who thought he was his father."

"If you bear his child, madam, I will kill it!" Cosgrove seethed.

"Then you see how important it is that we wait."

Cosgrove stared long and hard at her, his broad chest heaving. His rage was palpable, and though she had clearly gone too far, and never before felt such fear in the presence of any man, Thea held her head high in its presence.

The warrior began to pace, taking ragged strides the length of the cell, his hands balled into white-knuckled fists braced on his hips. It was almost longer than she could bear before he stopped and turned to face her. When he spoke, his words were spat forth with an edge.

"All right, madam," he said. "We shall have it your way, but it comes at a price. You shall have your reprieve . . . until we are certain. But then—oh, *then*, I promise you, you will wish you never gave your virtue to the likes of Ros Drumcondra!"

Stomping toward the door, he paused beside the drum table and swept it clean of basin, cheese and fruit, smashing the crock to shards on the cold stone floor. The nut-sweet brew it held bled toward Thea in a ragged, froth-edged circle, but she held her ground, standing tall, with the bearing of a queen, wrapped in the fur blanket.

Cosgrove cast daggers at her with his cold eyes, and then, without a backward glance, he crashed through the door and slammed it shut with force enough to set it off its hinges. Thea held her breath until she heard the key turn in the lock, and it wasn't until she heard his angry footfalls recede along the corridor that she flung herself across the bed and sobbed herself to sleep.

Chapter Twenty-two

If things went well, Thea would have at least a sennight's reprieve before Cian Cosgrove made any attempt to bed her, but that did not exempt her from his presence. Though he would not let her out, he haunted her chamber, brought her food—even lit the fire in her hearth, and had a bathing tub delivered to the cell from one of the other chambers. It was set before the hearth. A kettle filled with water was suspended on a tripod over the burning logs, and buckets of cold water were set about. Thea eyed it longingly, but days passed before she succumbed to the temptation of stripping off her clothes and submitting her tired body to the soothing water. It wouldn't even have happened then, if she hadn't heard Cian Cosgrove's loud shouts ordering lackeys about in the courtyard below and seen him ride out over the drawbridge just as the sun set. Hopeful that he had gone off to visit one of his whores, she tipped the hot water into the tub, tempered it with cold from the buckets, wriggled out of her clothes and climbed into the tub.

Thea groaned as she sank into the water. The warmth radiating from the hearth fire chased the draft leaking through the broken glass rattling in the window. She leaned her head back against the cold metal and closed her eyes, but she couldn't enjoy it. Her thoughts were too dark and frightening to let her relax. If only she hadn't been separated from Drumcondra in the passage tomb, if only she had come back with him his death might have been prevented. He had begged to go back once he realized they had come through the corridor into her time. That deuced corridor! It was a dangerous vehicle. There was no rhyme or reason to it, at least not one that she could make out. At first she thought her passage through it was to bring them together—two soul mates separated by time, united by a love that transcended it. It was a most agreeable fiction that had sustained her . . . until now. Drumcondra's death had cancelled that philosophy. All that remained was to discover the circumstances behind her disappearance as legend recorded it.

When the door came open in Cosgrove's hand, Thea gave such a lurch, water spilled over the side of the tub and splashed on the floor, just missing the fur rug she'd dropped there. He was staggering drunk as he lumbered close.

"You are easily flummoxed, m'dear," he said in a drunken titter. "I knew once you saw me ride off, you would take advantage of my little gift."

"You are castaway, sir!" she cried, eyeing the door he'd left flung wide behind him in his drunken haze. "How dare you compromise me in this way!" Drawing her knees up in the tub, she crossed her arms over her breasts. "We struck a bargain. Drunk or sober, I mean to hold you to it."

"Yes, well, I tire of the bargain, madam," he drawled, reeling closer. "Besides, there are other ways of pleasuring a man than those which result in getting offspring. It is time we explored some of those, hmm?" He dangled his hand over the edge of the tub and began stirring the water with his finger.

"Explore to your heart's content upon your whores, sir," she sallied. "I see no clergy here."

"You mean to hold me to that, too, do you?" he said, slapping the water. Droplets stung her face, and she blinked the water out of her eyes and tossed her dark curls, a soft outcry escaping her at the suddenness of the motion. "You marry that Gypsy bastard with a mere word, yet you demand a vicar sanctify our union." he went on, slapping the water again. "You were never meant for Ros Drumcondra. You were meant for me! The blackguard stole you from me."

"I cannot help that, sir. I had nothing to say in the matter. The fact still remains that we were properly wed, and if you wish the same privilege, you shall have it via the clergy. How else will your issue be legitimate?"

"*Properly wed*," he said, his face twisted in a drunken snarl. How ugly he was thus, with his scars puckering his cheek and drawing the corner of his mouth down. He looked like a rabid animal crouching over the tub. "What? You spoke some Gypsy gibberish and you call that properly wed?"

"Our vows were binding."

"Good! Say the same with me, and let us end this game of cat and mouse forthwith."

"You are not a Gypsy. That rite between us would be invalid, sir. Now, if you please, I beg you leave me in peace to finish my toilette, which you have so kindly provided."

"Enough!" he thundered. Reaching into the tub, he

hauled her to her feet, feasting upon the sight of her naked, dripping water in the firelight, despite her efforts to preserve modesty.

Thea screamed at the top of her voice as he lifted her out of the tub, tossed her down upon the bed, and dropped down beside her. He was aroused, the bulk of his manhood leaning against her thigh. Capturing both her wrists in one hand, he raised her arms above her head and explored her body with the other.

Thea screamed again, and he wrenched her closer still. "Scream all you will," he said. "No one will come to your aid. The only ally you had hereabouts brave enough to do that was Drumcondra's bitch of a mother. I killed her too—oh, aye, I killed them both—and I could just as easily kill you . . . but not before I've had my fill of you. So do not struggle if you want to keep any part of that bargain. Struggling only stimulates me. And if you think the few tankards I've drunk will spare you, dream on. One way or the other, you will relieve me, madam."

Nigel's words on Cian's lips covered Thea with gooseflesh.

His breath was coming short. Between vulgar moans he groped and pinched and pawed at her, and more screams rasped through her dry throat. All at once there was another scream so loud it nearly stopped her heart, and the great bird crashed through the cracked windowpane, talons first, shattering the glass, its wings beating the shards out of the way as it entered the room. Thea glimpsed a flash of onyx tinged with red in the firelight, as its eye sought and found its target and attacked in a flapping screeching frenzy, its talons firmly planting in Cosgrove's shaggy hair.

The bird's piercing screams at such close range vibrated in Thea's ears until they rang with the deafening din. Cosgrove let her go and staggered to his feet, battling with the bird whose sharp beak continued to pluck relentlessly at his scalp, beating a tattoo that drew blood. Free of her captor's crude embrace, Thea scrambled off the bed on the far side, rolling herself in the fur rug beneath her and crouching on the floor, her eyes wide in disbelief as she watched the struggle.

If Cosgrove had been sober, he would have rent the bird in two in his hammish hands. As it was, the minute he got a grip on the creature, groping blind in his stupor, its sharp beak canceled it. His hands and wrists were running with blood, his curses ringing from the rafters. Then, all at once, the falcon let go and soared above, circling in triumph as the warrior swung at it crazily.

Time was a monster that bore no reckoning. What seemed like an eternity occurred in mere seconds. At first, Thea was certain the bird would leave as it had come, through the window. To her surprise, it seemed to gloat, taunting Cosgrove, flying in circles just out of reach as he stumbled after it, arms flailing in the stale musty air. Thea watched in rapt amazement as Cosgrove spun, heaving and grunting, reeling dizzily in circles. He snatched up one of the fur rugs on the bed and began swiping at the bird with that, but still it eluded him.

Thea grabbed her gray muslin frock and cloak from the floor where she'd discarded them earlier, dressed herself, and tugged on her ankle boots. As bizarre as it seemed, the bird appeared to be luring Cosgrove toward the open door. The dizzying effects of strong spirits and the exercise combating the falcon had evidently overcome him. He had only one mission then, defeating the bird—Drumcondra's bird, the bird that had blinded him. It had his full and fierce attention. He seemed to have forgotten Thea altogether, and when the creature soared through the door he staggered after it, a fresh spate of blue expletives pouring from his lips.

Thea jumped to her feet and ran to the door. The bird's flapping wings created a cold draft funneling along the corridor, which attacked her moist skin, still damp from the bath, and made her shudder. She stood for a moment, watching the falcon soar back and forth at the end of the gallery, taunting the warrior toward the balustrade, enticing him to reach over the edge as he continued to swipe at it with the fur rug. All at once the bird's black eyes flashed toward her from the dusty haze at the other end of that narrow corridor. If ever a bird could speak, this one did now. Those piercing eyes said *run*, and Thea slipped into the hallway while Cosgrove was occupied, and melted into the shadows along the darkened east wing.

A chorus of bloodcurdling screeches from the falcon, coupled with Cosgrove's drunken outcry as he toppled over the balustrade railing, waging his attack upon the bird, spurred her on. Judging from his shouts from below, bringing others to the scene, the fall hadn't killed him. It had, she was confident, made an end to his amorous advances for a time. Bested by the bird and embarrassed before his men, Cosgrove's main priority would be his vanity. The commotion gave her just what she needed: time to escape. And with the bird's triumphant screams grown distant, she hurried down the back stairs to a narrow hallway that led to the kitchens, and stole along until she reached an alcove under the stairs. Hidden there, she watched Cosgrove's men stream along the corridor from the servants' area to where the warrior had fallen in the great hall. She held her breath as more came to his rescue, responding to his surly drunken commands.

Awaiting her chance to flee, she lingered there until it was safe enough to assume most in residence had gone to Cosgrove's aid. Then, with his bluster ringing in her ears, Thea crept along the narrow hallway to a rear servant's

door, and rushed out into the cold night air. Overhead, the
winter moon was nearly full. No one was posted at the
drawbridge. Every available man had gone to Cosgrove's as-
sistance. Thea glanced about. The way was clear. Scarcely
breathing, she hitched up her skirts and fled.

Wagons had come and gone during the day, leaving
tracks in the snow. Keeping well within those, Thea ran
on until she reached the wood, a close eye skyward in
search of the bird that had set her free. Had Drumcondra
reached from beyond the grave and sent his familiar to
save her? Whether he had or he hadn't, that was exactly
what had just occurred. With hope in her heart that the
falcon would not desert her, she continued traveling west,
picking her way from tree to tree at the edge of the grove.
The river gurgling in the distance somehow was a comfort.
She wasn't alone. Nature welcomed her then. Woodland
creatures ventured near, watching. Rabbits hopped from
their warrens, then a fox, and in the distance, the antlers
of a roe deer were visible in the moonlight at the edge of
the clearing. She thought of James, and of his expecta-
tions of bagging deer in the Meath hills, like the friend
he'd boasted of. There would be no hunting parties now.
Was she going mad? This was the least of her worries. She
was going to *die* here, to disappear from the pages of
recorded history just as Drumcondra had. She would never
see James again, or her father, her mother—anyone from
her time, come to that.

Thea glanced behind. None were in pursuit, and she
filled her lungs with the cold night air in relief, but she did
not slow her pace. Soon enough Cosgrove's men would
discover her missing and swarm over the valley. She dared
not stop to rest.

It wasn't until she reached the hillock the forest
bearded that her gaze swept the land between the clearing

and Falcon's Lair, and what had been the battlefield. The moonlight showed it clearly. It wasn't her imagination; the irregular shapes of what could only be the bodies of fallen warriors barely concealed beneath the snow littered the hills. What showed them to her were the hulking mounds that barely concealed the warrior's likewise fallen horses. Was Cabochon among them? Her heart sank, and tears welled in her eyes. Somewhere under that white blanket Ros Drumcondra lay dead, run through by Cian Cosgrove's sword. It hadn't really impacted her until now, seeing the sight with her own eyes, and she sobbed aloud despite the danger of attracting any of Cosgrove's men who might be keeping watch. What it did attract was a welcome sight. Above her the great bird appeared, its tether bells tinkling musically as it left the uppermost branches of an ancestral pine where it had been perching. Gliding low, it left the wood and circled the nearby hills. A last goodbye to its master? It seemed so to Thea, who was looking on through her tears.

The display was short-lived. One last pass over the land, and the bird soared back to the edge of the wood where Thea crouched watching. Dipping low, it loosed a melancholy screech that nearly stopped her heart. Was it an invitation to follow? Would it lead her away from danger, or straight to her doom? She had no choice but to trust it. Hadn't it just abetted her escape?

Her mind was made up in a heartbeat. There really wasn't a choice. Neither knowing nor caring where it would lead her without Drumcondra, Thea left the wood and followed the falcon westward.

Chapter Twenty-three

"People do not just disappear, Barrington," Nigel said, pacing the length of the Aubusson carpet in the drawing room at Cashel Cosgrove.

James hesitated. His viscount father was also awaiting an explanation from his vantage on the lounge across the way. As if he knew the answer. It was beyond the beyond. He was angry, to put it mildly. It would serve them both right, were he to blurt out the truth. He just might.

"What do you expect of me?" he said instead, throwing his hands up in exasperation.

"An explanation," Nigel pronounced. "You were with her, Barrington. What possessed you? How could you just let her hare off like that?"

"I was not with her, Cosgrove," James corrected him. "When I discovered her missing, I went in search of her and found her at Newgrange. She caught me off guard, took my horse and rode off—"

"After that Drummond chap, eh?" Nigel cut in. What a

fierce-looking image he presented with his scarred face and eye patch. His nostrils were flared, and his lips had gone white with rage. "What happened to the bounder? He was not with her when I saw her driving my Andalusian like a bedlamite in the hills west of Drogheda. And what happened to that horse? Do you have any inkling of the value of such an animal? No, of course you do not. I will be compensated for the loss, make no mistake about it!"

"Which loss, Cosgrove—your precious hack, or my sister?" James retorted.

"You go too far, sir! That horse is worth a fortune—hardly a hack—and your sister is my betrothed—"

"Not any longer, so it seems," James interrupted with a coarse chuckle.

"I will not stand it! I will not be cuckolded! Her behavior is unacceptable!"

"And what of *your* behavior, sir?" James shot back. "I've held my peace until now, but I will no longer. If you have lost her, you have driven her off with your insufferable abuse."

"Are you seeking satisfaction, Barrington? Because if you are, I am only too willing to oblige you. Declare your intentions, sir. Your veiled threats of calling me out are tiresome and inappropriate."

"Here now," the viscount put in, vaulting to his feet. "Let us not be hasty, gentlemen. Nothing is served in hostile bickering. We need to have Thea back. That is paramount here."

"I'll tell you what is paramount," Nigel seethed. "That both of you leave my house at once! Our arrangements are concluded—unless, as you imply, you wish to settle this with pistols or swords?"

"Your servant, sir!" James said, expanding his posture. "That will come later if needs must. In the meanwhile, we will remain at Cashel Cosgrove until Thea is found, since it is you who have driven her from your house, sir. Then we shall see if it wants pistols or swords. By God, if one hair upon her head has been harmed in this, you will rue the day you ever met the Barringtons!"

"That has already occurred," Nigel said. "Now then, I am still awaiting an explanation. Who is this Drummond individual—a Gypsy if ever I set eyes upon one—and what is he to your sister?"

There was a long pause. "I honestly do not know," James said at the end of it.

Nigel gave a deep nod. "I see," he said. "Well, let me tell you what I think. Your sister is a whore, sir—no better than a Penzance roundheels. She contrived to legitimize herself in an alliance with me while carrying on an affair with her Gypsy lover. She—"

James's white-knuckled fist interrupted the rest. Nigel staggered backward into the gateleg table, wiping blood from his nose.

"You earned the facer," James said, flexing his bruised knuckles. "Count yourself fortunate it wasn't a leveler. I don't happen to have a glove on me at the moment for a traditional calling out, but I shan't stand here and allow you to malign and slander my sister, you jackanapes! And I've heard all about your lightskirt."

"I was acquitted, you ass!"

"Ha! That does not make you innocent," James said. "Many a guilty man roams this planet set free by money drenched in blood."

Nigel lunged, but the viscount put himself between them, one hand splayed on each of their chests.

"Stand aside, Father," James charged. "You did not see the mark this bounder left upon our Thea's mouth. He drew blood, sir!"

"No, son, I did not," the viscount replied, "and it is fortunate for the bounder that I did not. Cosgrove, my daughter was never agreeable to a union with you. She accepted to please me, and would have honored the commitment to her dying day if she could have found one admirable trait to recommend you. Such is her character, sir. If she has fallen in love with another, you have driven her to it, and you have no one to blame but yourself. You are a boor, a rake, and a rattle. I release you from our bargain. And if you are fool enough to go up against my son on the dueling ground, I will pray for you. He's held a record at Manton's Gallery in London for two years running."

"You don't frighten me, Barrington," Nigel snapped, still dabbing at his bleeding nose. "This isn't London."

"How well I know it!" the viscount sallied. "There is neither chivalry nor honor here amongst your lot, I am sorry to say. And such shoddy behavior from *you*, who have spent half your life in England, sir, where it abounds! I am appalled. Why, your own father couldn't be coerced to put in an appearance at your wedding! What does that say to the world at large?"

"I care little for your opinion of me, sir," Nigel said, "and even less for that of the world at large. The fact remains that my intended has run off with another man, whilst enjoying the hospitality of my home. I mean to know why."

"Well, I cannot oblige you," said James. "The 'whys' needs must come from Thea, and while we wait for that, I would advise that you select a second, sir. This here between us is settled the instant I set eyes upon her again."

James stalked toward the doorway, but Nigel's bark turned him around when he reached it.

"Where the devil do you think you're going?" he said. "We haven't finished here. I want some answers, Barrington!"

"So far as I am concerned, we were finished before we commenced," said James. "And as to where I am going, I go to do what you have failed to do—find my sister."

Thea leaned against a tree trunk at the edge of the wood to catch her breath, which was puffing white in the darkness. The cold air seared her lungs and her sobs squeaked past her dry throat. Above, the bird came and went, impatient. She could not travel as fast as it could fly borne on the wind. Her feet were numb, bogged down in the snow; it had penetrated her ankle boots. There would be chilblains; it was inevitable. It didn't matter. History had it that she, too, had disappeared. Perhaps it was right that she die among her Gypsy husband's comrades . . . by his side. Perhaps that was where the bird was leading.

Her lungs burning, Thea pushed off from the tree and staggered on, her ears pricked for the tinkling of the bird's tether bells. When she couldn't see it clearly for the trees, it was the sound of the bells she followed. It wasn't the sound of the falcon's bells that pulled her up short, however. It was the thunder of horses' hooves that shook the ground beneath her. Cosgrove's men! So she hadn't crossed over. She was still in the past.

She glanced behind. The riders appeared like a dark cloud silhouetted against the snow, and she backed deeper into the wood and held her breath, praying they wouldn't decide to seek her there.

It was no use without a horse. What could she have been thinking to set out afoot in the dark, attempting to travel such a distance bogged down in the snow? They were nearly abreast of her—a dozen riders—when a hand on her shoulder spun her around to face a hunched, heavily cloaked figure lurking like a shadow among the trees. Though the hand had slipped away from Thea's shoulder, she still tingled from its touch, and she shuddered due to something other than the cold. She assessed it to be a woman standing there by the way the person moved, though it was nearly impossible to be sure of gender. The hood was pulled down so low that no features were visible. The figure did not speak, but gestured deeply in with a wide sweep of a cloaked arm, beckoning her to follow.

Thea hesitated, her eyes oscillating between the strange person at her elbow and the steady stream of Cosgrove's men riding past. Their number had doubled. It was only a matter of time before they turned back and searched the woods when they didn't find her elsewhere. Still she hung back, searching the sky through the trees for some sign of the bird; but it had disappeared when the riders came.

"Come daughter," the specter said, for that was what it seemed then—a specter risen from the evening mist. The weather was turning warmer. Soon the snow would melt, revealing Drumcondra's body, and Thea prayed that whatever was going to happen to cause her disappearance from history would be swift to spare her the sight. "My time is short. It must be now," the woman urged.

Something in the sound of that voice seemed familiar, yet distant, the words overlapping as if they were coming from an echo chamber. For a moment, Thea wondered if she had heard it at all or if it was only a whisper ghosting across her mind.

"Who are you?" she murmured.

"Come," the woman said, sweeping her arm wider still.

Thea started to follow, but the deeper she ventured into the forest, the darker it became, and the more she feared danger. Sight of the bird would have been a comfort then, but there was no sign of it, nor did she hear the tether bells. Could it be perched above, hidden from Cosgrove's men? Or had it abandoned her?

"Where are you taking me?" Thea demanded of the figure moving weightlessly before her. How odd that was for one so heavily cloaked. The woman almost seemed to float over the snow, while Thea meanwhile struggled, plowing through drifts linking the trees. "Wait!" she called. She could barely make the shape out now, though she was right beside her.

Acting on impulse, Thea reached out and threw the woman's hood back—only to utter a shriek that somehow managed to pass as a strangled whisper. The hood was empty. There was no one there.

"Do not fear me, daughter," the spirit said. "Have I ever harmed ye?"

All at once, recognition struck, and Thea cried, "Jeta . . . ?"

"Shhhh," the specter said. "The Gypsy dead can only help the living once, daughter."

"It cannot be?" Thea murmured. "I am imagining this. . . ."

"I am come to right a wrong that will not let me rest," the specter said. "I brought the pelerine to Si An Bhru. It was meant to bring ye both, but the Cosgrove killed me before the way was clear, and the corridor closed without ye. The magic wasn't strong enough to bring ye both without me, the guardian of the passage tomb. I travel it in spirit now, for that is where Cian Cosgrove struck the blow that killed me . . . in my time. But my son did not find me dead when he crossed over. I crawled outside to die in the wood and spare him the sight. Ye see me now, the way ye saw his ghost in your time, daughter. . . ."

"You brought my pelerine?" Thea was incredulous. "I thought . . . Drina . . ."

"I had it back from Drina before she set the fire."

"W-where are you taking me?"

"To . . . your . . . destiny . . ." the specter said, then it faded altogether.

Thea spun in circles, but there was no one there. She called Jeta's name, but there was no answer. Surely she had imagined it all. That was all it was; her imagination had gotten the better of her. Still, she searched the forest ahead and behind with narrowed eyes, praying for the darkness to give birth to something familiar, something real—some sign of the destiny the specter had promised.

It was then that she heard it: the tether bells. Above her, the uppermost branches clacked together, and pinecones fell. The bird! But it was leading her into the open on the far side of the wood. Should she not stay hidden? It only took a moment to decide. She had trusted the bird before. She would do so again. Had it not just saved her from the advances of Cian Cosgrove? Bounding over the drifted snow between the trees, she left the shelter of the wood and braved the open valley.

The lay of the land did not seem familiar here. She couldn't get her bearings. The air was warmer now. The snow had all but melted. No horsemen's tracks marred the frosty layer that remained, only what appeared to be wagon tracks leading . . . which way were they leading? North? West? Thea couldn't tell. She glanced behind for a glimpse of Falcon's Lair to fix her position, but another forest blocked her view. She was lost on the far side of a dense wood that bearded an unfamiliar glen. She studied the wagon tracks slicing through the hoarfrost. They were freshly made by the look of them. The moon showed them to her with clarity. There was nothing for it but to follow them up a hillock ahead, toward which the bird soared also.

The hills and valleys stretching before her seemed

unreal—a land enchanted, dusted with a sugary crust that twinkled like spangles in the moonlight. There was no sound save her boots crunching on the transparent surface. Keeping the bird in sight, she trudged on until she reached the top of the hill and saw what had made the tracks she was following. Below in the valley, nestled in a clearing at the edge of another stand of pines, a Gypsy camp appeared: wagons painted crimson, teal, and yellow, their brilliant colors muted by the darkness. A fire was lit beside them. Was it safe to approach? Thea hesitated. How she longed to warm herself beside that fire. But Cosgrove's men would surely stop there to inquire of her. Overhead, the great bird screeched and soared toward the wagons. Surely, it would not go where Cosgrove's men would kill it. When the falcon dropped out of the sky and perched upon the lead wagon, it was all the encouragement Thea needed. Bolting out of the wood, she scrambled down the hillock and plowed toward the wagons through the tall grass dusted white with frost.

All at once, a chill wind fanned her hot face as she neared the camp. A disembodied voice riding it grazed her ear in a hushed whisper. Though she spun in circles and nearly lost her footing in the slippery stuff beneath her feet in search of the author it, there wasn't a soul in sight, only a dog barking a warning to the sleeping Gypsies in the wagons below.

"Ye see me no more," the specter whispered across her mind, "though I be with ye always. Trust the bird . . . *his* familiar. Follow where it leads ye, daughter. Ye are the Falcon's bride."

Cold chills riddled Thea's body from head to toe, as the eerie voice was siphoned off on the wind. It died then, as suddenly as it had come, and she swayed as if she'd been struck. Movement at the Gypsy camp caught her eye. Two men came running, the dog at their heels, but Thea's eyes were riveted to the falcon still perched clucking and preening on the roof of the lead wagon. She stood her ground. It was useless to run.

Both men took hold of her. They were elders of the tribe, gray haired with weather-beaten faces, tanned skin like wrinkled leather, and eyes that shone silver in the fractured moonlight peeking through the clouds. The dog pranced at their heels, tail wagging. It looked suspiciously like pictures of a wolf she had once seen . . . somewhere. She couldn't remember—only that it had penetrating soulful eyes that reminded her of Drumcondra's. This dog had such eyes. How odd that she couldn't recall the source of that image. All aspects of her former life, the life she'd lived before Drumcondra, had faded into the mists of time.

"What is your name, child?" the eldest Gypsy said. "How have you come here?"

"Th-Thea . . . Theodosia Barrington—nay, Drumcondra," she sobbed, her breath coming short. "I . . . I followed the bird. I beg you, help me please. Cian Cosgrove's men seek me. They must not find me."

Both men gasped. The elder Gypsy made the sign of the cross, while the other tucked his hand behind his back and made the ancient sign against evil. Another came, a hunched gray-haired woman.

"It is she, Ina!" the elder whispered to her.

"Bring her—quickly!" the woman said.

The Gypsies propelled her along over the frosted grass at such a speed her feet scarcely touched the ground. The wolf dog bounded alongside, dipping its muzzle in the crust underfoot, wagging its long scraggly tail now and then, nudging Thea's hand with its wet nose as they sped her toward the barrel-shaped wagons at the edge of the clearing.

"Wait!" Thea cried. "Where is this place? I do not know it."

"Shhhh," the woman warned. Neither of the men replied.

"Please!" Thea said. "What year is this?" She had to know if the bird had taken her back to her own time of 1811, or if she was still in the troubled times of 1695.

"It is the Year of Our Lord 1747," said the elder.

Thea froze in place, pulling them both up short. She opened her mouth to speak, but no words came. Darkness closed in all around her. White pinpoints of glaring light starred her vision. Something at the back of her palate tasted of blood. She swayed as consciousness evaporated.

Mumbling words among themselves in a foreign tongue, the Gypsies scooped her up and carried her the rest of the distance.

Chapter Twenty-four

Thea came to lying on a straw-filled mattress, swaying back and forth with the motion of the wagon. She was wrapped in strong warm arms beneath soft fur, her head resting upon a man's bare chest. His scent drifted past her nostrils—*his* scent, darkly mysterious, clean and very male, of the earth and the forest, of musk and tanned leather. She would know that scent anywhere. How cruel were dreams.

She forced her moist eyes open to chase the vision, only to focus upon the soft mat of jet black hair curling beneath her face. Her eyes snapped open wider, and she vaulted upright on the pallet and cried aloud as strong hands pulled her into a smothering embrace.

"M-my lord!" she sobbed. "Oh, my lord. I thought you dead! Cosgrove said he ran you through with his sword. That you lay dead beneath the . . . snow."

Ros Drumcondra's huge hand cupped her face, his broad thumb flicking away her tears. His lips were warm as they took hers greedily, his tongue warm and welcome. He groaned, threading his fingers through her hair, his heart beating a ragged rhythm against her as he crushed her closer still.

He freed himself from her lips with a groan. "Did he . . . harm you?" he murmured through clenched teeth.

She shook her head. "The bird prevented it," she murmured.

All the breath in his lungs seemed to leave his body in the shape of a shuddering moan, and he clung to her, gentling more tears from her cheek. The tenderness of that only made more flow. *Please, God, do not let this be a dream,* she prayed.

Her hands flitted over his hard muscled torso and found the bandages that girded his waist. She gasped. Cosgrove hadn't lied. So many questions raced through her brain. So many emotions ran riot in her. It was more than she could take in.

"He *did* bring you low!" she said. "Do you know where you are? How did you come? What brought you? My lord, I do not understand. . . ."

"Nor do I," Drumcondra said. He lifted the fur that covered them. "It has to do with this," he told her.

The only light filtering in through the curtained window in the wagon was shed by the misshapen moon, which had thrown a shaft of light across their bodies. That was enough for Thea to examine the fur. She gasped.

"My pelerine!" she cried.

"I do not know what sorcery was afoot in Si An Bhru, but this fur was put there for a purpose. I do not know what that purpose was, but if it was to unite us in my time as I suspect, the magic failed, and you were left behind."

"Y-you did not see who put it there?" Thea said, praying that he had not seen his mother die by Cian Cosgrove's hand.

He shook his head. "When I emerged without you, I searched the chambers. When I could not find you, I went outside, but our tracks in the snow had vanished. And then I knew that time had once more separated us, and I rode for Falcon's Lair in hopes of finding you at the keep. What I found was the Cosgrove and his men laying siege to my stronghold again. I saw no sign of you ... or my mother. The keep was in flames. The land was littered with the dead. She must have perished with the rest. So help me God, if such is so, I will not rest until I find my way back to my own time and finish him once and for all."

Thea held her peace. He did not know what had happened to Jeta. Who was there to tell him unless it be she? He must never know. They had disappeared from the face of the earth. It must stay so if history were to play out as needs must. She wasn't going to die after all. The corridor had spat them out in a different era, where they were both safe—at least for now. She could hardly contain her euphoria.

"History tells that the bones of many of your band were found inside the passage tomb when it was renovated. They had not died violent deaths. They had escaped the Cosgrove's fury, my lord. Please God, your mother was among them. She was not at Falcon's Lair. I can vouch for that. If she were, I would not have needed to rely upon the bird to buy me free. She would have helped me. Besides, Cosgrove would have boasted of her death, I'm certain of it. He was vile and insufferable—just as Nigel, his descendant, is vile and insufferable." She abhorred the lie, but she dared not let on that Cian Cosgrove had gloated over Jeta's death in his drunken stupor. It didn't matter. Her account sounded logical enough. If only he believed her.

"What happened to you when we were separated?" he asked, tilting her face to look into her eyes.

The tale came spilling out of her, as much as she dared tell between wracking involuntary sobs that would not be put by. It seemed so like a dream, and yet she knew she was awake, existing forty-five years before she was even born among a band of Travelers.

"He said he saw you fall," she said. "He said the snow was crimsoned with your blood. . . ."

"The snow ran with the blood of many," said Drumcondra, "But mine was not among them. I fell, but came to earth in this time here now—horse and all. The corridor crosshatches these lands hereabouts in many ways and places evidently. The bird is the only one who knows the way of it now, with Jeta . . . gone. That mystery was hers alone to guard."

"What have you told these?" she said. "You must have told them something. They knew my name when I spoke it."

"I told them the truth," he said. "As much of it as I thought they would believe. They think I am descendant of the Drumcondras. The gold, I think, convinced them. It was still tied on Cabochon's back, when we crossed over. They had heard of such coin, but never seen the like. We will share it with them. My sudden appearing among them seemed otherworldly. These are Romany, my love. Such things as have happened to us are not unheard of among the Gypsies. It is the stuff of legends, aye, but as in all legends, there is a seed of truth. Whether they believed or no, they are our allies. All Gypsies are brethren—all Travelers, brothers of the blood. There is a code of honor among us that can neither be broken nor denied."

"Where do they take us, my lord—not back to Si An Bhru?"

"No," he murmured. "These times that we have come to now are hard for Gypsy Travelers. It has been so for our people since time out of mind, but this! It is obscene here now. My father tried to settle down and keep the border, leaning upon his Celtic heritage to hold sway over his Romany instincts. It did not serve him. It did not serve me, either. The wanderlust has always raged in me. It is in the blood, my Thea.

"These who have taken us in have fled from the north rather than settle the land for other masters. It is the only way that they can keep their heritage—the only way that it can be preserved for all the Travelers who will come after. In Spain, the Church no longer gives Gypsies asylum. Those men who will not settle the land and work it for cruel squires are shot. Their women and children suffer their ears to be cut off. How long before such happens here?"

"But this is madness!" she cried.

"We have a saying—*Jek dilo kerel but dile hai but dile keren dilimata.* 'One madman makes many madmen, and many madmen makes madness.' These have come south to gather any who might come with them to escape the madness. They will wend their way to the westernmost shore, and then double back and leave Ireland with any who would be out from under the yoke of cruel landowners until one day, please God, it will be safe to return. It is said that there are safe places for travelers in the Carpathian Mountains."

Away from the corridor, Thea reasoned. Perhaps it could be the answer.

"And if that fails, they will return to the east," he went on, "to India, and Persia, to their roots, until the world is sane again. They want me to go with them, to be their leader. The elders are soon too old to lead, and none among the young can match my reputation. If there is such a thing as destiny, I believe that this is mine, and I also believe that you were meant to share in it with me."

Thea raised his hand to her lips, and something sticky

on his wrist caught her attention. She examined both hands, and gasped. They were raw and weeping.

"What is this?" she cried.

"They had to restrain me," he said. "I would not go without you. I saw the bird. I knew he would bring you. When I tried to go in search of you, they tied me down. It was too soon. The wound would have festered. They only turned me loose when you were brought to me."

"My lord, do you want to go with these?"

"Will you go with me?"

"We cannot stay here," she said. "The risk is too great. Both of our worlds hold danger for us now—not that this does not. But as I see it, this path is the only one that will secure the future—*our* future—as it is laid down in history. Lost in another time, we shan't be found. We shall just . . . disappear."

Thea's words trailed off. She shook her head and buried her face against Drumcondra's chest. He must not see her tears. He must not know her heart. She was ill equipped to carry out a deception of this magnitude. He was too clever for her.

"You have not answered me," he said. "You hesitate. Why?"

"I will never leave you, my lord," she murmured.

"But . . . ?"

"My brother," she said. "He will think me dead, and father!"

"You are dead . . . to them. It cannot be helped, my Thea. You cannot exist in both dimensions; even I know that much. You must choose."

"I have chosen, my lord. It is just . . . if only I could tell them all is well. Only that."

Drumcondra thought a moment. "There may be a way," he said at last, soothing her gently.

"How?"

"Shhh," he murmured. "In due course. Hush now and rest. I cannot bear your tears. I cannot bear that I am the cause of them."

Thea stroked his face. His skin was hot and dry. "How badly are you hurt, my lord? The truth," she demanded. "I am feeling fever."

He ground out a chuckle. "Too badly to do you justice at the moment," he said, "but not badly enough to keep me from it for long. I mend, thanks to these who have a way with healing herbs . . . and now that I hold you in my arms again. I think I have run mad since last I saw you, Thea. I would have fought my way back and died on that battlefield before I would have left you behind, if the bird had not deserted me here among these, like this. You have so bewitched me, lady wife. I beg you, never leave me."

Thea drew him close. Her happiness should be complete, but it wasn't. Her conscience would not be appeased.

"What I do not understand," he went on, soothing her absently, "is how we were separated . . . and why we have come here, to this time. It means nothing to us."

Thea bit her lip. She could hardly tell him that his mother's death at Cian Cosgrove's hand had interrupted the magic and separated them. She could not tell him that Jeta was also responsible for their existence in this strange time, foreign to them both, where they could live out their destiny . . . where they could disappear. No, she could tell him none of it, else she risk everything, most of all, his love. He would never forgive her for keeping the truth from him. He would go back, and he would die a slow and horrible death at the hands of his enemy.

"Whatever alchemy is afoot here, we must accept it, my lord," she murmured. "We do not have a choice."

* * *

They traveled south at a leisurely pace, and left the snow and frost behind. Just as it was in her own time, such weather had been unprecedented, and was the topic of conversation wherever they stopped along the way. Many joined them once they heard the elders' tales, and the caravan grew at a steady rate as they turned westward.

Drumcondra mended quickly. In a fortnight, the Gypsy tinctures, salves and poultices had worked their magic, and he could sit a horse once more. The elders, Aladar and Palco, and Aladar's wife Ina, who had brought her to him, alone knew his real name, and were sworn to secrecy. Their vows were sacrosanct. He had passed himself off as a direct descendant of Ros Drumcondra. To all others, he was Drummond, and the role of leader fit him like a second skin. Thea was treated with respect befitting Romany royalty, outfitted in clothing suitable for a Gypsy princess, since to them any relation of Ros Drumcondra, a figure straight out of Romany legend, was a prince among Gypsies.

They were given the lead wagon to themselves. No one objected. Rumblings of astonishment were mild, and soon gave way to a greater press—persecution. Tensions ran high the while they traveled, as prejudices against them surfaced and grew to an ugly murmur. One sennight gave way to the next until a month had passed, and then another. When they reached Killarney, they turned the wagons northward again, intending to follow the coast to Galway then turn east-northeast and amble back through County Meath on a course that would, to Thea's dismay, take them dangerously close to Cashel Cosgrove and Newgrange . . . and the corridor. That, however, was still days off.

It was a soft night with the weather turned warmer when the caravan camped beside the estuary at Galway Bay. The air was brisk with the taste of salt on the wind, on the ghostlike mist that it couldn't chase. Thea had scarcely climbed into the wagon after the evening meal, when Drumcondra seized her in strong arms, swooped down and took her lips in a kiss that left her weak and breathless, her mouth no less set aflame than if he had seared it with a firebrand.

Taken by surprise, Thea nearly lost her footing. She laughed as he scooped her up and laid her upon the raised pallet fitted with feather quilts. It was warm in the wagon. A little brazier sufficed to maintain a comfortable temperature. Set in the corner and heaped with peat, the compact basinlike affair gave off radiant heat, while the fragrant smoke escaped through a chimney pipe in the roof.

Thea looked on shamelessly as Drumcondra shed his clothes and climbed in beside her. Her hooded eyes, lit with desire, slid the length of his bronzed torso in the shaft of moonlight peeking in at the wagon window. Those eyes flitted over his chest, and lingered on the magnificence of his aroused sex. It grazed her as he peeled away her clothing one piece at a time, commencing with the indigo-laced corset of carded wool. Loosening the drawstring on the embroidered waist beneath, he spread it wide, feasting upon her breasts, the tawny buds grown hard under naught but his gaze. He had the power to seduce with a look, to ravage with a whisper of that deep baritone resonance that delivered her name as it did now, riding a husky tremor. The skirt and petticoats came next. Thea arched her back as he slid them over her hips, down her legs, and then consigned them to the floor in a heap with the rest.

Rolling on his back, he took her with him until she straddled him. Thea's breath stuck in her throat as she gazed down into his eyes, dilated black in the darkness. They shone like quicksilver with reflected light from the wan moonbeam striking their bodies broadside. The fingers of a blush crawled up Thea's cheeks. Surely only light-skirts made love like this. His hardness throbbed beneath her. She gripped his shoulders as he cupped her breasts, his deft fingers grazing her nipples, lightly at first, in tantalizing revolutions that set loose a firestorm at her very core.

Thea groaned, her head thrown back as those skilled fingers slid the length of her body, following the curve of her waist, her hips, cupping her buttocks. Raising her as though she weighed no more than one of Isor's feathers, he lowered her upon his engorged sex, filling her with its hard, throbbing heat. Thea cried aloud at the swiftness of the motion, at the shuddering impact of his thick veined shaft reaching inside, delving deeper than he had ever gone before. He was holding back no longer. The wound in his side was too newly mended to stress, but that seemed not to matter to him, and he moved inside her, setting off undulating waves of icy-hot fire that scorched her loins, and knit her bones in rigid anticipation of excruciating ecstasy.

Just when she feared she could stand no more, he rolled her over, impaled thus, and gathered her closer still. Arched against his hard muscled torso, her body reached for him as if it had a will of its own. He took her deeper—slow, shuddering, heart-stopping thrusts that drained her senses. It was a possession, as if he were trying to absorb her into himself, as if all his hopes and fears hung in the balance of that one searing moment.

Thea took him deeper still. She couldn't help herself. The wild, pulsating climax that riddled her crippled her senses and paralyzed her mind. His undulations drained her dry—milked every drop of her precious essence until it sheathed his sex like a silken veil. He groaned, grinding his body against her in mindless oblivion. The thrumming sound reverberated through her body like a flesh-tearing wind, from his thick arched throat to the rock-hard member pumping, exploding inside her, leaving her weak and trembling in his strong muscled arms.

He didn't let her go. His life still throbbed inside her. In minutes he was hard again, reaching, probing, sending shock waves coursing through her belly and thighs. *Again.* His body, slick with sweat, moved against her in the moonlight, kindling desire, thickening her moist sex. *Again.* The sexual stream that joined them tightened, setting loose such heat as if he had burst into flame in her arms. *Again.*

"I cannot get my fill of you," he murmured huskily. All things passionate lived in that voice, those arms—that dynamic body joined to hers so totally it had gone beyond the physical plane of their existence, just as the corridor had taken them beyond the physical phenomenon of time. There was almost a facet of frantic desperation in their joining. It both frightened and excited her. She was answering the call of some primeval force as old as eons working in her then, in them both, for she could feel it in the power of his passion. It was almost as if he feared it was their last time together, as if he were trying to beat back the inevitable.

Rich, guttural moans bubbled up from his throat and filled her mouth as he took her lips and deepened the kiss in one swift thrust. Her breasts were not exempt from his ardor. His skilled tongue blazing a fiery trail along her arched throat, sidled over her curves and encircled first one hardened bud and then the other, drawing them into the warm silkiness of his mouth. Thea's head reeled like a castaway lord. His image blurred before her. She shut her eyes as the palpitating waves of white-hot fire rushed through her body, pumping through her veins, lifting her out of herself to another plane of existence, as if she could bear more tears in the cosmic veil draped about her. It was fast falling to tatters. They were hopelessly in love—matched in their passion—committed for life . . . But there was something wrong, a nagging, invisible, intangible something like a specter between them. Waiting to make itself known.

Thea knew what was troubling her conscience. Ros had a right to know what had happened to his mother, and she was keeping it from him. If he knew, he would somehow go back and extract Gypsy justice from her murderer, and she would lose him. Keeping it from him in those circumstances was justified in her mind, though she hated the deception.

Though she had her suspicions, she was almost afraid to probe him for the cause of his malaise. Still, that was exactly what she'd decided to do when he collapsed spent and breathless in her arms, his heart beating a heavy ragged rhythm against her breast.

Drumcondra lay back and clasped her to him. She was where she needed to be, where she was born to be, in the arms of the soul mate she had traveled through time to embrace. She had him . . . but not totally, and she wouldn't settle for less.

"We travel north again," she said, screwing her eyes shut tight against his heaving chest. "Will we return to Meath?"

"We pass through Meath and book passage for the east at the estuary in Drogheda," he said.

"You aren't going to seek out the corridor again, are you?" Her voice was anything but steady, and he pulled her closer in the custody of his strong arm, and soothed her gently. Thea's heart sank like lead in her breast at his hesitation.

"I shan't," he said at last, "but Isor shall. He must, if you would have me send word to your father and your brother."

Her breath stopped at her throat. She had almost forgotten, but he had not. Was there no end to the mystique of the man?

"Will they still be there, do you think?" he said.

"I cannot imagine them leaving without some word of me."

"It is not safe for you to go back," he said, "and I have other plans."

"What . . . plans?" She was almost afraid to ask.

"I have no need to access the corridor," he said, "when I can see for myself, with my own eyes what has become of my archrival."

"I do not understand," said Thea, nonplussed.

"If this is the year 1747, there is the possibility that Cian Cosgrove is still alive, albeit in his dotage. The way I calculate, he would be in his seventies, if some other adversary hasn't done him to death. We know he lived to father sons, who have passed my keep down through the generations as a Cosgrove holding."

Thea vaulted upright in the bed, her flushed breasts trembling against the fur throw. "Please, my lord, I beg you do not do this," she pleaded. "What is the point? We are safe and away. Whatever sorcery afoot here that has given us a chance to live out our lives in peace did not include this mad plan. I know it. I *feel* it. Why fly in the face of the fortune it has given us. As things are, history is undisturbed. I beg you, do not change it now!" All she could think of was Jeta's sacrifice—whatever trial she must have faced to reunite them, even in death. It was beyond bearing that such a feat would be for naught.

Drumcondra looked her in the eyes. His own were hard and cold. "I will see what has become of him with my own eyes, Thea," he said. "If he lives, he will wish he hadn't, and if he is dead, Ros Drumcondra will piss on his bones."

Thea sank back down and rested her head on his chest, her fingers combing the silky curls beneath her face. It was no use to argue with him. His decision was resolute. The mere thought struck terror in her heart, and she couldn't think why. If Cian Cosgrove were alive, a wizened old man, he posed no threat to her hulking husband, in his prime of life. Why had this news stricken her so?

"You cannot still be lusting after that castle," she said.

"No," he said, clouding. "I knew I could not ever make it my home once I slept again within its walls—they ran red with the blood of my children. I saw it waking and sleeping: rivers of blood, innocent lambs to the slaughter. Maeve earned her fate, I have no sympathy for her, but my children must be avenged—in this time or any other. The game we played, Cosgrove and I, would end in retribution, we both knew it. Anticipation made the wounding crueler and the dying that much more acute. He feared Gypsy magic, and was inept at his, else the game would have ended long since. It is not too late for justice, and by God I mean to have it however I may."

"What did you mean about the bird?" Thea murmured.

Do you remember the night I took you upon Cabochon to the Cosgrove?"

"How could I ever forget?"

He soothed her gently. "Do you remember the message the bird delivered?"

Thea gasped.

"He knows the corridor," Drumcondra said. "Write your missive, fair lady. When we reach the keep he will deliver it, just as he did then. He will not return until he has done so. And then, perhaps once that is done, you will be mine completely."

Chapter Twenty-five

James paced before the hearth in Nigel Cosgrove's study. Across the way, the viscount, his father, stood before the window, staring out over the courtyard through the sheeting rain sliding down the diamond-shaped panes; hardly an agreeable prospect. The guards had come and gone a dozen times as the weeks passed. They'd conducted their search throughout the county. They'd even made a thorough search of Newgrange inside and out, but there was no sign of Thea, and no evidence that she was ever there.

Everything was changed. The weather had turned warmer. Overnight, the snow was gone, except for stubborn patches dotting the soggy lawn here and there. The teeming rain had washed it all away. The downpour only added to the drear clinging to the very air in the ancient castle.

The guards had paid their last visit. There was nothing more that they could do. Nigel had gone to calm the countess, who was anxious to have her unwanted guests leave, and said so in no uncertain terms. That wouldn't award them much time. Having no patience for that chore, Nigel had ordered an herbal draught to be prepared to calm her, then he would join them. Looking toward his father's faded countenance, James couldn't help thinking he, too, would benefit from a dose.

"What's to be done?" he asked his father. "We cannot stay on here. There's to be a duel, or had you forgotten? How can we simply settle in and wait after that?"

"Where could she have gone?" the viscount said, as if he hadn't heard.

"I've told you where she's gone, Father."

"What—that drivel about the passage tomb being a time corridor? Are you addled, boy? She's run off with her Gypsy lover, plain and simple. We helped her!"

James rolled his eyes. "We did," he said, "and you were only too willing to take the Gypsy's gold. Look here, if she had done herself a mischief we would know of it. The guards have left no stone unturned from here to Drogheda."

"Well, m'boy, you'd best try and mend your fences with Cosgrove post haste. The Gypsy wasn't with her when the gudgeon sighted her on the downs west of Drogheda. His feckless ineptitude has lost your sister, and I shan't leave this place until I have her in my sights again. The coil must be unwound without delay. I cannot spare much more time to the bogs and byways of Ireland. I've urgent business awaiting me in London."

"Yes, sir," said James, dourly. "I know the sort of 'business' you have awaiting you there. She shall have to wait. You ought instead be thinking on what you will tell Mother, who sits at home expecting nuptials!"

"You forget yourself, sir!" the viscount barked. "Hold that insolent tongue! The day will never dawn that I let a greenling whelp dictate my affairs."

James let his breath out on a long sigh. "I am not liking that Cosgrove saw no sign of the Gypsy when he sighted her," he said. He was thinking of the corridor. Thea obviously meant to access it at another point of entry and reunite with Drumcondra. What if the Gypsy had tried to do the same? Had they missed each other and become separated in time? One thing was certain. Too much time had passed without word. Could they have passed each other, become lost? Cosgrove had seen the bird, and it hadn't been seen since. Was that a good sign or bad? There was no use explaining that aspect of the coil further to his father. The man's vision did not include the supernatural— but then, the viscount hadn't been where he had been, seen what he had seen. "But," he continued, "I strongly feel that the Gypsy must have been close by. If I am sure of nothing else in the muddle, it is that he would never leave her, and as long as they are aligned, Thea is safe."

"So! You *are* in league with the Gypsy!" Nigel bellowed from the threshold. "I thought as much."

Both men spun toward him.

Nigel strolled closer. "You can consider the betrothal dissolved, gentlemen," he drawled. "I do not accept damaged goods."

"That goes without saying, Cosgrove," James said. "My sister couldn't marry you even if you wanted her. She is already wed. To *him*."

Nigel staggered back apace. "She is what, sir?" he said.

"You've heard me rightly. My sister is wed to Drummond by Gypsy rite. You couldn't have her now in any circumstance."

James father's violet eyes faded to a murky, lackluster hue. All color but a tinge of blue in his lips drained from his face, and he sank like a stone onto the lounge.

"Forgive me, Father," James said. "I would have preferred to break the news less abruptly, but it was not to be."

"I want you out of my house," Nigel seethed. "Both of you! Now! Tonight!"

"We have unfinished business, Cosgrove," said James. "None of this would be if you hadn't misused my sister. You put your hands upon her. You frightened her and abused her—left a *mark* upon her. You must be called to account for that. Choose your weapon, sir, and inform your second. As soon as this benighted rain ceases, we meet on the dueling ground."

It was three days before the sheeting rain dwindled to a fine drifting fog that cloaked the land in a gauze of white not unlike the snow. Dawn brought no relief, and when they gathered for the duel in the meadow south of the castle, the mist was milling about their feet like restless ghosts.

The viscount insisted he stand second for his son, and Nigel called upon Boon to stand for him, which was highly irregular, James pointed out. However, in the interest of keeping the locals in ignorance of the duel, Nigel insisted, and they met in the meadow at first light. Regis, the reluctant butler, was enlisted to act as referee. He appeared like a wraith bearing a brace of dueling pistols in a leather case lined with burgundy baize. The seconds loaded the weapons. Nigel would have had first choice if the pistols hadn't belonged to him. Since they did, James was allowed to choose. Hefting both, he made his choice, Regis handed Nigel the other, and they squared off.

A small clump of bracken poking through the mist served as their starting point. Standing back-to-back beside it, they waited for the signal. James chose to duel in his shirtsleeves, while Nigel appeared fully dressed for the occasion. James hadn't fought a duel before, but he had served as second in several. How much experience Nigel had was unknown. Judging from his character—the very makeup of the man—James assumed he'd had plenty.

The signal was given. They were to pace the distance, stop on Regis's command, then turn and fire at will. Pistols cocked, they began to pace. Overhead, something stirred the air. James paid it no mind, in hopes that a zephyr would disperse the fog. Then he heard the tether bells, and looked up. Nigel heard them, too. He fired, but not at James. He fired blind into the fog toward the sound of the bells, a spate of blue expletives pouring out of him.

"Reload this, damn you—*now!*" he commanded, thrusting the smoking pistol toward Boon.

The valet moved to take it, but the viscount's bark arrested him.

"Hold, there!" he charged. "You've taken your shot, Cosgrove. 'Tis James's turn. Ready yourself to receive his fire!"

James hesitated, his breath suspended. No bird had fallen from the sky, but he didn't hear the tether bells any longer either. Nigel's expression was deadly. His jaw muscles had begun to tick, and his eyes had narrowed to slits as he turned his body slightly to the side.

"Reload the damn thing and give it here!" Nigel charged.

Boon had already done so, but he, too, hesitated, his eyes oscillating between the viscount, James, and his master, standing livid, his outstretched hand working in punctuation of his command.

"Sir, I beg your pardon," the valet said, his voice cracking in falsetto, "but the viscount is right, 'tis Mr. Barrington's fire."

"The devil take it!" Nigel thundered. "Fire, then! Take your damned shot!"

The viscount stepped back, squaring his posture, and

James leveled his pistol at Nigel. He had dead aim. It was an easy shot. There was virtually no wind. But for the fog, conditions were perfect. Across the field, Nigel's one-eyed stare was deadly. Was that a look of arrogance upon his face, or anger masking fear? It didn't matter. James could not countenance shooting the man down. He aimed the pistol toward the ground and fired.

"I have had satisfaction," he said.

Nigel wrenched the pistol from Boon's hands in a flash. "Well, I have not, sir!" he snarled through clenched teeth, the pistol wagging in his hand as he took dead aim at James.

From above and behind, the screech of a falcon and the tinkle of tether bells ripped through the quiet that had fallen over the meadow. James saw the spurt of fire blaze from Nigel's pistol just as a rush of air fanned his hot face, ruffling his hair. Something hard struck James's head with enough force to make him stagger. He fell to his knees, dazed, watching Nigel heave the spent pistol toward the low-flying bird that seemed to taunt him, strafing close before it soared off and loosed what could only be a cry of triumph.

The viscount ran to James's side. Across the way, raving like a madman, Nigel crashed through the mist, kicking at the tousled ground cover of furze and bracken for the pistol he'd hurled at the falcon.

"Am I bleeding?" James said, gingerly feeling his smarting head.

"You aren't pistol shot," his father said. Groping the ground through the mist, he produced a large flat stone wrapped with parchment tied with twine. He handed it over. "Cosgrove missed because that bird beaned you with this," he said. "If I hadn't seen it with my own eyes, I'd never have believed it. That creature dropped this stone—

I swear it seemed deliberate. You flinched, and Cosgrove's ball shot right past you. If you hadn't moved, the bastard would have drilled you dead center."

The bird's screeches echoed in the distance then, mixed with Nighel's shouts, his clenched fists raised to the heavens. It was over. Regis and Boon had left the dueling ground. Nigel stalked toward the viscount helping James to his feet. His eyes were glazed with rage.

"Get off my land!" he snarled, then stalked off into the mist.

James tore off the twine, and peeled the parchment from the stone. Smoothing out the wrinkles, he read:

> Father—dear, dear, James,
> My only regret is that I shan't see you again. I am safe with my husband on the other side of the corridor. Do not seek to find me. I am no longer in your time. I am where I want to be, where I was born to be . . . with my soul mate. There is no need to restore Falcon's Lair. We will not be returning. Go home, my dears, think of me kindly. Cause no falcons harm. Ever. The bird links us now and forever.
>
> Thea

James handed the parchment to his father. The viscount's eyes flitted over the page once, twice. He looked up nonplussed.

"Now do you believe me?" said James. Taking the parchment back, he stuffed it into his pocket.

"Harumph!" the viscount grunted. "She could be standing on that hill over there. You think this is proof of your 'corridor'?" James's crimped mouth and raised eyebrow replied to that, and the viscount perused the missive again. "What will we ever tell your mother?" he murmured.

"The truth," James said, "That she has run off and married her Gypsy lover."

"You may have that pleasure, m'boy. I wash my hands of this debacle."

"Just so," said James. "Now then, come! We have a wedding to cancel."

Chapter Twenty-six

The day was soft with rain when the caravan approached the castle. The bird returned at dusk. Swooping out of the misty sky, it came to rest upon Drumcondra's shoulder just as it always did upon completion of a mission, signaling its success. Clucking and preening, its head bobbing, feathers fluffed, the falcon accepted its reward. It plucked the scrap of meat Drumcondra had saved from the noon meal out of his hand, then flew off to perch upon the colorful lead wagon to devour the morsel.

They camped in the woods south of Cosgrove's land. Thea was occupied with the women preparing the evening meal. Ros had watched her throughout the day—for several days, come to that. He marveled at how well she took to camp life, as though she were born to it. She even looked the part, with her long black natural curls and sparkling eyes like precious gems shimmering beneath their sweeping lashes. For all of that, the farther north they traveled the more sullen and withdrawn she became.

The change had come over her once they'd crossed the border into County Meath. She should have been happy when the bird returned, the success of its task evident, but she wasn't. Drumcondra would not try to draw her out. His paying a call at the castle was at the root of it. She'd begged him not to go. When that failed, she'd pleaded to go with him, which was out of the question. Why she would fear his facing Cian Cosgrove as he was now, an old man in his dotage, he couldn't fathom. Was he not still in his prime? What threat could Cosgrove possibly pose? Still, she seemed in terror of it. That would not stop him. He needed to look upon his old adversary once more before he laid the feud to rest. It had been the main preoccupation of his life for far too long.

Hatless, dressed in dark clothing and cloaked in a woolen mantle, Drumcondra mounted Cabochon and whistled for the bird. It swooped down from the resting place it had chosen in the uppermost boughs of an ancient rowan tree, and perched upon his shoulder with flourish. Thea watched him in silence from her vantage beside the wagon, her gaze unreadable, and he walked the horse closer, ranging himself alongside her.

Seizing Cabochon's bridle, she stroked his long sleek neck. "Do not go, I beg you, my lord," she murmured, searching his face in the lantern light.

"You know I must," he said.

"Why must you?"

"What is it that you fear? That I cannot hold my own against a wizened old man? Have you so little faith in me? Have you forgotten who it is that I am?"

"I am not often given to premonitions," she said, "but something frightens me here now. We are safe, we are happy. Why must you tamper with that?"

"You have been spending too much time amongst the

old mothers," he scoffed. "They see grim specters in every shadow. It is how they pass the time. It is good practice for when they flummox the superstitious *Gadje*—the gullible non-Gypsy folk. Do not take them seriously, Thea."

Thea shook her head and set her jaw. "It is not the mothers," she said. "It is something I feel"—she thumped her breast—"here . . . inside."

Were those tears in her eyes? He swooped down and took her lips in a searing kiss meant as reassurance. He could almost taste her fear. He would not quarrel with her. He would need her when he returned, in his arms, in his bed.

Drumcondra nudged the horse with his heels. Thea's hands fell away from the bridle as Cabochon lurched forward, and he rode out into the night without a backward glance. It was best not to linger. The sooner he set out, the sooner he would return.

Once he cleared the meadow, the castle loomed before him, black against a blacker sky. Dark clouds hid the moon, yet there was enough light for him to see by reflected from the wet ground through the pearly haze that had begun to chase the rain. Besides, he needed no light to define this keep, these lands. They were emblazoned upon his memory, and he'd seen it in Thea's time, had he not? Little had changed over the years. The one thing he couldn't see was if there were sentries posted on the battlements. For that he needed Isor's eyes, and he straightened his arm and gave the bird flight. He would know by Isor's demeanor when it returned, and he reined in at the edge of a row of young saplings to wait.

Once, twice around the curtain wall that housed the battlements, and Isor returned to Drumcondra's outstretched arm clucking and preening. No wildly flapping wings foretold danger.

"Good bird," Drumcondra crooned, offering another

morsel. Nudging the horse forward, he gave the bird flight again, and rode out of the thicket toward the castle.

No sentries posted aloft? Cosgrove truly must be dead or in his dotage, Drumcondra decided. He crossed the courtyard and rode right up to the portal unhindered. No one was posted at the gates either. Unless protocols had changed since his day, it was too early for the changing of the guard.

Dismounting, he tethered Cabochon to a clump of bracken alongside the circular drive—all that remained of the sculptured gardens of his time—and banged the knocker. He knew other ways of gaining entrance, secret ways, but boldness had overtaken him. He had come to gloat and extract reparation. He would enter by the front door to mete that out.

Presently, the door came open in the hand of a rotund woman he took to be the housekeeper. She was clad in black twill, her white mobcap askew, tears streaming down her face, a tilted candlebranch in her hand dripping tallow on the terrazzo.

"Thank God you've come!" she cried, pulling him over the threshold, "And so soon! Why, Mr. Connor just went ta fetch ya not half an hour ago. This way . . . follow me."

Who did she think he was? Granted, he'd disguised his Gypsy ethnicity in dark clothes and a plain mantle, even to sporting a neckcloth, still he was totally nonplussed by her welcome.

"Do you always admit strangers to your master's house so easily, madam?" he said, as she lit his way up the staircase. "Is that altogether wise in these . . . times?"

"Who else could ya be at this time o' the night but the new surgeon from Oldbridge young master's gone ta fetch?" She stopped dead in her tracks. "But don't be tellin' him that I done like that or he'll skin me fer fair."

"You need have no fear of that," Drumcondra said.

She walked on, lighting his way along the corridor he could have traveled in the dark. Ros followed, trying to make sense of the situation from her babblings.

"What seems to be the press here?" he asked when those efforts failed.

"Didn't young master tell ya?"

"I . . . didn't speak with him directly, madam." Drumcondra's one concern was seeing Cian Cosgrove and leaving before 'young master' returned with the real surgeon. Could Divine Providence be that cruel? He hoped not. Only one thing was certain. This had to be done quickly.

"'Tis old master," she wailed. "He's dyin', and young master Connor nowhere near ready to take over here, the wastrel. He's not the man his father was—never will be. The place will go ta wrack and ruin, ya mark me words."

She was already speaking of her master in the past tense. Ros had come just in time.

"What is the nature of old master's malaise?" he asked. They had come upon more than one instance of contagion crosshatching the country. One couldn't be too careful.

"He's on in years," she said, "too old fer huntin' wild boar with the rest o' them. He took a dreadful fall. 'Tweren't his first, neither. He took a tumble over the gallery rail in another of his keeps when he was younger. Broke both his legs that time, he did. It left him with a dreadful limp. He was chasin' a bird what got inta the house if ya can believe it. That was before my time. Nothin's broke this time, but we think he's broke inside. He's been failin' ever since he come down."

"How long ago did it happen?" Drumcondra asked.

"Nigh on a sennight ago it was."

"And you've just sent for me now?"

"Young master had ta give the order ta go after ya," she said, bristling. "It weren't up ta us, or we'd have done straightaway."

Well, well! So that's the way of it, Drumcondra thought, the heir presumptive courting control. They had reached the master bedchamber—*his* master bedchamber. That still rankled.

He took the candlebranch from her. "I shall examine him alone," he said. "Do not loiter here. Run on about your duties. You'll be sent for if you're needed."

The room was in semidarkness. The sight of Cian Cosgrove in what once had been his bed tightened Drumcondra's posture, and set his jaw muscles ticking. Cosgrove was barely recognizable. Time had not been kind. His once handsome face was wrinkled now, made even more grotesque divested of the eye patch that would have spared him the sight of Isor's handiwork. Ros strolled to the foot of the bed.

"Who's that? Who goes there?" Cosgrove barked.

"Your worst nightmare," Drumcondra said, raising the candlebranch level with his face. "Do you not know me?"

Cosgrove squinted his rheumy good eye and lost what color he had. "*Y-you!*" he breathed. "It cannot be! You are youthful still. Are you a spirit come to haunt me?"

Drumcondra strolled around the bed and gripped Cosgrove's shoulder none too gently. "Does that feel like sprit, Cian?" he said.

"I *killed* you!" Cosgrove cried. "I ran you through . . . I saw you go down."

"And when the snow melted, did you find my bones upon that battlefield?"

"I assumed that Gypsy witch of a mother of yours dragged

them off and hid them somewhere before I killed her," Cosgrove sallied, the words edged with venom.

Drumcondra stiffened as though he'd been pistol shot. "What have you to do with my mother?" he demanded.

A triumphant smile curled Cosgrove's cracked lips. "There's no harm in telling you—a spirit. You cannot be real. I saw you die. I *saw* you!" He waved his hand feebly. Blood-speckled drool leaked from his lips, and he grimaced, speaking around a death rattle. "My deeds have come back to haunt me, eh? So be it! Your witch of a mother could not prevent"—he coughed— "your whore from setting fire to Falcon's Lair, but she did take back my betrothed's fur mantle, the thieving bitch, and took it to Si An Bhru. I have always wondered why. . . ."

"Go on," Drumcondra said. Cosgrove was fading, and he would have it all.

"I killed her there," Cosgrove said. "She was a sorceress, your mother. I saw her enter with that mantle, and I followed, but there was no mantle inside—only your mother. Somehow she made it disappear, but she did not possess the power to disappear herself! And so I killed her. When I returned to Falcon's Lair, it was aflame, and you came to the aid of the few of your men that remained. It was a glorious battle . . . you died nobly . . . for a Gypsy."

"Ahhhh, but I did not die, Cian. My mother was a sorceress, remember. Just look at me!" He whirled about, arms raised, head proud. "Does this look like a ghost?"

"That was over fifty years ago!" Cosgrove said, through another cough that spewed more blood-sullied spittle on the counterpane. "You cannot be real! What of my betrothed, eh? She disappeared as well. I told her of your mother's fate before she flummoxed me, the bitch, she and that bird— aye, she knew. Is she still young and fair as well? Am I the only one who has withered with age? I've outlived that blasted bird, though . . . your fine familiar."

Cosgrove was rambling, and rage moved Drumcondra to the window stiff-legged. *Thea knew.* . . . and she didn't tell him? This rotting pustule of a living corpse in the bed behind had told her . . . flaunted it . . . and she'd never spoke a word of it. Why? Because she knew if he knew, he would go back and kill this stinking living corpse, who had gone so addled that he could not tell the difference between the living and the dead. Her silence had allowed this evil wreck of a man to live out his miserable life in virtual comfort—let him take a wife and get an heir upon her after slaughtering Ros's children, his heir, and his unfaithful wife under his very roof—*his* roof!

Again Drumcondra saw the blood sliding down the walls, dripping from the ceiling, puddling at his feet. It was as if his eyes saw through a veil of red. Everything was crimson with the blood of the slaughter.

He threw open the window, and whistled.

"Here! What do you do?" Cosgrove said. "Shut that. I am cold!"

"Dead men are always cold, Cian," Drumcondra said as the falcon soared through the aperture and came to rest upon the studded leather gauntlet on his outstretched arm.

Cosgrove shrank back in the bed. "How can this be?" he cried. "Get it away from me! Get it away, I say!"

"Goodbye, Cian," Drumcondra said. "We shall not meet again this side of hell." He gave no command. Straightening his arm, he gave the bird flight, and turned away.

The creature did not seek Cosgrove's other eye this time. It dove now for Cosgrove's jugular and severed it with beak and talons. One long agonized cry left Cosgrove's lungs, then not another sound as his blood spurted everywhere—real blood this time, no illusion come to haunt Drumcondra. Trusting the bird to make a safe exit through the window once he'd fed from his kill, Ros turned his back and stalked out of his old master bedchamber, the falcon's contented clucking ringing in his ears as it ripped out Cosgrove's throat.

Chapter Twenty-seven

The bird returned before Drumcondra did, its beak and
feathers covered with blood. What could that mean? Thea
was beside herself with worry, and there was nowhere for
her to turn for reassurance. It didn't appear to be the bird's
blood that streaked its handsome feathers. Not the way it
strutted, clucked, and preened, traveling the roof of the
lead wagon like the victor in a battle. Whose, then? She
was almost afraid to wonder.

Cosgrove was the only soul aware that she knew he'd
killed Jeta. If he were alive, he would flaunt it, and Drumcondra would never forgive her for keeping it from him.
This was her greatest fear, the fear that spoiled her happiness. At first she'd been in terror of him going back to
confront Cosgrove for fear he would die in another time
and leave her bereft, but now there was another reason,
one even more devastating. Her courses had ceased to
flow, and her breasts were sore and swollen whether they
made love or not. She could no longer credit her nausea

each morning with motion sickness from the wagon listing over uneven ground before she'd broken her fast. Unless she was mistaken, she was carrying Ros's child.

Should she have told him? Not until she was certain. Would that knowledge have dissuaded him if she had? Thea doubted it. What it would have done, in her opinion, was create a distraction when he needed his wits about him. She had held her peace, and now she was having second thoughts.

She could never replace the children he had loved and lost. That wasn't what she wanted. To give him other children to love was her heart's desire, children that, in this time, destiny would allow him—children that his archenemy Cian Cosgrove could never take.

A knock at the side of the wagon lifted Thea out of her thoughts. She gave a start. It couldn't be Drumcondra. He would not knock. She poked her head out to find Ina, the wife of the elder Aladar standing in the mist.

"Shhhh," the woman whispered. "Aladar would not approve, the crosspatch. I am come to ease your mind."

Thea swept the heavy curtain aside, and the woman climbed into the wagon.

"To ease my mind?" she said. The old woman was intuitive to a fault. Could she have read Thea's angst over Ros's absence? She bade the woman sit, but the Gypsy remained standing, and it was Thea who sat instead. Her knees had suddenly gone wobbly.

The woman nodded. "To settle you . . . about the child you carry," she said.

Thea's posture clenched. "How did you . . . ?"

The woman flashed a wink and a triumphant smile. "What? You think Ina does not see the swollen breasts, the thickened waist, the sallow mask on that fair face?" It wasn't until that moment that Thea remembered Ina served as doctor, nurse, and midwife among the Gypsy band. The woman gave a knowing nod. "Lie down," she said.

Thea hesitated.

"Lie down, daughter," the woman repeated. "I'm not goin' ta hurt ye. We ask the question in your heart, and we have the answer, hmm?" She gestured toward the pallet. "Lie down. It must be done. There are . . . restrictions."

Thea did as she was bade, watching Ina remove the gold ring from her bulbous finger. She gasped as the woman plucked a long gray hair from her own head and tied it to the ring. Then, holding it like a pendulum above Thea's belly, she winked again.

"If the seed is planted, the ring will move in a circle," the woman said.

"How is that possible?" Thea scoffed, through a nervous laugh. "I do not understand."

"It is a method eons old, daughter," Ina said. "It is not to understand. You will see. Now ask the question in your mind. Go on, daughter."

It was silly, but Thea posed the question, a close eye upon the woman's hand, not the ring suspended over her belly, to be sure it wasn't Ina who answered the question and not the ring itself. But despite that the Gypsy's hand was frozen still, after a moment the pendulum began to swing and sway and move in circles over her.

Thea gasped again, and her hand flew to her lips.

"You see?" said Ina. "Lie still, daughter. Now we find out if the bairn is boy or girl—quickly, before your husband returns. Husbands frown upon such augur, though they respect it, aye, and fear it. If the child be a boy, the pendulum will swing up and down your body from head to toe. If a girl, it will swing sideways. Are you ready?" she didn't wait for an answer. "Ask your question, daughter."

Fascinated, Thea posed the mental question and screwed her eyes shut tight. She was almost afraid to know.

"Open your eyes, daughter!" the woman commanded.

Thea braved a look, as the ring began to sway from side to side over her, though the woman's hand and arm were still ramrod-rigid holding the hair it dangled from. It was impossible, yet it was happening, and Thea's breath stalled in her throat.

"A-a . . . girl?" she murmured.

The Gypsy nodded.

Thea's eyes were riveted to the pendulum moving mystically above her body. How was it possible? The woman's hand was perfectly still, and yet the ring was moving as if with a will of its own. Shuddering cold raced along her spine watching.

Thea started to rise, but Ina's sharp intake of breath halted her. "Wait!" she cried. "Lie still. It is not finished . . . look!"

Thea did look, resting on her elbows, and cried aloud as the pendulum began to take a different direction. Before her wide-flung eyes, it shuddered, swayed and began to swing toward her, then away—up and down her body. Once, twice, three times before it slipped from the hair and fell in her lap.

"What does it mean?" Thea murmured. Swinging her feet to the floor, she retrieved the ring. Ina put it back on her finger, folding her arms across her middle.

"You have not one but *two* bairns in that belly, daughter," she said. "One a girl, the other a boy. Congratulations."

"*T-two* . . . ?"

The Gypsy nodded. "The pendulum is never wrong, daughter," she said. "Now I tell ye why I've really come . . . about the restrictions. 'Tis true that you are *Gadje* in the

blood, but wedding one of us makes you as one of us—
subject to our rules, our traditions. Ye are *marhime* now—
unclean. The buckets we set out in the stream, the ones
for washing, cooking, and for the animals, you must not
use the one you have been using to wash yourself now. You
must use the one set farthest from the camp. That one is
for the *marhime*, those with child, or with their courses."

Thea nodded. "But . . . *two babies*," she murmured. She
could scarcely believe it. "Are you sure?"

The Gypsy nodded. "Do not fear. I will tend ye when
the time comes. All will be well, daughter, ye will see.
'Twill be our secret till ye tell your husband. Tell him
soon." Laying a finger alongside her nose, the woman
winked again, and left as abruptly as she'd come.

The last thing Thea needed then was another secret to
keep from her husband. Worry over that kept her awake,
though sleep was tugging at her eyelids. Another hour
passed, and it was nearly midnight when Ros returned.
One look at his hard-set scowl and ticking jaw muscles, at
his narrowed eyes glazed over with rage, and she knew her
worst fears were realized.

"W-where have you been?" she murmured. "The bird returned hours ago covered in blood. I thought . . . I've been
half out of my mind with worry."

"You knew," he said. "You knew, and you kept it from me."

She knew exactly what he meant. There was only one
thing that could have put such a look upon his face.

"You had no right," he raved.

"There was nothing to be done. Revenging yourself
against Cosgrove could not have brought your mother
back, my lord. You are not thinking clearly. If you had
gone . . . and died, what would have become of me . . . in a
strange land—in a strange *time*? Have you no care for
that?"

He ignored the question. "What else have you kept from me?"

"N-nothing," she murmured, thinking of the new life growing inside her. This was not the time to break that news. How could she bear it if he rejected the prospect?

"You never told me what occurred between you and Cosgrove when he captured you."

Thea hesitated. "He was castaway and he tried to force himself upon me. . . ." She wouldn't go into detail. She would not fuel his rage. "The bird . . . it saved me—lured him away, lured him over the gallery railing at Falcon's Lair. I thought the fall had killed him . . . until I heard him screaming for someone to stop me from escaping."

Drumcondra gave a crisp nod. "He broke both legs in that fall," he said.

Thea gasped. "How do you know that?" she breathed.

"Never mind. You know the history . . . you've said it. How does it say Cian Cosgrove died?"

"You've killed him!" She knew.

"I never laid a hand upon him."

Thea gasped again. "The bird!" she cried. "The blood! My God . . ."

"Be still! The others will hear. This is between us. You are my wife, and you have betrayed me. I will not be shamed before the others." He threw wild arms into the air. "Am I never to have a woman I can trust?" he cried. Upending their pallet bed with one sweep of his muscled arm, he scattered the bedding and everything near it helter-skelter. "Cuckolded by my first wife! Nearly burned alive by my whore! And now *you!*"

Tears welled in Thea's eyes. She flinched as if he'd struck her. No, he would never forgive her. This virile tower of a man would never stand betrayal after all that had gone before. The cold fingers of a chill crawled along her spine. He was right. She never should have kept the truth from him. He had the right to know. She had gone too far.

"D-don't," she sobbed. "I beg you . . . don't. It was self-ish of me, I will allow. I knew you would go back . . . do something foolish. I wanted you safe . . . with me. I wanted our life together—"

"The history," he pronounced through clenched teeth and lips drained white with rage. "How is it recorded? Speak!"

"It is recorded that Cian Cosgrove . . . hemorrhaged to death, an old man in his bed after a fall from his horse. . . ."

Drumcondra gave a deep nod. "That is how it is recorded, eh?" he snarled. "He saves face even in death. Bastard!" He leaned close in her face, his wild eyes blind with passion. "I'll tell you how and *why* he died, madam," he seethed. "He has at least one son—an heir—to carry on the benighted name of Cosgrove."

"You knew that, my lord," Thea interrupted. "How else would Nigel exist?"

"Silence!" he roared. "Do not speak. You would hear this. Be still and listen. He did fall from his horse. He was dying when I arrived. His son and heir had gone to bring the surgeon, but if we were to go there now, you would not find that surgeon. I would stake my life upon it. Unless I miss my guess, his heir meant to dally long enough for Cosgrove to die, so that he could take control. That, madam, is the murderous stock that spawned your Nigel."

"A-and . . . did he die as the records say?" Thea asked.

Drumcondra shook his head. "Nooo, madam," he said. "He saw death coming—looked it in the eye. My familiar tore his throat out. Oh, he bled to death, but it was Isor who bled him, not the fall. They would not put *that* in the family history, would they? The mighty Cian brought low by a handful of sinew and feathers. No! They gave him a nobler death for the world to see."

Vertigo starred Thea's vision. *Please, God, do not let me swoon!* She prayed, gripping the bedstead.

"How did you come here?" he said through a dangerous tremor. Gripping her upper arms, he shook her. "Are you a witch? What sorcery brought you here—brought *me* here?"

"You know it was the corridor, my lord," she defended. "Do you know where you were when I came to you among these that have taken us in?"

Drumcondra stared. It was as if an icy fist gripped Thea's heart meeting those tarnished green eyes. He never was wholly given over to the concept of a corridor that spanned time; neither was James, though they were all living proof that one did exist. Was it easier for this enigmatic Gypsy she had wed to believe she was a witch than to live with the knowledge that he might have prevented his mother's death if he had believed? Had her betrayal coming after all the others driven a wedge between them that could never be mended?

"You were on the other side of the forest south of Falcon's Lair, where that bird led me to find you," she said. Should she tell him his mother's ghost had a hand in reuniting them? No. He had already accused his wife of witchcraft. He would never believe it—never. She swallowed hard and held her peace.

"Who are you, Thea?" he said. "I knew naught of a 'corridor' until you appeared. You have bewitched me! From the first moment I clapped eyes upon you, hanging half naked in the passage tomb chamber, my soul was no longer my own. What have you done to me?"

"That bird returned hours ago," Thea shrilled, in a desperate attempt to change the subject. "You could not have been that long at the castle. Is this my punishment, then? You sent it home bloodied to frighten me out of my wits thinking you dead, my lord? Can you be that hateful?"

"I went to Si An Bhru," he said, "in search of your damned corridor—in search of my mother."

Thea's hands flew to her mouth, though he still gripped her arms. "Oh, my lord," she sobbed, "you will not find her there. She is dead." Was he addled? It seemed so. His eyes were wild with passion, the veins standing out in bold relief in his thick reddened neck. She seized his forearms, straining against his grip. Every sinew in him seemed stretched to its limit, like steel bands about to snap.

"I know that, woman!" he cried. "I sought the damned corridor to see if I could find her before—"

"You would have gone back and *left me here?*" she breathed. She was incredulous.

"Only until I put it to rights."

"You cannot 'put it to rights,' my lord. You cannot change history. We are where we must be in order to preserve it. This is the only way we can be together."

"Then I cannot live with it," he said. "If I were not with you in your time when Cosgrove killed her, I could have prevented it." An epiphany blazed in his dilated eyes. "*You* lured me away from that fire!" he cried.

"If I had not, you would have died there—we both would have. It was your mother, my lord, who set me on that course. She saved our lives—"

"And died to do it!" he concluded for her. "You expect me to live with that—celebrate my life at the expense of hers? You dream, madam!"

Thea searched his hard stare for some glimmer of redemption, some hope of forgiveness, but there was none. She saw again his mother's weary shape plowing through the snow that blanketed the castle courtyard, heard again the words that would haunt her for the rest of her days: *"Ye are the Falcon's bride . . ."* It mattered not to her enraged husband that Jeta had engineered their union from the very start, that Jeta had saved them from certain death, and sacrificed herself to do it. Her eyes brimming over with tears, she pried Ros's white-knuckled hands from her arms, snatched her mantle up from the floor where his rage had flung it with the bedding, and fled into the misty night.

Ros tossed the bedding back in place, albeit in disarray, and sank down on the edge of the pallet, head in hands. Cosgrove was dead, but it gave him no satisfaction. If his archrival died a hundred times it wouldn't be enough to purge the bloodlust in his heart. Recorded history had cheated him of his triumph. Ros Drumcondra, the Black Falcon, lived on in the persona of a renegade named Drummond, who would lead his people to safety, free them from the yoke of oppression brought to bear by prejudice and fear in another time, another place. Whatever sorcery it was that had brought it all about seemed not to matter. It was fact. He had revenged himself anonymously, and that was a shallow victory. He could almost hear Cian Cosgrove mocking him from the grave. He was on the verge of madness.

Heaving a ragged sigh, he raked his damp hair back with both hands. Where had she gone? His rage was such he scarcely realized his wife had quit the wagon. Sorceress or saint, he loved her. There was no question. But could he forgive her sin of omission? Whether he could or he couldn't, the fact remained that it wasn't safe for her to wander about these parts alone. This was a dangerous place, a dangerous time for Gypsies—evidently more dangerous than he had ever known. Suppose she were to blunder into that deuced corridor and travel back or forward in time? Access was tenuous through these parts. It could happen in a blink—*had* happened in a blink. That aside, they'd rode through many towns hostile to Gypsies along the way. They'd dodged stones thrown by adults—even children—dodged brimming chamber pots, had dogs set upon them, and been fired upon. Though there wasn't a drop of Gypsy blood in Thea's veins, she could be full-blooded Romany for the dark, wild look of her, especially clothed as she was now, in Gypsy garb.

Drumcondra staggered to his feet and climbed out of the wagon. The rain had stopped, and Finn, the camp dog, crawled out from underneath the wagon, padded close, and nudged his hand for nuzzling. He stroked the hound absently, meanwhile glancing about. There was no sign of his falcon. The horses were all accounted for. All was still. Nothing stirred. At least they hadn't roused the whole camp with their argument.

A pale three-quarter moon poked through the fleeting clouds. In its light, Drumcondra's sharp eyes picked out Thea's tiny footprint in the muddy track leading away from the camp. He started to follow on foot, but thought better of that once he'd gone some distance, and stalked back to the camp for Cabochon.

Drumcondra didn't bother with a saddle. Slipping on the bit and bridle, he mounted the animal bareback and walked him down the lane following Thea's footprints, clearly visible, the impression of her leather ankle boots well defined in the mud. He read her demeanor in them easily. They started out deep and wide, evidence of an angry stride. She had run here. Then, the footprints drew closer together. She had slowed her pace. She was dragging her feet now, suggesting that she had tired. These were the ragged steps of a weary traveler, or one borne down under a heavy burden, mental or physical. They almost looked like the footprints of an elbow bender for the way they reeled back and forth across the lane then stopped beside a stile alongside a low stacked stone fence, where she'd evidently taken a rest before moving on. He glanced about. Nothing moved ahead, though he couldn't see beyond a bend in the path, and he nudged the horse on. He had nearly come abreast of the meadow south of the castle. It loomed in the distance, black in silhouette against the scudding clouds, lit eerily in the moonlight. An uneasy feeling raised Ros's hackles, and made his heart race. He quickened Cabochon's pace from a walk to a trot, his eyes peeled for any nuance in the pattern of the tracks he followed.

She had come quite a distance. Where could she be going? Surely not to Si An Bhru. Nevertheless, the trail was leading off in that direction when he reached the crossroads. The forest thinned there on the south side of the road, and soon diminished altogether. Still, her footprints showed clearly in the mud of the road, though her strength was clearly flagging from the way she dragged her feet. And then, the footprints stopped abruptly. *Stopped*— right there, in the middle of the lane. The muddy stretch ahead was undisturbed.

Drumcondra reined his horse in, and Cabochon reared back on his hind legs, spinning in circles, forefeet pawing the damp air. Ros's keen eyes darted in all directions: before, behind, from side to side. Nothing. The land was open rolling green. He was an excellent tracker, but how could he track what didn't exist?

His heart pounding against his ribs, Drumcondra begged the inky darkness to give up Thea's slender shapely image. But no, his eyes had not deceived him. The footprints simply ceased right there in the middle of the lane. Searching the sky for some sign of his falcon, he raised his fingers to his lips and whistled—an ear-splitting sound that flushed birds from the trees in the forest behind. They soared skyward, all manner of sparrow, lark, lapwing, and thrush voicing their complaints at having been awakened so suddenly. Isor was not among them.

Chapter Twenty-eight

Thea stood at the crossroads. She had strayed quite a distance from the caravan without realizing it in her distraught state. She glanced about to get her bearings. Behind, to the south, a copse stretched down to the river. Cashel Cosgrove stood on a hillock to the north, standing out in bold relief against the dark night sky in the moonlight. She took a ragged breath. She hadn't meant to stray this far from the wagon. She certainly wasn't running away. She needed some time to sort out her thoughts. She had faced that she'd been wrong to keep the circumstances of Jeta's death from her husband. He'd had a right to know. But it wasn't a malicious omission; it was a selfish one. She knew when she made the decision that it would put him in a blind rage if he found out. But who save herself was there to tell? It had never occurred to her that Cian Cosgrove, of all people, would be the one to tell.

Thea started back the way she'd come. Ros hadn't followed her, which meant he was still angry. She couldn't spend the night in the wood. There was nothing for it but to return and try to make him understand why she hadn't told him. He also needed to know that she was with child, before he could accuse her of withholding that as well.

There was no sign of Isor returning, though he had been with her on the way, his magnificent wingspread silhouetted against the misshapen moon that lit her way. She passed the stile by the stacked stone fence, where she'd stopped to rest earlier. It wasn't much farther, just around the bend in the lane. She wouldn't stop to rest there now, though she was weary. Perhaps Drumcondra was asleep. Then she could crawl in beside him and not have to face his wrath again until morning.

The bend in the road loomed before her, and still no sign of the bird. Once she rounded the curve, the wagons should have been visible, but they weren't. She spun in all directions until the motion dizzied her, and she fell to her knees in the mud. They couldn't have moved on without her! There were no wagon tracks.

Thea scrabbled up and half ran, half staggered to the thicket where the camp had been. "My God," she realized. "They're gone."

By noon Drumcondra and the Gypsy men had combed the land all around with no results. The ragtag party fanned out searching the wood, the hills and dales, some on foot, some mounted. They searched clear to the banks of the Boyne River, and all the way to Si An Bhru, but there was no sign of Thea. She had vanished into thin air. Drumcondra's worst fears were upon him.

Still, they searched. He would not call an end to it, and he could not tell them what he feared—that she had once more breached the corridor. Half mad with worry, he drove the men like a tyrant until the sun began to sink low, then left them and rode Cabochon like a man possessed for Falcon's Lair. His last hope.

Drumcondra approached his wounded keep with a heavy heart. He hadn't yet seen it in this time. How sad it seemed, looming black in bold relief against the twilight sky. The sight pained him. The drawbridge stretched across a gaping cavern. The moat had been drained. He rode his magnificent Gypsy horse over the span at a gallop, slid from its back and crashed through the halls, throwing doors wide as he progressed, calling Thea's name at the top of his voice. He rummaged through the rubble, surged through the gallery, the kitchens, the servant's quarters, his voice echoing back at him as he went. He climbed up to the battlements, sifting through the twilight mist with narrowed eyes for some sign of life—of *her*—begging God to strike him blind if only He would show her to him just once more. But God did not accept the challenge, and though Ros stalked the halls like a madman until full dark, there was no sign of Thea.

In desperation, he scaled the stone steps to the battlements again and whistled for Isor, conspicuous in his absence. He whistled again and again, until the sound failed in his dry throat, and pounded the stone ledge until his white-knuckled fists were scraped raw. Isor had never deserted him before. He was with her—he had to be, and Ros could not find her lest the falcon lead him.

Wearily, he climbed down the slippery stairs and mounted his waiting horse. Thea was not here, and with a sinking feeling tying knots in his gut, he rode back to the camp, praying that the others had found her. His rage forgotten, nothing mattered to him then but having her back, in his bed, in his arms; but she had not been found, and he dragged himself into the lead wagon, the wagon they shared, pleading with the shadows to show her face just one more time.

Sinking down on the edge of the pallet, he dropped his head into his hands. He was slouched thus when Aladar, the elder, entered the wagon.

Ros's head snapped up toward his visitor. "Have they found her?" he begged.

The Gypsy shook his head. His wrinkled eyelids drooping sorrowfully made him appear older than his sixty-some-odd years. "We search no more tonight," he said. "We are hunted, my lord. We are watched. We dare not leave the women and children long unattended. It is not safe here now."

"We resume first thing in the morning," Drumcondra decreed.

The elder frowned. "My lord, we cannot tarry here," he said. "We are so close to freedom. Ships await us at the estuary that will carry us east. It will be a treacherous crossing at this time of year, but we must make it, or our pilgrimage is all for naught, and many will die. We must away before we have more serious threats to deal with than chamber pots and stones."

"I will not leave without her, Aladar."

"My lord, we *need* you!"

"And I need her!" Drumcondra retorted. "It is my fault she has run off, and I mean to have her back. The same dangers that exist for us here now exist for her as well—alone, afoot, while our kind are hunted down like animals, killed for no good reason but the sport of it, divested of their ears, their eyesight. I will not leave her here to that. Do not even think to ask it."

The elder hesitated. "She may already have been taken," he said, flinching at Drumcondra's reaction. Ros was like an animal set to spring, and the old Gypsy went on quickly. "It is what the others think. What other explanation is there? She cannot have vanished like a will-o'-the-wisp. If she has been stolen away . . ." He shrugged, wagging his lowered head.

Drumcondra stared at the elder. He couldn't tell him about the corridor. Travelers were a superstitious lot, but they would never brook this, and even if they did, they would fear it and shun him.

"I will not leave without her," he said unequivocally.

All at once, soft mewling sobs outside brought him to his feet, and Drumcondra threw back the blanket at the opening expecting to see Thea standing there; but it was Ina, blubbering into her apron.

"What do you want, woman?" Aladar barked, climbing down.

Drumcondra leapt from the wagon and seized the woman's upper arms. "Is she found? Where is she? Is she harmed? Speak!" he charged, shaking her.

Ina shook her head. "'Twas to be a . . . secret yet . . . awhile," she stammered. "Till she told ye . . ."

Drumcondra rolled his eyes. "Another secret?" he cried. What secret? His blood began to boil. He was going mad—he had to be. This was what madness was like, this twisting, racing agony of the mind that simmered in the blood and gave a man no peace.

"I . . . told her just last night. Just before . . ."

"*What?*" Drumcondra thundered, then in desperation to her husband said, "Aladar, what does she mean?"

"Be still, woman!" the elder charged. "Calm yourself and speak it plain."

"I saw her run off," Ina sobbed. "I should have followed. If only I had . . . She should not be taking risks now."

"You are rambling, old woman!" Drumcondra said, shaking her again. "Speak it plain!"

"She is with child," Ina sobbed. "Two bairns grow in her womb—a girl child and a boy child. We did the pendulum. . . ."

Drumcondra's hands fell away from the woman's arms, his addled brain groping toward sanity. He could do naught but stare. He knew well the accuracy of the pendulum. It had predicted the birth of his two murdered children what seemed a lifetime ago. Jeta had performed the ritual upon Maeve on both occasions. Jeta. His mother. It all came rushing back, crashing over him like an ocean swell, dragging him under. Gasping for air, he reeled off into the wood, staggering like a lord in his cups, whistling for his bird at the top of what was left of his voice.

The weather had turned colder. Patches of snow crunched underfoot. That was when Thea knew she had crossed over again. But where? What time was this? She shuddered. The cold was penetrating. Her homespun mantle was next to no protection from the chill. Why hadn't she worn her pelerine?

The sound of tether bells broke the silence. Overhead, Ros's bird soared, dipping and gliding, borne aloft upon a zephyr Thea could neither feel nor see, since it failed to flutter the pine boughs or ruffle the mulch at the edge of the lane. There was a strange comfort in the creature's presence. As long as she could see it, hear it, there was hope of returning to Drumcondra.

Again and again, she paced off the thicket where the wagons had been, hoping to come upon the corridor that would take her back. All the while, the bird circled overhead, its screeches fair warning that it tired of its vigil until it finally soared off toward the direction of Newgrange. Should she follow? There was no question. At least there would be shelter there; and then, once she'd rested, she could find her way.

She plodded on. If only there were some sign of life, some person to fix her position in her mind—*any* person. But nothing; no one was abroad. Not even the woodland creatures showed themselves, only the shrill cries of the falcon overhead gave evidence that any other creature lived but she and it. And then, in a blink, it was gone.

Thea spun in circles, searching the lightening sky for the falcon's familiar shape. Panic turned her blood to ice in her veins. Before her, the graceful mound of Newgrange loomed, its menhirs spearing the dawn in black silhouette. Patches of snow clung to the mound like patches on a threadbare quilt. She staggered toward it. The dawn breeze ran her through like a javelin, chilling her to the bone. At least inside she would be out of the wind. Clutching her middle as if to protect the new life growing within her, she trudged on to the place where it all had begun, the strangeness, the impossible pleats she'd sewn in time that had given her her husband—*her soul mate*—and taken him away again. In that terrible moment, she would have welcomed Jeta's ghost, repeating again her mysterious augur that she was the Falcon's bride. But there was nothing. Nothing but the hammering of her heart thudding in her breast, in her ears, in her throat, as she ducked inside the passage tomb abandoned by the living and the dead.

Groping the walls, Thea inched her way along toward the blackness inside. The lightening sky at her back provided little light for her progress, but she knew the way now. She would not venture deeply in. She meant to stay close to the entrance, for escape if needs must. All at once, a glimmer of light beyond the standing stone supports that divided the chambers caught her eye. She swayed as though struck. The fine hairs at the back of her neck prickled her skin. Objects being tossed about clanked and thudded. It was an angry sound. Someone was there. Raiding the tomb? Thea stood stock still. All the while she'd come, she'd begged Divine Providence for some sign of life, but now . . .

Footsteps! Carrying toward her. Thea flattened herself against the wall and held her breath. The sound had an angry ring to it, and more than one person was there by the sound. No . . . it was a man leading a horse—an Andalusian, like those in Nigel's stables. Shrinking back against the dank bleeding wall alongside one of the standing stone supports, Thea bit down on her lower lip until she tasted blood. She could see him clearly now. It was Nigel.

She was trembling so, bits of gravelly residue clinging to the wall she'd pressed herself up against fell away, betraying her presence. The horse, which had come abreast of her in the narrow passageway, already spooked by the close confinement, shied and voiced a sharp complaint, and Thea's heart sank. She was found.

And it was no use to run; the Andalusian blocked her way. Nigel threw down the reins and reached her in one stride. Seizing her arm in a white-knuckled fist, he yanked her out of the shadows.

"Well, well—what have we here?" he asked. He slapped the lantern he was carrying down in the stone basin alongside, and jerked her to a standstill. Sliding his familiar gaze the length of her, he took her measure. "How fetching you look in Gypsy garb. It quite becomes you, Theadosia. With that dark hair and those garish clothes, one might mistake you for one of the Gypsy dogs you've lain down with, eh?"

"Let go of me, Nigel!" she cried, trying to twist free to

no avail. His grip was like a vise. "What are you doing here?"

He whipped out a gold coin and flaunted it in her face. "Looking for more of these," he said. "I know this came from the lower regions of Cashel Cosgrove. You and your Gypsy lover left quite a trail behind in your haste to flee my gracious hospitality. What I want to know is where did it come from, and how did he know where to find it?"

"Neither is of any consequence," Thea said, struggling to free herself from his iron grip. "It isn't yours. It belongs to him."

"So it's his, eh? And just how is it that something dredged up from the dungeons of *my* castle could possibly belong to this Drummond person whom I never set eyes upon until you brought him into my home? This smacks of thievery."

Thea hesitated. Should she tell him? What harm could it do? He would never recover the gold. The Gypsies had it now in another time. It would finance their exodus to safer shores. If all had gone well, James and her father had the rest. She had to find out. Still she paused long and hard, for effect. If he were angry enough, he might forget the obvious—her strange appearance there. It was a dangerous game. She knew in her heart now that he was a murderer. He had killed the lightskirt. In a fit of jealous passion, he had brutally beaten and raped the doxy then slit her throat and dumped her in a Covent Garden gutter; she would bet her life upon it. She could see it in his eyes. She knew his capabilities. If she weren't very, very careful, she could well become another of his casualties. Left here in the passage tomb, who would find her? No one until next solstice, when the light flooded the tomb for a brief seventeen minutes once more to illuminate her bones. She shuddered as the dark thought slithered across her mind.

"My husband is a direct descendant of Cormac Drumcondra, whose gold it was," she said at last, "the inheritance hidden and to be handed down to Ros Drumcondra, his son, who . . . disappeared without a trace in 1695, and after that to any and all Drumcondra descendants so long as they lived. My husband stole nothing. The gold rightfully belongs to him. You and yours are the robbers. You, who have occupied the castle since you stole it from Drumcondra in a vicious slaughter of women and children, did not even know of its existence. How have you bloodthirsty lot deserved Drumcondra's gold?"

"Oh no, my dear," Nigel said, wresting her to a standstill. "When Cian Cosgrove won the keep, everything in it became Cosgrove property. Drumcondra descendants have no claim upon it. Never doubt that the gold is mine, and never doubt that I will have it back from your thieving Gypsy husband before the sun sets. Where is the bastard?"

"I do not have to answer you. Where are my brother and my father? Take me to them at once!" Thea commanded. But his look turned her blood cold. His face was livid white, his jaw muscles ticking. The black eye patch spared her precious little of the ugly scar slicing his face beneath. He smelled of stale onions and strong drink, making her grimace, the smell so strong at close range it threatened to make her retch. Her upper arms were numb from his grip, and his buffeting was making her dizzy.

"I sent them packing," Nigel said.

"When?"

"Two days ago."

"Good!" Thea rejoiced. "You shan't have their share back, then."

Nigel let one of her arms go then drew back his hand, and struck her full in the face with his open palm. "You bitch!" he seethed. "There are laws against thievery. Robbers dangle at the end of a gibbet, even here in Ireland. Keep that in mind whilst I ask you again. Where is your husband?"

"You will see him soon enough," she hedged, reeling from the blow. It stung her cheek and made her eyes water, but she blinked the mist back. She would not give him the satisfaction of her tears.

"He is to meet you here, then? I should have guessed." He hoisted her up on the Andalusian and mounted behind her. "Well, when he doesn't find you here, he will come to Cashel Cosgrove, where I will be waiting to make a widow of you, madam! Then the guards may have their way with you."

Kneeing the agitated horse, who was clearly out of sorts for having such a burden imposed upon it in such a tight space, Nigel Cosgrove rode out into the dreary gray dawn, his head bent low to clear the opening, and made straight for the castle at a gallop.

Chapter Twenty-nine

Ros had crosshatched the surrounding land from the Gypsy camp to Drogheda and all that lay between three times before he saw the falcon. He had been searching along the riverbank when he spotted the bird alighting in the uppermost branches of an ancestral rowan tree. Whistling hoarsely, he extended his arm, and the bird swooped down and came to rest upon his leather gauntlet.

"Where the devil have you been, eh?" he growled. Seizing the bird's tether between thumb and forefinger, he took its plumed leather hood from the folds of his cloak and fitted it in place, tying it with the aid of his teeth. "There!" he said. "Though I wouldn't put it past you to find the deuced corridor blind."

The bird clucked. It sounded for all the world like a burst of mocking laughter. Its head bobbing up and down in its plumed finery, it traveled the length of its tether along Drumcondra's forearm, which was a short distance, indeed.

"When you are ready to take me to her, I will restore

your sight." Drumcondra said, kneeing Cabochon toward the camp.

Aladar came running to meet him as he crossed the thicket. Drumcondra shook his head that he hadn't found her, but the elder continued to come, his posture rigid. Drumcondra knew from the old Gypsy's demeanor, from the wiry spring in his step and set jaw, that he wasn't going to like what the man was going to say.

"My lord," Aladar said, sketching a dutiful bow. "*We really must press on.* We are watched here. We have stayed in this spot too long, and have aroused the curiosity of the townfolk from Oldbridge. Men were sighted spying upon us from the copse not an hour ago. They knew they'd been seen, and they ran off, but they will soon return in greater numbers. I am sorry for it, but we must away. Townfolk burned a Gypsy caravan to cinders just south of here not a fortnight ago. Many died."

It was time to tell the elder who he really was, and he sat him down and did so. When he'd finished, the old gypsy's complexion had turned to ash, and Drumcondra sank down upon a fallen tree at the edge of the copse.

"I have heard of this," the elder said, "but I never thought to see it firsthand."

"There is no other explanation for her disappearance," Drumcondra said. "Her footprints stopped in the middle of the lane as if some creature had swooped down and picked her up. It is how I came to you—how she came to me. This is why I continued the search on my own. There was no need to burden you and the others.

"It all began at Si An Bhru. My mother was the guardian of that secret until Cian Cosgrove killed her. She and the bird knew how to access the corridor. The bird alone is the key now. I have found him. Now I must find *it*. We are as one, the bird and I."

"But that I am in the presence of Ros Drumcondra himself!" the elder murmured. "I can scarce believe it. The others . . ."

"Mustn't know," Drumcondra concluded for him. "Ros Drumcondra disappeared from recorded history in the Year of Our Lord 1695. It must remain so. That I appear to you here now is nothing more than destiny. That, too, must remain so. History cannot be changed. Ros Drumcondra has faded into the mists of time, where he must stay. Drummond will lead your people to safety, and his issue will follow after him. It is what must be, but I cannot go without my lady, else all this be for naught. She carries my seed, Aladar."

"What must we do?" the old Gypsy despaired. He threw his arms into the air. "We cannot go, we cannot stay. *What*, my lord? Enlighten me. My humble brain is addled with all this."

"No less than mine, my friend," Drumcondra said. "I go now again to Si An Bhru. That is where it all began; unless I miss my guess that is where it will end. If I do not return by noon, break camp and travel eastward to the quay. This lane winds in that direction by the passage tomb. If you do not see me there you will know that I have crossed over. Do not tarry. Go to the docks straightaway and arrange for passage. God willing, I will join you there with my lady wife before the ship sails."

"And if you do not, my lord? We need you to lead us— even more so now that I know . . . who you really are."

"Remember, you must not tell the others," Drumcondra said. "Whatever magic is afoot here, if it is my destiny to do so, it will be."

Thea saw the falcon before she saw Ros following her and Nigel at breakneck speed from the direction of Newgrange. She saw him before Nigel did, and her heart tumbled over in her breast. Astride the magnificent Gypsy horse, he looked like a creature of myth riding out of the mist—head bare, his dark hair combed by the wind that spread his mantle wide. Beneath him, Cabochon fairly flew over the land, his feathered feet and forelegs gouging clumps of wet sod out of the patchwork hills softened by the melting snow.

The bird swooped low, knocking Nigel's beaver hat from his head.

"What the deuce?" Cosgrove cried, espying the bird as it soared off into the mist. He slowed his horse. "So that is how it is to be. That bloody bird dies today!"

Nigel whipped a pistol from his belt that Thea hadn't even realized he carried, and fired a shot into the mist. She screamed, and the bird screeched in reply. Nigel had missed.

Nigel loosed a string of expletives at his failure. He had the implements, but he couldn't reload without stopping, and Thea was in the way. The ground shook beneath them with the vibration of Cabochon's heavy hooves tearing up the landscape behind. Nigel did turn then, and loosed another spate of blasphemies. Ros was gaining upon them, closing the distance between with precision, great speed, and expert handling of his mount. It was as if man and horse had become one entity, and Thea thrilled at the sight. Tears welled in her eyes and in her throat. Ros hadn't abandoned her. The minute she saw the bird, she'd known he could not be far behind.

"My husband comes," she said. "You were so anxious to see him, should you not turn round and ride the other way? Or are you a coward to the end?"

"Shut that acid mouth!" Nigel warned. "The fool rides straight into a trap. I've posted sentries aloft. They lie in wait for your thieving husband, madam. How fortuitous that you've unwittingly become the bait to lure him. That makes me reconsider. Once we've done, you have a choice. You may remain as prearranged, and be my consort, or face the gibbet. The choice is yours. It matters not to me. As I always did prefer the inventive spirit of a lusty whore to the bland resolution of a 'lady,' I'd just as soon see you swing."

Thea stiffened in his arms. She was caged against him. He had positioned her between the reins fetched up against his body on one side and the pommel on the other.

All at once, a piercing whistle ripped through the quiet. Almost simultaneously, the great bird soared out of the mist, flying right at Nigel. Thea cried out, covering her head with her arms as the two collided, the falcon's talons firmly fastening in Nigel's pale, damp hair. The Andausian's shrill complaints as the bird's wings beat it about its head and withers echoed, amplified by the mist. The horse tossed its long silky mane, shaking its head from side to side, trying to dislodge the bird from its rider, but Isor's talons held fast. Terrified, the horse slowed its pace and reared back on its hind legs, forefeet pawing the misty air. Whirling, it skidded. The tousled wet grass had been in need of scything before winter set in, and it was a snarled morass now from neglect. The horse's feet become hopelessly tangled in the tall wet mess, and the animal went down with Nigel and Thea, a heap of churning legs and rippling horseflesh.

Thrown clear and landing in a cushion of furze, Thea scrabbled out of the way as Drumcondra—abreast of them now—dove from Cabochon's back. He drove Nigel back to the ground with a shuddering thud as Nigel started to rise. For a split second, her husband's eyes observed Thea's face. His scalp drew back, his sharp eyes narrowed, riveted. At first she thought he was trying to be certain she hadn't been hurt in the fall, but a quick glance downward revealed the puffy red swelling of her cheek from Nigel's blow. His hesitation was costly. From inside his waistcoat, Nigel produced a knife that opened with a spring mechanism, and slashed out with it.

Isor, meanwhile, soared skyward, circling the situation as Ros whipped his own dirk from his turned-down boot and parried Nigel's thrust. The racket of tether bells upset the floundering horse, whose cries trailed off on a fugitive wind that had suddenly risen. Its thrashing and shuddering suggested a broken leg. There was no time to address it. Both men had squared off, their dirks gleaming in light reflected from the drifting mist as they circled each other.

The two men employed footwork more exemplary of duelists thrusting swords than paltry daggers. A slash of red on Drumcondra's arm pried a gasp from Thea's dry throat; they'd moved so fast she didn't see the thrust that had put it there. Tripping over the floundering horse, the men continued to strike at each other.

"Where is my gold?" Nigel hollered through a grunt as he lunged forward.

"You have no gold," Drumcomdra panted. "It is mine."

"The guards will think differently," Nigel retorted. "Your neck will stretch if I do not kill you here."

Thea's hands flew to her lips. Her husband was staggering. He had come too soon from a serious wound to wage the kind of war he did here now, slip-sliding in the slick wet grass, and she prayed that something—*anything*— would end it.

All at once Isor swooped down, just as he had when Nigel struggled with her on the battlements what seemed a lifetime ago. Talons first, it landed on Nigel's head again, its talons gripping his hair. Nigel cried out as the sharp claws and pecking beak pierced his scalp. Turning his attention to the bird, he straightened up from his crouch and began slashing at it with his blade between lunges at Drumcondra.

Twice, the falcon let go and landed again for a better grip. Loose feathers rode the air. Thea couldn't tell if they had been slashed from Isor's body, or if they simply had been loose and ready to fall as a matter of course. Black and white and mottled gray, they drifted down around her.

Ros's shirtsleeves were both bloody now, and a cut on his face was bleeding also. Seeing a chance, he sprang through the air and dove for Nigel—but his arms closed upon empty air as he hit the ground with a thud that shook the patch of earth Thea stood upon. Nigel and the bird were gone. So was the Andalusian.

Ros surged to his feet and spun in all directions, but there was no sign of Nigel or the falcon. Thea rushed into his arms, and he clasped her to him in a crushing embrace that siphoned her breath away.

Neither spoke. There was no need. Drumcondra's fingers traced the outline of Nigel's hand raised in bold relief on Thea's face, and groped her body feeling for injuries. When the hand came to rest on her belly and lingered there, she covered it with her own and stood on tiptoe to reach his lips.

It was a long, breathless kiss that buckled her knees, and he scooped her up in his strong arms and stalked toward Cabochon, pawing the ground with his feathered feet a few yards distant.

"W-where has Nigel gone?" Thea murmured.

"It doesn't matter," he replied. Settling her on Cabochon's back, he climbed up behind her.

"Where are we, my lord?" she said.

"Not where we need to be," said Ros.

"Was it Nigel who crossed over . . . or did we?" she asked, almost afraid of the answer.

"We will soon see," he said. And he wheeled the stallion around toward Newgrange.

Chapter Thirty

It did not matter which time they traveled in; just to be cocooned again in her husband's arms was all that mattered to Thea. There was no way to tell from the terrain, since the snow had all but melted in both dimensions. She didn't even try. Cradled against Drumcondra's hard muscled chest, she listened to the ragged thrumming of his heartbeat hammering beneath her face. She breathed him in deeply until she was full of his evocative scent, of the musky, woodsy, dark and mysterious depths of his very maleness. Even in this circumstance, need raged in her, strumming chords of arousal at the center of her existence.

"Have you forgiven me?" she murmured.

"I would not have if you had died from this mad ramble," he said. "Never run from me again, wife. Do not make a madman of me ever again."

Thea nuzzled closer. "I did not run from you, my lord," she said. "I only meant to put some distance between us for a little. I could not bear your rage, particularly because you were right. I never should have kept the circumstances of your mother's death from you."

"You should have spoken this then, instead of running off."

She shook her head in contradiction. "No, my lord," she said, "you were in a blind passion. I quite deserved your wrath. But I was selfish still, and would have done it all over again to keep you safe."

"When were you going to tell me you are with child?" he asked.

"When I was certain," she told him.

Drumcondra snorted. Thea couldn't decide if it signaled acceptance or rejection of her explanation.

"What I do not understand," she went on quickly, "is why the falcon led me back to my time in that moment."

"Isor metes out his own brand of justice," Drumcondra said, moving against her with a soft groan. His growing arousal rubbed her thigh. She leaned into the hot bulk of it throbbing against her, titillated by the sound of his rumbling voice alone. It was just as it had been the starry night he carried her thus to flaunt her before Cian Cosgrove. All that seemed to have happened in another lifetime. She almost laughed. It had!

"Where is Isor now do you think?" she murmured.

Ros shrugged. "Wherever he has led Nigel Cosgrove," he said. "He will return once that justice is done. I do not question my familiar. He has never failed me in the past, nor will he in the future, wherever that is. He will always be here at my side in time of need. I owe much to that bird. As you do, also."

Thea thought on it. Yes, she did owe much to the bird she had once so vehemently feared and hated. Her mind reeled back to the battlements, when the creature had swooped down and taken Nigel's eye, to the night it helped her save Drumcondra from the fire, to the very hour it crashed through the window in the chamber where Cian Cosgrove held her captive and lured him away for her escape. She sighed, and sighed again, remembering more and more instances. So many times it had attended her. So many times she had misunderstood its motives, yet it had stood by her all the same.

It was nearly noon. The mist had dissipated, and the day was bright with the promise of sun behind the dense cloud cover. Drumcondra scanned the sky, but it was vacant of birds. Then he whistled and, from behind, Isor dropped down from above and landed upon his broad shoulder in a flutter of flapping wings. Ros snaked a tidbit from a pouch beneath his mantle, and offered it. Gobbling the scrap of juicy meat, the falcon clucked in appreciation, and settled down as they approached the passage tomb.

They had almost reached the menhirs when the falcon suddenly took flight again, heading toward Newgrange and into a sudden rain shower. Drumcondra turned his mount and followed.

"Where will it lead us, my lord?" Thea asked. "You would not be happy in my time."

Drumcondra gave it thought. "No more than you would be in mine," he finally said.

"And . . . your mother?"

Drumcondra shook his head. "No," he said. "I have realized the dead cannot be brought back to life. Only God can do such magic. History cannot be changed, else the whole of Nature be unbalanced. Were we to return to my time, it would either be before she died, to live again those days—that sorrow—or after, and pray that somehow I did not die when Cosgrove ran me through."

"And if we return to that caravan?"

"I do not know," he said, his voice somber and deep.

"Are you willing to take such a chance . . . in a foreign land, for that is what must be. In that time when our kind are hunted like animals, driven from their home and made to wander to the four corners of the earth in search of freedom? Are you willing to bear my children in such a world, give over a gentlewoman's privileges and live the life of the Gypsy Traveler at my side?"

Thea looked him in the eyes. They had taken shelter from the rain among the trees on the south side of the lane nearby Newgrange, and the falcon, with them still, had perched in the uppermost branches of an ancient oak, its tether bells tinkling.

"Yes, my lord," she murmured.

Ros crushed her close and took her lips in a fiery kiss that rocked her soul. All things impassioned under heaven lived in that heart-stopping kiss, and when their mouths parted, hers still reached for his begging more. There, at the edge of that damp, fragrant forest, dodging raindrops, he brought her to the brink of climax with a single kiss. She was on fire for him.

"Good!" he said, pointing. "Look!"

Thea craned her neck westward, and saw wagons appear through a curtain of fine sheeting rain. Splashes of teal, red and yellow defied the drear with blazing color, rumbling along the muddy lane. Thea gave a squeal of delight, and threw her arms around her husband's neck.

Whistling for his bird, Drumcondra extended his arm, and the falcon swooped down to perch upon his leather gauntlet. Together, all three rode out to meet their destiny.

Epilogue

Nigel Cosgrove trudged eastward through the snow. How had it come there? A moment ago there was naught but soggy grass and mist ghosting over the land. When had it snowed? Reloading his pistol, he put the Andalusian out of its misery, loaded his pistol again and plodded on toward Newgrange. That must be where they'd gone. The cowards must have fled before he had a chance to catch his breath.

The passage tomb was all but hidden under a mound of snow when he reached it. Nonplussed, he strode on, remembering the keep on the outskirts of Drogheda he'd followed Thea toward until she literally vanished before him. He must be having lapses. People didn't just vanish.

It took a good deal longer to reach those hills afoot than it had on horseback, of course, but reach it he did to blunder upon what seemed like two ragtag armies warring. The hills were strewn with the dead and dying, the snow crimson with their blood. In the background, the keep was afire, its whole west wing engulfed in flames belching thick black red-rimmed smoke into the air.

Nigel crept closer, unarmed but for his paltry blade and dueling pistol he'd reloaded with his last pistol ball, which he was saving for the falcon. These men, however, were fighting with swords—some mounted, some on foot. They hadn't noticed him yet, which was a miracle, since it was open country. But for a scant low row of snow-covered bracken shrubs hemming the hillock where he crouched, there was nowhere to hide.

Nigel searched the hills in all directions for Thea and the Gypsy, Drummond. There was no sign of Thea, but there was Drummond mounted upon the magnificent white stallion in the center of the foray. Stepping out from behind the shrub, Nigel leveled his pistol; but he didn't get a chance to fire. Another warrior, who seemed oddly familiar, wearing a similar eye patch to his own, ran Drummond through on his left side. Nigel watched the Gypsy stiffen and fall, but he never hit the ground. Nigel blinked, and man and horse were gone! As if the ground had opened up and swallowed them. He shook his head, and blinked to clear his vision. He must be seeing things again.

On his feet now, his sanguinary stare riveted to the warrior with the eye patch, Nigel had attracted the attention of both warring factions, which were converging upon him from different directions. The stench of char and blood and death rose in his nostrils. There was nowhere to run. In all the chaos playing out around him, all he saw flashing before his wide-flung eye as the warriors closed in upon him, was the lifeless body of the half-naked lightskirt lying where he'd dumped her in the Covent Garden gutter, the hilt of his dirk protruding from her chest. . . .